THRILL ME TO DEATH

"Sizzles like a hot Miami night."
          —*New York Times* bestselling author Erica Spindler

"Sultry romance with enticing suspense."
                              —*Publishers Weekly*

"Fast-paced, sexy romantic suspense. . . . A book that will keep the reader engrossed in the story from cover to cover."
                                        —*Booklist*

"Roxanne St. Claire's got the sexy bodyguard thing down to an art form. . . ."
          —Michelle Buonfiglio, Lifetime TV.com

"St. Claire doesn't just push the envelope, she folds it into an intricate piece of origami for the reader's pleasure!"
          —*The Winter Haven News Chief* (FL)

KILL ME TWICE

"Sexy and scintillating . . . an exciting new series."
                              —*Romantic Times*

"*Kill Me Twice* literally vibrates off the pages with action, danger, and palpable sexual tension. St. Claire is exceptionally talented."
          —*The Winter Haven News Chief* (FL)

"Jam-packed with characters, situations, suspense, and danger. The reader will be dazzled. . . ."
                                        —*Rendezvous*

Also by Roxanne St. Claire

The Bullet Catchers Series

Now You Die

Then You Hide

First You Run

What You Can't See
(with Allison Brennan, et al.)

Take Me Tonight

I'll Be Home for Christmas
(with Linda Lael Miller, et al.)

Thrill Me to Death

Kill Me Twice

Killer Curves

French Twist

Tropical Getaway

Hit Reply

ROXANNE ST. CLAIRE

HUNT HER DOWN

POCKET STAR BOOKS

New York   London   Toronto   Sydney

Pocket Star Books
A Division of Simon & Schuster, Inc.
1230 Avenue of the Americas
New York, NY 10020

This book is a work of fiction. Names, characters, places, and incidents either are products of the author's imagination or are used fictitiously. Any resemblance to actual events or locales or persons, living or dead, is entirely coincidental.

First Pocket Star Books paperback edition September 2009

POCKET STAR BOOKS and colophon are registered trademarks of Simon & Schuster, Inc.

For information about special discounts for bulk purchases, please contact Simon & Schuster Special Sales at 1-866-506-1949 or business@simonandschuster.com.

The Simon & Schuster Speakers Bureau can bring authors to your live event. For more information or to book an event, contact the Simon & Schuster Speakers Bureau at 1-866-248-3049 or visit our website at www.simonspeakers.com.

Cover design by Min Choi
Art by Gene Mollica

Manufactured in the United States of America

10 9 8 7 6 5 4 3 2 1

ISBN 978-1-4391-0221-3

This one is for Dante

I cherish the memory of the baby you were and
hold tight (futile, I know) to the child you have been.
More than anything, I stand in awe of the man
you are about to become. I just love being your mom.

ACKNOWLEDGMENTS

Some days it feels like I work in a vacuum, all alone with these fictional folk. The truth is, there are a lot of real, live, amazing people who help me make each book better. A million thank-yous go out to all of them. In particular, there are a few shoulders I leaned on a lot for this book:

Jim Vatter, retired FBI agent, good friend, world-class neighbor. I'm sure it seems like you can't walk your dog without being inundated with questions about evidence, criminals, procedures, and that pesky palm tree disease.

Deputy Becky Herron of the Monroe County Sheriff's Department, for taking the time to answer questions and provide information about Marathon, Florida law enforcement, response to kidnappings, and geography.

Kenneth A. Smith, U.S. Immigration and Customs Enforcement Office of Investigations, for directing me to valuable information about drug trafficking and money laundering.

Kim Whalen of Trident Media Group, my agent and advocate and phenomenal beta reader. You are brilliant and beautiful!

The marvelous and incomparable Micki Nuding, who is truly an editorial gift to me, and the entire team of supportive professionals at Pocket Books, who work tirelessly to publish, package, and sell my work. I can't thank you enough!

My posse of peeps, my dearest of dears, my circle of writers, who are with me from Chapter One to The End. You know who you are! Must give a shout-out to Kresley Cole, for a ridiculous amount of perspective and laughter, and Marilyn Puett, for the HGFR installments to inspire me. And major props to the pool party plotters, who helped me craft this one: Kristen Painter, Lara Santiago, Lee Duncan, Maggie Lynch, Babe King, and Carrie Hensley (special thanks for the GPS For Blondes assistance).

Always and forever, my precious family, Rich, Dante and Mia. Nothing would matter without you. (And a great big dog bone to Rojo Loika, who loves my Pepper and inspired Goose.)

HUNT
HER
DOWN

PROLOGUE

THE UNIVERSE GAVE them rain the night of the delivery. A drenching summer downpour that swept in from the Everglades and turned Miami's expressways into one long blur of red and orange over slick pavement. The kind of rain that would hide anything, or anyone.

Maggie blinked once, then again quickly to ward off bad luck, but also to make sure the blur was on the window and not in her eyes. She'd been teary ever since Lourdes had sneaked her that stupid fortune cookie this afternoon.

She slipped her fingertips into the front pocket of her jeans and ran a nail over the edge of the paper she'd folded into a tiny square, every word committed to memory.

"Now that love grows in you, then beauty grows, too."

When the universe spoke, Magdalena Varcek listened. That's what her grandmother taught her. *Follow the signs the universe sends you,* Baba would say.

This one was kind of hard to miss. And there was only one thing to do: she had to tell Michael tonight. He'd know what to do.

She closed her eyes and imagined his face, his reaction to her news. She loved to think about his face. The way she got lost in his soft brown eyes. His perfect mouth, the little bump on his nose, the way he kissed, the way he—

She looked up and caught Ramon's unrelenting gaze on her in the rearview mirror. She'd once thought those sultry Venezuelan eyes were sexy, that curled lip of a smile was dreamy. But now her stomach flip-flopped for a whole different reason when she looked at her boyfriend. If he knew what she'd been doing in that shed behind his father's house, he'd kill Michael.

And his father would kill her.

She didn't want to die at eighteen. Especially not at the vicious hands of El Viejo. Ever since Ramon had brought her home like a stray cat, his father had looked for excuses to get rid of her. She was only allowed to stay so she could be a free nanny to little Lourdes.

In the front passenger seat, Carlos tapped his fingers to some imaginary tune, his head bobbing like a fool's, his chubby jowls wiggling as he chewed and cracked gum. He'd probably snorted a gram before they left. He said something to Ramon in Spanish and threw a look over his shoulder at Maggie.

Ramon unhooked the car phone from the console, the red brake lights in front of them illuminating the rattle-snake tattoo that ran up his forearm. She used to think that was the last word in sexy, too.

After dialing, he asked, "Where are you, bro?"

English, so it had to be Michael on the other end. Viejo and Ramon didn't always include him, but she'd told him about tonight's job, and he was pretty good about worming his way in. She liked to think that was so he could see her.

Maybe when the guys were unloading the crates, she could give him the signal. Move one bracelet to the other arm . . . *meet me in my room.* Move two bracelets . . . *meet me in the shed.* Three meant *follow me when I leave the house.* And he usually did.

"They're through? Already?" Ramon turned to Carlos and muttered something.

He whizzed down the next exit, water hissing under the tires as he sped through the deserted industrial section near the airport. In a few minutes, he pulled into the lot in front of the warehouse, the words AJ Cargo and Shipping barely visible in the rain.

El Viejo's Stash House was more like it. But Alonso Jimenez wasn't there tonight. He usually was, but something in the silent looks volleying between Ramon and Carlos told her that things weren't exactly going smooth and easy this time. Starting with the rain and ending with Juan Santiago puking on Chinese-food poisoning, so that Ramon freaked and brought Maggie in his place. At least the Chinese food delivery had included her message from the universe.

She touched the paper again, scanning the empty lot for Michael's car. Nothing but three AJ Cargo trucks lined up near the loading dock in the back.

Michael would be following a fourth one in at any minute, and the men driving it would help Carlos and Ramon unload furniture boxes from Caracas, sofas and chairs stuffed with bags of cocaine that had traveled from Colombia to Maracaibo, Venezuela, then shipped out of Caracas.

Ramon had told her the whole thing. And anything Ramon told her, she passed on to Michael because, well, he was kind of low on the totem pole in this operation and even if it was a drug business, he was ambitious. She loved that about him.

God, she loved everything about him.

"Sit up here and don't get out of the car, Maggie," Ramon ordered as he threw it into reverse.

How would she get to Michael then? "What if—"

"What if nothing," he said harshly. "When Mike calls and tells you he's on Hialeah Drive, you flash the brights three times." He tapped the turn signal stick on the steering wheel. "Just pull it like this. You know how to do that, Maggie? Or are you so stupid you can't flash the brights?"

She glared at him.

"We'll come out and open up the cargo door and you wait."

"And when you're done?" Could she talk to Michael then? Give him the sign?

He backed up to a dilapidated fence that separated this parking lot from the next, a good hundred yards from the trucks and the loading dock.

"When we're done, we're done," Ramon said. "You don't get out of this car, understand? If we gotta move fast, you have to be ready to drive."

"What if Viejo calls and needs you? Should I come and get you?" she asked.

Ramon just shook his head. "He won't."

He threw open his door and Carlos did the same on the passenger side, and they hustled off while she got behind the wheel. The motor was still running, and the wipers smacked from one side to the other, clearing the windshield for a split second before it was drenched again. *Smack, slap, smack.*

Were they giving her a message, those rhythmic wipers? Baba would say . . . *listen. Smack, slap, smack. Smack, slap, smack.*

Mich . . . ael . . . Scott. Tell . . . him . . . now. This . . . is . . . it.

She dropped her head back to watch Ramon disappear around the back of the warehouse, the air-conditioning blowing her hair off her face, the wipers thwacking their cryptic messages.

Mich . . . ael . . . Scott. Tell . . . him—

She startled when the phone rang. "Hello?" The only reply was a mix of a choke and a soft intake of breath. "Michael?"

"What the hell are you doing there, Maggie?"

"Juan's sick. He was throwing his guts up."

Under his breath, she heard him swear. "You're supposed to be taking Lourdes to the movies."

She liked that he kept track of her schedule. "She went to a sleepover 'cause Ramon was losing it, screaming that he needed me here. But now I can—"

"Don't go in to the warehouse."

"I won't. I'm just going to flash the lights when you turn on Hialeah. I won't get out of the car." His concern touched her and she tucked the phone deeper into her shoulder, wishing it were him. "Michael, um, listen. Can we meet later?" The silence on the other end lasted one beat too long. "Michael? Did you hear me?"

"You have to get out of that car. *Now.* You have to get out of there, away from there."

She frowned, confused. "Why?"

"Because you do. You're not supposed to be here tonight." His voice was strained, the tone sending a chill down her. "I mean it. Get the hell out of there. Fast."

Just as he said it, she heard the rumble of a truck turning into the lot and caught the AJ Cargo logo between wiper swipes. The delivery.

She twisted in the seat to see down the road. "Aren't you behind these guys?" she asked.

But he was gone. The line was dead. Why would he tell her to leave?

And why hadn't he called when the truck was on Hialeah, like he was supposed to? They needed to get the cargo bay door open.

Should she do the brights now? If she didn't, Ramon would kill her. If she did, and this wasn't the delivery, then El Viejo would kick her ass from here to kingdom come anyway.

She curled her fingers around the stick and pulled once, yellow light spilling onto the rain-slicked asphalt. After a few seconds, she let go and the pavement went dark. She waited the same amount of time, then—

The driver's side door popped open.

"Get out!" Michael pulled her out, yanking her harshly from the seat.

"Hey! What are—"

He whipped her out as if she weighed nothing, pulling her by her shoulders into his face. His breath was warm, his face furious.

"Go through that fence and run to the next block and get the hell out of here." His eyes burned darkly.

"Michael, why—"

"Just do it!" he ordered. "Go as fast as you can. Don't stop. Don't come back. Just run, Maggie. *Run*."

He pushed her away, madder than she'd ever seen him.

She stumbled and looked back at him. "Michael! I have to—"

"God *damn* it! Go!"

She lunged, grabbing his shoulders. "Listen to me!" she screamed. "I have to tell you something—"

"Just go!" He shoved her toward the fence again, but she braced her legs and refused to move.

"No," she insisted, digging her sneakers into a crack in the wet asphalt. "Not until you tell me what's going on."

He took hold of her shoulders and squeezed so hard his fingers dug into her bones. "Get the hell out of here right now. That's all you need to know."

Lights from a car illuminated his face, and he forced her down, behind the car.

"Michael, stop it. Why are you doing this?" Tears mixed with rain, stinging her eyes and cheeks.

Headlights illuminated the lot and his eyes flashed as he nudged her once more toward the fence, then vaulted away.

Slowly, she rose in shock, staring after him as he ran full speed to the warehouse. She saw him shake out of the jacket he wore and drop it to the ground, revealing another jacket underneath. With yellow letters on the back . . .

FBI.

Oh God. Oh God, *no*.

He stopped, looked over his shoulder to where she stood, and even in the darkness, in the distance, she could see him saying something. To her? What was he saying?

Then there was light and noise and the world seemed to explode. Spotlights poured blinding whiteness over everything, drawing a gasp from Maggie as she faltered backward.

She spun and lunged for an opening in the fence, her sneakers splashing into puddles, her legs almost buckling as she tripped over gravel and cracks. Rain sluiced over her face, into her mouth.

A gunshot cracked and voices cut through the deafening rain.

"FBI! DEA! Get out of the truck! You're under arrest!"

Four, five, six more gunshots, staccato and deafening.

She slowed, stopped, and pressed her hands to her chest to ease the pain of her heaving breaths. She had to see. *Had* to. Grabbing a strip of wood along the top of the fence, she hoisted herself up, blinking into the rain and lights and chaos.

Men surrounded the delivery truck, guns drawn. One of them yanked open the door and pulled Jorge out. Then Stephan on the driver's side. More men swarmed the warehouse. In the flood of light, she could easily read the large yellow letters on their backs.

Her heart dropped right down to her toes, leaving a black, empty hole in her chest. Michael had betrayed them all. He was a fed. A narc. A liar.

She clung to the fence, her hair plastered over her face, her lungs bursting, her heart breaking as the ugly truth hammered down on her as hard as the rain.

One of the agents threw Jorge on the ground and clamped him down with a boot and gun to the head. Two more ran into the back, pistols straight out and ready to shoot.

Agents and cops poured out of the warehouse, first with Carlos in cuffs, then Ramon, his long black hair streaming wet in his face, spewing obscenities as he tried to jerk free. An ambulance screamed into the parking lot, blue lights flashing; then the paramedics were running into the warehouse.

Where was Michael?

Frozen, she watched in horror as they took a stretcher inside. Minutes dragged by until they came back out, carrying Michael. As the stretcher passed Ramon, who was cuffed and slammed against the side of the building, he turned and spat on the body.

"Cabrón!" Bastard.

At the ambulance, they covered his face with a sheet.

Closing her eyes, Maggie let go of the fence and

dropped to the wet ground. Her stomach rolled, the nausea caused by something other than what she'd suspected for the last few weeks.

He'd used her. He'd played her. He'd strung her along, made her think he loved her, all the time coaxing information that she got from her boyfriend. All the time making her believe he cared.

She was nothing more than a way to get to Ramon, and through him, to El Viejo.

Thank God he was dead—otherwise she'd go to jail for killing him herself.

Ramon was right. *Bastard.*

She reached into her pocket and pulled out the fortune. The universe spoke to her, all right.

Stupid, stupid Magdalena. You have been royally fucked once again.

She started to roll the paper into a ball, rocked by the sudden need to throw it down and grind it under her foot as if it was Michael Scott.

But then she stopped and cupped her hands over it, the urge to protect it strong. The urge to protect the beauty that grew inside of her.

That was the real meaning of the message in the fortune cookie.

She tucked the paper back into her jeans pocket and then, just as she'd done the last time someone betrayed her, she ran for her life.

Only this time, she wasn't alone.

CHAPTER
ONE

Fourteen Years Later

ALL HE WANTED to do was make a clean getaway.

But Dan Gallagher knew the minute he stepped out of the Bullet Catchers' headquarters that this exit would be anything but clean.

Leaning against his Maserati was the one person who wouldn't let him get away with anything.

"Slinking out so soon?" Max asked, crossing his arms over his massive chest, his hair still sweaty from the company touch football game.

"Slinking is generally done through the back door, Roper. I'm going out the way I came in."

Max narrowed dark eyes at Dan. "Out for good?"

"Out for now."

"You're crushed."

Dan laughed. "No, but if you don't get out of my way, you will be." He pulled his keys out. "I got a plane to catch."

"Not taking a Bullet Catcher jet?" Of course he didn't move.

"Nope. It's personal business."

Max just cocked his head, never wasting a word. They hadn't had "personal business" they didn't share in twenty years.

"Come on," Dan said. "I'm seriously late getting to the airport."

"Did she tell you everything?" Max asked.

Dan glanced up to the second-story window overlooking the drive, to Lucy Sharpe's private library and office. She'd probably gone to the back patio to celebrate with the others. These were happy days for her company. For her.

"She didn't have to tell me anything. It's all over her glowing face. And I'm delighted for her."

Max choked. "Delighted?"

"What?" Dan countered. "You don't believe I'm not happy that a woman I've worked for and been friends with for years has found . . ." Freedom from whatever misery had kept her in an emotional prison for a long time? He'd never had the key to that jail cell, but Jack Culver had proven himself more than capable. "Has found bliss," he finished.

"Delighted and bliss in the same speech?"

"Shut up. She's happy, and I'm . . ." Free to move on. "Happy for her. We're all just one big, happy Bullet Catcher family. And a growing one, at that." At Max's look, he just shook his head. "I swear to God, I'm not lying."

"You're rationalizing. Which is another word for *lying*, only to yourself. And while your ability to bend the truth has served you well in countless undercover situations, this is real life."

Dan scowled at him. "Did aliens come and take Mad

Max Roper? Or has marriage and fatherhood turned you into Dr. Phil? And since when isn't a UC situation real life?"

"I'm worried about you."

"Fear not, my man. I've never been better. I'm free."

"Free."

"Yeah. Free. Lucy, in case you haven't surmised from her radiance, has made the ultimate commitment with Culver. Do I agree with her choice of partners?" He shrugged. "Not my problem. Do I wish it was me up there perusing a baby name book? Hell, no. I know you think you've cracked the code with Cori and little Peyton, and maybe you have. But I don't want that key. I like the status quo."

Unrelenting brown eyes narrowed. "More rationalizing."

"Call it whatever you want." He gave Max's meaty shoulder a smack with the file in his hand. "Now go eat some charred meat like a good Rottweiler. You're missing the party and all the gossip about the reasons behind my leave of absence."

"A leave of absence, with a Bullet Catcher dossier still warm from the Research and Investigative Department printer?"

The son of a bitch didn't miss a trick. "Just grabbed a file on an old friend I might look up in the Keys."

"You're going to Florida? Cori and I are going down to Miami tomorrow, to her place on Star Island. Why don't you stay with us for a few days?"

"And get psychoanalyzed by the two of you? No thanks. Anyway, I'll be a couple of hours south, in Marathon."

"Doing what?" Max pressed.

"Fishing."

"You don't own a tackle box. What's going on down there?"

"Nothing." He hoped. "I'm taking some time to my-self. See an old friend. Learn the difference between a trout and a . . . nother kind of fish."

"Who's the old friend?"

It was a waste of time to try and sidestep him. "A young lady I knew from my Miami days."

Max's wheels visibly turned. "Not the girl from the Venezuelan money laundering ring?"

Dan sighed. "Do you have to have a memory like a steel trap?"

"How could I forget? For one thing, the takedown of Alonso Jimenez and company was a major operation that involved the DEA and the FBI. And, not exactly a *lady,* as I recall, though she was young then."

He bristled at the comment. "She's fourteen years older now."

"So instead of licking new wounds, you're going to open old ones?" Max asked.

"The only thing I'm planning to lick is salt with my tequila."

"You sure that's smart, when you're on the rebound and all?"

Dan leaned right in his friend's face. "Let's get this straight, Roper. I'm not on the rebound and I don't need you to judge what's smart and what's not." He pulled back. "But since you're so damn nosy, I still have access to some of the FBI sites and I noticed that Ramon Jimenez got out of prison recently."

"El Viejo's son?"

"Yeah." Everyone who knew the case knew Alonso Jimenez was universally referred to as "El Viejo"—the old man. "I just want to make sure she's okay."

"You think he'll go after her?"

Dan shrugged. "She was never implicated or arrested, and, per my request, she was left out of the trial since her testimony was superfluous, considering all the evidence we had. As far as she or any of them know, Michael Scott—my cover name—was accidentally killed that night in friendly fire. That's the way the agency wanted to play it. But Ramon has had a long time to put together the truth, and he might have figured out the leak was his girlfriend. He's a rat bastard, and I don't trust him."

"So what's your plan? Spring your real identity on her?"

"God, no. And she'll never recognize me, because that cover was thorough and the guy she knew had brown eyes, dark hair, and a prosthetic nose. I just want to check out where she lives and works, make sure she's safe. She goes by Smith now, so she's probably married with kids."

"Could be an alias and she's living in fear that they'll find her."

The same thought had occurred to him. "If that's the case, then I'll introduce myself as a former FBI agent who thinks she should be aware that Ramon Jimenez is out of prison. Then I'll leave, and she'll be safer. This is strictly a standard security check after a prison release. After I'm done, I'll be back." Probably. He gave Max a tight smile.

"Culver is a fact of our life, now," Max said, a warning in his voice. "Can you live with that?"

"Look, I know Lucy and I flirted with possibilities. But it would have screwed up a great friendship, and I'm not interested in . . ." A *baby*. "Anything that would tie me down. She knows that, and so do I."

Finally satisfied, Max moved. "Call me when you get there."

Dan reached for the car door. "Why would I even need a wife, when I have you?"

"And the invitation stands. Cori has a week of board meetings at Peyton Enterprises, and I'm going to go apeshit and melt in the heat. Hang out with me in Miami Beach."

"You're so full of it. You love all that time with Peyton."

Max beamed at the mention of his two-year-old. "It doesn't suck."

"Who woulda thunk it? Max Roper morphs into Father of the Year."

"Don't knock what you haven't tried."

Dan circled his throat and mock-choked, then took one more glance at the library window. He'd never have gone there with Lucy, so she really was better off now. He climbed into the car and shut the door.

Snapping on the CD player, he cranked up the volume, then took off down the driveway with the familiar relief that once again he'd successfully dodged a bullet.

"Oh, please, not *again*." Maggie clunked the empty tray on the service bar and put her hands over her ears but it did nothing to drown out the music echoing through Smitty's. "I swear, I'm going to go down to Margaritaville myself and shoot Jimmy Buffett for recording it."

"That'll just make 'em want to hear it more." From his favorite bar stool, Gumbo Joe threw her a wide, yellow-toothed smile. "Anyhoo, you're the one who put a jukebox in this joint, Lena. Smitty'd roll over in his grave if he saw how you turned his nice little watering hole into a tourist trap full of northerners who want to get wasted away again."

"Smitty, God rest his soul, *ought* to roll over in his grave, for the debt he left me in." She flipped the service door up and slipped behind the bar, dumping the empties into the recycle bin. "And I see the transformation from bait bar to tourist trap hasn't stopped you from swilling one dollar AmberBocks every Friday night, Gumbo."

"Well, a man's gotta drink after a hard day of trawlin'." He took a swig to underscore the statement while Maggie headed to the cash register to ring up the pitcher of draft she'd just served.

She hip-nudged Brandy out of the way, but not hard enough to make the superskilled bartender splash a drop of the tequila she was pouring. "Don't forget the lost shaker of salt."

Brandy gave her a wry smile and lifted the tequila bottle. "Every time that tune comes on we sell more of this shit, and the markup is pure profit, partner. That song is what you would call a good sign."

"*Ka-ching!*" Maggie exclaimed as the drawer popped open.

Brandy turned, expertly threading her fingers around six shot glasses. "Oh, and speaking of good signs. Look who just came in. Your boyfriend's back."

Maggie froze, a little thrill tickling her tummy. "Don't care."

"You lie, Lena Smith."

"I never lie, Brandy Istre, and you know that. But I'm not looking, because I don't care."

"You should look, because, whoa, he is even hotter than the last two nights he's been in here, checking you out like you were his favorite library book."

Maggie rolled her eyes, closing the cash register with a quiet click. "Whatev, as Quinn would say."

"In case you change your mind, he's sitting down at the two-top by the window," Brandy continued. "He's looking at the table tent as if he's actually considering a dollar beer, but we know he's an import kind of guy. Look at those clothes, all Ralph Lauren expensive. I bet he came down in his yacht. Yep, he's looking out at the marina, running his hand through that dirty-blond hair, and over his jaw." Brandy dipped a little closer to whisper the rest of her play-by-play. "I don't think he shaved today. He wants your poor li'l thighs to get all rosy with a rash."

Maggie laughed, hiding her weak knees and high hopes.

The last two nights he'd been there, he'd just ordered a Heineken, nursed it, and then left. But the entire time, he'd watched her. No, he *pinned* her with eyes the same green as the bottle she served him, making her tense and prickly and . . . aware.

She turned from the cash register, and looked right at him. Another lightning bolt rocked her, this time right between those poor li'l thighs.

Holy mother of all that mattered, the man was *edible*.

Neither one looked away, and Maggie could have sworn those perfect lips tipped in a smile. She managed to breathe—no mean feat.

"Shots are up, Mrs. Smith!"

His eyes flickered when Brandy called out the order.

Maggie instantly transferred her attention to the service bar, where Brandy stood with a hand on her narrow hip and a smug smile on her elfin features.

"Why'd you have to call me that?" Maggie scowled as she ducked under the bar to get to the other side.

"Thought you didn't care."

"Well, there's no reason to make him think I'm still married."

"Sure there is—now you have to talk to him. Get your butt over there and tell him you're a widow."

Maggie shot her a vile look and scooped the tray full of shots in one hand. "Look, if I want to get a good look at his ass as he runs screaming out the door, I don't need to mention my dearly departed husband. The teenager at home usually does the trick."

"The teenager is at his uncle's fishing for two days . . . and two *nights*." Brandy leaned her whole body over the service bar to make her point. "And the merry widow hasn't had sex in four years."

"Four years?" Gumbo Jim slammed down his bottle and let his jaw drop. "Lena, that's a damn sin. Smitty would've wanted you to get laid once in a while. You're a beautiful woman, for God's sake."

Next to Jim, Tommy Sloane inched over and pointed at her. "You know, a hymen can grow back. I read that in *Penthouse*."

"A brain can grow back, too, Tommy, so there's hope for you yet." She nodded to a tall, dark-haired man who walked up to the bar and took the stool at the opposite end. "Brandy, you have a new customer. You're going to want this one."

Brandy glanced over her shoulder, then let out a low whistle. "Holy hell, the place is swimming in high-quality testosterone tonight."

Maggie balanced the tray. "Go get 'em, tiger. Our song's still playing." She headed toward the group from Philadelphia, who were already a little loud and loose. As she leaned to set down the drinks, she couldn't resist lifting her gaze to the two-top at the window.

He was staring. Hard. Right down the scoop neck of her top.

Oh, had she forgotten to wear a bra? They were small but mighty, as someone had once told her, and every once in a while the girls went free. She smiled at the customers she served, but the twinkle in her eye was for *his* benefit.

She'd also purposely worn the tight hip-hugging jeans and a little extra makeup. It was true; she didn't *care* if he came back for a third night—but she hoped like hell he would. Especially tonight . . . the one time she didn't have a thirteen-year-old and his dog waiting at home.

Tonight, Magdalena Varcek Smith was going to have some fun.

Straightening, she nodded to him. "I'll be right there," she mouthed, taking the empty glasses from the table and wending around some chairs to make her way over.

He made no effort to hide his long, slow appraisal of her, the hungry gaze leaving a trail of heat and a thousand chills over every well-admired inch of her. By the time he got back up to her face, she'd reached the table and slid into the chair across from him.

"You want a Heineken?"

"Among other things." He added an imperfect, slanted, utterly decadent smile that took him from jaw-dropper to heart-wrecker in a pulse beat.

"Name 'em," she shot back.

He dropped his elbows on the table and folded his arms, a move that emphasized the power and size of his shoulders, and leaned closer. She got a whiff of peppermint and spice, a dose of raw sex appeal, and a chance to see that no, he hadn't shaved.

"Mrs. Smith. Are you married?"

His question was direct, simple, and delivered with a

baritone that made her wonder if his chest rumbled when he spoke.

"Not anymore." She met him halfway across the table. "Are you?"

"Not even close."

"Well, now that we got that little detail out of the way, how about we finally introduce ourselves?" She held out her hand, bracing for the electricity she just knew was going to zing up her arm. "I'm—"

"I know who you are." He didn't shake her hand. Instead, his long, strong fingers plucked at one of the silver bangles on her wrist. "You make noise when you walk, you know that?"

She just stared at him, unable to look away.

"I've been hearing you jingle in my sleep."

Oh boy. He was good. "What's it sound like?"

"Trouble."

She laughed. "I'm no trouble at all. Everyone calls me Lena, and I'm the owner of this fine establishment and jingler of your dreams. What's your name?"

"Dan."

"Just Dan?"

"For now, just Dan."

"How about for later?"

"That assumes there is a later. I don't want to be presumptuous."

She crossed her arms and matched his position, as into the game as he was. "Go ahead and presume. We've been dancing around each other for three nights. How long are you in town?"

"How do you know I don't live here?"

"Because I know everybody who lives in Marathon, which means you're a tourist."

"Are you going to close up again tonight?"

Another zing went through her, this time more of a mental alarm than a sexual buzz. "Maybe."

Since she'd just said she was the owner, it made sense she'd close the bar. But these days, she couldn't be too careful. Not after she'd read the prison release list on that website. Ever since, she'd carried Smitty's pistol in her handbag, made a habit of looking over her shoulder, and had one of the regulars walk her to her car.

And sent Quinn for long weekends at his Uncle Eddie's, so he wasn't home alone when she worked late nights.

"Can I meet you tonight?" he asked. "So we could talk when you're not working."

Talk. Right. "It could be late."

"I don't mind."

"We make last call around one."

He nodded and stood, looming over her, easily surpassing six feet. "I'll be back at twelve thirty."

She pushed herself up, pulled by that gaze and something else. A sensation that numbed her fingertips and toes.

Familiarity. That was it. There was something weirdly *familiar* about him.

"Have you been in here before?" she asked. "I can't shake the feeling that we've met."

He just gave her that wicked half smile again, revealing the slightest overlap of his front teeth, the imperfection wildly attractive on an otherwise perfect face. "Maybe in another life." He reached out and slipped his fingers right under her hair, flicking the three silver hoops so they clinked against each other. "See you later . . . Lena."

She didn't move a muscle as he walked away, didn't take a breath or blink an eye.

Lena. He said it as if the name amused him, as if he knew she didn't even think of herself as the name she'd adopted the day she showed up at this bar.

But he couldn't know. No one knew. Except Smitty, who'd given her a new, safe, sane life, along with a completely different name.

" 'Scuze me, miss? Can we get another round?"

She just held up a hand, making her grandmother's silver bangles ding against each other. A tendril of déjà vu curled up her spine and raised the hairs on the back of her neck.

From another life? If so, it must have been a good one.

CHAPTER
TWO

DAN PARKED THE rented Porsche directly across from the bar at twelve twenty-five. He had damn good reasons for coming back to Smitty's night after night since he'd arrived in the Keys.

He wanted to be certain she was safe. He wanted to know how she'd fared over the years. He wanted to make sure none of the "tourists" were plants from the Jimenez family, looking for retribution. He wanted . . .

Her.

Magdalena Varcek had grown from a teenager into a glorious woman, with sultry dark eyes and masses of chocolate curls and a translucent complexion that hinted at the Hungarian blood she had claimed made her part Gypsy. She had the same sass and spunk, the same playful smile, the same glint of erotic invitation in her eyes, but now it was all part of a woman's package, and ten times more attractive because she knew exactly how to use it.

She'd always been a sex pistol, but now she was a freaking AK-47, loaded and clearly looking for a target. All he could think of when he looked at her were those secret, steaming, sexy nights in the shed when nothing was off-limits. Nothing.

Well, *she'd* been off-limits. But that hadn't stopped him. He could have gotten his information a half dozen other ways, but something about Maggie Varcek made him crazy and achy and more willing to take risks.

Which was why he was sitting in this car right now, just as crazy as he had been then.

Once he'd seen her, smelled her, heard the siren call of her silver jewelry and throaty laugh, he just kept coming back with unanswered questions. What in the world ever brought her to this place? Why?

And other questions, like . . . would she taste the same? Move the same? Scream when he made her come?

He pushed the car door open and climbed out, already tasting the first kiss, the first heat of her skin.

Maggie would never know who he was. One night. One time. All his questions answered, all his needs met, all his curiosity sated.

How could anyone get hurt by that? Her signals were unambiguous, and he was just responding the way any red-blooded male would. It didn't matter that he knew more about her than she knew about him. Tomorrow, he'd be gone.

Inside Smitty's, only a few people were left: two guys at the bar, a couple making out at a table, and some twenty-somethings doing sloppy shooters with limes.

The waiflike blonde named Brandy looked up from wiping the bar and curled a come-hither finger at him. He took one of the empty seats and matched her conspiratorial smile.

"She made last call five minutes ago," Brandy said.

"Guess she was eager to end the night," Dan suggested.

"Or start it." She turned to the fridge, pulled out a Heineken, and snapped the top against a bottle opener near her hip. "This one's on the house, Mr. Dan-with-no-last-name."

He took it. "Gallagher. Thanks."

Two seats down, a man turned and looked sharply at him.

Dan nodded, immediately remembering the dude who'd come in five minutes after he did. He looked pretty damn sober after camping at the bar for three straight hours. He had a draft in front of him, but it was flat and the glass had no condensation.

He'd been nursing that drink for a long, long time.

"How ya doin'?" Dan nodded to him, noticing the Mediterranean features, the black hair and olive skin contrasted with eyes so pale blue they were nearly silver.

"What did you say your name was?" the other man asked.

"Dan Gallagher. You?"

"Constantine Xenakis."

Dan tilted his bottle in greeting. "Just in from Athens?"

"Something like that. Where are you from?"

"New York."

The other man shifted over one seat, keeping one between them but obviously inviting conversation. "What brings you to Marathon? Business or pleasure?"

"A little of both," Dan said, vague by habit. "What about you?"

"Business is a pleasure."

The barmaid stopped her wiping right in front of them and looked from one to the other. "Look at you two. The man gods have been good to Smitty's tonight."

" 'Scuze me, sweetheart," Xenakis said, reaching over to put a friendly hand over hers. "Can you give us some privacy?"

She backed up, surprise and a little disappointment darkening hazel eyes that had gotten a retouch of mascara since Dan's last visit.

"Anything you want." She walked to the opposite end of the bar and Dan waited, curious as to why the stranger would prefer to talk to him than flirt with the obviously interested bartender.

The other man turned toward Dan, locking on him with an intense gaze. "You here to see Mrs. Smith?"

Dan just nodded, not willing to commit to anything.

"She's a fox," Xenakis said, lifting his beer. "How'd you meet her?"

"Here," he said.

He settled back on the stool a little, eyeing Dan. "When?"

"A few nights ago. Why?"

"No reason. I noticed her."

Who wouldn't? "She's noticeable, that's for sure."

The other man looked side to side, as if he wanted to make sure no one could hear him, then leaned a little closer to Dan, his silvery eyes piercing. "Have you had any luck?"

Was he serious? "Why, have you tried and failed?" Dan asked.

He got a long, hard look in response. "I never fail."

"Good for you." But he was the one nursing a flat beer, and Dan was the one with the midnight rendezvous.

"Don't think for one minute I don't know why you're here, Gallagher. I can't be the only one after it."

"I'm sure the line is long for Ms. Smith's attention."

Dan lifted his beer and gave the guy a warning look. "But there's only one in the queue tonight, pal."

"You're not getting it tonight."

What the hell? Dan drank and turned back to the bar, hoping to end the conversation.

"I'm serious," he continued anyway. "You are not getting it."

Dan set the bottle down. "I don't discuss my personal life with strangers."

The man laughed softly. "You can keep your personal life all to yourself. You're not getting her fortune."

Maggie had a fortune? That wasn't in the Bullet Catcher dossier. "You want some advice?" Dan asked coolly.

He got a raised eyebrow in response. "No."

"Well, I'm giving it." Dan added an edge to his voice and leaned closer to deliver his message. "Stay away."

The other man just smiled. He stood, put a bill on the bar, and gave Dan a half-assed salute. "You might think you're real good, Gallagher, but trust me, I'm better."

Dan watched him leave, memorizing his gait and posture, and every detail he could. Including the bulge of a gun on his hip.

"You know that guy?" he asked Brandy when she came back to his end of the bar.

"Wish I did." She glanced at the door as it thudded closed. "I managed to find out his name is Constantine and he's Greek."

"Does he come in here a lot?"

"Never. All he did was ask questions about Lena, even after I told her she was, uh, taken tonight." She added a saucy wink. "But I really think he was hanging out to see if you'd reappear or not."

"Of course I'd . . ." The door next to the service bar

opened and Maggie stepped into the dim bar, her eyes sparkling at the sight of him. "Reappear."

"Hey." Her smile was warm and wide and glistening. She'd put lip gloss on for him.

"Hey yourself. How was the night?"

"Long." She eased onto the bar stool next to him, sending the softest scent of cinnamon perfume mixed with the citrus from a lot of limes she'd probably squeezed that night. "And yours?"

"Longer."

That made her laugh, soft and low, drawing him closer. "I'm done now."

He nodded in Brandy's direction as the bartender disappeared into the back carrying a load of clean glasses in a dishwasher bin. "Letting your employees do all the dirty work?"

"She doesn't work for me, she's my business partner, and Milk Dud's still in the kitchen. Dudley's our chief cook and bottle washer. Anyway, I'd do the same for her if she had a hot date."

"Is that what this is?" He fought the urge to slip his hand into her curls. They were so soft and plentiful, framing her pretty face and cut so that wisps of dark hair fell over her finely arched brows.

"This is whatever you want it to be," she said, taking his beer. "May I?"

Without waiting for a response, she took a long, slow swig, the creamy skin of her throat undulating with each swallow.

"*Mmmm.*" She put the bottle down and pointed at him, the bracelets clinking on her arm, instantly reminding him of days gone by. And nights. "Now, you don't drink another thing and I'll let you drive the yacht."

He gave her a surprised look. "You have one?"

"No, but I figured you did."

"Sorry to disappoint. Just a Porsche."

"That's almost as good."

"Rented."

She nudged him. "You want to lose me forever? Let's go."

"Where?"

"Sightseeing."

"At midnight?"

"Sure." She slid off the barstool and tugged his hand to do the same. "That Porsche ought to do some damage on the Seven Mile Bridge, and we can sit under the palm trees at Bahía Honda beach and . . . talk. That's what you wanted to do, right?"

So she still liked outdoor sex. "Right."

The lights of the Key's signature bridge stretched so far it looked as if it ended in Cuba. Dan glanced from the endless stream of white lights to the woman on his right, who kept the conversation so light and teasing that he really didn't have a chance to ask many questions, or tell her much about himself.

Of course she wanted to keep it impersonal. To her this was a hook-up, plain and simple. She dodged the few questions he asked, and the only new tidbit of information that he learned was that Smitty, her husband, had died four years ago of a brain tumor, leaving her his bar, which evidently was deep in debt. She'd brought in a partner to help share the burden and they had some plans for renovation and growth, but it was slow going.

Nothing about her security, safety, home life. None of the things he ostensibly came to find out.

"What about you?" she asked, adeptly turning the questions away. "I still don't know your last name."

"Gallagher."

"Oh, that explains the Emerald Isle eyes. What's your business?"

"I'm a security specialist."

"What does that mean? You install alarms?"

He laughed. "I am the alarm. I'm a bodyguard, a personal protection specialist."

"Really? That's very cool." She reached for his right hip and he flipped his hand from the gearshift and snagged her wrist before she touched him.

"It's on my ankle, but that's not a smart move."

"You have a gun on you?"

"Yep."

"Me, too."

He shot her a look. "You carry concealed? Are you licensed?"

"I'm friends with the deputy sheriff." She wrinkled her nose. "Does that count?"

"Only if he's the one to arrest you. What do you have?"

"A .22 pistol."

A water gun. But still, why carry? "I didn't think there was an inch of your lovely body I hadn't checked out. Where you hiding your iron?"

"In my purse."

"Where it would do absolutely no good if you were attacked."

"Spoken like a genuine bodyguard. Don't worry, it's just for peace of mind."

"Have you been threatened?" His brain flashed to the big Greek fortune hunter at the bar.

She didn't answer, but pointed to a turnoff as they

reached the end of the bridge. "That's Bahía Honda State Park. If you park way down at that other end, we can easily jump the gate."

He gave her another look of disbelief. "It's closed?"

"Come on." She tapped his arm. "Like anything we're doing tonight is going by the rules. Live dangerously."

"I'm a bodyguard."

"All the more reason for me to feel perfectly safe. Honestly, I've been here a million times for night fishing. It's fine. Marathon goes to sleep at eleven, and all the criminals are down in Key West."

He parked, and in minutes she had them over an admittedly pathetic gate, and guided him by the closed concession stand, bathrooms and showers, then up a path to a secluded beach. Palm trees and heavy foliage lined the sand, providing shade in the day and shadows at night.

"Here's a nice spot." She found a patch of grass, tucked under a tall palm and within view of the silver-white waves and cream-colored sand.

Dropping down, she wrapped her arms around her legs. "Isn't this pretty?"

He scanned the entire deserted area. "Pretty out in the open."

She reached up and tugged his hand to pull him next to her. "This is much safer than, say, my living-room sofa, where we both know the conversation would end in five minutes."

The conversation might end in five minutes anyway. Talking wouldn't do a damn thing to address the low, burning need he'd been feeling since he'd seen her again.

"Is Lena short for something?"

"Magdalena."

"Beautiful name," he said, leaning back on both hands, studying her. "For a beautiful girl."

She smiled thanks. "It's my grandmother's name."

He knew all about her 'Baba,' who'd raised her after her mother disappeared with a nameless boyfriend. He knew that when her grandmother died, sixteen-year-old Maggie had run away to Florida to look for her mother but found only Ramon Jimenez in a turnpike restaurant. That's where their personal histories intertwined for almost a year. Along with their bodies, after a few months of secret flirting.

"Where's your grandmother?" he said, treading carefully over ground he'd covered years ago.

"In that great big fortune teller's tent in the sky."

He'd even heard her use that line before. "Sorry to hear that."

"It's okay, now. I get messages from her all the time."

He remembered that, too. "What does she say?"

She shrugged. "She warns me. She coaxes me. She uses the universe to send me advice and guidance."

"And how does she do that?"

"Can the patronizing voice, will you? I know you don't believe me, but you wanted to get to know me, and this is me. I notice words and numbers and phrases and song lyrics and . . . signs. Baba used to say 'Follow the signs the universe sends you, Maggie.'"

He glommed onto the name, the first time she'd used it. "She called you Maggie?"

"Everyone called me Maggie when I was young. I think of myself as Maggie."

"I like it." So much better than Lena. Maggie was the spirited, wild girl who made him nuts with her mouth and her fingers and her bracelets. "I'm going to call you Maggie." That way, when he screwed up and used the wrong name, she'd never notice.

"Call me anything you want," she said with a nudge. "Just call me. Ha-ha."

"Why'd you change it?"

"Smitty called me Lena, and it stuck."

"How long were you married?"

"Aw, Dan." She leaned closer. "You really want to talk about my husband?"

He turned his head, which put them face-to-face. "Do you?"

"I don't . . ." She inched to him. "Really . . ." A little closer. "Want to talk at all."

He could feel her breath on his mouth, see her eyes shutter close. "One more centimeter, Maggie, and it's gonna be all over."

"No, it's gonna start."

Closing the space, he let his lips brush hers, and just that little contact tightened his groin and made his hands itch to touch her.

If she had any earthly idea who he was . . .

She pressed her lips to his and branded him with silky smooth gloss and the tip of her tongue.

Soft. Sweet. Wet. Warm.

He relaxed into the heat of her lips. Her cool, dry palm on his cheek, guiding his mouth into the right place. After about thirty seconds, he took them both to the grass without breaking the kiss, pulling a soft moan of consent from her throat. Partially on top of her, he slid his thigh over hers, turned her into his body, and deepened the kiss.

This was all he wanted—one more time with Maggie.

He was transported back to the smell of sticky Miami

nights and sweaty clandestine trysts. The burning, insistent desire to be inside her. Anywhere. Anytime.

Her legs wrapped around him, her crotch molded to his hard-on.

"Another life, huh?" Her words against his lips pulled him back to reality. Had she figured it out? Remembered him from just one kiss?

"I really don't believe in all that," he said, sliding a hand over the curve of her hip and headed for the sweet rise of her backside.

"But you feel familiar," she said, rolling against him again. "And trust me, I don't do this that often."

"Then why me?"

"I don't know." She inched back, considering him. "Something about you made me feel . . . adventurous."

"Everything about you makes me feel . . ." He opened his hand over her backside, pulling her into him a little. "Good."

She smiled as she kissed him, sucking in his tongue and flattening her hands on his chest, then sliding them up to his shoulders. In one easy move she wrapped a leg around his, so that his erection had nowhere to go but between her legs.

She was right. All so familiar.

He squeezed her buttocks and pushed her hips against his, the sound of their breathing, their gentle groans, and his thundering pulse drowning out the distant surf and surrounding hum of a million insects living in every tree. Like old times.

She arched into him and let him put her completely on her back, rolling on top of her to mimic sex with all their clothes on.

Exactly like the first time he'd seduced her.

In the shed. Late at night. A long, hot, dry hump that left him painfully hard and gave her what she called the best orgasm she'd ever had with her jeans on.

They were headed right back there. Fast.

"Touch me," she whispered, pressing her breasts against his chest. "Here. Please."

"Maggie . . . are you sure?"

"I'm sure," she said, rolling against his cock, "that when you call me that name, in that voice, with that . . . pressure . . . right there . . . that I'm going to . . ." She breathed into his ear. Then licked it. "Come."

Exactly like the first time.

He knew precisely how to make this woman lose it. Her nipples were little grenade pins. One touch. One tweak. One bite. That's all it took.

He eased under the tank top, sliding up her warm, tight belly, loving how her muscles clenched in anticipation. He closed a hand over her sweet, small breast, letting out a slow exhale of pleasure. He palmed her nipple and pulled it to a peak. "Beautiful, sexy Maggie."

He breathed her name, grateful she'd given him the reason to use it as he kissed his way down her throat, over her top and lifted the material up to her chin.

"Yes," she whispered. "Please, kiss me there. Kiss me."

He closed his mouth over the dark brown bud and instantly she reacted, rocking and rolling against his erection, mixing ecstasy and madness down there, making him so hard his balls felt like they could explode.

Sucking one breast and kneading the other, he rode her again and again, sliding his cock up and down her crotch, his zipper scraping her denim, knowing it was hollow intimacy but not caring because she wanted this release.

Her skin was moist and smooth, her hips were slow

and hungry, her fingers dug into his hair as she guided him between her breasts to kiss and lick and curl his tongue over the peaks. She whispered his name, moaned with gratitude, whimpered with need.

Under his mouth, her heart hammered. In his ear, her breath whooshed. She writhed and squeezed and bit down on his shoulder. And then she rocked with a vicious little fury that bruised his blood-stiffened cock, giving in to her climax.

"Oh my God." She fought for steady breaths, but didn't quite find them. "I have to tell you, I can't remember the last time I did something like this."

He could.

She pushed him off her a little, scrutinizing his expression, reading it wrong. "Oh, I'm sorry. I guess that was awfully one-sided."

"Nothing was awful," he said, rolling on to the grass next to her. "Two-sided isn't going to happen in the middle of a state park."

She opened her mouth to protest, then closed it. "You want to go back to my house?"

"I am going back to your house." He ran his finger along her lower lip, plumper from the kissing. "But seven miles of bridge is going to give you plenty of time to change your mind and let me leave you at the door."

If she didn't, he'd gratefully spend the night with her. But he'd disappear before she woke up.

Because too many more instant replays of the past, and Maggie Varcek was going to realize that Michael Scott didn't really die that night, and the "other life" she knew him from was in Miami fourteen years ago. No cover was *that* good.

"Then I'll have time to think about it," she said.

He cupped her face, kissed her again, then helped her up. "Let's go then."

He'd done this before—slept with her under false pretenses, used her for pleasure and purpose. He wrecked her life once, and sex with Maggie again could not—

The sudden screech of a car alarm screamed through the night. For a second they froze; then Dan reached down and snagged his gun, and automatically thrust Maggie behind him.

"They're all in Key West, huh?" He bolted forward, pulling her with him. "Stay behind me," he called out over the deafening wail of the alarm.

"My bag is in that car," she reminded him breathlessly.

The bag with her little .22. He ran faster, rounding the concession stand and keeping them both low as they reached the car. In the shadow, he could see a man at the passenger side, crouched over.

He took a warning shot over the car and over his head.

The thief pivoted away from the car and took off.

"Is he alone?" Maggie whispered in Dan's ear.

He squinted into the dim moonlight, the waning quarter giving him enough of a shadowy glimpse to sense a familiarity in the clothes and the muscular build and crisp moves of a highly trained runner.

That was no street thug breaking into a Porsche in an empty lot.

That was the Greek fortune hunter.

CHAPTER
THREE

"I NEVER TOLD him about Quinn." Maggie slumped on her sofa, the move fluttering the credit card receipts Brandy had laid on the coffee table while she completed her Saturday morning accounting. "Does that make me a liar, on top of a slut?"

"First of all, you didn't sleep with him, you made out on a beach. Little wild, but not bona fide slutty. Second, you didn't lie, you just didn't tell him your entire life history." Brandy tapped the calculator. "Honey, we kicked ass last week."

No one knew her entire life history, Maggie thought as she lifted a mug and powered down more coffee. Only Smitty, and he was gone. "Good thing we kicked ass, since I sent the rich guy packing before he got through the front door. I just didn't want to tell him I have a son. It's such a mood-killer."

"Mood-killer? Who are you kidding? You use that kid as a freaking shield." She held up her hands in front of her face. "'Back away from my body. I have a child. Do not try to get close. I have a child!'"

Maggie smiled and tucked her bare feet under her, smoothing the sleep pants she still wore and imagining what she'd have on, or not, if she hadn't sent that man away last night. "Very funny, but I told you the real reason I changed my mind about sleeping with him."

"Uh-huh." Brandy fought a smile. "That would be the 'stop before you do something you seriously regret' message from the great beyond, in the form of an attempted carjacking."

"It wasn't a carjacking. But don't you think it's completely weird that Dan is certain the guy who did it was the same one who was in the bar chatting you up all night?"

Brandy cleared the calculator. "As much as it pains me to admit it, the chatting was about you. Sorry, I don't buy his theory. They were just two alpha dogs growling over you, and he just wants you to think he's some superpowered bodyguard so you'll have sex with him and not the other dog."

"Except we were already on our way to having sex when that happened, and he was dead certain it was the same guy."

"Right. Some customer followed you to Bahía Honda to steal the Porsche? Then what was he doing while you were doing the horizontal hoo-ha up on the hill?"

Maggie sipped her coffee. "And, if he wanted to steal the Porsche, why would he have been on the passenger's side?"

"To steal your purse. Or maybe he was going to hide in the back and attack when you got in," Brandy suggested as she tapped the receipts into a neat pile. "Now, would you like to know exactly how much money we made last week? Another year of weeks like this and you can pay off the second mortgage. Then one more year and we can start the renovation."

Maggie dropped back on the sofa with a groan. Years of debt, followed by years of renovations, followed by years of more debt before they ever saw a real profit. That wasn't going to get the money in her bank account soon enough to pay for Quinn's college. And speaking of Quinn . . . Regret took another stab at her chest.

"What kind of mother am I, hiding my son? Now how do I tell him? 'Oh, by the way, when we were "talking" last night and I shut you up with the total maneater kiss? I didn't want to come clean about my son.' "

Her gaze moved to Quinn's seventh-grade school picture on the table, filling her with love. "I live for the kid, and I would die for him. It's just that . . . I don't know. Last night, I wanted to be . . ."

"Screwed?"

She pulled her legs up and hugged. "Loved."

"From a bar hook-up?"

"I know. It's just that there was something about that man. He even said it. It was like I knew him in another life."

"Oh, please. He was smokin' hot and smooth as silk. Another life? What a line."

"Hey, it worked. But I just don't think a man like *that* would be remotely interested in a woman who has a teenager."

"I'll go file these." Brandy stood up and cracked her back with a groan. "Look, what's to be interested? He lives in New York, not Miami. Use him for what he's offering, get your rocks off a few times, and kiss him good-bye. You've got one more night of maternal freedom. Who cares if he knows you have a son or not?"

"He might not come back tonight."

Brandy snorted as she headed to the office. "Oh, he'll be back."

Alone, Maggie picked up the other picture on the end table, taken their last Christmas as a whole family. Smitty with his insanely wide smile and shiny bald head, one arm around Maggie, the other around a skinny nine-year-old, glowing like he'd found buried treasure and was keeping it all for himself.

Except if Smitty had found treasure, he'd have bought a bigger boat and spent the rest on live bait, and told Maggie it was securely in the bank.

"Uh, Lena. You been cleaning?"

"No."

"Then you better come in here."

Maggie pushed off the couch and headed toward the third bedroom she used as an office, where Brandy stood with one hand out to a completely empty file drawer. "Any chance Quinn had the sudden burning need to go through the last twenty years of bar tabs? Because this puppy's been wiped out."

For a moment, she just stared, unable to comprehend. Then she slowly turned and took in the rest of the office. Nothing looked touched. She pulled open another file drawer. Empty. And the top desk drawer. Still full of junk, but the red folder where she kept unpaid bills was gone.

"Someone's been in here—oh God. The strongbox!" Maggie dropped to her knees to her hiding place under the desk where she kept their most important papers. The deed to the bar, passports. Quinn's birth certificate.

"Brandy, call Deputy Nusbaum. Someone robbed us."

"What about your jewelry? Anything else?"

Maggie darted down the hall to her room. She yanked

open the top drawer of her dresser and let out a groan. The pink cloth–covered jewelry box was moved to the left. She flipped the top, and the tiny diamond ring that had been Smitty's mother's was still there. Along with Baba's tarot cards. Next to the box, the tarnished silver container that said Baby's First lay open; a single yellowed tooth lay in a lock of flaxen hair.

She put her hand on her stomach, the violation so intense she almost gagged. Someone had broken into her house and touched her personal treasures.

"Nusbaum's on his way," Brandy said from the doorway, snapping her phone closed. "Goddamn teenagers looking for drug money."

"They were neat, then. I never even noticed when I came home. I just went to bed." Maggie closed her eyes, the realization hitting hard. "I'm so glad Quinn wasn't home last night."

Lola James strode across the expanse of her office, her three-inch heels snapping to the rhythm that propelled her forward. The familiar beat of the way she lived her life: fast, steady, ferocious.

She picked up the ringing PDA, not bothering to look at the ID. She knew who it was. Instead, she glanced at her reflection in the corner window, which was far nicer than the view of downtown Miami. She smoothed the hip-hugging skirt and lifted her chin to admire the strong lines of her jaw. Then her eyes focused on the view outside the offices of Omnibus Transport, LLC. It beat the last place she had, in South Miami, and the hellhole before that in Hialeah.

But she could do so much better.

That's what she'd done with her private real estate, and

what she'd do with her company. Always, always moving up. Getting better. Getting more and more *attractive*. She'd done it to her body, her face, her home, and her business was next.

"Just come up the elevator and knock," she said as she answered the phone on the fourth ring. No need to seem anxious. "I left the main door open, and there's no one else here on a Saturday."

No one but her, and she'd work *eight* days a week if she could. Not that she didn't enjoy her weekend nights. She'd certainly enjoyed *last* night. She brushed her palms over her breasts, remembering how they'd been admired and attended to. Yes, she'd enjoyed that man a lot.

But she had three minutes until this one arrived, so she dropped onto her chair and touched the laptop to bring it to life. Lola never wasted anything, especially time. At twenty-three, she was already almost a millionaire. You didn't get there by taking breaks and thinking about men who'd adored you for a few hours.

Well, some breaks. And some men.

While she waited, she clicked through the air-shipping schedule for the evening, and dashed off a quick note to the CEO of a furniture company in North Carolina who'd just signed on as Omnibus Transport's latest customer. That one gave her a twinge of satisfaction.

After all, furniture delivery had always been the humble roots of this little empire.

The elevator dinged and she touched the button on her desk to unlock her door, a security measure she'd learned from her father. Standing up, she rounded the desk to position herself in front of it. She'd make him sit of course, the only way to get a height advantage on a man of six-two.

The door opened slowly and she met the steely eyes of Constantine Xenakis, thief, mercenary, and one of the finest specimens of male to ever cross her threshold. She took a slow ride down his incredible body, but her gaze stopped at the tan box in his hand.

The thrill of victory was so intense she shivered. "Well, that looks promising. A lockbox."

"There was nothing else close to what you wanted in her house."

"Maybe she carries it with her."

"I thought of that, but wasn't able to get her bag. She's got muscle." He took three long strides to her desk and clunked the box on her desk. "Or . . . someone else has beat you to the punch."

She curled her lip. Impossible. "Maybe Maggie did get some protection. She's probably heard that Ramon is out."

"She goes by Lena, and she doesn't just have a bodyguard, my friend. She has one of the best in the business. A Bullet Catcher. That's with capital letters. Top man in the company, too, so she's paying a handsome fee for his services. Unless . . ." He looked hard at her. "You planted him there."

Lola dismissed the suggestion with a wave. "Nope. You got this, and if you got what I wanted, nothing else matters. You didn't open it, did you?"

"Of course not." He eased into one of her guest chairs, lifting his legs to land a pair of scuffed Docksiders next to the box on the desk in a move both rude and arrogant.

No matter. She touched the lock. "Can you get this off?'

"Yes."

"Then do it."

He grinned. "Lock removal's an extra grand."

"Fuck you, Con." Not for one minute did she believe he hadn't opened the box before he brought it here. But he wouldn't keep what she wanted, because then he wouldn't get the ten thousand dollars she'd agreed to pay him for it.

She yanked open the top drawer of her desk and pulled out her little pink-handled revolver, aiming it at the box.

"Oh, for Christ's sake." He slammed his feet down and took the gun from her hand. "And I thought you were elegant."

The dig stung, but at this point, she didn't care. Her heart rate was up and her palms were damp. She was so close. So, so close to finally winning Alonso Jimenez's biggest game.

Con stood, reached into his pants pocket, and pulled out a tiny silver cell phone, which he set on the desk, then a key ring, which he squeezed, popping out a short metal prong. He put it in the lock, twisting once, then again. The lock released with a soft ping.

She took off the lock and slowly lifted the dented lid. Her father used to tell her that sometimes the most valuable treasures were hidden in ugly places.

Of course, he said that when he squeezed her face and tried to erase the insult by jostling her chin. The heartless bastard.

There wasn't much in the box, but that was okay. What she wanted was very small. But all it held was . . . papers.

She lifted one after the other. Insurance. Deeds. A birth certificate. A passport? A wedding license?

That was it. Legal papers.

She sifted through again, checking corners, fluttering the documents. "It's not here."

"It's nowhere else in her house. I looked in all the places where women keep things."

Glaring daggers of accusation, she leaned forward. "If you doublecross me, you lying, thieving bastard, you'll be sorry."

"Calm down, Lola. I have to get to her another way than a B and E into her house or bar. I have to talk to her, which I would have easily done if that Bullet Catcher hadn't beat me to it."

"I agree, and I have just the thing to make her talk. Leave."

"What?"

"Go out in the hall. I'll let you back in. I want to show you something, but you need to leave first."

He got up with an amused look on his face and walked out, closing the door with a solid click, but she followed him and double-checked the lock. You couldn't trust a thief.

Then she headed to the wet bar, crouched down, and opened the cabinet, which, of course, didn't contain a drop of alcohol.

Reaching into the back, she touched the digital pad hidden behind a false door and entered the passcode. At her desk, a soft snap told her it worked. She returned to her chair, placing her hands under the front of the desk and inching out the false bottom.

There were two items on the left side. She picked up one, a photograph of a boy not more than twelve. She closed the drawer, closed the wet bar door, too, then buzzed Con back in.

She handed him the picture. "Use this to get it."

He glanced at the boy, then up at her, disgust in his eyes. "A kid?"

"I suppose you'd want more money."

He set the picture down, making no effort to hide his disgust. "No, thanks."

"Oh, please, you're suddenly developing morals?"

"I'm suddenly developing a deep distaste for your style." He picked up his phone and headed back to the door. Damn it, she had no choice.

"Seventy-five thousand," she said quickly.

Con hesitated and looked over his shoulder, his silvery stare cold. "A hundred."

"Fine." What was a hundred thousand when she stood to make a hundred million? "Take it," she said, waving the picture.

"I don't need it." He left without another word.

Alone, Lola sat back down, disappointment seeping through her. Not because of the money she'd just spent, but because she thought she had Viejo beat. But the momentum in the game was definitely not on her side.

She lifted up a crispy parchment deed, the marriage license, the birth certificate, and let them flutter to her shiny desk. Useless crap that didn't . . .

For a moment, she didn't breathe. She just stared at the words in front of her and felt her jaw loosen.

Constantine Xenakis might just have earned his ten thousand dollars. Because if information was power, this little tidbit was a nuclear plant.

Magdalena Varcek. You little vixen.

The game had just shifted Lola's way.

CHAPTER
FOUR

BY FIVE O'CLOCK on Sunday afternoon, Dan lost the fight.

He'd done really well, too. He hadn't gone back to Smitty's. He hadn't gone back to Maggie's little house less than two miles from the marina next to the bar. He hadn't succumbed to what he knew was a very bad idea . . . one more night with her.

More specifically, one more night of sex with her.

If she somehow figured out who he was, she'd want to kill him. If he slept with her and disappeared *again*—well, nothing could justify that. She deserved better.

He'd even packed his bags and checked out of the resort, with every intention of getting into that rented Porsche by noon and heading straight up U.S. 1 to Miami to spend a few days with Max and Cori and little Peyton. Maybe he'd call the Bullet Catchers' office and run a background on Constantine Xenakis. That's all he needed to do.

Nothing had to be done . . . in person.

Yet, he turned onto the street where she lived. He still had that nagging belief that he recognized the vandal who'd broken into the car, so he just couldn't leave. It wasn't safe for her.

Then he turned the corner and saw her.

Man, it wasn't safe for *him*.

She was splayed over the hood of a white truck, sudsy water rolling all over the place, her arms wiping furiously. Tiny jeans shorts barely covered her heart-shaped butt, a bushel of curls tied up like a palm tree grew out of her head, and the skimpy pink tank top had to be soaking wet as she laid her whole screaming-hot body over the front end of the Silverado.

Whoa. Could he possibly have her, just once, and then leave the same way he appeared? Quickly and mysteriously and without explanation?

Could he possibly *not*?

She hadn't yet noticed the Porsche idling at the stop sign two houses away. Throwing the sponge down, she pushed off the truck, landing on her bare feet and brushing stray, wet hairs off her face with the back of her hand. She turned to the house and yelled something.

She wasn't alone.

He tapped the accelerator, revving the engine enough to make her whip around and squint down the street, raising her hand to the setting sun, and taking a slow step backward when she realized what car made the noise.

She tilted her head toward the house, calling again.

Dan rumbled forward, closing the space slowly, until he stopped at the end of her driveway. He lowered the passenger-side window.

"You missed a spot, sweetheart."

She threw a look over her shoulder, then ambled to his car, walking slowly enough to torture him. The wet top was plastered to the peaks of her breasts, and if her shorts were any shorter, they'd qualify as a bikini.

When she reached the car, she propped her elbows on the window ledge. "I thought you went back to New York, Irish."

"You really think I'd leave and not say good-bye?"

"You really think I worried about it?" She tempered the tease with a wink, her face glowing from a little sun and sweat, her eyes just as sultry in sunlight as they were under a moonbeam.

"I figured you needed some breathing room."

She inhaled with great exaggeration. "Okay, I've breathed. Good-bye now."

Good-bye? He gestured for her to back away. "Let me park."

"No." She didn't move.

"Why not?"

One more little look over her shoulder gave it all away. "You're not alone, are you, Maggie?" For one instant he imagined the fortune hunter would stroll out of the garage, and his fingers actually fisted as a wave of jealousy rocked him.

She soothed it with a pretty smile. "I do like it when you call me that."

"So get rid of whoever has you watching your back, and I'll call you Maggie all night long."

She collapsed a little on one arm. "Not for all the Maggie-calling in the world could I get rid of . . . him."

"I could." Because now that he'd seen her again, there was no way he was leaving until he got what he wanted. And he wanted her.

"I can't," she said again.

"Whoever it is, Maggie, ditch him." He reached across

the passenger seat and put his hand on hers. "I want to be with you tonight."

"Oh." The single syllable came out like a soft sigh. "No."

"No you don't want to, or no you can't ditch your . . . company."

"No it's not company." She sighed and shook her head. "Look, I haven't been completely open with you, Dan." She nudged her head farther into the car. "I didn't tell you this the other night. I have a . . ."

A door slammed behind her, and a big brown dog came barreling up the driveway, barking wildly.

"A dog." He finished for her, smiling as it bounded to the car and threw his paws up next to Maggie. "A huge one," he added as a giant chocolate fur–covered face and a tongue the size of a small country filled the window space next to her.

Dan shut off the engine, opening his door when another sound from the driveway caught his attention.

"Yeow! Holy craptastica! I swear to God, Mom, if you know the owner of this car, I just died and went to heaven."

A golden-haired boy, smooth faced enough to be twelve but broad enough to pass for fifteen, pointed at the Porsche, shaking his head. "I'm freakin' out."

The kid transferred his attention to Dan, who climbed out of his seat and continued around the car, drawn to the deep green eyes, the clefted chin, the too-cool-for-his-own-good posture of the boy in front of him.

Maggie, holding the dog by the collar, looked from one to the other as the animal tried hard to break her grip and jump on Dan.

And a dog *could* have knocked him right over. A soft breeze could have flattened him at that minute.

"You have a son," he said, finishing what he now knew she was trying to say.

"Yeah." She got a good grip on the dog.

Dan's attention was riveted on the boy, who was just as riveted on the car.

"Dude, shoot me now because that is my effing dream car!"

"Quinn, please."

"Mom, I have a *poster* of it on my wall. No sh-kidding."

Dan didn't take his eyes off the kid, every single detail of his appearance and demeanor suddenly so sharply in focus. "You hiding anyone else in that house, Maggie? Any other secrets? Any other surprises?"

"No," she said quietly. "It's just us. Honey, this is . . . a friend of mine, Mr. . . . Gallagher."

"You *do* know him." The boy punched his fist in the air. "Yesss!"

Dan finally turned to look at Maggie. Her color was high as she gripped the dog's collar with both hands. "This is Quinn." She tilted her head, an apologetic smile on her face.

Why should she apologize?

The boy bounded toward the car, his jaw open just about the way Dan's probably was.

"And, this is our dog, Goose," she added.

"Goose." He sounded as befuddled as he felt, every synapse in his brain misfiring.

"I know, I know," the boy said, practically dancing around the car and gingerly touching the hood. "Maverick would have been a better name."

Dan reached down into years of undercover training,

digging for a way to not react or respond. And while he was digging, maybe he could find any possible explanation for what he saw, other than the obvious.

But none came.

"You thought he'd be your wingman," Dan finally said. "So you named him Goose."

Quinn whipped around to Dan. "You like *Top Gun*, too? Cool." He grinned, revealing neon bands through silver braces. Braces that were so new, his two front teeth still overlapped slightly.

Dan's tongue automatically traveled over his own front teeth, the slight misalignment as familiar to him as the green eyes he saw in the mirror every morning. The same ones staring at him right now.

The truth gripped him like a fist, shaking him down to his feet, leaving him reeling.

He had a son.

A *son*.

He turned to Maggie and casually bent down to scratch the dog's ears. "So what are you two doing tonight?" Some quick stealth work and math needed to be done. "How 'bout we all go out for dinner?"

Her eyes widened, but the boy snorted. "In this? Is the Pope Catholic?"

Maggie rolled her eyes and laughed softly. "Quinn."

He turned at the chiding note in his mother's voice. "Can't we? I mean, he invited us."

"I certainly did," Dan agreed, dangling the keys in front of Quinn. "Can you drive yet?"

He put his hand on his chest and pretended to choke. "Dude. I wish."

"You must be close to that age." But thirteen would be the *right* number.

"He's only thirteen," Maggie said.

Oh, man. "I guess that would be pushing the law a little to let him drive," he said easily. "But the jump seat's big enough. Let's go for a ride."

Quinn beamed. "I'm in."

"I'm . . . wet." Maggie said, obviously torn.

"It's a rental." Dan put a hand on her shoulder and reached for the passenger door. "You can bring the dog, for all I care."

She laughed, hesitating just a little.

"Mom, we are *so* going in this car."

Defeated, she put up her hands and stepped forward, then stopped. "Wait. I have to lock the doors."

"Definitely, since we were burglarized the other day," Quinn said.

"You were?" Dan looked from one to the other. "When?"

"The night . . . we went out."

"You two went out?" Quinn's eyes popped. "Seriously?"

"Sort of," Maggie added.

"Yes," Dan said right over her words. "So go lock every door in the house, and we'll take her for a spin."

The kid hesitated, more out of disbelief than disobedience, but Maggie pointed to the house. "Go. He knows what he's talking about. He's a bodyguard."

"No way!" Quinn almost jumped out of his skin. "That is tight, dude! Hang on. I need shoes, too." He turned and jogged back down the driveway to the house with Goose close on his heels.

"Wow," Maggie said, swiping at one of the curls that fell on her face. "I should have such a carrot to dangle all the time." She stepped back, biting her lip. "I'm sorry I didn't tell you about him."

"Why?" *Because he's mine?* Of course she couldn't know, but the reality still rocked him.

"Why didn't I tell you, or why am I sorry?"

"Both."

"I didn't tell you because, I don't know, raising a teenager is . . . not . . . what most men want to talk about. I'm sorry, because it feels like I deceived you and that doesn't sit well with me."

He reached out to push that curl aside for her. "First of all, I'm not most men. Second, if that loses you a date, then the idiot wasn't worth your time. And third, I'm the one who deceived you."

Which anyone with decent vision could see, if they compared her son to him. Of course, people see what they expect to see, and she obviously never expected to see Michael Scott again. Still, he had to get to the truth fast, because she *might* figure it out.

She frowned. "How did you deceive me?"

"I don't have to leave for New York for a while. I'm staying longer, and I should have come into the bar and told you."

"Why are you staying?"

He tilted his head and tapped her chin. "Like you need to ask."

She let out a little exhale of satisfaction.

"He seems like a great kid," Dan added, glancing at the house.

"He is. He's amazing. And . . ." She closed her hand over his, and pressed it to her cheek. "So are you."

Baba, send me a sign. It's Maggie, calling for help.

Nobody answered.

Maggie curled her legs under her, fitting nicely into

the undersize backseat of the sports car, listening to the two males in the front discuss cylinders, horsepower, and torque.

She glanced at the clock on the dashboard. Did the numbers 9:28 portend great things?

That they'd get married on September 28? That he'd kiss her nine hundred and twenty-eight times in their lifetime together? Or just tonight? That'd work, too.

She and Quinn had just spent four hours with the most delectable man she'd ever met, and all the three of them had done was laugh over burgers and basically have more fun than she'd had at a dinner since Smitty died.

Who needed a sign? *Face facts, sister. You're over the moon for this guy.* Totally crushed out, as Quinn would say.

She looked up into the rearview mirror just as Dan caught her fighting a smile. He gave her a sly wink and the Fourth of July exploded in her stomach.

Not only was he a prime gorgeous hot, sexy hunk of human male, he also asked Quinn a zillion questions and listened to the answers. He never made fun of the teen talk, never excluded him from the conversation, and kept everyone laughing.

And made her blood boil with lust.

Could she possibly have a great guy to be around her son and a lust fest for herself?

But how could there be a future? Her mind whirred with possibilities and obstacles. He lived in New York. Would she move to New York?

In a heartbeat. The one that had been hammering her chest for the last three hours. Of course, she'd have to sell the bar, and after all Brandy had put into it, that would be tough. But maybe if she—

"Can I, Mom?" Quinn turned and asked the question, dragging her from the most ridiculous and premature line of thought she'd ever had.

"Uh, it's kind of loud back here." She put her hand to her ear. "Can you what?"

Dan looked in the mirror again, the smile in his eyes looking a lot like the one in Quinn's. "That's because the engine's in the back," he explained.

No, it's because she was spinning stupid fairy tales.

"Can I put the stereo on full blast?" Quinn asked. "They're Bose surround-sound speakers. Okay?"

She nodded. Maybe the first song would be a sign from the universe.

A guitar solo blared and Quinn shouted something over it, so Maggie just closed her eyes and conjured up her own signs. But all she could think of was the way Dan had kissed her and touched her on the beach. What would happen if they went further? Should she?

She sneaked a peek at his shoulders, at the dark blond hair that brushed his collar, at the hair-dusted forearm resting confidently on the gearshift.

She shouldn't, but, whoa, she wanted to.

"Can I change the tune?" Quinn asked, sliding it to the classic rock station he liked.

A rocker wailed. "You . . . shook me all night long."

Okay, Baba. Got it. Heard that one loud and clear.

Maggie listened to the crashing rock and roll and felt her whole body coil into a knot the rest of the way home. She stayed wound pretty tight while Quinn took his captive audience on a tour of his room to examine his car posters, and the two of them Googled exotic sports cars for a little while.

When Quinn finally went to bed, she lit a few candles

on the screened-in back porch, got Dan a beer, poured herself some wine, and left plenty of room next to her on the rattan sofa. It was dim, private, and romantic, with the smell of the sea in the air and wind brushing palm fronds together. Perfect.

When he joined her he seemed completely at ease, in no way put out by having to spend all those hours with a teenager.

"You've really been terrific to him tonight," she said. "Thanks."

"No need. He's an awesome kid," he said. "Smart and inquisitive. Great sense of humor."

"He's very dry-witted," she agreed. "Sometimes downright sarcastic."

"Hey, he's a teenager. He's doing his job," he said, sitting down next to her. "I'm glad I got to know him."

Did she detect a strange note in his voice? The same one she heard when he said he was staying in town . . . something was just not right.

"I have to ask you a question," she said, lifting her glass. "And you have to promise to be completely honest."

That got her a rueful smile. "Of course."

"Because something you said, and did, has kind of been niggling at me all night."

The smile disappeared. "Really? What?"

"When we got in the car to leave tonight, you had to take a duffel bag out of the backseat to make room for me."

He took a sip of his beer, not looking at her as she continued.

"But right before that, you said you'd decided to stay a few extra days. So, when did you decide that? As you pulled up and saw—"

"You in those shorts." The answer was fast—and a little too slick? "I drove around the corner, saw paradise plastered on the hood of a Chevy, and changed my plans."

God, she wanted to believe that.

"Now I have a question." His tone was serious, and his expression matched.

"Fair enough. Shoot."

"You must have been pretty young when you got married, huh? I mean Quinn's thirteen and you're . . ."

It wasn't the first time she'd heard this. "I was nineteen when he was born," she said, heat rising to her cheeks because she'd just demanded honesty, and he'd countered with the one and only thing in her life that didn't get that same treatment. "And, yes, I married young."

He would assume, as everyone did, that she and Smitty had to get married. And she would tell him the truth: that she and Smitty married when Quinn was a year old. No one had ever questioned anything beyond that. They'd met when she was two months' pregnant, and almost from the beginning, they'd been complicit in the lie.

Except she'd insisted on putting the truth on Quinn's birth certificate.

"So, did you meet your husband in high school?"

"Um, no." She'd told the story enough times and it was so close to reality that it even felt genuine. "I dropped out of high school, and came down to the Keys really young. I got a job working in the kitchen for Smitty because I was too young to serve alcohol, and we . . . well, it was pretty much love at first sight." Maybe not love. Maybe . . . need. Love came later. "We ended up getting married when Quinn was about a year old."

She never actually said Smitty was Quinn's father, but everyone made the assumption.

Except something about his expression said he didn't believe her. "Why didn't you get married before he was born?"

Why was he looking at her like that? "Lots of people wait. And I was really young. A lot younger than Smitty."

He nodded, obviously thinking it all through, and for some reason, didn't seem quite . . . satisfied.

"He was twelve years older than me," she added.

Still, he didn't respond.

"What's the matter?" she asked, fighting a little wave of defensiveness and embarrassment. "A lot of people live together before they're married," she said, her voice sounding weak to her. "And have babies."

The romance of the moment slipped a little, along with her heart. He didn't like her story, she could tell. Well, he'd really hate the rest of it, then.

Quinn's not Smitty's child. I was a drug dealer's girlfriend who had an affair with a narc.

He picked up his beer and took a drink, then set it down a little hard. "Did you call the police?"

Call the police? For what? Then she realized what he was referring to.

"When we were robbed? Of course. Actually, it's a sheriff in Marathon, and they did a full report. But they'll never find who did it."

"What'd they take?"

"Well, it was weird," she said, lifting her wineglass. "They took only paper: old receipts, bar tabs, and a strongbox from my office, which had some legal docs and paperwork. But they left the small diamond ring in my jewelry box."

"Any prescription drugs?"

She shook her head. "I don't take them, but they only

went into two places. My office and my bedroom. Nothing else was touched. For drugged up kids, they were neat."

"No electronics? Laptop? TV?"

"Nope."

"And it happened Friday night?"

"Yes. Why all the questions, officer?"

"Can't help it. My FBI background comes out."

She barely covered the tiny intake of breath and managed not to sound shocked. "FBI?"

He nodded slowly, watching her reaction carefully. Too carefully.

"I didn't know you were with the FBI."

"That's what I did before I joined the Bullet Catchers, the firm I work for now. I was an FBI agent."

She sipped her wine, but it stuck in her throat and swallowing felt impossible. "Well, you're welcome to look around for clues, but I'm pretty sure it was just a random robbery."

Could any FBI agent—or former one—find her name in the old files from the Jimenez drug bust? Could they know her history? She'd never been contacted after she ran away from that life, but it always hovered in the back of her mind.

An FBI agent would hate how she'd lived. *She* hated how she'd lived. Or maybe he already knew.

She sat a little straighter. "So, how long were you with the FBI?" She forced her voice to be casually interested, not riddled with shame.

He nailed her with that green gaze again, direct and meaningful. "A long time."

Oh *God*. He knew exactly who she was. And if he didn't, he would. He'd run a check, and her name would pop right up in some federal computer.

But not Smith. It would say Varcek. Didn't matter; it was only a matter of time. This party had officially ended.

She stood up. "You know, it's getting late and I have to work late tomorrow night so I better get some sleep."

He didn't move. "Why?"

Why? Why did she live with a drug dealing son of a money launderer when she was eighteen, and screw around with an undercover federal agent? Why did she run away and never look back, pregnant with that bastard's kid? Why did she change her name, her life, and her world? "Why what?" Her voice cracked.

"Why do you want me to leave?"

She blew out a breath, and offered a shaky smile. "Because, as you may recall, I have absolutely zero ability to resist you, and my son may or may not be asleep at this moment, and if you spend even one more second here, I will surely jump your bones and take a ride. So, good-bye. And thanks for dinner. I had a blast."

He reached up his hand and tried to tug her back down. "We can just talk."

She gave a dry laugh. "Yeah, that was some sparkling conversation on the beach."

"No, I'm serious. I have . . . something I want to tell you, Maggie."

I bet you do. "My name's Lena. I haven't been Maggie for a long time. That girl is . . . dead. Got it?" She underscored that with a look that said she would not talk, she would not confess, and she would not let some former FBI agent dredge up her past and smash it into the face of her unsuspecting son.

His expression grew darker and even more intense, but he didn't say a word.

"So, please. Up and out, Irish." She worked to keep her voice easy. "Night's over."

Very slowly, without taking his eyes from her, he stood. Then he put his thumb on her chin and rubbed it, the gesture pulling at something elemental in her.

"All right, *Lena*," he said softly. "We'll talk . . . later." He lowered his face and kissed her so softly she barely felt it. "Good night."

She didn't move as he walked away. She listened to his footsteps on the tile floor, heard the front door open and close. Following him, she twisted the dead bolt.

His car started up with a loud rumble, then disappeared into the night. She dropped her head against the door and closed her eyes.

The first tear that slipped out surprised her. She *never* cried. She hadn't cried since Smitty died. And before that, not since she'd been a teenager in trouble.

She wiped her face hard—but that didn't get rid of the hollow pain in her heart.

CHAPTER
FIVE

ALONSO JIMENEZ KEPT his head low, his right hand on a pistol in one pocket, his left hand on the riveted handle of his dagger. Nighttime in the warehouse barrio of Las Marías, Venezuela, was no place to wander alone and unarmed.

Especially for El Viejo.

But his normal circle of protection couldn't be trusted to accompany him on this trip. No one could. He'd made this visit three times in the past six months, and he'd run into trouble on a few occasions, but nothing serious. He'd been very, very lucky so far.

There were so few cars in Las Marías that he stopped when he heard an engine, slipping into the shadows to let the vehicle rumble by. Pressed against the dilapidated wood boards of a building less than one block from his destination, he turned his head to flatten himself as much as possible as the car passed.

A few seconds ticked by, and the car slowed.

He swore under his breath. He was old, and past his prime for street fighting. But the engine revved again and the old heap continued on its way, so Alonso did, too.

Around the corner he stepped into a littered alley, rats skittering at the sound of his footsteps. It grew darker as he moved deeper to the side door of a stucco-sided warehouse, pausing to listen for the car, or anyone who might have followed him.

Only his breath. His heartbeat.

One was quick, the other, sadly, getting slower every day. The cancer that invaded his body was taking its toll, no matter how much he tried to deny it. Just as it had for Caridad, his beloved wife, time was running out. And he had yet to finish the most important project of all. When he was done, to the victor went the spoils.

Well, to the boy.

He sheathed his knife so he could slip a key into the padlock on the metal side door. Silently he unlocked it and opened the door just enough to slide inside.

He paused in the musty darkness, giving his eyes a moment to adjust when he closed the door behind him. When he could see shadows, he rolled an empty barrel he kept near the opening against the door, standing it up so that he'd hear it scrape the floor if someone tried to get in. There was no internal lock; that would just be a signal that something extremely valuable was in this "abandoned" warehouse.

A rat scratched the rafters, but other than that the place was silent.

Alonso felt his way to the left, his fingers scraping the rotting wood of empty shelves. Five more steps, then four to the right until he reached the crates. He touched one, following the lines of the splintered wood until he found the opening. He reached for the crowbar he'd left on a shelf last time and just as his fingers closed over it, the scuff of metal on concrete echoed through the warehouse.

The door was shoved open so quickly that he didn't have time to get his dagger. He dove to the floor, crawling between two crates, the crowbar in his grip.

A hushed whisper, a low male laugh. The rough tones of barrio Spanish.

They knew he was in here, or suspected it. And even if they didn't find him, would they find what he was hiding?

He couldn't risk making a sound by reaching for his weapon. So he waited, dead still.

A crate moved across the floor, gritty dirt against cement. Feet scuffled, and a few words were exchanged in hushed whispers. If they had a light, he'd know it by now. And he'd be dead, or killing one of them.

"Que hay aquí?"

What was in here? More money than any of these *maracuchos* had ever seen in their lives.

Listening to the slow and steady beat of his pulse, Alonso waited.

One of them kicked a crate and called the others. *"Pesado."*

Of course it was heavy; it was full of gold. He swallowed, keeping his mouth closed so his tongue didn't click on the dry roof of his mouth.

He heard the sound of their moving one of the crates, discussing how to open it.

A motor revved, and a shout from the street stopped everything. *"Anda! Anda!"*

Yes. Go. Now.

The first prickle of relief started in his chest as one of them moved to the door. Then another. Then the third. They spoke, too quiet for him to make out the words. A little laughter. Another shout from the street.

They left the door open when they ran out, which

gave out the tiniest bit of light. He waited, listening for the sound of the engine to fade away before he carefully pushed himself up from his hiding place. He took a few silent steps, the dim light from outside giving him a fairly clear view of the storage area. All of the crates appeared to be as they had been, except for the ones he'd emptied, piece by tedious piece.

He had a job to do. And a grandchild to do it for.

He lifted the crowbar to raise the lid of the crate he'd come to empty, just as he heard the infinitesimal whisper of a breath behind him.

Whipping around with the bar raised, he flung himself on instinct without seeing his attacker. The crowbar smacked against a head, the crack of the skull snapping through the warehouse walls, instantly followed by a yelp.

Alonso took another vicious swing as the man fell to the ground, landing the blow right on his temple. That silenced him. But was it enough?

He whacked again, thudding the skull one more time, then again, and again, until his attacker lay completely still.

Alonso looked at the door, waiting for the next one, the crowbar in his right hand, his knife in his left.

Had this one been alone? Had he been the only one to suspect something of value might be in the old, abandoned warehouse?

Nothing stirred, not even the rats.

After a minute, he dragged the body to the crate he'd emptied last time.

Alonso Jimenez was a strong man. He might have a cancer in his body, a broken family, and a wrecked life, but he was still El Viejo. He hoisted the body into the crate, closed it, and returned to the one he'd been about to open. He jabbed the bar in and grunted as he pushed, the hinges squeaking. Then he reached in for a very heavy hammer to close the intruder's coffin.

He quickly finished his business, got what he needed to make this next deposit, and slipped back into the night, satisfied. Almost satisfied.

He wouldn't be truly happy until young Quinn Smith was home.

After seventy-two miserable tequila-soaked hours staring out at the ocean from a different room at the same resort, Dan still didn't have any answers. The questions just kept piling up.

Quinn had lived his whole life, thinking another man was his father, so what difference did it make if he spent the rest of it with that mistaken notion?

Maggie was clearly running from her past; what right did he have to blow it up in her face and wreck her life?

Dan had just dodged the commitment bullet with a woman he knew well and nearly loved; why the hell would he seek it with a virtual stranger?

And the biggest question of all—how would Maggie feel? He had no doubt that she'd seen what happened that night in Miami, and knew he'd betrayed her and used her to rat out the whole operation, so the chances that she'd be overjoyed to have a reunion with Michael Scott were nil. More likely, she'd use her little .22 right between his eyes. Or legs.

She hadn't figured it out yet, but wasn't he living on borrowed time? Couldn't she see the genetic imprint of him on her son?

It didn't matter if she did or not. He had to tell her the truth.

Otherwise he'd have to go on knowing he had a son living on this earth whom he didn't know. Not to mention the financial responsibilities. Maggie was obviously struggling, and he could make her life easy with the stroke of his pen.

Was it the right thing to do . . . or the wrong thing?

One thing he knew: he owed Maggie honesty. Then he had to respect what she did with that information. If she chose not to reveal the truth to her son, he would abide by that. He'd still give her money and whatever she needed, but he wouldn't force his fatherhood on Quinn.

He waited until he was fairly certain she'd be at the bar, early enough so that there would be few customers. As he parked his rented car in front of Smitty's, the last vestiges of sunshine faded. He didn't want to tell her at home, when Quinn was there, and not while she worked the bar or cleaned tables. Hopefully he could talk her into one more midnight rendezvous.

As he climbed out of the Porsche, a loud bark pulled his attention and he spun around, seeing Goose, and then meeting those very green eyes that had haunted him for two days. The hero worship he'd earned over their dinner was replaced by cold teenage distrust and disgust as Quinn yanked the leash and pulled the dog back.

"Hey, Quinn."

"What are you doing here?" Quinn demanded, the big Australian shepherd winning the tug of war and gaining ground. The boy's flip-flops snapped on the pavement as Goose dragged them both closer, a bushy tail whipping side to side, that massive tongue waving with each loud pant.

Dan closed the space and knelt down to rub the dog's neck. "I stopped by to see your mom."

"She doesn't want to see you." He yanked the leash, as if to say *don't touch my dog*.

Slowly, Dan stood. "Why's that?"

"Beats me." He brushed his hand over his hair in a gesture so familiar, Dan almost laughed. In a few years, when the kid had a beard, he knew exactly how he'd rub that, too.

And, shit, he kind of wanted to be around to see it.

"She didn't tell you?" Dan prodded.

Quinn managed to inch the dog back. "I don't know. It's, like, not my business, and I don't really get her all the time, but whatever you did to her the other night . . ."

"I didn't do anything to her," Dan said quietly. "What happened?"

"She cried all night, that's what. I hate that."

So did he. "Then I really better talk to her."

"No, you really better leave her alone." His gaze flickered to the car for a second, and regret darkened his face. "Just . . . leave us alone."

He fought the leash one more time and started off.

"Where are you going?" Dan's question was natural, and came out without thinking.

Damn. He cared. Already.

"None of your fucking business." Despite the tough guy talk, maybe because of it, he suddenly sounded very young, and vulnerable.

"Quinn, don't talk like that."

He shrugged. "Whatev. You're not the boss of me."

And that, son, is where you are wrong. But Dan said nothing as Quinn jogged away, trying to keep up with Goose, who'd moved on to the next interesting scent.

He headed in, rethinking his plan for a late night

meeting. There might not be time for that. Or the opportunity.

The bar was empty except for one older man at the far end, watching ESPN on the flat screen, the vague smell of stale beer and conch fritters in the air.

Brandy looked up from a magazine and gave him a wide, friendly smile. "Well look what the hundred thousand dollar Porsche dragged in."

At least *she* didn't think he ought to leave them alone. "It's a rental."

"So I've heard. And it tells me a lot about a man who rents a car like that as opposed to, say, a Taurus."

Dan smiled as he leaned on the bar, resisting the urge to look around for Maggie. "What's it tell you?"

"That you're rich."

"Only that I have expensive tastes." He tapped the bar and glanced around. "She here?"

Brandy cocked her shiny blond hair toward the door next to the back bar. "In the office. Want me to get her?"

The office. Perfect. "Can I go see her?"

She frowned, considering. "She hasn't talked much about you the past few days. I thought maybe the crush got crushed." Then she pointed a finger at him. "My godson, on the other hand, hasn't talked about anything else. That's how I know what your rental cost." She looked hard at him. "You evidently made quite an impression on both of them."

He nodded and took a few steps toward the office. "Is it unlocked?"

"Yeah. Go ahead. She'll wished she had worn a little make up, but go on. Make her day."

"That's my plan." He turned the knob without knocking and stepped right in, peeking around the door just as she looked up from a metal desk covered in papers and forms.

"Oh," she whispered, her whole being stilled by the sight of him.

Her face was pale except for faint shadows under her eyes. She obviously hadn't slept much. And he was about to make it all so much worse.

"Hey." He didn't wait for an invitation, but slipped in and closed the door, twisting the latch position as he faced her. "You should keep this door locked if you're back here with any appreciable amount of money."

"Not appreciable. But thanks."

There was one chair with a little hole in the cane seat. A reject from the bar, no doubt. It wasn't offered.

"How are you?" he asked.

She lifted a shoulder. "Fine."

He waited, but she didn't say anything. "I'm fine, too," he finally said, taking the chair that wasn't offered. "Thanks for asking." He winked to make it playful, but she just sucked her bottom lip in a little and watched him warily.

"So . . ." he said, hands on his legs. "We need to talk."

"I don't want to talk, Dan." She set down a pencil and crossed her arms. "I don't want to hear what you have to say, or flirt with you anymore, or make out under the stars, or get all tangled up in you. I really don't know how to make that any clearer."

He scratched his face, definitely confused. She didn't know yet, so why was she so defensive? "Why?"

"I don't owe you an explanation. I don't owe you anything."

He took a deep breath. "I owe you . . . the truth about something."

"No, you don't. You don't owe me anything. Just leave and we'll call it—"

"Lena! I need you!" Three whacks on the door followed Brandy's call. Then the locked handle jiggled. "Now!"

They were both up in a shot, Dan turning the lock to whip the door open at the panic in Brandy's voice. "Remember the Hispanic guy you told me to watch out for? With the snake tattoo up his arm?"

Ramon.

"I didn't notice that tattoo at first and served him. Now he's at the bar. Mean as spit and demanding to see the owner."

Maggie paled and put her hand to her throat. "I want him out of here."

"Stay here. Both of you." Dan pulled Brandy into the room with one hand, and put another on Maggie's shoulder. "I'll handle this."

Without waiting for a response, he strode back into the bar and took the empty seat on Ramon's left, getting a dark look and a fraction of a nod when he did.

"How ya doin'?" Dan asked, his voice low.

Ramon slid him another look. "Fuck off."

Good to know he hadn't changed. "You know who I am?"

"A prick."

"That and house security. So you don't want to piss me off. All you need to do is go out the same way you came. Now."

Finally he got Ramon's full face, which had become a little craggier in prison, and still housed plenty of hate in deep-set black eyes. "Kiss my ass, Mr. House Security. I know the owner. And I'm not leavin' until I see her."

"That isn't going to happen," Dan said calmly. "So you can leave now."

Ramon took a very long swig of beer, then set the bottle down and gave Dan one more death stare. "She's got something of mine and I'm not leaving without it."

Ice dribbled through Dan's veins.

Of course. What else would Ramon think? The kid might not look like him, but the math would work in his favor. Magdalena Varcek was *his* lover fourteen years ago, too.

The ice turned to adrenaline and something else very dark. Possession. As Ramon reached for the bottle, Dan grabbed it out of his hands. "No more. Out."

With surprising speed, Ramon whipped his fist around, but Dan clipped it with the bottle. Glass smashed against flesh, cracking as beer and shards hit the bar and they both leaped up, Ramon's bar stool clattering to the floor.

"Motherfu—"

Dan threw a fist into his cheek, then one into his gut. When he doubled over, Dan grabbed his arm and twisted him around into a chokehold, one easy move. He jerked away from the bar and yanked Ramon's arm higher. "Time to leave, pal."

With a solid shove, he got him to the front door, and used Ramon to push it open and thrust him outside.

"Where's your car?" Dan demanded, still not letting him loose.

"Down there." He jerked his head toward a narrow street that ran alongside the bar. "Fuckin' A, man, let me go."

Dan didn't let up, scanning the streets for a possible accomplice and seeing no one. Around the corner was a row of parked cars by a Dumpster and side entrances to the buildings.

He twisted the arm as he tightened his grip around Ramon's throat. "Which one?"

"Here." He notched his head toward a subcompact.

"Locked?"

"No. The keys are under the front seat."

"Open it." He let him reach the handle to pull open the door, then thrust him into the driver's seat with one push, racking his Glock before Ramon took his next breath.

"What the fuck, man?" He held his hands back and stared up at Dan in disbelief.

"Here's what the fuck, man." Dan crouched down and got in his face, pointing the barrel between terror-stricken eyes. "If anyone ever sees you anywhere near this place again, if you make any effort to so much as breathe the same air as Maggie Varcek, if you even think about having contact with her, you're a dead man. Is that clear?"

"Yeah." He glared at Dan, his eyes shooting back and forth as he surveyed his face. "Who *are* you?"

"Her bodyguard." Dan leaned forward. "And I take my job very seriously."

"Oh, yeah? So do I. And I have business with her."

"What business?"

"She has a fucking fortune and it's mine!" His black eyes burned. "I want it back."

Dan lifted the gun and touched it to Ramon's sweaty forehead. "Get out. Don't come back."

He stood, keeping his arm steady, then slammed the door and kept the weapon aimed straight while Ramon dug under the seat for the keys, turned on the engine, and drove away.

Just as the car pulled out of sight, he caught movement in a doorway to his left. He instantly braced his weapon and locked on the shadow; then Maggie stepped onto the street.

Her face was pale, all light gone from her eyes, her generous lips drawn to a tight line. "I want you to leave."

That was a fine thank-you. But he swallowed the sarcasm and chalked her reaction up to fear of the gun. "Not yet. Quinn's out there alone, and so is that lunatic."

"You called me Maggie Varcek."

Yes, he had. Stupid, but he had. "Let's go find him."

Her eyes widened. "No. I'll find him and you . . . you . . . just stay away from me and my son."

"I can't, Maggie." He hated to do it like this, but there was no time. "Because . . . he's not your son."

"*What?*"

"He's our son."

CHAPTER
SIX

AS IF HER whole insides had exploded from the shock, Maggie's brain went blank, and her heart just . . . stopped.

"Who are you?"

"Later. We need to find Quinn and get him home. Ramon wants something, and it might not just be revenge."

He was right, but— "Not until I know who you are."

"You knew me as Michael Scott."

The entire world rolled, taking her along with it. He must have seen her sway, because he lunged forward to grab her as she lost her balance. Instantly, she wrangled out of his grip.

"You're dead," she spat the words. "He's . . . dead. I saw his body. I read about the . . . trial. He was shot by another agent. Michael Scott is *dead*."

He just shook his head, as if he had no words to counter that.

And honestly, words weren't necessary. Because she was staring at Quinn, twenty-five years older. How could she have missed it?

One by one, the pieces, and truth, fell into place as she covered her mouth and a fist-size lump formed in her throat. "You were in disguise."

He nodded.

"You weren't really killed that night."

He took a step forward, lifting his hands in a slight gesture of surrender. "Maggie, listen to me."

Her heart thundered so loud in her ears that the words sounded garbled. "No, no. You get out of here."

"I'm sure you hate me right now—"

"Right *now?* I've hated you for so long, I . . . I can't even tell you. I don't know how to tell you how much I hate you. You have no—"

"We have to find Quinn." He grabbed her arm again, but this time his touch wasn't playful or friendly. Oh God, had she really been flirting with the monster who'd used her and betrayed everyone around them? Kissing him, practically begging for sex? Dreaming of more? Worried he could trace her past through the FBI?

Trace her past? He *was* her past.

"They know where you are, Maggie. If Ramon does, then any of Viejo's men do, too. It wasn't that difficult to find you." He tightened his grip, engulfing her wrist and leaning closer to drive his point home. "You can skewer me after we get that boy home and safe."

As numb as she was from shock, she knew he was right. She let him lead her to the street, but questions bombarded her.

"But why now? No one's tried all these years." *Not even you.* "Now two of you show up in the same week?"

"Ramon just got out of prison. That's why I'm here. And they could know more about you than I did. That you have a son. A son who is out there right now walking his dog, oblivious. Does he have a cell phone?"

"Sometimes."

She hesitated one more second. Shouldn't she go on her own? Or get someone from the bar? Someone she trusted? Should she get in a car with a man who lied and used her? Made her fall in love with him and then betrayed her?

"Or you can stay here, locked in the office," he said sharply. "That's fine, and smart. But I'm going to find him, so tell me where the hell he might be. *Fast.*"

She yanked her hand out of his and marched. He was right about one thing: she'd skewer him later.

"Does he have a regular route or a place he always walks the dog?"

"Sombrero Beach. He usually crosses the highway right there at that light, and takes Goose to a dog-friendly park down there." Unless one of his friends called and he went to meet them. Then he could be anywhere.

In the car, she dragged the seat belt over her as he started the engine.

"Turn right here," she said, leading them down the road to the park. With Ramon around, Quinn definitely wasn't safe. She focused every brain cell on the need to see that lanky body loping along with a dog on a leash.

She called Quinn's cell three times, getting voice mail every time.

The quiet streets of Marathon seemed dark and menacing, and the neighborhood looked nothing like the peaceful, residential beach town it was. Thickets of palm trees and hibiscus bushes formed dangerous shadows, and walls around yards and driveways became hiding places as the sun disappeared in the west, leaving darkness behind.

She could practically hear the universe laughing at her. Talk about life playing a joke on you.

Michael Scott wasn't dead. He was alive and dry-humping her on the beach last Friday night.

"Oh God," she moaned.

"Do you see him?"

"No." But she looked, hard.

"I was going to tell you tonight," he said.

She snorted softly. "Uh-huh."

He didn't respond but stayed focused on the road and the sidewalks. She did the same, squinting into the shadows, her worry for Quinn at war with her misery over Michael. Dan. Whoever the hell he was.

"Why did you have to pretend to die?"

"It was always the plan. Sometimes we did that with UC jobs. Undercover," he added, as though she might not know what he meant. As though she hadn't followed the trial while her stomach grew huge, and Quinn was born.

While Smitty took her in, cared for her, gave her a home and a whole new life. He was the only one who knew. The only one who forgave her for being a stupid, immature, trusting kid.

"Was it in the plan to screw the girlfriend of one of the guys you were trying to entrap and arrest? So you could get secrets and inside information?"

He still didn't react, didn't even blink or glance at her. He just kept rumbling along at five miles an hour, scanning every inch for her son.

She tried to think, to come to terms with how her life had just turned upside down. Failed on all counts.

"Were you going to tell me . . . about the baby?" he finally asked, making the tension worse.

"I thought you were dead."

"I mean then. In Miami. If we hadn't busted Viejo's ring. Or . . . weren't you sure . . . he was mine?"

She closed her eyes as though he'd jabbed his fist into her chest. She had that coming.

"I wasn't much more than a child myself, and I wasn't sure about anything. But based on timing and birth control . . . I was pretty sure. And I . . ." She wet her lips. "I was planning to tell you that night. I thought . . ."

We might run away together.

"You thought what?"

"I had some stupid and romantic notions."

"Well, you were eighteen." Meaning, he had no such notions.

All history. Ancient history. She shifted in her seat and pointed at the grassy area and a low wall that ran along a park and Sombrero Beach as the street dead-ended.

"He takes the dog to that park."

Dan whipped the car into the first parking spot and threw it in Park, then looked at her, his eyes much softer as he put his hand on her leg.

"We'll find him. I give you my word, we'll find him."

"Your word?" she spat, jerking her leg away. "A man who lied from the day I met you, used my youth and my trust and my *body* to get information, pretended to be killed, and then disappeared while I hitchhiked, pregnant and broke and starving, to the Keys? I have your trustworthy, sincere *word*?"

She blew out a disgusted puff of air, reaching the door handle to flip it open, when his gaze moved over her shoulder and disintegrated to horror.

She spun around, and all she could manage was a strangled noise at the sight of Goose meandering along the fence, sniffing the ground, his leash dragging in the grass.

Dan threw open the door and jumped out, his weapon drawn before his feet hit the ground. Goose barked and charged, but Maggie was out of the car almost as fast, and her sharp order stopped the dog.

Moving on instinct and adrenaline, Dan ran around the low wall that surrounded the park, surveying the empty playground and deserted beach. He stayed perfectly still, listening for any sound, hearing only the dog bark and Maggie call for Quinn.

And there was something else: the distant hum of a motorboat. The sound wasn't coming from the ocean; it was across the street.

At the car, Maggie was struggling to get the dog into the small backseat, still shouting Quinn's name.

"Do those canals lead to open water?" he asked, pointing to the houses that lined the cul de sac across from the beach.

"Yes. They all lead to a little bay, then straight out to the ocean."

No car had passed them on the way out, and Sombrero Beach Boulevard was a dead end. If someone took Quinn, they might have taken him by water.

Dan darted through the first yard, straight to a canal in the back. He stopped at the water's edge, peering to the end of the waterway where a single-engine outboard fishing boat powered out, making way more wake than was legal.

Dan tore after it, following the seawall that lined all the

waterfront property. The boat had no lights on, and he couldn't tell how many people were on board, but it was too small to have a cabin below.

It was just a little fishing boat like the ones a zillion tourists rented every week, but no one drove a boat that fast in a canal without a reason. At the end of the short waterway, the boat veered to the left and revved toward the open water.

Dan ran down to the next dock, hoping to get a clean shot to stop them before they got away.

"Can I help you?" A man's head popped up from the stern of a thirty-foot sport fishing boat tethered to the dock, a soda can in his hand. "This is private—" He froze at the sight of Dan's gun.

"I need your boat. You'll get it back."

The guy scowled and opened his mouth to argue.

"Move!" Dan ordered, and the man did, scrambling up on the deck and untying one line with shaky hands as Dan did the other.

"What are you doing?" Maggie came tearing down the dock, her hair flying, her eyes wide.

The man waved her off. "Go away. He has a gun."

Dan barely looked at her as she bounded onto the boat dock. "I think he might be headed out to the ocean."

She jumped into the boat and slammed her hands on the wheel. "Bill, we need the keys! Somebody took Quinn!"

"Jesus, Lena, why didn't you say so?" The man flipped a set of keys attached to a bright orange floaty. "Go!"

As she turned the engines on, Dan hopped in. "Thanks," he said to the owner. "We'll get it back."

Maggie pushed the throttle forward and gunned the motor as Dan went to take the helm.

She speared him with a look. "I'll drive. You shoot. Carefully."

With the agility of a seasoned boater, she rumbled away from the dock, holding up one hand in gratitude to Bill while she powered the boat into the darkness, wisely keeping all the lights off.

"They went left, into the bay," Dan said.

He didn't have to add "hurry" because she was already breaking every law of land and sea, and he loved her for it. As soon as they cleared the peninsula that formed the canal and hit the open water, he saw the other boat in the moonlight.

"There," Dan said, squinting to see what they were up against.

"Are you sure he's on it?" she asked.

"No, but we're not going to quit until we find out."

She bore down on the throttle and the other boat reacted by picking up speed in the opposite direction, kicking up a huge wake.

Maggie matched its speed, the big sport fishing boat easily gaining on the little outboard.

"Stay down as low as you can," Dan ordered, moving into position with his weapon straight ahead. "There may be bullets."

"Please don't shoot my son."

"Keep her steady and don't panic. I don't want to shoot anyone if I don't have to."

They were within a hundred and fifty feet of the other boat when the first shot nicked their starboard side.

"Get down!" Dan commanded, diving toward the bow cushions to line up his own shot, holding on since their velocity raised the bow a good forty-five degrees above the water. Maggie ducked behind the windshield but held her speed.

He could only see one person—a driver—but suspected someone else was on board to take that shot.

"You know where the bow spotlight is, Maggie?"

"Yeah, it's on a remote. I've got it right here."

"Slow down a little to lower the bow, then aim it directly on that boat, and when I say hit it, blind them and don't stop moving. Just keep driving straight for them until I say turn."

"Got it."

They closed in at thirty feet, and another bullet hit their boat. But he still couldn't see the boy.

Fifteen feet. Ten. "Hit the light!"

Instantly, white light poured over the water, the blinding beam spotlighting the little boat. The driver looked over his shoulder, another man dropped down to his knees in the back, covering his eyes, but no one else was visible.

"Turn starboard!" he yelled.

She whipped the boat at exactly that second, and Dan took a shot, purposely aiming to miss but let them know he meant business.

"Stop your boat!" he yelled, punctuating the demand with another shot, skimming the port side.

Maggie adjusted the beam so it kept them in light, handicapping the shooter and revealing something dark on the deck.

Quinn, bound and flopping around like a hooked fish.

Despite his visceral reaction, Dan steadied his aim.

"Quinn!" Maggie's voice lost all its earlier calm, cracking at the sight of her son. "Oh God, don't shoot," she begged. "That's Quinn on the deck."

"Hand him over," Dan demanded. "Give him up or you don't take another breath."

He shot again, careful that the bullet couldn't ricochet off the side and hit Quinn.

The driver and shooter shared a look, while Maggie maneuvered the boat closer, keeping the spotlight on them while they blinked and cowered.

Dan stood straight on the bow, protected by their blindness, his Glock aimed at the shooter. They were both Hispanic, but he didn't recognize either one from his days with the Jimenez family.

"Throw the gun in the water," Dan ordered.

They squinted into the light, defeat on their faces. The shooter in the back lifted both hands in surrender, a revolver in the right.

"In the water," he shouted.

After a beat, he obeyed, his weapon splashing as it hit.

"Stop the boat. Now!"

The driver pulled back on his throttle and Maggie did the same, easily matching their slowing speed. When they idled to a stop, so did she, just as Quinn rolled over, revealing duct tape over his mouth.

"Get over there," Dan said to the driver, using his gun to point to the other man. "Next to him."

With both of them together, Dan could shoot either one at any time. He climbed over the port side rail, balancing as his boat dipped in the water before he eased himself to the other deck.

Keeping the gun aimed on his targets, he used his other hand to reach down and help Quinn, who looked at him with eyes full of terror. And tears. Fury careened through Dan. The bastards made his kid *cry*.

Behind him, he heard Maggie move into position to

help get Quinn on their boat. With his feet bound, he struggled, and Dan turned just enough to negotiate a way up to the other boat, when Maggie shouted and a body thudded against Dan.

He grunted with the force and lost his balance just as Quinn fell over the side and hit the water hard.

"He's tied up!" Maggie screamed. "He'll drown!"

Dan managed to whip around and slam his elbow into the first face it met, but the other man pounced on him, knocking his gun out of his hand and sending it sailing across the deck. Dan got in a kick to the gut of the other guy, but the first one was already at the helm. He flattened the throttle, sending Dan tumbling backward to his knees, rolling into cushions, the weapon still two feet from his reach.

He twisted in time to see Maggie scrambling, ready to dive in after her son. The driver whipped the boat in the opposite direction, taking the outboard perilously close to the dark spot where Quinn had gone under.

Leaping to his feet in one jump, Dan dove into the black water, instantly grabbing the boy's shoulder as they both sank deeper.

Dan forced his eyes wide, just in time to see the proper blades churning closer to chew them up. He looped his hand through Quinn's bound hands and thrust them both lower, using all his strength to go under the hull, then kick them away just as the spinning prop whirred by.

In a second, the boat was gone and he swam Quinn up, sensing the panic in his body. As soon as he broke the surface he heard Maggie screaming, and he ripped the tape off Quinn's mouth so he could gasp in air.

"Stay with me, Quinn," he insisted, pulling the boy along. "Stay with me."

Quinn nodded as Dan swam them to the back of the boat. Maggie flipped the lock on the gate of a small diving platform and reached down, dragging Quinn up as Dan gave him a mighty push to the deck.

As the other boat disappeared into the darkness, Quinn turned to Dan in gratitude, the water dripping down his face mixing with his tears.

Dan dropped to his knees, put his arms out, and hugged his son for the first time.

CHAPTER SEVEN

MAGGIE TURNED OUT the bedside table light and kissed Quinn's smooth cheek, whispering good night. She'd been sitting with him for the past hour, soothing him and answering his questions as best as she could.

The one thing she'd strived to teach her son was to be honest, and she felt like the biggest hypocrite on earth. But right now, in this mental state, at this time of night, with so much unknown, the best she could do was assure him that he was safe and that she would do whatever was necessary to keep those men away from him.

She stepped into the hall, glancing toward the kitchen. Dan stood in the soft stove light, wearing nothing but camouflage drawstring pants slung low enough to reveal every muscle down to his hips. He must have changed out of his wet clothes and showered, because his hair looked damp. Stone still, he stared out the window, a mug poised inches from his mouth.

He turned as he heard her approach, his eyes narrowed, his jaw clenched.

"How is he?"

"Asleep. Confused. Scared out of his mind." She went to the coffeepot and grabbed a mug from the cup tree Quinn had made for her in summer camp about ten years ago.

She touched the bear's brown head, imagined little fingers painting it just for her, and swallowed a lump. She'd almost lost him.

"Thank you," she said softly. "You saved his life."

She kept her gaze on the coffee as she poured a cup and dipped the spoon into the sugar bowl. Her hands were steady, but she jumped at Dan's touch on her shoulders, and spilled half the teaspoon on the counter.

"Look at me," he demanded, adding some pressure.

She exhaled softly, set the spoon down, and let herself be turned around. The scent of soap and skin was overwhelming this close, as was the sight of his unshaven face, his parted lips. She looked up to meet his gaze and tried to step back from the sheer force of it, but the counter hit her hips.

"Did you tell him?" he asked.

"No. I need some time to get used to the idea first. It's not just something you blurt out after the kid just went through the scariest ordeal of his life. Give me time."

"Of course."

She put her fingertips on his hard chest to push him away, but he didn't move and her hands barely dented the solid muscles underneath. "I need to get used to the idea that you're here. And alive. I buried you a long time ago."

He stepped back, but not very far. "Your cell phone rang," he said, pointing to the table. "A text, I think."

She reached for it and as she did, he snagged her arm,

his hand warm as it closed over her skin. "By the way, you drive a mean boat."

They held each other's gaze for a long moment. "Smitty taught me," she said. "He did a lot of things for me. He took me in when I was pregnant and broke. He gave me a home. He loved me. He married me. And he raised my son as though he were his own. He made a lot of mistakes and wasn't always the man I wanted him to be, but he was Quinn's father in every way but biological. Don't forget that."

"All I said was that you drove well."

She slipped out of his grasp and picked up the phone, thumbing to the text.

You have a fortune I want. Let's make a deal. She stared at the message, frowning, then read the words out loud to Dan, the ominous implication sending a shiver through her. "I don't have a fortune."

"Ramon thinks you do. And so does that Constantine Xenakis. They both said the same thing: you have a fortune they want."

She pressed a few buttons, trying to figure out who'd sent it. "Well, they're both delusional. I'm mortgaged up to my eyeballs, my truck isn't worth the paper your Porsche rental agreement is written on, I sold my husband's last boat at a serious loss, and put the little bit I made into a college prepay program. I don't have two thousand dollars in the bank, let alone a fortune." She held the phone up. "Should I reply or call the sheriff?"

"We should contact authorities, absolutely. Who sent the text?"

"Unknown caller. Blocked ID." She looked up at him. "What does it mean? Is it a threat? A ransom? They didn't get Quinn, but who's to say they won't try again?"

He rocked back on the kitchen chair, the muscles in his chest and stomach outlined by the move. "Kidnapping is something I know a little about, and I can tell you that was a well-executed and planned event. Maybe Ramon was in on it. They were sitting outside the bar all that time, waiting for Quinn. Who better to distract you than your ex-boyfriend?"

True. Maggie finished fixing her coffee, thinking. "You think Ramon believes Quinn is his, and now that he's out of jail, he wants him?"

"A damn stupid way to get custody, if you ask me, and frankly, it stunk of El Viejo."

She refused to think about the word *custody*. "Ramon's father? He's been out of jail for six months. Why try something like this now?"

"So you've been following them?" Dan asked.

"Of course." She took a seat across from him, placing her mug on the table near his. "I've been on a website to monitor his release, and praying the whole damn family would disappear off the face of the earth and take my messy history with them."

"I've done some checking, too. The rumor is that Ramon and his father are on the outs, but I don't know that for a fact. I do suspect that Viejo is back in business, and, as much as I can determine from available information, he's staying clean enough not to be arrested. His visa allowed him to move back to Venezuela.

"Isn't that where his younger brother lives?" Another drug-running money launderer.

"Lived. Esteban Jimenez dropped dead of a heart attack about three days after the bust, or we'd have had him, too. Viejo lives on Esteban's old coffee plantation outside Maracaibo."

She closed her eyes and let out a soft grunt. "How can I possibly explain this to Quinn? He'll never understand that I lived like that, with those animals. And that you . . ."

For a long moment, the kitchen was silent. She finally looked up at him, not at all sure what to expect. "I do have to tell him, don't I?"

"You have to do what you think is right. And I'll . . ." He frowned, hesitating. "I'll go along with your decision. But in the meantime, we have to protect him. I think he should be out of here altogether while we figure out who did this."

He'd go along with her decision, but he'd already started making his own. "He's my responsibility," she said. *My son.*

"I'll protect him. Maggie, I respect that he's yours and you've raised him. But protection is my business. I can put him somewhere safe, where no one will be able to get to him. You want that for him, don't you?"

She nodded, looking at the coffee. "Of course I do. But for how long? How do we figure this out? Do I have to live in fear forever? First I'm robbed, then this . . ."

"No coincidence, by the way," he said. "Neither was that break-in to my car. You have something, and someone wants it."

A fortune? "Sorry, but the only thing of true value I have is Quinn."

"Did you take something when you left Miami?"

"I ran away in the middle of the night during a raid on the warehouse. I took the clothes on my back."

"Maybe your fortune is knowledge," Dan said, locking his arms behind his neck. "Maybe all you know about Viejo's defunct drug-running business is considered valuable."

"I hardly paid attention," she said, looking out the window. "And wouldn't Ramon know far more than I know?"

"Think harder, Maggie. What could be considered a fortune?"

She closed her eyes and remembered the little piece of paper she'd held that rainy night in Miami.

"I had a fortune that night," she said softly. "But I doubt it's worth anything."

"You did?" His chair inched down.

She laughed a little in embarrassment. "I got it the day . . . you died. From a Chinese restaurant food delivery. It said: 'Now that love grows in you, then beauty grows, too.'"

"A Chinese fortune?" The slight urgency in his voice surprised her.

"Yeah, I thought it was a message from the universe. I thought it was about . . . our baby."

"A Chinese fortune you got the day of the bust?" His gaze sharpened to knifelike.

"Yes. I took it as a sign that I should—" She looked down and twisted her coffee cup, lining up the handle to the right. "Tell you I was pregnant."

The front legs of his chair smacked on the tile floor and he stared at her, his expression stunned disbelief. "How? How did you get one? Who knows you had it?"

At his tone, she frowned. "Lourdes gave it to me."

"Ramon's little sister? How did she get it?"

"I don't know. Why?"

"Because *that's* what they want, Maggie." He shot up from the chair so hard, the table shook, splashing coffee. "The fortune you had."

"Have." She blinked at him. What was he talking about?

"What?" He practically pulled her out of her seat. "You still have it?"

"I think I do. It's hidden in my grandmother's tarot cards." She brushed by him and started toward the hallway. Had the thief taken it? She hadn't even checked. "But why would anyone want it?"

"For a hundred million dollars."

She missed a step. "Excuse me?"

"The fortune in the cookie. That's what we were looking for the night of the bust. It was the location of a hundred million unlaundered dollars."

"Are you serious? But it was just a phrase, a saying in a Chinese cookie."

"It was much more than that. It was the key to where the Jimenez family was hiding too much money to dump into standard accounts without being noticed." He followed her into the bedroom, nudging her to move faster. "You know that El Viejo not only moved cocaine from Colombia through Venezuela using that bogus shipping company, but also laundered the money his operation made all over the U.S., the Caribbean and Europe."

"Yes, I knew that."

"The reason we had to conduct the raid that particular night was because a message that Viejo had been waiting to receive came in that day, and we had to intercept it. It was from his brother, and it was the location of the money."

She switched the light on her nightstand and rounded the bed to get to the dresser. He had to be wrong. Her fortune had no such information on it.

"Wouldn't a message from his brother have been hidden in the furniture shipment that came into the warehouse? Did you look in all those furniture boxes?"

"Of course—that's why the bust happened that night; otherwise we might have waited. But there was no message in the shipment, just tons and tons of cocaine. Certainly enough to shut them down and put them all away. But the other undercover agent in the operation found out that the message had come in a Chinese food delivery that day."

"Juan Santiago," she supplied, remembering him clearly. He was the one who'd testified at the trial, the one mentioned in the news. She'd fallen for his act, too, never knowing that he was an undercover federal agent in their midst.

"He discovered a fortune from a cookie in Viejo's possession when we arrested him that night. But the best minds in the FBI couldn't crack the code, if there was one."

Maggie opened the drawer and pulled out the jewelry box. "If Viejo had the message when he was arrested, why do you think this one has anything to do with the money?"

"Some of us, including me, thought maybe the message came in pieces as a precaution. Others thought we'd been duped entirely, and there was no money. We never found any other messages, and God knows we searched that house. We never found the money, either, even after they all went to prison."

She lifted Baba's precious Buckland Romani tarot cards and cut the deck in the middle, between the Sun and the Queen of Cups, where she'd long ago hidden the fortune, now yellowed with time.

"Just like I remembered." She handed it to him. "Now that love grows in you, then beauty grows, too."

"A typical meaningless cliché."

Not to her. "What did you expect? A Swiss bank account number?"

"I just hoped for something more obvious," he said, examining it carefully. "El Viejo isn't that sophisticated, and this wasn't the CIA."

"What did his say?"

He just shook his head. "To be honest, I don't remember."

"So if this is connected to the other message, what good is it now, anyway? Plus, after fourteen years, surely the money is gone."

"I could get the other Chinese fortune easily. I'm sure it's still in the files in the FBI office up in Miami, since this part of the case is still considered pending. And we don't know if the money's gone. Viejo couldn't even get to it until six months ago, and his transactions are closely watched. If he has it and is washing it through a system, it would have to be in very, very small amounts. Plus, the only person believed to know its exact location, Esteban Jimenez, is dead." He turned it over and looked at the numbers. "One-zero-three-eight."

"Maybe a combination lock or a safe deposit box?" she suggested.

"Or an address. Maybe the other one has a street name on it. Although I seemed to recall it had some numbers, too." He studied the words again before he looked at her. "Can you remember exactly how you got this?"

"There was an afternoon meeting, to plan the delivery I guess, and I was shuffled off to watch Lourdes. When I went into her room to find her, she had two fortune cookies."

"How did she get them?"

"I have no idea. She gave me one, and after that I was

totally wrapped up in my message. She was barely ten, and not really aware of the business going on in that house. I doubt she knew that she had something valuable."

"Maybe Ramon gave her his on purpose," he said. "Maybe giving one to her was part of the fail-safe system. Maybe he suspected someone was undercover. I wasn't in that meeting."

"But you were in on the delivery that night."

He must have heard the accusatory note in her voice. "You weren't supposed to be there," he said. "You were supposed to be at the movies with Lourdes, both of you out of the house."

"But Juan Santiago got sick, and he was—one of . . . you. Oh."

Dan nodded. "Viejo decided to stay home at the last minute, so Juan—Joel is his real name—had to pretend to be sick, so Viejo didn't somehow get word of the bust before agents got to him. I didn't know Ramon would insist on taking you in his place. When I saw you there . . ." His brows drew tight at the memory.

"You made me run away."

"I knew bullets would fly. I knew I was supposed to be 'killed.' It was the best I could do for you under the circumstances. I thought you'd go back to Viejo's and be put in government protection. That was my plan all along, but when you disappeared . . ."

"You never tried to find me."

"I knew you'd be fine, especially once they were all under arrest. I knew you'd survive, and if I had found you, I'd have had to tell you the truth."

She stepped away, a wave of familiar hate rolling over him. "God forbid you'd be honest."

"There was nothing to be gained. For either of us."

"Whatever. It's history." *Her* history, like it or not.

"No, it's not." He gripped her wrist, demanding her attention. "I never wanted your role to be revealed, Maggie. I never wanted you involved in the trial. That was always paramount to me, and one of the reasons I pushed to 'die' at the scene, so I didn't have to reveal to a jury where I got some of the leads. Without me testifying, it was just a matter of presenting the evidence we found at the warehouse. I never intended for you to get hurt."

"Well, you may not have intended it, but what you did hurt like hell. Par for the course."

"What does that mean?"

"I've been lied to since I was born. My mother spewed them in her once-a-year calls to me, my husband wasn't the most honest dude to walk the face of the earth, and, of course, there was you, the granddaddy of liars in my life. So forgive me if I'm not about to shower you with trust. You have zero credibility."

She pulled away and closed her fingertips around the fortune he held. "So, I'll take that." She slid it from his fingers. "Until we give this to whoever wants it, my son's not safe. This is ransom. And they can have it."

"You can't turn over a hundred million dollars to a former drug cartel and known money launderer. Or to anyone, for that matter."

"I don't care about the money. I only care about one thing on this earth: Quinn. If this little piece of paper puts him in jeopardy, then I'm giving it to the people who want it, to be sure he's safe."

"It belongs to the United States government."

"Oh, please. Don't go all FBI on me now." She took a step back with the paper. "I'll text whoever wrote to me right back. That Greek guy, Ramon—hell, I'll hand it over to El Viejo himself. I just want my son out of harm's way."

"Are you crazy? Maggie, do you think they'd let you live? Even if you gave that to them? Knowing what you know?"

"What do I know? Only what you've told me, and that's always questionable. And even if you are telling the truth, they have no idea you're alive, let alone standing in this room." She turned away. "This is mine, and Quinn is mine, and you can't just waltz in here and take either one. No."

"He's my son, too. And you know damn well neither one of you would ever be secure. Don't you remember what those people are like? El Viejo is ruthless and brutal. Life means nothing to him. Not yours and not Quinn's."

She couldn't deny the truth of that. "But until they have what they want, Quinn's not safe."

"Oh, he'll be safe. I'll take him to Miami tomorrow, where he'll be surrounded by ten-foot walls and under the constant watch of a personal protection specialist with the size and disposition of a grizzly bear."

That sounded really good at the moment. "And then what?"

"If someone wants this fortune that bad, it confirms one thing: the money is still there. I'm going to find it and then turn it over to the FBI in a very public announcement, letting Viejo and anyone connected with him know that it's gone. Then you can rest easy."

His approach made sense, it was safer, and he was right about Viejo. He'd never let someone live who had that kind of information on him. "How can you do that? And how long will it take?"

"By ten o'clock tomorrow, I'll have every single public

and private record on the background of Constantine Xenakis. By noon, I'll be in the 1A files at the FBI office in North Miami Beach to get the other fortune. With the two fortunes in hand and the resources of my company, we can have the code broken in hours. By tomorrow night, we could be home free."

He made it sound so easy. "What if they want retribution? What if they want to hurt Quinn just for vengeance?"

He reached for the memory box in her open drawer. He lifted the lid, the golden curl and baby tooth looking absurdly small next to his masculine finger.

"Then I'll find every damn one of them and kill them myself." His expression was dark with emotion, surprising her with the force of it.

She really had no choice. "All right. I'll go with your plan. But if anything happens to my boy, I'll kill *you* myself."

CHAPTER
EIGHT

QUINN POPPED OUT his earbuds when Dan pulled up to the guard gate at the entrance to Star Island, the boy's eyes wide and his jaw slack. Dan couldn't help watching his expression of shock and delight in the rearview mirror.

"Dude. This place is insane. We're really staying here?"

As if he sensed the excitement in Quinn's voice, Goose lifted his head and uncurled from the comfort of a tight leather seat in the back of the Porsche.

"We are," Dan said, handing his license to the guard.

"Awesome. I bet they have a ballin' pool."

Dan and Maggie shared a look that silently said they had no idea what ballin' was, but it must be good.

"They have twelve thousand square feet of mind-boggling luxury stocked with a theater and an aquarium and plenty to make sure you're not bored."

Quinn let out a low whistle, leaning forward as they drove through the gated entrance, looking far more like he was headed into a vacation hotel than a 24/7 secure compound.

As the Porsche purred down the island's only road, Maggie and Quinn tried to see the houses blocked by large walls and thick foliage.

"Who is this Cori again?" Maggie asked. "And how much does the universe love her?"

"I don't know about the universe, but Max Roper sure does. She's on the board of her deceased husband's mall management company, and after she married Max, they moved to wine country and Max runs the West Coast operations of my company. A couple of times a year, they have to come here for board meetings. We're lucky this is one of those weeks."

They pulled into the wide drive, and Dan entered the code on the keypad. The iron gate opened slowly, inviting them into lush grounds. As the driveway curved, the stunning expanse of a contemporary Spanish-style villa came into view.

Quinn choked. "Holy crap."

Before Dan had even stopped the car, the front leaded-glass doors opened and Max stepped out, looking almost comical with a two-year-old in his arms.

"The size of a bear, maybe," Maggie said. "But not the disposition. Not the way he's looking at that child."

"Fatherhood has mellowed him, it's true. But he'd still kill you for looking sideways at his principal. Believe me, I've known the guy since he gave me a black eye in kindergarten."

Seconds later Cori stepped into the morning sunshine, her long dark hair pulled up in a youthful ponytail, her wide smile genuine as she darted to greet Dan with a hug the minute he climbed out of the car.

"A woman, a kid, and a dog," he whispered as she gave him a kiss. "I owe you for this."

Before she could answer, Goose bolted out of the back seat and jumped on her.

"He's harmless," Dan assured her, going for the collar as Maggie came around the front, commanding Goose to sit. Over the barking, Dan made the introductions as Quinn unfolded himself from the backseat.

"Hi," he said, a little unsure of himself. "Sorry Goose jumped like that. He's really a good dog."

"It's all right," Cori said, reaching out a hand. "I'm Cori Roper."

He shook it and then looked at Max. "Hey. Cute kid."

Normally that's all it would take to turn the big guy into a ball of mush. A compliment to Peyton usually resulted in Max's goofiest smile and a five-minute dissertation on his son's latest accomplishment.

But Max merely stared at Quinn. After an awkward beat, he reached out his hand. "Max Roper. And this is Peyton."

"Hey, little dude." Quinn reached up and stuck a playful finger in the baby's face, and instantly had it grabbed and giggled over.

Max's gaze slipped to Dan, and a lifetime of nonverbal communication screamed the obvious.

He knew.

Maggie stepped forward. "I really can't thank you enough for letting Quinn stay here," she said to Cori. "I hope it's not an imposition."

"Not at all. Max abhors these weeks in Miami, and he's happy for the company while I'm out." Cori reached out and slipped an arm around Dan. "And this one is a fixture in our family."

Dan smiled down at her, surveying her face for a clue.

Did she know, too? He got nothing but her guileless smile. "Thanks, Cor," he said, giving her a squeeze.

Goose was already bolting as Quinn struggled to hold him.

"Why don't we take him to the back," Cori suggested. "The yard's completely fenced in, and the dock is gated off. Would you like to come and look around, Maggie?"

She guided them around the side of the house, leaving Dan and Max to get the bags. Dan popped the front well, practically feeling Max close behind him.

Peyton cooed and Dan lifted the bags out, not turning to respond to the child as he normally would. Instead, he waited for the ax to fall.

Is he yours? Have you told her? Do you realize what this—

"Does Lucy know?"

Dan froze while lifting his duffel bag. Didn't see that coming.

"That I'm here, and you're protecting Quinn? Yes. In fact, she's going to call in a few minutes with some reports I asked for."

"But does she know you have a son?"

He turned and met the challenge in Max's dark eyes, an expression he'd seen a million times. "What's much more important is that Quinn *doesn't* know yet, so don't say anything. Do you think Cori can see it?"

"Doubtful. She didn't know you at that age. I did. How about Maggie?"

"I told her. It's been kind of rough on her. She thought I was dead, you know."

Max nodded, tugging Peyton a little closer. "What're you going to do?"

"I told you last night. Find the cash, turn it over, and get the Jimenez family off Maggie's and Quinn's backs."

Max's thick brows furrowed. "That's not what I mean."

"What *do* you mean? What am I going to do with a kid? How am I supposed to be a father to him? What does this do to all that freedom I just acquired?"

Slowly, Max grinned, then slid a look at his little boy. "You know what I love about the guy, Peyt? You don't have to say a thing. He'll just spill his guts all over the sidewalk and I don't even have to ask."

Dan held in his curse in deference to innocent ears.

"Let's go inside," he said instead, heading toward the door, Max chuckling behind him.

In the cool marble foyer, he dumped the bags and stabbed his fingers through his hair, turning to Max.

"I had no idea," he said. "If I'd known she was pregnant . . ." He'd what? Sent money? Called on Christmas? Tried to talk her out of keeping the child at all? "Anyway, I didn't, and now I have to deal with this. So I'd appreciate a little less humor and a little more sympathy."

Max looked at Peyton. "See? Guts. Everywhere." He set him down carefully, giving him a hand until he was completely steady on his two-year-old feet. Then Peyton shot off like a rocket.

Max led them deeper into the house, past a towering curved staircase and formal living area and into the much less ostentatious family room. Toys and trucks and a playpen vied for floor space, and Dan had to scoop up a few stuffed animals to drop onto the leather sofa.

"I'd ask if you're sure, but he's a clone," Max said.

Dan spread his hands along the back of the sofa, exhaling. "I don't know when and how or even *if* Maggie's going to tell him."

"Then I better keep our old high school yearbook under lock and key. Because one look at Danny Gallagher, class of '85, and he's going to see which way the DNA twirls."

"Yeah, I got your drift on that."

"Don't let him find out the wrong way," Max said quietly. "It's going to be hard enough as it is."

Cori's laughter preceded the group into the room through an arched opening from the patio. Quinn led the way, letting himself be pulled by Peyton.

"He's strong for a little thing," he said, pretending he was about to fall.

Peyton looked up and beamed a two-toothed grin. "Kin." He pointed at the boy and stomped his feet with excitement. "Kin."

"He likes you," Dan said. "I can never get him to say my name. C'mere, Peyton. Give Uncle Dan a hug." Dan reached his arms out and Peyton toddled over, drool sliding down his chin.

He threw himself into Dan's arms, then climbed up on his lap.

"What d'you say, monster?"

Peyton slapped a damp palm on Dan's face and gave him a loopy smile. "Kin."

Son of a bitch, could everyone see the resemblance?

On his belt, his cell phone rang with the first few notes of "Lucy in the Sky With Diamonds." He saw Cori and Max share a look as he set Peyton on the floor and stood up.

"Can I take this in your office?" he asked.

"Of course," Max said, lifting a knowing brow. "You need privacy."

"No, I need to put this on speaker." He cocked his head toward Maggie, waving her toward him. "C'mon. You should hear everything firsthand."

Cori swooped in to gather the baby in her arms. "We'll finish the tour with Quinn, then."

In the plush jungle-themed office, Dan put his cell phone on the coffee table and did the audio introductions as Maggie settled onto the zebra-striped sofa across from him.

Lucy, being Lucy, asked no questions about Maggie. But then Lucy, being Lucy, probably had a full top-secret FBI file in front of her, had memorized every detail about their former relationship, and had deduced the rest between the lines.

Dan pictured the woman he'd called boss for the past seven or eight years, seated at her massive antique table, no doubt dressed in a cream or white silk designer suit, six-hundred-dollar shoes hanging from her perfectly manicured toes as she crossed her mile-long legs, her black hair loose and long.

The image usually pulled at something basic in his gut, but today he felt nothing but the urge to look at Maggie, her jean-clad legs tucked under her, flip-flops on the floor, a thin T-shirt clinging to her narrow frame. She nibbled on her thumbnail, listening, then looked up and caught his gaze.

She couldn't be more different from Lucy if she tried.

She held his eye contact, her expression dragging at something even more basic and raw in his gut. Was that because she was the mother of his child? Or was this just ordinary garden-variety lust? He'd fought the feeling all night long, sleeping on a lumpy sofa in her enclosed patio, knowing she was right down the hall.

"Let's start with Lourdes Jimenez," Lucy said. "We needed to go to a Level 3 background check, because no such woman seemed to exist."

"But you found her," he said into the speakerphone, not looking away from Maggie.

"Of course. The problem was that no one with that name was documented as being related to Alonso or Ramon Jimenez. Level 2, which accounts for marriages, divorces, and changes in Social Security docs, also came up empty. But then we tackled legal name changes and bingo."

"So who is she now?"

"Lola James, the president and CEO of a Miami-based shipping company called Omnibus Transport, a rapidly growing freight and cargo company,"

Dan snorted. "Don't tell me she's gone into the family business of drug smuggling?"

"Yes and no," Lucy said. "Omnibus is one hundred percent clean, without even a shadow of a misdeed. Ms. James has a perfect record, with no obvious ties to the drug world. The company is highly profitable, she's a well-documented workaholic, and her employees are loyal and long-standing. But here's where things get interesting."

"They always do," Dan said.

"Omnibus Transport is a new name for an old company that Lourdes bought, formerly known as AJ Cargo. The original warehouse is still listed as property owned by Omnibus, although her offices are downtown. And the house once owned by her father, Alonso Jimenez, is also an Omnibus asset, although Ms. James lives in a condo on Brickell Avenue. The house wasn't confiscated by the feds because Jimenez paid his fine in cash, and Florida law prevents the government from confiscating property of a felon if they pay."

"Who lives in the house?"

"As far as we can tell, no one. I'll send all this in an e-mail with documentation and addresses, phone numbers, et cetera, Dan. You can check it out."

"Will do. What else do you have? Anything on Constantine Xenakis? I wasn't entirely sure how to spell that name."

"I know how to spell it," Lucy said flatly. "And I already had a file an inch thick. An employee file."

Dan shot forward. "He was a Bullet Catcher? When?"

"Briefly, before you joined the company. He did one job, a diamond drop. Then I let him go."

"Why?" Despite his suspicions about the guy, Dan could easily see him as a Bullet Catcher. No wonder he'd moved over when he heard Dan's name. No doubt he recognized it.

"I let him go on gut instinct, nothing tangible. Some diamonds were missing from the drop, but they later reappeared. There was just something about him I wasn't sure I could trust, despite some exemplary skills. But it was early in the start of this company, and I didn't think he was what I wanted."

"So what's he doing now?"

"From what I can tell, living well in Tarpon Springs, Florida. But not employed. Not gainfully, anyway."

Dan dropped back on the sofa. "My guess? He's a professional thief, a hired mercenary. He doesn't want the fortune," he said, directing his comment to Maggie. "Someone's paying him to find it."

"It wouldn't surprise me," Lucy replied. "But, beyond what I just told you, I have nothing new on him, except that I assume he freelances his services, so he could be working for anyone. Oh, and I know you were going to arrange access to the evidence files in the FBI's Miami office. I'm friends with the new SAC there, Thomas Vincenze. Have you ever met him?"

"No." But who wasn't friends with Lucy?

"He's just taken over that office after some time in Los Angeles. He owes me a favor, so I put a call in. He's expecting you in an hour."

"Great. I've already been in touch with Joel Sancere, my partner on the case. He knows I'm coming in."

"Now pick up privately, Dan." It wasn't a request.

He took the cell phone off speaker and put it to his ear. " 'Sup?"

"I know you're on leave, but I may have a job down in Florida. Since you're already down there, I thought you might consider it."

He looked at Maggie, who was still curled on the zebra stripes, studying him carefully.

"I don't know." There was a lot of ground to cover with Maggie, and he hadn't even started yet.

He heard a soft sigh. "Dan, when are you coming back to work?"

"Someday."

"That's not good enough for me."

Dan laughed. "Nothing's good enough for you. See ya, Juice. I'll be in touch." He flipped the phone closed and caught Maggie's smile.

"Efficient, isn't she?" she asked.

"You have no idea." He stood and offered her a hand. "Do you think you can handle a trip to the Miami FBI offices?"

She nodded, letting him pull her up. "Yeah. I think Quinn is in good hands here."

As he opened the door, Peyton shot by, followed by Quinn.

"We're going swimming," he said, throwing the announcement at Maggie as he bounded by. "The pool is like a thousand feet long!"

As he disappeared, she looked up at Dan. "He may never want to leave."

Alonso Jimenez slammed his massive hands on the table, breathing so hard and so slow that he could feel his nostrils quiver with each shaky inhale. His fury couldn't be contained.

Across the table, the blood drained from his men's faces.

"Viejo," Pedro said. "Think of your heart."

"Think of yours!" he spat back. "Think how it will feel when I rip it out of your chest and feed it to wolves for letting a woman outsmart you."

Both men shifted uncomfortably, looking anywhere but at Alonso. Fear, respect, and shame kept their eyes averted. Not that he'd really hurt them. He had so few loyal men left, he couldn't afford to lose even a stupid one.

"And now she's hiding him, of course. You've ruined the opportunity, now, when time is of the essence and my . . ." *Days are nearly over*. But they could never know about the cancer. No one could, until he'd finished and replaced lying, stupid Ramon with his only hope—a grandson he'd never met. "My needs are not yet fulfilled."

"I can find him, Viejo," Roberto said. He was older, and his loyalty to the Jimenez family ran deep. But Pedro? Viejo couldn't even look at the filthy cheat who was in the game for the money only.

That's all he could find to work for him now, and why his activities had to stay secret and be handled on his own. But getting his grandson to Monte Verde couldn't be done alone.

"Give me time, and I can find him and bring him

to you," Roberto repeated, his dark eyes burning with intensity.

No, he could never kill this man. Time was, he would have picked up a butcher knife and driven it through his heart to make an example, to maintain his power. But his power, like his body, was faltering, and loyalty like this man's was more valuable than examples.

"You tried and failed," Alonso said. "Now he is hidden and protected."

"I will get him," Roberto said defiantly. "For you, Viejo. I will find your grandson and bring him to your plantation. He belongs at Monte Verde. He will start the next generation."

Roberto was also very good at saying exactly what he thought Alonso wanted to hear.

"*I* will find him," Alonso replied. "I have many resources." That was a lie. He had one resource, and it cost him dearly. But he'd paid the fee gladly all these years, rewarded with knowledge. Pictures. Even a videotape of Quinn playing in the park with a big brown dog, a fair-haired boy who obviously favored Caridad's side.

Across the room, the ancient fax machine trilled with an incoming call. The next shipment must be on its way. He pushed himself up, using both hands, his strength sapped just from this conversation.

He blocked the machine from their view. The readout that lit with the sender's phone number had long ago burned out, but he knew who was transmitting this information. The same person who would find his grandson.

As the paper inched into the tray, he saw that a strange design trimmed the paper, as though the sender had used some sort of official document to write the information.

This should just be a confirmation that the shipment

had been sent from the code name they used: Michael Scott. Alonso frowned, glancing over his shoulder at the two men who shared a look of hope, like chastised children who prayed the worst they would get was a tongue-lashing.

Half of the paper was through the machine now, enough to pull Alonso's attention from his men to the message.

This was an official document. It was a certificate of some sort.

His belly tightened, because anything out of the norm was never a good thing. He'd been expecting a shipping number, an arrival time, a cargo code.

Finally the document completed printing, and the machine shut down, releasing the paper. Alonso lifted it, frowning as he worked to translate the English, much better at speaking the language than reading it.

Certificate of Birth.

Birth . . . he understood that.

Quinn Varcek Smith.

He certainly understood that.

Mother. *Madre*. Yes, Magdalena Varcek. He recognized that name, of course.

Father. *Padre*.

He sucked in a breath and felt his treacherous heart skip one beat, then another.

"El Viejo?" Pedro asked. "Bad news?"

Bad news. Horrible news. Impossible, wrong, despicable news. His head grew light, his chest felt squeezed by a vise, his powerful fingers trembled.

This could not be real. This was a cruel and vicious joke, played by someone who wanted to speed his demise. The words shattered and changed and ruined everything.

There was the code name he'd been expecting, but never, never like this.

Was it possible? Had *she* been the betrayer, not Ramon? Had he blamed the wrong person all these years? Did he have men out to kill a son who had not done anything except the crime of stupidity by not watching his woman more closely?

Bile rose in his throat as the harsh reality settled over him.

The boy was not his blood.

Then what did he have left to live for? Nothing. Absolutely nothing but revenge.

He stepped back from the machine, holding the paper as if it burned his fingers. She had to die. No, no, it had to be worse than death.

The whore who had ended his life as he knew it, ruined his business, and put him in prison, had to suffer first. Alonso folded the paper to cover the hateful words.

The *puta* would watch her own son die. Then she would pay for her betrayal with her life. And when that was over, he'd have one last man to kill.

Michael Scott. This time, his death would be real.

CHAPTER
NINE

ONCE MAGGIE KNEW Dan's former identity, she easily picked up the nuances that made the man she knew similar to the man who walked into the FBI offices with her. Not that his cover hadn't been thorough, but there were subtleties in his speech patterns, the way he moved his brows and hands, even his gait and posture, that were his regardless of hair color or the shape of his nose.

Not so with Joel Sancere. As the stocky, stiff-backed, military-buzzed FBI agent marched to greet them in the lobby, Maggie stared in amazement that this man was the sloppy, slacky Juan Santiago who had seemed to be kept around more for his off-color jokes than his role in the drug dealing.

In a tailored suit, crisp white shirt, and square-knotted tie, there was nothing slack about FBI Supervisor Sancere.

"Dan Gallagher, you son of a gun." He reached his hand straight out to Dan and gave it one snap of a shake. "Great to see you again."

Dan returned the shake and immediately turned to

Maggie to make the introductions, even though he'd already told her exactly what to expect. "This is Joel Sancere, currently the supervisor of—which squad are you running now?"

"Major thefts and violent crime," he said. "But I've worked my way through most every division we have. Mrs. Smith, I understand you are helping us once again with an open investigation. Thank you."

Like she'd *helped* on purpose last time.

"Supervisor Sancere," she said, shaking his hand and looking him in the eye. He had to know how Dan got inside information all those years ago, but she refused to feel ashamed.

His attention was back on Dan. "So you did it, huh?" he asked, a look somewhere between admiration and chastisement in his eyes. "Why am I not surprised? You were always a rule-bender."

"Getting into the evidence room?" Dan shrugged. "I know people. But I'm afraid they won't let Maggie in there."

"That pushover SAC? He might." Joel shook his head with distaste. "The guy's a mess."

"I admit I was surprised when you didn't get the job."

Joel waved a hand as if he didn't care, then leaned closer and lowered his voice. "Like you've known for years, Dan, it's who you know, not how well you do the job. And this one?" He pointed a thumb over his shoulder. "He knows *everybody*."

"Who knows everybody?" Another man came around the corner to the lobby, smaller in stature and breadth, slightly balding, with sharp brown eyes behind rimless glasses. "Are you Dan Gallagher?"

Maggie had to agree with Sancere; the "boss" was a mess. He hadn't even ironed his shirt and clearly thought shaving was optional.

"I'm the special agent in charge, Thomas Vincenze." He shook Dan's hand and then nodded to Maggie. "You ready to go Gallagher? I've had the ev clerk pull the 1As and bulkies for you."

Dan hesitated, looking at Maggie. "You want to wait here in the lobby?"

"I'll take care of her," Joel assured him. "We'll be in my office."

If Dan noticed the blood fade from her face, he didn't react. He just nodded his thanks to Joel and disappeared out the lobby doors with Vincenze.

"This way," Joel said to Maggie. "My hole is in the back."

She started down the hall, wondering how to make small talk without going to the past, the place she wanted to avoid.

"So," he started, "have you met the infamous and incomparable Lucy Sharpe?"

The question surprised—and relieved—her. "I spoke with her on the phone before we came."

"No sparks?"

She gave him a confused look.

"Between her and Dan. Rumor has it they're an item, didn't you know?"

Another surprise, but this one at her reaction to that news. What did she expect? That he'd never been attracted to another woman? A man like that? "He didn't mention that."

"It's just a rumor, mind you. Lots of those where that operation is concerned. They're sort of shrouded in mystique." He laughed as they reached the door to his office, and gestured for her to go in first. "And money."

"I'm really not that familiar with the company," she said, crossing her arms and not taking a seat. How long would it take Dan to find that fortune?

"Bet you were surprised when he showed up after all these years, huh?"

Even five minutes with someone who had this much on her past was too long.

He ambled around his desk and sat in a creaky chair. "Sit down, Maggie. Oh, I'm sorry. Do you want something? Coke, coffee?"

"No thanks." She sat and glanced around, looking for something to change the subject. But there wasn't even a family picture or diploma or anything she could use to make a comment.

"Did you recognize him?"

"No, I didn't." She looked directly at him. "But I really wouldn't have recognized you."

He smiled, obviously taking that as a compliment. "I don't do much UC anymore, but I was pretty good at it back in the day."

He leaned forward, and there was a subtle shift in his features from amiable to something rougher. "You don' remember your old pal, Juan?" The thick Spanish accent had a hint of something mean, and she sat back a little to get away from it.

"I do now."

Instantly, he was himself again. "Sorry. I'm sure this is awkward for you."

"A little." She gave him a tight smile. "I appreciate that you understand that."

"Let's just proceed as friends, Maggie. I think what you're doing to help is a noble thing, and we're grateful."

"I'm happy to help," she said, keeping it as vague as possible.

"What do you have? One of the 'missing fortunes'?" He air-quoted the words and added plenty of sarcasm.

"I take it you don't believe they are the key to . . . anything?"

"Never have. That was Dan's theory, and some others. Me? I was there that night with El Viejo. He made no effort to hide or conceal the fortune he had. It's nice folklore—a hundred million in missing cash—but I doubt it ever existed. And if it did, Esteban went to the grave knowing where it is."

"Not even Ramon?"

"The minute those agents busted in, El Viejo knew exactly where the leak came from. Ramon is persona non gratis with him, I suspect."

"I really don't know that much about it," she said coolly. "I'm just trying to help Dan."

"You haven't answered my question. Do you have one of the fortunes? Because if you do, even a rogue investigator like Gallagher wouldn't be foolish enough to keep that from the FBI, would he?" When she didn't answer, he leaned forward. "*Do* you have one, Mrs. Smith?"

"Not anymore." It wasn't technically a lie. She'd hidden the fortune in the one place she thought was completely safe—Quinn's backpack. If he was in a safe house, then so was his backpack.

"It's okay, Maggie," he said, reclining his chair casually. "Dan will eventually tell me; we're good friends. You don't have to worry about what's safe to say or not."

"Thank you," she said. "And please, don't feel like

you have to babysit me. If you have a meeting or something . . ." *Please go to it. Now.*

He flicked a hand. "It'll wait. Tell me what you've been
doing all these years? Living in Florida, still?"

"In the Keys."

"Husband? Kids?"

"My husband passed away about four years ago, but
I have a son, Quinn." Before he could take a breath or
ask how old, she pointed to his bare walls. "I don't see
any pictures of a family, Supervisor Sancere. How about
you?"

"No time, I'm afraid." He added a sheepish smile. "I'm
here more than I'm home, and when I'm not, I'm traveling on a case. How old's your son?"

"Old enough to drive me crazy half the time," she said
quickly. "Have you completely given up undercover work?
I would imagine it's quite exciting."

"Not as exciting as it was for Dan."

Could he mean what she thought he meant?

"A guy who stomps all over the regs like he does tends
to do quite well UC," he continued. "So he's a teenager
then, your Quinn?"

It was a direct volley and she knew exactly what he was
trying to figure out—the math. Was the baby Dan's . . . or
Ramon's?

Blessedly, she heard footsteps and Dan's voice in the
hall. *Thank you, Baba.*

Dan's face was dark as he entered. "All right, Maggie.
We can go."

She stood, grateful for the reprieve, but trying to read
his expression. She couldn't. She glanced at Joel. "It was
nice talking to you."

"Wait a second. Dan?" Joel stood, also frowning at the

other man. "What's the matter? Something wrong with the evidence?"

Dan dropped his hands into his pockets and nodded slowly. "It's gone."

"The fortune?" Dan didn't seem surprised that Joel made that assumption. "Are you kidding me? What did the clerk say?"

"She has no explanation."

"But did you check the notes for a copy of what was on the fortune?" Joel asked. "Anything in those files had to have been recorded in the notes."

"I got it," he said. "But that's not quite as reliable."

Joel blew out a breath and looked over Dan's shoulder as if he expected the SAC to charge in any second. "What did I tell you about that guy? He can't even run an evidence room."

"There has to be an explanation," Dan said.

"There might be," Joel said. "A whole lot of files from the midnineties were taken up to storage in D.C. I know you'd think that something that small would be in a 1A file, but it could have gotten transferred. I'll look into it for you."

Thomas Vincenze tapped on the door, snapping a cell phone shut with his other hand. "C'mere, Dan."

He stepped out, and Maggie hesitated for a second as Joel gave her a very hard and suddenly accusing look.

"Pretty big coincidence that this disappears right after Ramon gets out of prison and you show up again. Don't you think?"

She bristled at the comment and the tone. "Excuse me?"

"This is still my case, Ms. Smith. Not . . ." He notched his head to the door. "His." He took one step closer. "And I know you didn't ask, but allow me to give you some unsolicited advice."

"No, thank you."

He leaned closer to whisper it anyway. "If you think you can trust that man, then you obviously don't have a very good memory."

"So what happened with him?" Dan asked when they got into his car. "You don't seem happy."

"Neither do you."

"I'm not. A key piece of evidence is missing." He started the car but didn't pull out. "What did he say to you to upset you?"

Did she seem upset? She thought she was holding it totally together. "He said exactly what I expected, mostly in subtext. Tell me about the notes you got."

"Don't want to talk about it, huh?"

"Actually, no. Drive."

Instead, he pulled out his phone and hit a few buttons to bring up a text. "Here's what was in the evidence notes, which aren't as reliable as the physical fortune. It said 'Success is failure when turned inside out.' And on the back, four numbers again. Five-nine-two-five."

"What can we do with that?"

"Run the words and numbers through some cryptography software, brainstorm possibilities with addresses and GPS, parse the words for clues. With two fortunes we have twice as much as we did first time around, if my theory is correct."

"We don't know that my fortune wasn't just a regular old cookie. The clue could have been on the one Lourdes had."

"Or anyone in the house that afternoon, but everyone else was arrested that night and searched." He turned the ignition on and headed out of the parking lot.

"Not Lourdes."

He nodded. "We should visit her. But first, there's somewhere else I'd like to stop by." He pulled out and headed toward the expressway entrance. "The search was thorough, so I don't expect to find anything, but I do think it's interesting that the house is still owned by the Jimenez family."

Great. Just where she never wanted to go again.

He flicked the blinker and pulled onto the highway. "You don't mind, do you?"

"Of course not."

"Will you tell me what Joel said that upset you?"

"He implied that I might have something to do with the missing fortune, and he doesn't like that you're nosing in on his turf."

"He's never liked me. He's a stand-up guy, an agency man to the core, but very competitive and jealous. Don't let him bother you."

She nodded, trying to take the advice to heart, looking at the traffic out her window. "He also said you and your boss were an item."

"Then *really* don't take anything he says to heart."

He whipped the car into the next lane and accelerated, weaving through traffic as if it were the Indy 500. They skirted a truck, and threaded between a van and an SUV. She filed his silent but powerful response and stayed quiet all the way to Coral Gables.

Each mile, the landscape grew more and more familiar, and as he maneuvered through the lush hallways of banyan trees that shaded the pricey neighborhood, she broke the silence. "I remember the first time I came here."

"You were, what? Seventeen?"

"Eighteen." Scrawny, scared, and scarred by Baba's

death and the harsh reality that her mother, wherever she was, didn't want anything to do with her. "In fact, I met Ramon on my eighteenth birthday and, of course, I took that as a sign that he was meant for me."

"You were here a few months before I was," he said.

"I remember," she said, closing her eyes for a moment. "I remember the day I met you."

"You do?" He seemed surprised.

Of course it wouldn't have left an impression on him. "I was so happy there was another gringo around. Someone who would speak English to me other than Ramon and Lourdes." She laughed softly, shaking her head. "I had an instant crush."

"Me, too."

"You did not," she shot back. "You had an instant insider."

He turned onto Granada, then cut his gaze her way again. "Maybe crush is the wrong word. But there was instant . . ."

"Lust."

A smile pulled at his lips. "That, too."

Funny thing, lust. She'd felt the same chemical response when he'd walked into her bar that she felt when he'd walked into the dining room at Viejo's house. Like wings were fluttering in her stomach and her whole body wanted to just . . . attach to his.

"Here we are," he said. "Just like old times."

They were on Alfonso Street, which looked even more rich and elegant than she remembered. Until they reached the gate, where signs of abandonment flourished.

"It doesn't look like anyone lives here," Maggie said as they drove the length of the two adjacent lots Viejo owned. The house was blocked by live oak trees and thickets of palmetto palms, except for one little corner of the second floor that rose above the highest branches.

They exchanged a look, and he slid the Porsche up to the curb about a block away. "Let's check it out."

Dan shook the wrought iron gate set into the chipped and faded stucco privacy wall. The entire place felt forgotten and neglected, except for one addition to the entrance: a state-of-the-art security access keypad on the other side of the gate. That, oddly enough, looked sparkling new.

"I remember the old key code," Maggie said. "One-one-two-nine." She used to wonder if November 29 would be a lucky day for her.

Dan tried it, but, predictably, nothing happened. "Let's go around to the side entrances," he suggested.

They started down the eastern perimeter of the property, moving along a narrow pathway between the stucco wall and a wild, ten-foot-high jungle of shrubbery, so thick that Dan had to hold branches back for them to pass. When they reached the side gate, that whole section was buried by oleander and hibiscus trees.

"If only we had a machete," Maggie said, pulling back thick palm fronds to get closer. "See that row of bricks along the foundation of the wall? One of them, the third from the left, I think, wasn't grouted in and Ramon hid a key there so he could get in after El Viejo locked up for the night. But I doubt it's still there, or still works this gate."

Dan tore at some of the branches and ivy covering the large iron gate, testing it. "No keypad access here. Maybe all this shrubbery is enough to keep someone out."

"Can you hold these branches back while I dig down there to look?" she asked.

He made an opening so that Maggie could get on her

knees and work the bricks as she'd seen Ramon do. The third brick was loose in the grout.

"Got it." With one good yank, she was able to slide the brick out, set it aside, then gingerly reached her hand into the hole.

And touched the edge of a key.

She rocked back on her heels and looked straight up at Dan. "This, my friend, is a sign from the universe." She held the key up to him.

His grin, a little crooked, gave her a kick in the tummy.

"Nice work, Maggie May."

And the old nickname pretty much left a boot mark on her heart. She could still hear his voice, whispering in her ear when they were alone and he slipped his hand under her shirt. *Maggie May . . . then again, she may not.*

"Let's see if it still works," he said, obviously not sidetracked by memories.

He helped her up and they headed to the gate, where he inserted the key. The latch unlocked with one turn, and he pushed the ten-foot-high gate open against the thick Florida crabgrass so they could slide in.

For a moment, they just stared in silent disbelief.

What used to be a spacious and gloriously landscaped expanse of prime Coral Gables real estate clearly hadn't been pruned, cleared, or inhabited for a very long time.

Dan led them along the wall, away from the water, toward the main house. Untamed brush grew everywhere. The swimming pool, enclosed in shreds of dried, torn screening, was completely drained, cracked, and coated in mossy fungus.

At the far end of the property, near the water and tucked into a wall of protective shrubbery, there were a few grassy slopes. Viejo had carted in tons of dirt to build a miniature valley where he'd planned to grow coffee. The endeavor was a disaster; Miami didn't have the climate or the soil. But the hills stayed, along with the tool shed the workers had erected. *Their* shed.

She didn't look. Instead, she took in the brown patches of grass where sun had broken through the foliage and burned it, while other areas were jungle green and thick. The back of the three-story hacienda was in total disrepair—faded, chipped, with numerous barrels missing from the Spanish tile roof, and the ones left behind were shadowed with black mold. Every window was gray with filth, and closed tight.

"Remember what a showplace it was?" Maggie said softly. "Viejo was maniacal about the landscaping and maintenance."

"Look at that rusty patio furniture. Same stuff. I guess they never moved anything out." As they got closer, Dan used one hand to keep her behind him, the other poised for access to a weapon she knew was under his shirt.

They passed the patio and walked down one side of the house, trying to peer in dirt-encrusted windows, until they reached the utility room. When Dan stopped and tried the lock, Maggie looked around, transported back to the nights when she'd used this exit to steal out and meet him.

A yellow piece of paper in the bushes caught her attention. She plucked it out—a post office delivery notification. Someone tried to deliver a package to . . .

"Michael *Scott*?"

Dan turned from the door. "What?"

"Look at this." She held the paper to him. "And look at the date. One month ago, someone tried to deliver something to Michael Scott. A dead man who never officially lived at this abandoned house."

"An oversize package from New York," he said, studying the paper hard before slipping it into his pocket. "We can track that. But now, I really want in." Kneeling down, he pulled out a key ring, and used something to work the lock.

"You carry a lock pick?" she asked.

"Security works both ways." In a few minutes the knob turned and he gave it a push, but it didn't open. "It's bolted from the inside."

"Not when I lived here," Maggie said. "Do you have a tool to break the dead bolt?"

"Yep. It's called a Glock." He tapped along the frame of the door a few times, then unholstered his gun and motioned for her to get back. The shot echoed over the water and made her ears ring as the door popped open.

The dank smell of mold and humidity hit Maggie as they stepped in, along with a rush of memories.

Once when she was folding clothes back here, he'd come to talk to her. To arrange a meeting. He'd pressed her up against the hot, rumbling dryer and they'd kissed, insanely close to getting caught, but unable to stop.

Because she thought he cared.

"Come on," he said, reaching to pull her into the house, his expression determined.

She followed him into the kitchen. The smell was putrid, the air was heavy, and everywhere she looked, she remembered the shadowy, unhappy life she'd lived here. Always bound by a false sense of security, the property of one man and the playmate of another. No, the *informant* of another.

But he'd been so *good* to her.

She stole another glance at him, bracing for the rush of revulsion for what he'd done to her, but getting a different rush altogether.

Damn her body. Damn her hormones.

Damn *him*.

"It's as if nothing has been touched since the day the FBI finished the investigation," he said, oblivious to the storm of emotions whipping through her. "Even the dishes are still in the cabinet. The booze in the bar. The chairs around the table where he held every meeting."

The table where she'd sat next to Ramon and across from Dan while her teenage heart took flight. *Get a grip, Maggie*. She was no better now than then.

"What are you looking for?" she demanded, her voice harsher than she'd intended.

"Clues. Hints. A reason to explain why there are all those locks, but the place has been untouched. I want—" He froze for a minute, listening to a loud pop from outside.

Her heart jumped at the sound of gunfire, but then she realized what it was. "A boat," she said. "On the canal."

"I know." He took a few steps toward the doors that lined the back. "That's a go-fast, a Cigarette boat."

The low, staccato throb of a racing boat rumbling up the waterway got closer and louder. It almost masked the sound of a car pulling up to the front of the house.

"Did you hear that?" she asked, just as the boat stopped with one loud thump of a mighty, unmuffled engine. Right in the back of the house. "Someone's in the front, too."

Dan grabbed her arm and twirled her toward the utility room, pulling out his gun as he shoved her into hiding. The second she stepped into the room, the front door opened, followed by heavy, male footsteps on the terra-cotta tile, punctuated by the soft digital ring of a cell phone.

"I'm in. I don't know. It could be another fucking false alarm."

Had they set off a silent alarm?

"Get up here, now. I'll search the place. It's probably another goddamn squirrel in the third floor."

She inched farther behind Dan, who looked over his shoulder and pointed to the door. "Go."

Together, they moved soundlessly past the washer and dryer to the door; then Maggie touched the knob. She twisted the handle, praying the door didn't squeak.

The footsteps grew louder, closer. Biting her lip, she pushed. It silently opened as the man's footsteps crossed the kitchen.

Dan nudged her forward, closing the door behind them without making a sound.

"Go!" he urged quietly, shoving her toward the path, rounding a huge row of bushes that provided the same cover as when they'd slip away for a midnight tryst by the water.

They couldn't risk crossing the yard to reach the gate they'd used to get in; parts of the property were too open. She knew instantly where they were going.

The tool shed.

As they darted forward, she heard movement on the other side of the bush. Someone was coming up from the water, blocked from view. With his arm still around her, Dan kept her low as they ran, slowing occasionally to try to get a peek at whoever was out there, but more focused on hiding.

They rounded a curve in the property, followed the

thick treeline, and Dan dove them both over the first small hill, and rolled to the shallow valley. Stiff crabgrass poked at her face and arms, as his hard, solid body held her tight. The smell of earth and oak and brackish canal water punched her nose, her breath whooshing out as they landed.

"Stay down!" he ordered, crawling up the side of the hill the minute they stopped moving.

She caught her breath, steadied herself, and watched him get into position.

They'd used that lookout before to check the lights in the house, to make sure they were completely alone. They'd made love under the stars on this very hill.

He reached his hand out, indicating that she climb up next to him. She did, her jeans dragging over the grass, her fingers digging into the dirt.

Through the greenery, they could see the dock, a starburst-painted racing boat bobbing on one line. In the other direction, the foliage blocked their view of the house.

"Move it!" The man's voice echoed from the house. "We might as well do it, now that we're both here."

Closer. Coming right toward them.

"The shed!" Dan said, rolling them both in the direction of the small metal shed twenty feet away.

They ran, staying low, reaching it in seconds, but stopped at the sight of a massive sliver bolt and a fist-size padlock holding the small double doors together.

"Behind." Dan pushed her around to the back of the rectangular structure, then pressed her against the warm metal, covering her completely.

"Why don't you just confront them?" she whispered. "You're armed."

"I don't want them to know we're here until I find out why they are. And I want you safe. Stay quiet and still."

The tiny building shook as someone worked the heavy-duty lock, the bolt grinding noisily, then one of the two doors thudded open.

Maggie listened for any clue to what they were doing, protected by the strength of Dan's body. Inside the shed something scraped the flooring, the gritty, earsplitting sound of metal against metal.

"Christ, that makes my teeth itch," a man said.

The response was a grunt of raw male exertion.

"Son of a bitch, this fucker's heavy." Same guy.

"Just get it in the boat. And quit complaining. The one coming tomorrow's going to be twice as bad. This shit has to move, and fast."

Their voices shifted outside the shed now, moving away. Maggie stayed stone still, braced for the possibility that someone would suddenly pop around the corner and shoot them. Dan remained pressed against her, the front of her body warmed by the sun-drenched corrugated metal. He kept his right arm up, his weapon poised to fire.

But the men's voices were down at the dock, and there was a loud thump as something hit the wood. Then the thunder of the racing-boat motor starting up.

Dan inched his head to the side of the shed, holding Maggie in place.

"Only one's on the boat," he whispered. "The other one'll probably go back to the house."

They waited, ready, breathing softly, the sun burning and the bitter boat exhaust mixing with the humidity. In the distance a door slammed, followed by the sound of a car motor starting up, then disappearing.

"Think he's gone?" Maggie asked.

"Possibly. Probably."

"But he didn't come back and lock the shed."

"I know. Let's check it out." Dan led her around the front, where one of the doors gaped open. He stuck his head in and Maggie tried to see around him.

"What's in there?"

"Absolutely nothing." He ducked to get into the opening, and she followed.

The place was so full of memories, she almost choked.

In reality, it was just eight by five empty feet, with nothing but a crumpled piece of trash in the corner. Dan bent to get it, smoothing the paper and holding it toward the light to read it.

"Enclosed items," he softly read. "Five wrenches, sixteen hammers, fourteen boxes of shank nails . . ." He skimmed the rest of the list. "It's some kind of packing list."

"Look," Maggie whispered, indicating the recipient's name at the top of the list.

Michael Scott.

"Something tells me . . ." Dan said softly as his gaze scanned the paper again. "Viejo's business is definitely thriving again."

Behind the shed, trees rustled and snapped into place. Before she could breathe, Dan pulled her against the front wall, so that anyone glancing in wouldn't see them inside.

Five seconds passed, then ten. Then the door ground across its metal track, followed by the sound of that industrial-strength lock and bolt, locking them in a pitch-black, hundred-and-ten-degree dungeon.

CHAPTER
TEN

ONLY ONE THING got Lola out of the office in the middle of a busy workday, and that was a soul-shattering, head-clearing orgasm delivered by a man who lost every shred of control over her beauty. Her business gave her the power high she'd craved since childhood, but sex with the right man—a man who absolutely folded in half over her physical perfection—*that* was irresistible.

And the man she'd met in SoBe last Friday night had provided exactly that. He'd begged for her, drooled over her looks, praised her symmetry—he'd even used that word when he sat up in her bed and watched her prance naked around the room.

Like she was doing right now. At the height of a busy Thursday, with clients calling and accounts receivable growing, Lola had driven to her Brickell Avenue condo after he called and spoke so dirty and sweet on her phone.

She stepped back from the mirror in her master bed-room, the backlighting from the balcony twenty-eight floors above downtown Miami and Biscayne Bay perfectly accenting her toned thighs, her flawless C-cups, her flat stomach, and, best of all, her exquisitely beautiful face.

Her father had been so very wrong.

"You're pretty, Lourdes," he would say, in English, so that no one would understand him and think he was saying sweet things to his little girl. "Pretty ugly."

Well, look at me now, Viejo. Pretty *pretty.*

The insults were all the worse because they were secret, insidious, vicious, and swift. The same way he'd kill a man for looking the wrong way in a meeting, Viejo would shred her. All she could do was run and hide. In her closet in Coral Gables, and at the farm, she'd climb to the balcony through the attic and weep.

But now? Now he understood what ugly was. All the things that mattered to him—his son, his reputation, his home, his life—had gotten very, very ugly.

She smiled, running her hands down to the completely waxed flesh between her legs. She'd even managed to make sure his last good dream went up in smoke, too.

The light tap on her door didn't surprise her. The doorman was never where he was supposed to be in this building, and her man was anxious to get his hands on her.

Anxious was good. Desperate was better. Out of control turned her absolutely crazy hot.

This guy was all of those things, and none of that had affected his performance the other night. He hadn't been hugely endowed, but what he lacked in size he made up for in frantic need to touch her. Not fantastic-looking, but meaty and strong. Anyway, she didn't want someone who was better-looking than her. What would be the point of that?

She grabbed a short silk wrap, tying it loosely enough to let her breasts show as she peered through the peephole.

For a minute she couldn't even remember his name. Did she even *know* his name? Who cared? It was better this way. Anonymous made it hotter.

Opening the door slowly, she treated him to a smile. "Hi."

"Hi yourself." He swept up and down her nearly naked body with a slow, wildly appreciative grin. "Fuckin' A, you're magnificent."

She opened the door wider, inviting him in.

"I'm supposed to be at work," she said, holding a cheek out for him to brush with his lips. "But you lured me away."

He grinned, looked around the condo, and let out a low whistle. "This place is even nicer in the daytime," he said. "I still can't believe you're that much of an earner in your twenties." He ducked down as if he was looking around. "We alone? No sugar daddy waiting in the wings to watch, right?"

"Nope. But I have a business to run, so . . ." She opened the robe. "Let's get busy."

His nostrils quivered as he tried to steady his breath. "Hang on, honey. Let me savor the moment." He moved deeper into the condo, his gaze torn between her decor and her body. "Really nice place. I didn't get to look around the other night."

"You can look at me." This wasn't a real estate meeting, for Christ's sake. "Follow me." She curled her finger playfully and headed to her bedroom.

"Don't I even get a drink first?"

For the first time since she'd met him, her internal alarms went off. The night he'd hit on her in SoBe, he'd been a total animal, completely into her. The call to her office with his sexy come-on was a pure booty call, too.

Now he wanted to turn this into a date? A chat over cocktails?

"If you want a drink, there's a restaurant downstairs," she said, her voice cool. "Otherwise, the bedroom's this way."

"I just want to . . . relax."

"I don't want you relaxed." She let the robe fall to the floor, and stepped back so he could see the whole package. "I want you worked up."

"Oh." He stared, perfectly slackjawed. "Like a fucking piece of art."

That was better. She turned slowly, pivoting so he could drool over her ass, her perfect back.

He jumped her so hard, she sucked in a breath as his body thwacked into hers from behind.

"Hey." She tried to duck out of his grip, but he brought his hand up and squeezed her tit, then slid it to her throat, tightening his hold.

"Cool it," she insisted, trying to wiggle out, trying to turn to him. "I don't like it rough."

"We're not going to do it rough." He let her twist around face-to-face, pulling her tighter as he kissed her. His lips were limp. His tongue was lackluster.

Nothing was like what she remembered from last time. She opened her mouth to try to get the feeling back, just as he yanked her around so he had her from behind again, wrenching her arms behind her back and locking his forearm over her throat.

"Stop it!" she choked, trying to kick him. She got in one swipe when she saw the knife. He pointed it right at her temple and her whole body turned to water, her bowels threatening to release, her stomach clenched against a gag of fear.

"What the hell do you *want*?" she said. "I'm offering it to you. You don't have to get violent with me."

"I'm not going to get violent," he said, his voice lower and more menacing from behind. "We're going to make a deal . . . Lourdes."

Son of a bitch, how could she be so stupid? "Who are you?"

"I'm your fortune hunter."

Fuck!

"You don't have to give it to me, Lourdes. I don't expect you have it anymore. But you sure as shit better know what it said. And tell me the truth, because I know just enough to know if you're lying. And every time you tell me a lie, I make a cut." The tip of the blade grazed her cheek. "I won't kill you—but I'll make damn sure no plastic surgeon can ever make you magnificent again."

She stayed very, very still, her eye muscles straining to see the knife without moving her head.

"Why do you want it? It's useless alone."

The blade pressed cold and sharp on her cheek. "No questions. Just answers. Words. Numbers. Answers."

The pressure increased, along with the first pinch of pain as something warm dribbled down her cheek. Blood.

"You're the one who wanted to play chess with the big boys, Lourdes."

Another sting as the blade trailed over her cheek.

"And I can make a chessboard out of your pretty, pretty face. Big, fat, red scars that will never go away. Then I'll start on your sexy body. I'll put so many fucking flaws on your skin, no one will be able to look at you."

She tried to swallow. Tried to think.

"Then you'll be pretty." More blood dribbled down to her mouth, warm and salty as it mixed with a tear. "Pretty ugly."

She closed her eyes and made her choice.

Dan slowly peeled his body off Maggie's back, giving them both air and space, but not enough of either one.

"Can't you just shoot the lock off?" she asked.

Dan put his fingers over her mouth. "Wait."

They did, silent and still inside the airless metal box, time ticking at the same rate as Maggie's heartbeat, which he felt pulsing through her.

"I can't shoot it," he said when he removed his hand as a signal that she could talk again. "It probably wouldn't shoot off, anyway, and I'd leave a mess."

"You're worried about how it looks?"

The place was black, small, airless, and so sweltering it was almost impossible to think. "I don't want them to know we've found where they hide the shipments. They'll change their strategy."

He got down on his knees and started feeling along the bottom, at the crevice where the siding met the metal floor, searching for any place where rust and time could have made the structure vulnerable.

"It's cheap tin," he said. "Cuttable."

He made his way to the back, then up the wall to the vent. The eave was barely six feet, and he couldn't even stand straight. The back vent was closed tight, the bolts rusted, eliminating any chance of popping it out. He wouldn't risk the front one; it would be too noticeable.

"We'll cut our way out," he said. "A clean slice where the back corners meet that no one will notice and we can slip out of without them ever knowing we've been here.

I'll come back and see if I can get a look at what they're shipping tomorrow."

"You have a knife that will do that?"

"No, but I'll call Max, and he'll come down." Giving them about forty minutes in a hot box with very little air and space. He crouched down. "Close your eyes."

"Why? I can't see a thing anyway."

"I'm going to flip open my phone, and if you look at the light, it'll delay how long it takes to get your night vision."

He closed his own eyes and pressed Max's speed dial by touch, but she covered his hand with hers, stopping him.

"Wait. He can't leave Quinn."

"Quinn's with Cori, and that place is as secure as Fort Knox."

Max answered on the first ring, and Dan quickly explained the situation, gave him a location, and put a rescue plan in place.

"What's Quinn doing?" Maggie whispered.

Dan relayed the question to Max, who chuckled in response.

"He's teaching Peyton the name of every fish in the tank," he said. "He's a great kid, Dan. Smart as a whip and funny. Not bad to have around, for a teenager."

He had no right to feel the twinge of pride; he hadn't raised Quinn. But he felt it anyway, and smiled. "I know he is. Be sure he's inside the whole time you're gone."

"Don't worry, we've got him under wraps, and I did the security in this house myself. It's impenetrable."

"Then get down here before we spontaneously combust."

Dan pressed the end button and opened his eyes, still not seeing even a silhouette of Maggie. But he could feel her heat, and he could smell her scent. Salty, spicy, sweet. The scent of Maggie in the shed.

The first bead of sweat trickled down his neck.

"Take off your clothes," he said, ripping his own T-shirt over his head and wiping his face with it.

"You're a riot."

"I'm not joking. We're both wearing jeans, Maggie. We need air on our skin to keep our temperatures under a hundred. And stay low, because heat rises. In fact, you should lie on the floor and let as much of your skin touch it as possible. It'll keep your temp down."

Next to him, he felt her shift position and heard her zipper scrape.

He couldn't resist. "There's a sound I've heard in here before."

"Oh, boy." Her laugh was dry. "That didn't take long."

"What? We're not going to talk about it? Here? In this place where there's a lot of . . ."

"History," Maggie said.

"Memories," he countered.

Down to his boxer briefs, he lay back, the metal slightly cooler than the warm air.

He heard denim slide over her legs, and pictured what was happening less than two feet away. He could roll, reach . . . and feel hot, damp, silky skin.

"Good memories," he added softly. "I hope you know that."

"Mmm." The response was noncommittal. "I guess you want my top off, too?"

Always. "You'll stay alive longer." He might die of need, though.

Cotton brushed flesh, and heat pooled around his balls, making them tight and sweaty.

She exhaled and the metal creaked as she lay down, probably an arm's distance from him. He couldn't see, but he could imagine. She had a bra on today, he'd noticed earlier. Did she still favor little wisps of panties, all lacy and feminine?

"Can you see yet?" she asked.

He wished to God he could. "No. Nothing. You're completely safe with me."

That earned him a soft snort of disbelief.

"I would never touch you now, Maggie. First of all, we'd die of heat stroke. Second . . ." He couldn't think of a single reason not to touch her except the danger to their internal thermometers. And the bone-deep knowledge that once he did, he wouldn't stop. "I just won't."

He heard her body shift, imagined her turning on her side, sensed her looking at him, even though she couldn't possibly see him in this complete darkness. But he could feel her breath and the warmth that rolled off her skin. His was damp, sweat prickling his whole body.

"What was it about this place?" she asked softly. "The minute I got in here, I was . . ."

Hot. Excited. Wet. Ready. She was all kinds of things, and thinking about them sent a gallon of blood south.

"Willing to try anything," she finally said.

He pictured her bare legs, long, lean, tanned, crossed at the ankles. The way her breasts sloped down when she rested on her side. The deep tips of her nipples. The glint in her eyes when she wanted to try something . . . different.

"It wasn't the shed," he whispered. "It was us."

"You always brought out a risk-taking side of me," she said, a smile in her voice.

"It was mutual," he agreed.

"It was . . . fun." Her voice was no more than a whisper. "Scary sometimes, but thrilling. I've never done anything like it since."

"Good." The burn of possession mixed with arousal.

"Good?" she scoffed at the word. "I suppose you haven't been with another woman since."

"I've been with plenty," he admitted. "But none . . . like that."

"Like what?"

Man, he didn't need this. Didn't need to think about what they'd done in here. How they'd done it.

"Stop talking about it, Maggie."

He stood suddenly, placing his hands flat on the back wall, bracing his legs wide.

"What are you doing?"

The equivalent of reciting the alphabet backward. Anything to stop thinking about Maggie in the shed.

"I want to work on this vent some more." He tried the nut again, but even with a tool it wouldn't have loosened. "If I can open the slats, we'd have a little light and air." He stuck his fingers in, but it was sealed with rust. The front vent let in more air, but its slats were at an upward angle, letting no appreciable light in.

Perspiration ran down his sides, and heat waves rolled through his body. He returned to the floor, engulfed in blackness and humidity. Forty minutes until Max got there. Anything could happen in forty minutes. And everything.

He laid his gun inches from his fingertips and closed his eyes, hoping the old trick would help his vision adjust faster when he opened them.

Maggie shifted again, moving her arms up with a frustrated, uncomfortable sigh. He pictured her lifting her hair, cooling her neck. She was sweating, too. He could smell the salt on her skin, and feel the heat shimmer around her. So close he could imagine the taste of her.

"Do you think the chance of getting caught made it more exciting?" she asked.

Was she doing this to torture him, or was she just as turned on as he was?

"Everything made it more exciting."

"It was always so . . . desperate," she barely whispered.

Desperate. Frantic. Furious. The rush to get in her made him all of those things.

"But I guess that was all an act to get me to tell you everything."

"No," he said simply. "It was genuine desperation."

He could have sworn she moved closer. If he just brushed his right hand a little along the floor, he'd touch her. Again.

Against his will, his cock stiffened. He bent his knees slowly, quietly, widened his legs, and took a slow breath.

"Remember the time I stripped by candlelight?"

"Jesus, Maggie, are you trying to kill me?" Blood hummed in his head as he remembered Maggie unbuttoning a cotton blouse, with nothing underneath. Maggie bending over and dragging jeans over her round, sweet ass. Maggie on the floor, under him. On top of him. On her knees in front of him. Teasing and taunting and taking him into her tight, slick body.

A sound escaped his lips as a droplet of moisture formed on the head of his cock.

"Why didn't we get heat stroke back then?" she asked.

"We did. We just called it something else." Mind-blowing sex.

"Yeah." Her voice was wistful; then she was quiet for a

long time. Breathing softly, not moving. With each passing second, his balls pinched with need and his cock beat with a blood rush, and his brain exploded with images of her body and the sounds of her orgasms and the flavor of her velvet skin.

"I need to ask you a question." Her voice was low, soft, and way too sexy.

"Anything." He turned just a little, ready for—anything.

"What are you thinking about right now?"

Your mouth. Your breasts. Your sweet . . . "Viejo. And what these guys are doing."

A finger jabbed his shoulder. "That was a test, Dan Gallagher."

He squinted into the dark, wishing that his damn night vision worked better. "What kind of a test?"

"Lie detector. And you . . ." The sudden touch of her hand on his hard cock shocked him. ". . . failed." She gave it the slightest squeeze, branding him. "*Now* I recognize you, Michael Scott."

"Very funny. Okay, you win. I lied." It took every ounce of self-control not to slide against her fingers. "But if you don't move your hand, it's gonna be real obvious, real soon."

She released him, leaving him aching. "You're thinking about things we did in this shed."

"And things we still might."

She inhaled softly but sharply. "You wouldn't."

"No, I wouldn't. That doesn't mean I don't think about it when I'm undressed, in the dark, six inches from a woman I think is the sexiest on earth." God, he wanted her to touch him again. Just put her palm right . . . there . . .

He slid his own hand down, unable to stop, unable to

resist replacing hers for one maddening second. He managed not to move, except to cringe with need, and take a slow breath.

"You okay?" she asked.

"What do you think?"

She shifted next to him again, the sound of her palms grazing her own skin, the image of her touching herself suddenly vivid behind his closed eyes. Clenching his jaw, he stroked his shaft again, squeezing for the fierce pleasure and pain of it, then letting go.

Sweating profusely, his throat bone dry, he fisted himself to fight the urgency of his erection. Next to him, Maggie moved some air, fanning herself.

"You know what night I remember the most?" Her question cut through the airless silence.

"They were all pretty sweet."

"I remember the time you found me here asleep at four in the morning."

"That was stupid," he said, more gruffly than he meant to. "You could've gotten caught, waiting for me like that."

"But you did come."

"A few times as I recall." The first, in her mouth.

"Ha-ha. Very funny. Do you remember how you woke me up?"

She really *was* trying to kill him. And succeeding. "Sort of."

"You do remember."

"Maggie, I remember everything. That's why I was so good at undercover. I have a photographic memory." And the photos she made for his mental album were well worn from many nights of remembering.

"So you remember exactly what we did that night?"

Of course he did. Did she want him to say it? Right here in the dark, is that what she wanted? She'd worn a denim skirt with nothing underneath, and he spread her legs, put his mouth on her and . . . "I licked you."

This time, her breath sounded unsteady. Maybe she was just as gone as he was.

That thought was enough to make him lose the battle not to touch himself again. His back bowed with the next secret, silent swipe of his palm against his swollen dick.

"Yes, you did." She sighed ever so slightly, but he still saw nothing but blackness and his fertile, full-color imagination. "Right between the legs."

One more time. Up. Down. Up. Around the head. Needing . . . tight . . . flesh.

She was beautiful down there, delicious and responsive. He could see her glistening, taste the moisture, feel the soft tuft of hair against his mouth. He wanted to be there right now. All he had to do was turn, and touch, and taste.

"You never said a word." Against his arm, he felt her breathe the words. So close. So, so close. "You just turned me upside down."

And she'd put him in her mouth while he had her in his. That was the moment their illicit affair went from crazy lust to . . . intimacy. Maybe even more than that.

"There's a number for that move, you know." He had to keep this light.

"I'd never done anything like that before." She exhaled softly, so close and warm he had to roll his palm again, squeezing his dick between his fingers. Wishing it were Maggie. With his hand wet with his own juice, he glided down the shaft, reaching his rock-hard balls, burning for that hand to be hers.

Just one touch. A fingertip. A pinch. A single stroke from her soft palm, and he'd have release. He opened his mouth, ready to say her name, ready to—

"And I've never done it since. Only with you."

Everything scorched. His brain. His hand. His stiff cock as he stroked again, soundless, stealthy, responding to the image of her legs around his head, her lips on him at the same time, the fierceness of their climax as he shot into her mouth and she came in his at the same moment.

"Sometimes I think about that." Her voice cracked with the admission. Maybe she was doing what he was doing: touching herself, pretending it was real. Stroking, stroking, stroking without making a sound. The pressure built up to the point of pain.

"Actually," she whispered. "I think about it a lot."

He came, shooting one violent spurt in his hand, then another, then another. He fought not to move, not to jerk with the release. He clenched his teeth so hard he could crack his jaw, but he never made a sound as relief rocked him.

Except for his heart, which pounded his ribs relentlessly.

"Did you hear that?" She sat up.

Oh, *man*.

"I heard someone out there."

He couldn't hear anything but the blood rushing in his head. Then a single tap on the back wall of the shed.

"Max?"

"To the rescue."

Maggie shot up and Dan blinked, hearing her dressing. He did the same, surreptitiously wiping his hand on his boxers. Once his jeans were on, he watched the first sliver of light as Max's knife sliced through the corner of the shed.

"Make it clean," Dan said. "And easy for us to get back in."

Max didn't answer, but the sound of the knife screeched louder as it moved along the floor, making an L-shaped metal flap for them to climb through.

Just as Dan popped his head into his T-shirt, sunlight illuminated the shed, momentarily blinding him.

Maggie was already on her knees, ready to crawl through.

Max reached in and gave her a hand. "Careful, the metal edge is sharp."

She eased through the opening, disappearing into light.

Dan took another slow breath before following. "No sign of anyone in the house?"

"It looks vacant, but I stayed way clear of it."

"We'll come back at night," Dan said as he kneeled down to follow Maggie out. "And figure out what the hell's going on here."

"Bet it was hot in there," Max said as he emerged.

"Hot as hell, and dark as night," Dan said.

"He has lousy night vision," Max told Maggie.

Dan turned to bend the metal back into place. Did the bastard have to reveal all his shortcomings?

"He must," she said. "Because after a few minutes, I could see everything."

Dan just closed his eyes and swore.

CHAPTER
ELEVEN

MAGGIE'S HEAD WAS spinning from hours of brainstorming, conference calls with a former national security adviser cryptographer, and the residual buzz she still felt from the heat that had melted her in the shed.

And it wasn't caused by the sun.

If her body betrayed her with one more crackle of desire, she'd scream. How could she forget who Dan was and what he'd done? How could she steal glances at him and fantasize? How could she let his loss of self-control in the shed twist her into one big knot of need?

At ten o'clock, she used Quinn as an excuse to slip away from the guesthouse living room they'd turned into a "war room," pausing to watch Cori on a second-floor balcony, walking with her baby in her arms.

It made her ache for her own son, and remember why they were here: for his protection.

Quinn and Maggie had rooms on the first floor, in one of multiple wings shooting off from the *Architectural Digest*-worthy home. At Quinn's room, she tapped softly, then pushed the door open. Goose ambled over for a sniff and rub, then jumped back to an overstuffed chair across from the foot of the bed.

"You got a lot of sun today," Maggie said, sitting on the queen-size bed and reaching out to brush honey gold hair back from Quinn's brow.

He wrinkled his nose. "Doesn't hurt, though. Don't make me put that aloe sh . . . stuff on it."

She just narrowed her eyes; it wasn't the time for a language lecture. "Did you have fun?"

"Are you kidding? This place rocks."

She surveyed the sharp angles of his face, the full shape of his mouth. How could she not have seen the resemblance the minute Dan Gallagher walked into her bar? How could Quinn not see it now?

Because when you're not looking for something, you can miss it.

"So, you okay?" she asked, hoping to get something more than a monosyllabic answer.

He shrugged. "Yeah."

"Come on. Talk to me."

"Nothing. It's all good."

"Quinn," she said. "Come on."

He exhaled and shook his head. "All right. I mean, the whole boat thing still kind of creeps me out, but . . ." He plucked at the silky comforter on the bed, averting his eyes.

"But what?"

"I know why I'm here."

Her heart fluttered. "You do." How much did he know?

"It's like protective custody. Witness protection. Whatever you call it. You ever gonna tell me what's going on?"

Eventually. "We're trying to figure that out."

"Mom, who are these people?" He waved a hand at the

room that dwarfed the one he had at home in scale and decor. "We don't have friends like this."

"Honey, a long time ago I . . . I knew that man, Dan. And . . ." Oh God, was it the right time? Should Dan be here when confessions were made?

She never wanted to lie—it was her ruling mantra of motherhood. Yet his entire conception was built on a lie.

"Well, duh," Quinn said. "It's pretty obvious you guys were tight."

"Really?" Were they that transparent?

Before he answered, Goose's head shot up in alert, followed by his bark and a soft tap on the door.

"How's it going?" Dan asked, stepping in. "You hanging in there, Quinn?"

Their smiles kind of matched, and Maggie's chest tightened.

"Yeah, I'm cool," Quinn said. "Can't believe there's no flat screen TV in the guest room though. It's so ghetto."

Maggie laughed at his sarcasm, and caught the spark of something in Dan's eyes as he said, "Yeah, call the management and complain, will ya?"

Connection—that's what that look was. They thought alike, made the same smart-ass comments. Dan had just realized it, and so did she.

"So when were you guys going to tell me that you two already knew each other?" If Quinn's question threw Dan, she couldn't tell.

"Soon," they replied in perfect unison.

"How 'bout now?"

"All right," Dan said. "Now's good." He glanced at Maggie, a question in his eyes as he gave Goose an easy scratch and took over his chair. "It was before you were born, when your mom lived in Miami."

"When you were a waitress there?" Quinn asked. "Before you moved to Marathon?"

Damn. She hadn't had a chance to tell Dan the story Smitty had made up.

"How'd you meet?" Quinn asked.

Maggie stayed silent, heat warming her cheeks. It wasn't just Quinn's conception that embarrassed her; it was how she lived. That dark and degrading part of her life when she chose to sleep with one criminal to keep a roof over her head, and screw around with another one because she found him irresistible.

"I was an FBI agent," Dan said.

Maggie managed a breath, and Quinn's eyes widened as Dan's cool quotient rocketed into the stratosphere.

"Seriously?" He sat up straighter in bed.

"And I interviewed your mother for a case involving one of her . . . customers."

God, he lied so smoothly. How could she forget that? And why wasn't she contradicting him?

"At the deli?" Quinn asked.

Dan glanced at her. "It was someone I was trying to arrest."

This was her opportunity to set the record straight. To tell the truth, and teach her son what his mother was really made of. She opened her mouth, then closed it.

Gutless.

"That's what this is all about, isn't it?" Quinn looked from one to the other. "I heard you guys talking in the car about someone in jail. That's who tried to kidnap me, isn't it?"

"Yes," Maggie said quickly, gratefully. "We think there might be a connection. That man recently got out of prison and Dan came to warn me. Then those men took you in the boat, so until we know who it is and why, you're staying here."

"Can you figure it out and get them?" he asked Dan.

"Probably. That's what I do, and I work for a company that excels in precisely that sort of thing. In the meantime, you're safe here."

He grinned. "In the ghetto."

Maggie forced a laugh, but Dan's chuckle was genuine as he stood. "And you haven't even seen the garage. Prepare for major Ferrari action."

"No way!" Quinn almost popped out of bed.

"Not now," Maggie said, pushing him down, along with her shame and guilt. "Tomorrow. Now you have to sleep."

Dan reached for her hand. "And you have to go back to the war room, Ms. Smith," he said. "I think we're close to a breakthrough. Can you talk to Max? I'll be right there."

Was this just an excuse to be alone with Quinn? What would he say? Did he feel it was his job to tell Quinn the truth? Would he think that would be sparing her somehow?

She kissed Quinn on the forehead, and slipped out of the room. When she stepped into the wide hallway she paused, leaned against the wall by the door, and listened.

"Are you serious about the Ferrari?" Quinn asked.

"Yep. A cherry red Testarossa. Max'll take you for a ride. Guaranteed."

"Oh, man, that is so fuckin' cool."

Maggie cringed at the curse.

"Hey," Dan said sharply. "No ride if you talk like that. It doesn't impress me, and it makes you sound stupid."

"Yeah, okay." He actually sounded contrite.

Maggie closed her eyes, fighting an unexpected wave

of emotion. This is what Quinn needed. A man to tell the truth. A father figure.

Not a father *figure*. His real father.

"Listen, I want to talk to you about something," Dan said. "About your mom. When she was younger."

Oh God. For a moment, there was just silence. Maggie ignored the thump of her heart, breathlessly waiting for the next word.

"What?"

"I liked her. A lot."

"Yeah? So why you telling me?" Quinn asked.

Was she imagining sharpness in that question? Had he just looked into Dan's matching green eyes and figured it out?

She fisted her hands, ready to respond or be there for Quinn.

"Because I want you to know that I still like her. A lot. Even after that conversation we had the other night."

What conversation?

"Dude. As if I couldn't tell. Your tongue hangs out like Goose's when you look at her."

"It does not. Well, maybe a little," he added.

" 's cool, man." Quinn was working so hard, trying to be this man's equal, trying to be tough. "Just remember one thing. I get a learner's permit in less than two years, and I heard you say you have a Maserati."

Dan laughed. "Is that blackmail?"

"Just sayin'. You like my mom. I like your car."

"Cars. Plural."

"Oh, wow." Quinn made a choking noise. "Shoot me now."

"Go to sleep." Dan's voice, still warm with laughter, was getting closer to the door.

Maggie hesitated for just one second, just as Max's large frame ascended the stairs at the end of the hall.

"The thing about Dan is," he said quietly as he walked closer, "you don't really have to eavesdrop to find out what he's thinking."

"I'm not . . ." She smiled, admitting defeat. "All right. I am."

"All you have to do is give him an opening," Max continued, "and you'll know more about what's going on in that deceptively complex head of his than you want to."

"Deceptively complex?" Behind her, Dan's voice was rich with disgust. "Because I'm slightly more evolved than a caveman?"

"And much prettier," Max shot back.

Dan closed the bedroom door and added a wink to Maggie. "He's always been wildly jealous of me. What's up, Max?"

"I think you were right. I just ran every conceivable satellite coordinate, and guess what the latitude of a good portion of Venezuela is?"

Maggie straightened. "Ten degrees, thirty-eight minutes north." The very numbers on her fortune.

"Exactly," Max said, giving her an impressed look. "Did you know that?"

"Not offhand, but my husband was an avid fisherman and we lived by GPS. I can't believe I didn't think of it." She looked at Dan, excitement shooting through her. "That can't be a coincidence. If we put it together with the other numbers, I bet we get the longitude."

"I did," Max said. "Come and see where that puts you."

"Let's go," Dan said, his hand on Maggie's back as he

lowered his head to whisper softly in her ear. "And you can thank me later."

Thank him—for lying?

Maybe she should. Maybe she would.

Several hours and what seemed like fifty-nine different permutations of possible GPS coordinates later, Maggie hit the wall. Max had long ago been sidelined by his wife's request that he come to bed, leaving them to work into the night, a situation that didn't seem to bother endless-energy Dan, but left Maggie yawning and tense.

They hadn't discussed what transpired in Quinn's room, too focused on all the GPS and satellite possibilities, mathematical and otherwise, nit-picking through every word on two fortunes, translating them into Spanish, searching for cryptic meanings, squeezing blood out of her gray matter to figure out a puzzle that seemed impossible to solve.

She was a GPS pro from all those years on a fishing boat with Smitty, but that's where her cryptography skills ended.

"I can't look at that anymore." She waved a page of notes to the massive flat-panel screen with the satellite image of Venezuela, dropping her head back on the sofa. "It's there, I'm sure of it, but we just don't have enough to nail it."

"We're so close," Dan said, stabbing his hair with two hands. "There are only so many ways we can cut the numbers, so many different combinations of latitude and longitude, minutes and seconds, and possible directions. One of them has to be in Venezuela. One of them has to be the location of the money."

She sighed, curling deeper into a light cotton blanket

he'd brought out a few hours ago from one of the bed-rooms. "Let . . . me . . . just . . . think."

Dan sat at the end of the sofa, tucking Maggie's feet behind him. From beneath closed lashes, she watched him, focused and strong and smart, and sexier than any man she'd ever known.

She wanted so badly to move her feet to his lap. That's all it would take. He'd be hard and ready and . . .

He zoomed in on Maracaibo and squinted at the satellite image, and she watched his hands work the laptop on the coffee table. So masculine and capable. Hands that could do amazing things to her. That had done amazing things to himself that very afternoon.

Her gaze drifted up to his bicep, tightening, relaxing, then tightening again. Her stomach did the same thing.

"Of course," he murmured, half talking to her, half to himself, "the latitude on your fortune also includes everything else six hundred miles north or south of the equator anywhere in the world, including the middle of Africa, the lower tip of Indonesia, and part of the Malaysian peninsula."

She knew he was right. Latitude and longitude coordinates of minutes only gave you a fairly large geographic area. But further divided into seconds, those coordinates were far more specific, right down to an actual street block.

The numbers they had could be either minutes or seconds.

"We have two sets of numbers," she said. "And even though one of those sets matches a latitude across Venezuela, the other can't be the longitude in minutes, because it isn't anywhere near Venezuela. And if the numbers you got from the FBI files are the longitude in *seconds,* then it doesn't really help us."

"There have to be more fortunes," he said softly.

Obviously.

"Because this one," he continued quietly, "could take us across the fattest part of Venezeula. But you know what's in there?"

He leaned forward, studying the screen on the wall, his jaw set and accented by beard growth. How would that feel against her thighs?

It would feel scratchy and . . . good.

"The Jimenez coffee plantation. Somewhere west of Maracaibo is a place called Monte Verde. What better place to hide your money than on your plantation?"

She looked at his thighs, spread wide as he leaned over the laptop keyboard. She'd seen those thighs in the dark that afternoon. Watched him steal a secret release. It had taken everything in her to keep from helping.

"And miles of impenetrable rain forest, fathoms of muddy rivers, and endless, rolling, impassible mountains." He rubbed his beard, then turned to her. She closed her eyes tight. If she faked sleep, he wouldn't talk . . . or touch . . . or test her control again.

"A hundred million dollars could be anywhere in that country, Maggie. What we need is a short list of who could possibly have . . ." She felt him lean closer, could smell his scent as he got nearer, the weight and warmth of him over her body. "What *you* need is sleep, Maggie May."

His fingers touched her hair, brushing it off her face.

Should she open her eyes? She knew what she'd see. Attraction in his jade green eyes. Desire. Arousal. The same stuff that was electrifying her own body. Everything she'd been fighting with common sense and bad memories.

He grazed her lower lip with his fingertip, or maybe the

pad of his thumb. It was just a little calloused and smelled clean and masculine.

Then he was gone. She heard the table lamp click, saw darkness behind her lids, heard his footsteps around the counter that separated the living area from the kitchen.

She stole a peek, catching his profile as he opened the refrigerator door and stood silhouetted in the light. One hand threaded his hair, the other reached in to get something.

She heard the hiss of a bottle cap, and the scuff of his footstep behind the sofa where she lay. He put a hand on her shoulder, warm enough that it couldn't be the one that held the beer or soda he'd just opened. Gentle enough that the touch was more tender than sexual. Long enough to make her ache to roll over and invite him to join her on the couch.

He pulled the blanket higher and tucked it under her chin. She almost let out the little mew in her throat, the gesture was so sweet.

Just as she nearly lost the battle and opened her eyes, he murmured, "You're so different."

Different? Different from what she used to be? Different from someone else? Or just different . . . from what he usually liked?

His footsteps headed to the front door. She peeked through her lashes again to see him stand for a moment in the darkness of the patio and unlit pool; then he closed the door and left her alone.

She put her hands on the blanket where his had been, the need to have him near so powerful that it took her back to when that same man—with a different name, different face, different hair—did precisely the same thing to her body. Funny thing, that physical chemistry. It really must be pheromones or scent.

Throwing off the blanket, she sat up. He couldn't have gone far.

Outside, she stood in the doorway, scanning the dark, empty patio that easily sat thirty or more in various arrangements of tables, chairs, and chaises. She peered at the house, seeing one light—her room. Was he in there, waiting for her?

"I'm over here."

She turned toward the shadows of a tiny cabana, where a double-width chaise was tucked under an arched overhang. A brown bottle was balanced on his stomach, his laser gaze sharp even from twenty feet away.

"What are you doing?" she asked, walking toward him, the breeze in the palm fronds and the brush of her long cotton skirt the only sound. She lifted her hand to push her hair off her face, and Baba's bracelets fell down her wrist, adding a ping of silver against silver, and a sex-charged memory, into the silent night.

"Right now I'm counting stars." As she approached, his perusal dropped to her chest, to the rhinestones flickering across her breasts. "Is that a dragonfly or a butterfly winking at me?"

She ran a finger over the tiny pink and green stones sewn into her top. "You tell me. You've looked at it enough tonight."

He grinned, white teeth against tanned skin. "About a hundred times, I think."

"What are you doing?" she whispered, reaching the side of the chaise.

"Having a beer. Want some?" he asked.

"Yeah." She gave him a nudge with her knee. "Scoot over."

She shouldn't do this. She shouldn't slip between the armrest and his rock-hard flank, shouldn't let her flouncy skirt flutter over his khaki shorts and bare calf, shouldn't share his beer and thoughts.

But she did. He handed her the bottle and she took a solid swig, then returned it to his stomach, leaning back against the angled cushion. "Good, but not Heineken."

"What can I say? Totally ghetto."

She laughed softly.

"I thought you were dead to the world," he said.

"I woke up when you left."

"Sorry. I thought you were asleep—I had a massive epiphany and you didn't answer me."

That she was *so different?* "What was your revelation?"

He slid his gaze away with a sideways smile. "It's a secret now."

"You wouldn't tell me the truth anyway." She turned to get more comfortable, the move pressing her breasts against that lovely bicep. "Besides, it doesn't matter."

"What doesn't?"

That she was different. "How many fortunes we have," she said. "Even if we get two more of them, with eight more numbers, we have what? Maybe sixty-four different combinations of latitude, longitude, minutes, and seconds, east, west, north, south?"

"So we track them all. I have the resources."

"You still can't convince me that all that money's still hidden after all these years." She tapped the beer bottle with her nail. "Give."

He handed it to her. "Listen, if a hundred million dollars got laundered in the six months Alonso Jimenez has been out of prison, the FBI would know about it, and I would know about it. And these people wouldn't be going to all this trouble to get your fortune. Someone could be dribbling it into banks and accounts, but not more than five percent of it. There are too many safeguards in place to track that kind of cash."

She sipped, then rolled back into the space he'd made for her, balancing the bottle on his solar plexus, keeping one hand around it, her arm resting easily on his stomach muscles.

"So what do we do next, Irish?"

He gave her a half smile at the nickname. "In the next few minutes, or tomorrow?"

"I know what you want to do in the next few minutes." His pants weren't totally tented yet, but she could see a bulge growing. No force of nature could stop her from looking at it. Imagining it. Wanting it.

"Pretty obvious, huh?" He took the beer.

"Mmm hmm." She curled her fingers around his bicep. "That's why I came out here."

He finished the drink and set the bottle on the ground next to him. "Really."

"To talk." Liar, liar. "About Quinn." That ought to quench his passion.

"Don't worry, Maggie, I had no intention of blowing your old cover. If he thinks you were a waitress, that works for me."

"It's not 'an old cover,'" she said, hearing the resentment in her voice.

"It's not? You were a waitress in Miami? News to me."

"I was, for about one lunch rush. Then I got fired. And met Ramon." She shifted, trying to move away but the chaise was a tight fit. "It's the story Smitty used to tell people when I worked for him at the bar, and I never contradicted it. Not even tonight, when I should have."

"Maggie, listen to me." He turned to face her. "Not all lies are bad. If your husband wanted to spare your boy the grief of certain things, why not? He wanted Quinn to think he was his father, right?"

"But that doesn't have anything to do with what we told him I did before he was born." The waitress story *had* been a cover. A benign and shameless change of history.

"You told him you were a waitress to protect him. His self-image and his pride, right?"

"Both of their prides," she said.

"A lie to protect someone is not a lie."

"Straight from the Gallagher Book of Bent Rules."

"They've worked well for me."

"Everything works well for you. You don't have to change history. You walked away from that parking lot in Miami a hero, while I walked away a pregnant tramp. You went on to glamorous jobs, important assignments, enough money to buy cars I can't even pronounce, and I'm worried about paying the orthodontist."

She sounded bitter, but couldn't stop. Hell, she *was* bitter.

"I'll pay for the orthodontist," he said quietly.

"Yes, you will."

"And clothes, and college, and cars. Whatever he—and you—need."

And then he'd be guilt free. She blew out a breath, not liking being *bitter* any more than she liked being *different.*

"Can I ask you a very personal question, Maggie?"

"Honey, we're way past personal. Shoot."

"Why did you choose to keep Quinn? You were so young, and you had options."

"I know. I considered abortion and adoption, but neither one felt right. And then Smitty said he'd marry me."

"So you married a man you didn't love to give Quinn a father?"

"I loved him. I wasn't *in* love with him, but . . ." He gave her a better choice, and a good life. "You wouldn't understand."

Reaching down, he lifted her chin to hold her gaze. "Try me."

"He was my friend more than anything. In the beginning, a sounding board and, of course he was my boss. Then he became a really, really good friend. It felt like . . . love. Sort of."

"Actually, I do understand that." His voice was rich with sincerity.

"Do you?"

"A boss, then a friend, feeling like love but not quite love." He gave her a quick smile. "I totally get that."

She scooted higher, searching his face, wanting to know more. "Tell me about her."

"No."

"Why not? Because you'd have to be honest, and you're not capable of it?"

His jaw loosened in frustration. "No, because I don't happen to want that person here right now, on this chaise, in my head. I have you. And that's . . ." He turned more, lining their bodies up. "Really good."

"Well, I have no qualms about Smitty being out here on this chaise. He was a great guy, and a terrific father. Quinn loved him, and I often wondered how he was going to take the truth when I told him."

"You'd planned on telling him? Before I showed up?"

"I knew I'd have to, someday."

"Why?"

She rested her cheek on his shoulder, her hand still lying on his chest, her leg almost curled over his. When a long second passed, he repeated the question. "Why would you have to tell him?"

"Because I put your name on the birth certificate. Well, I put Michael Scott on it." Before he could ask the obvious question, she held up her finger. "I couldn't put Maurice Smith on that document because it was a lie, and Quinn would be grown up and maybe dealing with something medical, and he'd think he knew half his DNA and didn't. I put Michael Scott on that because it was the truth. And because . . ."

"Because why?" Dan prodded.

"Because my mother put 'unknown' on my birth certificate. You remember my mother, don't you? I know I talked about her back then."

He nodded. "I know she let your grandmother raise you, and when your Baba died, she was supposed to come for you, but didn't."

"You do have an amazing memory. Did I tell you that she called?"

"When? Recently?"

"God, no. When Baba died. She called me and promised me she'd come to get me. But she didn't show. For weeks and months. I was almost eighteen and really didn't need my mother, but I wanted her." She remembered that state social workers became the enemy. Along with bankers who put Baba's house into foreclosure. And neighbors who wanted her out of there. She couldn't trust anyone. Her mother had no relatives, no friends. School was a nightmare. "So I just . . ."

"Ran away." He stroked her arm comfortingly. "You

told me a long time ago. You came to find her, but couldn't."

"And that's why I kept Quinn. I was determined to be a better mother than the one I got."

"And you are. You're a breathtaking mother."

She felt a smile pull. "He'd probably disagree sometimes, but thank you. Smitty always thought I was pretty good, too."

"How did he feel about the birth certificate?"

"I never told him." He'd never asked, either. "I just did what I thought was right and kept the birth certificate locked away. But it's out there now. Someone stole it when they thought they were getting the fortune in my lockbox."

Dan's fingers stilled on her arm. "They got much more than that. They got something that could be used against you."

"I know," she said, tucking closer to him. As if by just touching him, she'd be safer.

He didn't say anything, but slipped his arm around her, cradling her. He moved his hand to her hair, stroking the curls and letting them twirl around his finger. There was nothing between them but the thin fabric of their clothes and the heavy night air. And a whole lot of history.

"What were you planning to tell Quinn about Michael Scott?" he finally asked.

She looked up again, searching his eyes. "That his father was a man who worked undercover for the FBI and was killed in a drug bust. If he wanted to research that and find out who you were, and who I was, that would be his choice when he's an adult." She hesitated, searching for the right way to say whatever she had to say. "Guess that'll be easier now that he's met you. But I'll have to eat some crow for all the lecturing I've done about lying."

She pushed herself up. "Ever since you showed up here and admitted he was yours, I've prayed that your ability to lie with ease is not hereditary."

"I don't lie about everything, Maggie. That's the job I've had, working undercover. If I adjust the facts, it's always with the goal of stopping someone bad or protecting someone good. I do have ethics."

"Oh puhlease." She rolled her eyes and gave him a poke in the arm that rattled her bracelets. "Face it. You. Can't. Tell. The. Truth."

The staccato words were like gauntlets, being thrown one at a time at his feet.

"I can tell the truth," he shot back. "Ask me anything, absolutely anything, and I will tell you the unadulterated, honest-to-God truth."

"Like truth or dare?"

"Without the dare. Although"—he pulled her a little closer and entwined his leg with hers—"that idea has merit."

It would be so easy to play a game like that. To drop this conversation and do what both of their bodies were primed and ready for. So easy, so much more fun. "You'll just lie, and I won't know the difference."

"Maggie, come on." She heard the frustration in his voice. "Give me a chance."

"You'll tell me the truth about anything? No matter what I ask?"

"The truth, the whole truth and nothing but the truth." He raised his right hand. "I swear."

"All right," she said, thinking back to various things that had happened in the past week, and the events and people that made her curious. "Let's start with Lucy Sharpe."

He just smiled. "Why am I not surprised?"

"Is she the boss-friend-almost-love person you don't want on this chaise?"

He opened his mouth, but nothing came out and she jabbed him, friendlier this time. "Told ya," she said smugly. "You can't do it."

He exhaled, defeated. "She is the woman I was referring to, yes."

"You love her?"

"I love her as a friend." At her look, he added, "That is the truth. I am not in love with her. I never have been, despite rumors to the contrary. I care deeply for her as a friend, and I am happy that she's found someone."

"Ohh." She gave him a teasing smile. "More than I even asked for."

"See? Honest to the core." He caressed her arm slowly. "When's the dare part start?"

She narrowed her eyes. "I'm not done."

"Fine," he said, slipping a finger under the sleeve of the T-shirt, getting a rise of goose bumps on her flesh. "Ask away."

Okay. If he was finally going to be honest, she was finally going to get some important answers. "What would you have done back there on that rainy night in Miami, if you'd known I was pregnant with your child?"

He brushed his finger over her skin again, looking like he wished to God he hadn't promised the truth.

"I would have done exactly the same thing," he said quietly. "Only I would not have let you disappear, and I would have taken care of the baby and you. Forever."

The word made her heart tumble. Or was it the sentiment? *Taken care of?* "You wouldn't have married me."

He swallowed hard. "No, but I sure as hell wouldn't have let you make it alone."

"I wasn't alone," she said simply.

"Are we done with this game yet, Maggie?"

It wasn't a game. "Nope."

"What else is left? What else do you want to know, Maggie?"

She had one last critical, must-know-or-die question. She looked up at him, wet her lips, and asked the question that had kept her awake on countless nights. "Did you care about me? Even a little? Even for a minute?"

"Oh." The word slipped out as he pulled her completely into him. "Much more than a little. And for much longer than a minute."

She felt his heart hammer against her, as if she were the lie detector machine and his red line just shot off the paper. "You're lying."

"No, I'm—"

"You just said it. You don't think it's a lie if you're protecting someone, and you're trying to protect my feelings. Thank you, but I'd rather have the truth."

"Here's the whole truth, then." He inched his face back to hold eye contact. "Whether you want to hear it or believe it or accept it. I took major, stupid, reckless risks to be with you. I could have gotten my information a lot of different ways, and none of them had to include nights in that shed or secret trysts that endangered my life and yours."

Could that be true?

"I didn't seduce you for information, Maggie," he insisted, his muscles tense from head to toe. "I touched you and teased you and *took* you because I could not resist you."

He moved just enough to press his erection into her, making his point, sliding his hand down her back, over her waist, and letting it settle on the curve of her hip.

She couldn't resist him, either. Then . . . or now.

"I couldn't be in the same room with you and not get hard. I couldn't be alone with you and not want to be inside of you. I couldn't be inside of you and not need to come." He leaned as close to her mouth as he could get without making contact. "Which is still very much the case."

He kissed her, opening his mouth immediately, rolling his tongue into her mouth. She took it and gave him her own, heat spiraling through her as his hands moved over her body, bunching the material of her skirt in his fists to drag it up over her thighs.

"Do you believe me?" he demanded into her mouth, his hand mighty and strong as he curled her into his hardness. "Do you?"

"I believe you," she whispered, letting her body sink into his.

"You'd better." He rolled on his back and pulled her on top of him, the skirt nearly up to her hips and the searing contact of his hand on her bare thigh making her gasp.

She arched against him, opening her legs enough to give his hard-on direct access to her crotch, the rhinestones perilously close to his mouth.

"No more stupid questions, then," he growled, one hand under the lace edge of her panties, the other on her head to force her mouth back to his.

She dizzily kissed him, sucking in a breath as he rubbed

the rhinestones over the bare breasts underneath, the roughness instantly shooting hot pangs between her legs.

He bunched the material and pushed it higher, driving her hips into his and holding her so he could drink in the sight of her breasts. He lifted his head to suck, then lick, then drag his tongue across her flesh to tease the other one.

Desire twisted and tensed between her legs. He flipped her on her back in one move, reaching behind her to drop the angled head of the chaise flat into a bed.

"You picked this seat with this in mind," she said, sinking into the thick, padded cushions, the weight of his body on hers.

"No." At her look, a slow smile pulled at his lips. "Maybe."

She gave him the look she saved for Quinn when she asked if he'd folded his laundry.

"A guy can hope, can't he?" He walked his fingers over the rhinestones and paused at the hem of her T-shirt, then slid it almost to her chin.

His gaze dropped to her exposed breasts, scorching them.

"One more question," she said, stiffening her arms and denying him the ability to take the top off.

"No more questions." He tugged the material, but couldn't finish the job. Giving up, he lowered his head and his mouth, transferring all his attention to her breasts.

Pain and pleasure and excitement collided under his tongue and lips, firing sparks through her body, tensing her muscles, making her hips writhe.

She needed to think, but all she could do was *feel*. All she could do was tunnel her fingers into his hair, and guide his head to the other breast, and sigh with each wave of sexual bliss that rolled over her.

There had to be some truth she could wrest from him to douse the fire, because this was headed one place. Fast.

"I have to know one more thing . . . first," she panted.

He lifted his head, his lips wet, his green eyes heavy with arousal. "All right. One more question. Then let me take this top off, Maggie. Let me . . ." He reached between them, sliding his hand down past her bunched-up skirt, low enough to stroke her thigh, then press against the silk of her panties.

Soaked, sticky silk.

"Let me." His voice was rough with need. He followed the lace with one finger, then slipped inside, branding her core with one slow stroke. "Please . . . let me."

She rolled against his finger, making him slip in deeper. So easy. It would be so easy, and sexy . . . and stupid.

So, so stupid. And so, so good.

"You like that," he coaxed with a soft voice, his thumb on her clitoris, his index finger circling her sex-slicked opening, his power over her as strong and relentless as ever.

"One more question," she said, forcing the words from a mouth that just wanted to moan and plead for more. "And one more truthful answer."

"Then . . ." Moisture and heat surrounded his fingertip, making it impossible not to slide deeper. "I want to be in here." Deeper. "I want you, Maggie." Deeper. "I want—"

"Will you leave me again?" The question was out of her mouth before it even consciously formed in her brain.

He froze. "What?"

Talk about the truth. She had it in just one look. She

didn't know what made her ask the question, didn't even realize how much it mattered.

But suddenly it mattered a lot. "Will you make love to me and leave me again?"

Still silence.

"I don't get the question," he finally said. "What are you looking for? A formal commitment? A promise? Some kind of pledge about the future?" He made it sound like she'd asked for the moon.

Maybe she had. But the question—and his response—did the trick.

She rolled out from under him and sat up, pulling her T-shirt over nipples still wet and hard from his mouth.

He looked shell-shocked.

"I don't know what I'm looking for," she admitted. "But I have a son to think about—your son. I have to know. When Quinn is safe and everything's normal, are you leaving? Going back to New York, back to your life and out of . . . ours?"

He opened his mouth and she put her hand over his lips.

"Don't give me some Dan Gallagher version of the truth."

Three, four, five endless seconds ticked by.

"Yes," he admitted. "I'm leaving. But that doesn't mean—"

"Yes it does." She stood, the skirt falling over her legs.

Finally she could think straight. Both the past and the future looked like heartache, with him.

"Good night." She bent over and kissed him softly on the forehead. "I really appreciate the honesty."

CHAPTER
TWELVE

COULD THIS BE possible? Did they have the best Thursday night *ever* or had she counted the receipts wrong? Brandy knocked her knuckles on the bar and stared at the readout. There had to be a mistake. She needed to run the numbers again.

"Hey, Milk Dud," she called out. "What time is it?"

The kitchen door punched open and Dudley Matheson beamed at her, a navy bandanna wrapped around his shaved head, his blue eyes bright, considering he'd been cooking, washing, and working his damn ass off since four that afternoon *and* he loathed the nickname.

"Snapper spawning hour, my friend." He held up a small cooler. "Got the chum here, and Jimmy's picking me up in five minutes at the dock."

"Really? It's that late?" She'd lived in the Keys long enough to know those little buggers mated after two a.m., and the hard-core fishermen were out there to catch them in the act. "No wonder I'm beat."

"That last table of tourists couldn't say die, huh?"

She shrugged. "They will suffer tomorrow, that's for

sure. Had a couple of hundred on the tab when they finally closed." She pointed at the calculator. "Contributing to what appears to have been a stellar night."

"Kitchen's done and locked up," Dudley said. "You going out the front? I'll walk you to your car."

She made a face at the pile of receipts. "I want to run these numbers one more time so I can call Lena with the right amount tomorrow."

He shook his head. "No can do, boss. Lena left strict orders that you are not allowed to walk to your car alone with cash."

"I won't take the cash, Dud. I'll lock it up. And I'm parked next to the kitchen door, so there's nowhere for you to walk me. You go out the front, I'll lock it behind you, and I'll leave through the back."

His look said he didn't like the plan.

"Come on." She jumped off the stool and pulled her key ring from the pocket of her shorts. "You've worked too long and too hard to miss this boat ride to snapper heaven."

He hesitated, but she marched right by him, unlocked the door, and held it open for him.

"You sure, Brandy? I don't mind waiting."

"I'm fine." She hit him on the shoulder. "Go forth and fish. Catch enough so we can fry it and sell it at a ridiculous profit tomorrow. I'll give you a cut."

He grinned and blew a kiss to her, heading straight out to the marina, where there were enough engines running to assure her that all was right in the home of twenty-four-hour fishing. She locked the door and went back to the numbers which, miraculously, were dead-on the first time.

She finally turned out the bar lights, locked the cash in the office, grabbed a soda for the road, and trotted through the kitchen that Milk Dud had cleaned within

an inch of its life. Shutting down the last lights, she un-
latched the dead bolt and stepped outside, lifting the Diet
Coke to her mouth.

The can flew forward as the force of a man's body
pushed her down to the sidewalk, and his body covered
hers.

Son of a bitch! More mad than scared, she fought to lift
her head, but a powerful hand pressed it down.

"I don't have cash," she managed to say.

"Where is she?" The voice growled in her ear.

What did he say? "I don't have money," she repeated.
Could she give up that five hundred in cash? Yes. The rest
was credit cards, thank God. Would he make her go back
in? Then what would he do to her? She struggled to turn
and see her attacker. "I swear to God, my kitchen guy
took the bank."

A knee slammed into her back, knocking her breath
out in one painful swoosh. "Where is Maggie Varcek?"

Maggie Varcek? "I don't know what you want."

Something prodded her back, right behind the heart.
Holy shit, this dude had a gun. Her veins went icy. "I have
five hundred," she said quickly. "Inside. Please, don't hurt
me."

"Don't fuck around," he rasped in her ear. "Where is
Maggie?"

Maggie? "Do you mean Lena? My partner?" Was her
name Varcek before she married Smitty? Wasn't that
Quinn's middle name? Panic made her mind go blank.

"She's not here," she said, unable to see anything but
his arm in a long-sleeved sweatshirt. Was it the guy with
the snake tattoo?

"I know that." He knocked her head down with the
heel of his hand, pressing her cheekbone to the concrete.

"You tell me where she is, right now, right this minute."

"She went out of town. With . . . her boyfriend."

He yanked some hair. "Where?"

"I don't know. Miami." It was a big city. He'd never find her. "I swear to God I don't know."

"And the kid?"

"Yes, he's with her. But I swear, I don't know where they went. I *don't*. Don't hurt me."

"I'm gonna hurt you." Her stomach turned, fear flattening her. "I'm gonna hurt you so bad, you'll want to be dead. Tomorrow."

She fought for a breath, terror squeezing her chest. Tomorrow he'd hurt her, or she'd want to be dead?

"Please. I can't . . . help you." Tears she didn't even realize she'd been crying soaked her cheek and dribbled into her mouth.

Voices floated up from the marina, some of the men laughing.

He released his grip, maybe looked up. She tried to jerk free, but he smacked her back down again. "I'm not fucking around, Brandy." The use of her name punched her like the knee in her back. "I'll be back, and I'll get what I want."

The voices grew closer, and then he was off her. She stayed perfectly still, half expecting a bullet in her head, half hoping she was about to wake up from a really bad dream.

His footsteps faded away, and so did the unknowing saviors from the marina. Shaking down to the bone, she slowly pushed herself up, then managed to stand, turn to the door, and reach for her—

Damn it! Her keys! She searched the shadows, the whimpering sound from her throat not even recognizable as her own.

The bastard took the key ring. Which had her car keys, house keys, bar keys . . . She let out a soft moan.

Lena. She had to call Lena. She pulled out her phone and pressed the speed dial with trembling fingers, her gaze darting up and down the street in terror. This side was silent. Around the front, there was activity near the marina.

She took a few steps in that direction, willing Lena to answer, but it clicked into voice mail. Half certain he'd be waiting around the next corner, she headed to the marina, grateful as hell that her best friends were fishermen.

"How exactly did you get this appointment?" Maggie peered through the windshield of the Porsche, checking out the four-story office building tucked between two much glitzier towers.

"Oh, the usual Gallagher technique."

"You lied."

He threw a wry grin as he took his seat belt off. "I convinced Ms. James's efficient assistant that I was a potential new client checking out cargo companies and only had one hour this morning. She said she'd get me in." He handed her a cell phone she recognized as her own. "You left this in the guesthouse. So now I'm number one on your speed dial."

Of course he was.

"You need to call or text me if you see Lola James come or go while I'm up there. But I'm hoping she's the workaholic that file says she is, and I'll catch her in the office."

Maggie had gone through the paperwork as they drove over the causeway from Star Island to downtown Miami, knocked out that his company could get that much information from a name. Flipping the file open again, she glanced at the picture of a beautiful Latina woman holding court at a business networking event, printed from the pages of a glossy magazine.

"I'd have never recognized her in a million years," she said. "There's no way that homely little girl grew up to look like that."

"That's the work of a fine Venezuelan plastic surgeon—they're world class. What surprises me is that her company is legit. At least on paper. I'm going to go find out more."

She closed the file folder and held out her hand. "Keys?"

"You're not going anywhere."

"No, but you're not leaving me without air-conditioning. Keys."

He put them in her outstretched hands, closing his fingers around hers and drawing her closer. For a minute, she thought he was going to kiss her, but he just gave her that look—the same one he'd seared her with when she walked away from what he offered last night. A warning that it was coming, like it or not.

"Go." She pushed him back, trying to pull her hand and the keys from his grip. "Go pretend to be a client."

He gave her hand one more squeeze; then he left, striding across the parking lot, his broad shoulders square, jeans fitted over narrow hips and the hard thighs she'd ridden for a few blissful minutes last night.

Once he was inside the building, she watched the glass doors glinting in the sunlight as they opened to let in and out a few people who couldn't possibly be Lola James.

Five more minutes passed and a man with long dark hair emerged, throwing on a pair of sunglasses the instant he stepped outside and looked around. Something about his gait, his posture—

Ramon! It was Ramon Jimenez. She peered at him,

reaching for her cell phone as he approached the same dark blue compact car she'd seen him get in when Dan ran him out of the bar.

She couldn't lose him. He was a critical link to the kidnapping, the fortune, and El Viejo. She hoisted herself over the console and stabbed the key into the ignition. Would Dan kill her for following a dangerous man? Or would he be disappointed she'd lost track of him?

She hit 1 on her cell phone, glancing at the options on the screen. What if he was talking to Lourdes right then? She opted to text, quickly typing in *Ramon here* just as the blue car backed out.

She hit Send, then threw the phone on the passenger seat, using all her might to depress the gearshift and follow the pattern on top to get the car in reverse. To the right and straight back. She slammed it down and pushed, grinding the gears in the process.

"Damn." The clutch! She had to get the clutch down before the gearshift worked.

Ramon's car stopped at the curb, waiting for a break in traffic. If he headed east, she was in luck. West? Could get ugly.

He turned right, and she threw a thank-you up to Baba and the universe.

As soon as he passed her, another car got behind him. That was okay; she could still see him. She turned the wheel, gave the clutch a little pressure, and slipped the gear shift into first. Then she hit the accelerator and shot like a rocket, narrowly missing the back end of a parked car.

"Son of a—" She eased up on the gas, almost stalling. God, this thing was delicate. Dan made it look so *easy* to drive.

Ahead, Ramon got in the left lane, headed straight for wide and busy Biscayne Boulevard, clogged with Friday lunch hour traffic. She managed to jerk over one lane to the left, grateful that the low speeds meant she could stay in first gear.

On the passenger seat, the phone rang just as the light changed and Ramon slipped into the left-turn lane. She had to speed up to get there while the arrow was still green, the engine screaming for a better gear.

Palms sweating, she blocked out the telephone and pressed the shift and clutch at exactly the same moment, finding that spot so the gear would slide into second just as Ramon made the turn and the light went yellow.

And the goddamn car stalled. Grunting in frustration, she hit the brake, twisted the key, restarted it, and slammed on the gas, flying into the intersection just as the arrow disappeared and the phone stopped ringing.

She whipped the wheel to the left, cruising to a spot where five cars separated her from Ramon.

Working her way through traffic, she cut off one guy and gave a wave to another who let her change lanes. Then Ramon slid into the right lane, a few hundred feet from the next intersection.

She glanced into the rearview mirror, prayed for an opening, and the phone rang again.

It had to be Dan, furious that she was gone.

Ramon turned right and she careened into that lane, still not used to the billion horses that powered this thing, and still four cars behind him. Without a signal, she rolled into the turn with one hand and grabbed the phone with the other, hitting the speaker button and tossing it back on the seat.

"I know, I know, you're going to kill me. But I have

Ramon in my sights, he's headed across Flagler and I just want to see where he's going. Then I'll come back and get you, but I didn't want to miss the opportunity to follow him. He could go back to Viejo's house; maybe there's been another drug delivery. So did you see Lola?"

"Lena, what in the hell is going on?"

"Brandy!" Maggie choked in surprise. "I thought you were Dan."

"I was attacked in the street at two in the morning by some thug asshole who wanted to know where you were." Panic was not a sound she was used to hearing from Brandy, and the fear in her voice made Maggie sick.

"Oh God, I'm so sorry."

"You are Maggie Var . . . something, right? That's your name? 'Cause that's who this guy wanted."

Very, very few people on this earth knew her as Maggie Varcek. And almost every one was part of the Jimenez family. "Brandy, you have to be so careful."

"No shit, Sherlock! He's coming back today. He already told me. And he has my keys to everything!"

"Where are you now?"

"At Milk Dud's place. I'm not leaving, I swear. And I don't even want to go near the bar. I'm scared, Lena."

"Don't be. I'll get you help, I promise." Superman bodyguards. Dan would send an army down there.

Traffic thickened as they approached Second Avenue, and Maggie's head reeled. If Ramon was right there, could he have been the one threatening Brandy last night? It was only a few hours' drive from here to Marathon.

"Did you see what he looked like? Was he Hispanic?" One of Viejo's men, maybe.

"I couldn't see a thing. He held me down on the ground and had a gun in my back and—"

"Oh Brandy." Maggie moaned with sympathy. "I am so sorry to drag you into this."

"Into *what?*" she demanded. "What the hell is going on, Lena?"

"It's complicated." She heard her friend snort on the other end. "Really, it's life and death. Oh, crap, I'll never make that left. Hang on a second!"

She checked the rearview mirror and punched the gas, grinding the gears as she cut off another car to get in the left lane. She powered through a light that was more red than yellow, screeching into the left turn and praying that didn't get Ramon's attention, even though his little car was now eight ahead of her. And two were view-blocking SUVs.

In the brief silence, she heard the soft beep of an incoming call. Dan, no doubt.

"Where are you?" Brandy demanded.

"In Miami, and I don't even want you to know more than that. Quinn is in a safe house, totally protected. And I'm . . ." Chasing an ex-con down Biscayne Boulevard. "Trying to find out who threw him in that boat the other night, and how we can stop them."

"What do they want from you, Lena?"

Ramon caught the empty lane and zoomed ahead, forcing her to do the same.

"A fortune."

She caught the gear and the lane and held him in her sights as he approached a bridge over the Miami River, continuing south. She glanced at the blue street sign hanging over the intersection. Brickell Avenue.

"A fortune from you? Good luck with that."

Brickell Avenue? Where Lola James lived?

"Listen, Brandy, I have to go." She had to call Dan and tell him where she was. "But do *not* leave Dudley's house, and make sure someone is there with you all the time. By tonight you'll have professional protection. I promise. And they'll arm the bar."

The incoming call beeped again.

"Okay," Brandy said. "But this really sucks, closing the bar and all. We made a ton of money last night."

"Just be safe—that's all I care about. I gotta go. I love you. Be careful."

"You, too."

The connection ended just as Ramon moved into the much slower right lane and the landscape changed to palm-lined sidewalks and sky-high condo buildings perched on man-made rises along Brickell Avenue. He jammed on his brakes, zipping into a tight U-turn and parking in a spot across the street.

She drove right past him, almost pounding the steering wheel in frustration, looking for a space that wasn't there.

In her side-view mirror, she watched Ramon get out of his car. She had no option but to wait for a truck to pass, then make her own U-turn, which put her in front of a handicapped spot. She took it while Ramon crossed the street.

The cell phone rang and she didn't even have a chance to say hello after she pressed talk.

"Where the hell are you, Maggie?"

"I followed Ramon, and he's going into—"

"*What?*"

"Just listen to me," she insisted. "I followed him to 2180 Brickell Avenue. Isn't that the address in Lola's file?"

"Don't even think about it, Maggie. Get back here. *Now.*"

She did think about it, but not for long. Following Ramon on foot was stupid and dangerous.

"Okay. I'm only ten minutes away." She pulled out of her spot and worked back into traffic. "But listen to me. Someone attacked Brandy last night. Someone who called me Maggie Varcek. No one knows me by that name except you and the Jimenez family. What did Lola say?"

"Nothing. Just hurry up and I'll tell you."

"Be right there." She saw Ramon disappear into a condo building. "But, Dan, please, I need you to get someone down to Marathon to protect Brandy. That guy said he'd be back today. And he has the keys to the bar."

"Done. Now drive, fast, Maggie."

Traffic was on her side on the way back, and she spotted Dan waiting outside the office building. While he headed for the car, she braced herself for a barrage. *You shouldn't have done that. I told you to stay there. What were you thinking?*

"Good work," he said as he got in and yanked on his seat belt. "How'd it drive?"

She managed a smile. "Like a dream." She pressed the clutch and eased into first without a pop. "I thought you'd be furious that I followed him."

"I was. And worried when you didn't answer the phone, but I'd've done the same thing."

She merged into traffic and threw him a look. "Bodyguards for Brandy?"

"Lucy's working on getting a team down there today."

Taking her hand off the gearshift, she placed it on his arm. "Thank you. What happened with Lola?"

"She's missing."

"Missing? What do you mean?"

"She left the office yesterday afternoon and didn't come in this morning."

"She must be home. Ramon just went into her condo."

"Let's go find out. According to her assistant, it's very unusual for Lola to miss a Sunday, let alone a normal workday."

While he replayed his conversation, Maggie retraced the route down to Brickell Avenue until they reached the condo.

"There's his car," she said, pointing to it; then she turned to the condo entrance. "And look at that. There he is."

Ramon was far enough away that they couldn't make out his expression as he paused in the arched entryway to light a cigarette. Dan had the seat belt off and his hand on the door before she took her next breath.

"What are you going to do, shake him down in broad daylight, on the street?"

"I'm a little more subtle than that. Drive around for ten minutes, then come back for me."

"I'll find a place to park."

He peered at the row of parallel-parked cars. "Doubtful." He leaped out of the car before she'd even brought it to a full stop and she drove on. She expected him to walk toward the condo, toward Ramon, but instead he crossed the street and headed right for Ramon's car.

This time he didn't look sexy. He looked like a man capable of killing someone.

Still watching him, she touched the accelerator, then looked back at the road—and slammed on the brakes with a gasp, screeching inches from Ramon.

She held her breath, half expecting him to recognize her, but he just flicked his cigarette onto the hood of the Porsche and sauntered to his car.

Chapter
THIRTEEN

AY, MEIRDA! RAMON resisted the urge to flip the bird at the moron chick in the sports car. But his frustration was really aimed at someone else.

Where the fuck was his sister?

First she tried to end-run him by sending someone else to shake down Maggie. Then she didn't show for their meeting at the office. And now she wasn't home at all.

At least he hadn't told her everything he knew. She was a conniving *puta*, no matter what she called herself or how much she rearranged her face and their father's business. But as long as he was on El Viejo's hit list, he needed her. That's why he'd told her about the fortunes. Next thing he knew, she was lying, and now she disappeared.

He yanked the car door open and slid in.

An arm shot out from the backseat and crushed his throat, making his eyes pop open as he choked.

"You really ought to lock your doors."

He sucked in a breath and looked up at the rearview mirror, tilted so it landed right on his attacker. Mother of God, it was that prick who kicked him out of the bar. Maggie's muscle.

The man loosened his chokehold, but replaced it with the cold nose of his gun.

"What the fuck do you want?" Ramon's gaze slipped to the glove box. Had he been in there? Had he found the only thing of value he owned?

The man dug the muzzle of the weapon deeper into Ramon's neck. "Were you making trouble in the Keys again last night?"

Ramon didn't dare move, but studied the mirror reflecting both their faces. Blazing sun torched the leather seats as the temperature rose in the little car, forming beads of sweat on Ramon's upper lip. This mother didn't even look lukewarm.

When he didn't answer the question, the guy jabbed the gun harder. "How's your sister?"

Ramon's eyes widened, staring back at the cool green eyes. No one knew Lola James was his sister, except his father. Was this one of Viejo's hit men?

"Did she have want you want? Did she keep it all these years?"

He knew that? Then it couldn't be one of Viejo's hit men. Besides, he was in bed with Maggie, this one, so he probably had one of the fortunes already. And there wouldn't be time for talking when his father's men found him.

"I don't know what you want from me, man, but you ain't gettin' it. Get the fuck out of my car and leave me alone."

"What'd you two talk about, you and Lourdes? Planning your old man's funeral?"

"You yankin' my balls for fun, bro?"

"I'm not having any fun," he said. "And I'm not your bro."

If this guy did work for Viejo, this was the last conversation he was ever gonna have. Didn't he have anything left to bargain with? One more time, he cut his gaze to the glove box.

"Shit." He dragged out the word, flipping his hair out of his face. "I faced badder motherhumpers than you in prison." He reached for the keys he'd left under the seat but that arm whipped around for another crunch of his windpipe.

"Do you *want* to go back there, Ramon?"

"Fuck you," he managed to choke. "You can't send me there."

"Oh, no? I did once already."

Ramon tried to break the hold, but that just made the guy clench tighter. "Who . . . are . . . you?" he rasped.

"You used to call me Miguel. Amigo Miguel."

What?

"Michael Scott was my official name."

No way. No effing way. His gaze shot to the rearview mirror to see his captor's face again. Impossible. Different eyes. Different hair. Different man.

The fucking FBI narc was . . . *not dead?* Holy shit.

"Now why don't you tell me exactly what you're trying to get from Maggie, and why you keep showing up and hurting my eyes with your ugly face. What are you up to, Ramon? Have you been over to the old house lately? Doing business again?"

The grip loosened enough for Ramon to speak, but even swallowing hurt like a bitch.

"No," he managed. He didn't dare go anywhere near that house. Viejo's men were all over the place—here, down in the Keys. Man, he was so marked for death it wasn't funny.

And if this *wasn't* Viejo's hired assassin, was he really Michael Scott?

Wait a minute. *That's* why Lourdes wasn't here. She wasn't screwing him with the fortunes—she'd turned him in. He heard she did deals with the feds, determined to make her company all squeaky clean and legit. Of course. Lourdes had done this deal.

Couldn't Viejo see who the *real* traitor in the family was?

But the money, or the hope of it, was the only way Ramon was going to prove to El Viejo that *he* wasn't a traitor, that *he* hadn't been the one to leak stuff to the FBI. He still belonged in the family.

"Prove it," he said gruffly. "Prove you are Miguel."

The other man laughed. "I don't have to prove anything since I'm the one holding the gun, but go ahead. Give me a little test."

He'd taught his friend Miguel a very little bit of important Spanish, but mostly he taught him curse words and dumb sayings, laughing his ass off at the way Michael would screw up the pronunciation. One of those sayings had become a joke between them.

"La vida es breve," Ramon said. Life is short.

The other man smiled. *"Vámonos pa'l carajo y vamos a joder toda la fregada noche!"* His smile widened as he loosened his grip enough for Ramon to easily breathe again. "I finally found out what it meant, you dirty bastard."

Holy shit. He even butchered the words in the same goddamn way. Michael Scott, the one person who knew that Ramon hadn't leaked family secrets, was *alive*. And that meant that the one person on earth who knew

Ramon was innocent of what Viejo accused him of . . . was sitting here in his car.

The first coil of hope started to unwind in his chest. What would it take? If he really was a fed, money probably wouldn't work. But . . . fame and glory and a big score might do the trick.

"Amigo Miguel," Ramon said, a slow broad smile on his face. "It's good to see you, man."

"Get real, Ramon."

"I'm real, bro. I'm real."

"Real desperate."

Ramon attempted to turn, to look him in the eye. "Why don't we make a deal?"

He got a doubtful look in return. "I don't know what you want, but you don't have much to barter with."

"That's where you're wrong, Miguel. I have a hundred million dollars."

One eyebrow notched in interest. "Then you should get a better car."

"I'm going to lean forward, now. Very slowly." Ramon inched slightly toward the glove box. "I'm going to open that little door."

"I don't think so."

Ramon was undeterred. "And I'm going to reach in and pull out a tiny piece of paper worth a hundred million dollars."

"Is that right?"

"If you don't believe me, fine. But you have a choice. You can keep it for yourself, or you can turn it over to your bosses at the FBI and get lots of ribbons and honors, or whatever the fuck you get in the FBI for turning over millions in drug money for the government."

"You get to stay out of jail. Which is all I can offer you."

"But you have something else I need, amigo. You have the truth."

He got a look of interest and distrust in response.

"I'll show it to you, if you'll let me get it."

Miguel nodded a fraction. "You so much as touch a weapon and you're dead."

He had no doubt that was the case. He flipped the latch and the glove box door dropped open, revealing the rental papers. Behind him, the man inched to the right, looking for a gun hidden in the glove box, of course. There was none. His gun was under his seat.

Very slowly, Ramon slid his hand inside the opening, his fingers grazing the edge where he'd tucked the fortune. Nothing.

"Fuck," he whispered, reaching deeper. He knew it was there. He'd made the decision not to take it up to Lourdes until he saw the other ones she said she'd—

"Are you looking for this?"

He opened his hand and revealed the tiny Chinese fortune, right under Ramon's nose. The bastard already had it.

"How many are there, Ramon?"

Son of a bitch. How could he barter now? "Four."

"Who has the other one?"

"Maggie," he said, knowing that wasn't new information.

"Who else?" he demanded tapping Ramon's jaw with the gun.

What difference did it make? Lourdes had already betrayed him, so he was back to making deals with feds. "My sister and the FBI. But that piece of paper is worthless if you don't know how to read it."

"Maybe I do. I have GPS."

Shit. The bastard knew everything. No, not everything. "But not the clues. You don't know the clues."

"But you're going to tell me, aren't you?"

"For a price."

The man laughed softly. "The price is my bullet in your head."

"I will tell you everything, if you tell Viejo the truth."

"About what?"

"Who fed you information. Who in that group was your inside source."

"Why would I tell him that?"

"For the glory of finding your country a bounty of one hundred million dollars. Would you?" He knew he sounded desperate, but, right now, he didn't care. "And because *mi amigo*, we were friends."

"No, you were a drug dealer and I was an FBI agent."

Ramon looked hard at him. "We *were* friends. And El Viejo is going to have me killed if someone doesn't tell him the truth."

Miguel looked uninterested. "What's this? Longitude or latitude? Minutes or degrees?"

"Will you tell him for me?"

"I can maybe get you protection." He flicked the fortune. "When I find the money."

"What if it's not there?"

"Then you're probably a dead man. Because as I recall, your dad's a vindictive and pitiless son of a bitch."

Ramon took a deep breath. Lourdes had abandoned him. His own father wanted him dead. This light-eyed version of Michael Scott was his only hope. "There are four fortunes. Each one has numbers and words. The numbers are the coordinates. On every fortune there is a word that begins with the same letter as the direction, telling you if it is longitude or latitude. Two of the fortunes have minutes, two of them have seconds."

Miguel read the fortune. "A little can go a very long way." Flipped it. "Seven-one-three-zero." Then he looked hard at Ramon. "Interpret that."

"The W in *way* says it is west, or a longitude reading. I had main longitude, so that is seventy-one degrees thirty minutes west longitude."

"Who has the precise seconds that you add to this?"

"My father, originally. So the FBI has it now."

"And the other two? Which one is which?"

"Will you help me, Miguel?" Ramon asked. "*Will* you?"

"Depends on whether or not you're lying. The other two fortunes?"

"My sister has the latitude seconds; Maggie had the latitude main. All four together will give you want you want."

Ramon watched him fold the paper and slip it into a pocket on his T-shirt. He still couldn't see any real resemblance to the man he'd once considered a friend, but he had no doubt.

"Will you help me, *mi amigo?* For old time's sake?"

"Lay low. Stay out of sight and out of trouble. I'll find you."

"Gracias."

As Miguel climbed out of the car, Ramon reached forward, digging for his gun. Outside, his old *friend* held up the pistol.

"Looking for this?" He dropped it in his pocket and walked away.

That was too easy. Way, way too easy. The fortune still in his hand, Dan scanned the street, his gaze landing on Maggie as she closed the driver's door of the Porsche and headed toward him, sunlight streaming through yet another flimsy skirt, her dark waves bouncing with every step.

He met her on the sidewalk, his grin widening with each of her steps.

"What are you so happy about?"

"That your skirt is see-through."

"Doesn't take much, does it?"

"And I'm also kind of happy about this." He held up the fortune he'd found in the first place he'd looked. Too, too easy.

Her jaw opened as she snatched it from his fingers. "No."

"Yes."

"Are you kidding me? He just gave it to you?" She held it out to read.

"Not exactly."

"You threatened to kill him."

"A little."

She read it. " 'A little can go a very long way.' " She looked up at him, her eyes bright. "See that? You said 'a little' and those are the first words. That's what my Baba would call a sign. Just like the parking space that opened up for me." She turned the paper over, reading the numbers. "And where do these fit into the GPS scheme?"

"According to Ramon, that's the main longitude. And he explained how to read the code on each fortune."

"Seriously? That was a very fruitful meeting."

"Yes, it was. Maybe a little too fruitful. Let's go see Lola." He took her hand. "And you're not staying out here alone. Plus I might need you to distract the doorman by standing in front of the window and letting him gape at your legs."

"Whatever it takes."

The door to the lobby wasn't locked, and the front desk was unmanned, with a little note that said "Receiving delivery—will return shortly."

Maggie shot him a victorious look. "Baba's hard at work today."

"Someone's helping us, all right. But I don't think it's your grandmother."

The elevator required an access key, but in less than thirty seconds, the car arrived and a redhead stepped out. She made sexy and unsubtle eye contact with Dan before walking by.

"See that?" Maggie said. "The universe is definitely on our side today."

When the car stopped at the twenty-eighth floor, Dan held her back. "I'll ring the bell, and you stay behind me. No matter what, you let me take the lead."

There were only three units up there and he strode right to 28C, remembering the address. He rang the bell, knocked, and rang again. Nothing.

The lock pick took a minute longer than when he worked on Viejo's house. But Lola—or the universe—had assisted by not bolting her door.

"Ms. James?" he called as he opened the door.

The only sound was the ticking of a grandfather clock. He took a step in. This place was definitely a notch up from her office. Hardwood floors with expensive Oriental carpets, designer furniture, original art.

"Lola?" he called again, Maggie following him.

The living area had a corner balcony, the sheer curtains offering a hazy view of the bay and Miami Beach across the water. The room was spacious, and led to a dining area and kitchen, and two bedrooms beyond that. Every single item was placed just so, not even a throw pillow out of alignment.

Except for the silk robe that lay on the floor.

Dan glanced at it, and at Maggie. Why would a woman

who lived in such pristine perfection leave her robe in the middle of the floor?

He moved deeper into the condo, giving the kitchen a cursory check, then stepping into the hall that led to a bedroom, guest bath, and an office.

Maggie stayed in the living room while he searched the bedroom and found nothing, including a quick look in drawers, jewelry boxes, and the porcelain cups of an Oriental tea set displayed on her dresser. Everything was so tidy, it was pretty easy. The bathroom, closet, and dressing area were way past orderly and into nutcase neat.

He paused in the hallway and motioned to Maggie. "I'm going to check out the office."

The office was more of the same. A lot of white, a lot of clean, a lot of perfection. None of the drawers were locked, and he searched in every possible place.

The computer was off, a printer and scanner next to it, words flashing in green on a tiny panel on the top.

Fax successfully sent.

Dan lifted the lid, where a paper lay facedown on the glass. Slipping a nail into the corner so as not to compromise any DNA or fingerprints, he inched it up and over.

His gaze landed on three words: *Quinn Varcek Smith.*

Behind him, Maggie gasped. "It's his birth certificate."

At the bottom of the document, Dan stared at the line that said *Father: Michael Scott.*

He pressed the redial button to get a number. The first five digits told him exactly who it had gone to.

"Fifty-eight is the country code for Venezuela," Maggie said. "She must have sent it to her father."

"And she must have hired that Greek thug to steal it from you."

"I'm not a thug."

Dan spun at the sound of the male voice, drawing his weapon faster than his next breath.

Constantine Xenakis stood in the hallway, empty hands away from his body, silvery gaze slicing Dan. Even with the nonthreatening posture, Dan automatically stepped in front of Maggie and lifted his weapon to the intruder's face.

"She hired me to get a Chinese cookie fortune and I failed." He tilted his head in a nod of respect, or disgust. Hard to discern.

Dan refused to respond, waiting and watching.

"Then she asked me to use a kid to get what she wanted."

"And you failed at that, too," Dan said.

"Not failed. Refused. But she doesn't know that, and I'm here to tell her."

Dan narrowed his eyes, not trusting anything about this. "She's not home."

Xenakis glanced behind him as though he didn't believe that, then beyond to the office, and the desk. "You looking for the fortune?"

Dan didn't answer.

"Is it your kid, the one she wants to use?" he asked Maggie. "I thought so. What you want is in her office, downtown. I know exactly where the fortune is and I assure you that you will never find it. I can get it for you."

Dan took a half step forward. "I won't pay for it."

Xenakis gave him a curious look. "You might. You haven't heard my asking price. Do you want the fortune or not?"

Behind him, Dan felt Maggie step a little to the side, exposing herself. He moved instantly to cover her.

"Yes," she said. "We want it."

"Never bargain with a terrorist, sweetheart," Dan said.

"Or a thief," Xenakis added with a slow smile.

"Get it and we'll talk," Dan said. "How long will it take?"

"Assuming Ms. James is still out of the office, I can have it shortly after her assistant locks up for the night." He reached into his pocket and Dan tightened his finger on the trigger. "Here's my card." He handed it over, then tilted his head over Dan's shoulder. "Nice to see you again, Ms. Smith."

He turned, walked through the living room, and left through the same door he must have broken in through. The bastard was good.

"Let's go," Dan said, lowering his weapon and glancing at the card, which had only a name and cell phone number.

"You don't want to search the living room and kitchen?"

"I doubt we'll find it, but yes."

"Maybe he will get it for us," she said, gesturing toward the door. "He seemed credible."

"He's playing both sides against the middle." Dan picked up the birth certificate and rolled it. In the living room, they both paused at the robe. "This is really out of place for our OCD resident."

He crouched down and lifted the silk, and stared at the four dark droplets dried into the floor.

"Is that what I think it is?" Maggie asked.

He looked up at her. "If you think it's blood, then yes."

CHAPTER
FOURTEEN

CONSTANTINE XENAKIS WAITED until Enriquietta, Kiki to her friends and lovers, stepped out into the late afternoon sunshine. Since it was five thirty, that meant the CEO of Omnibus Transport was not in. Otherwise Kiki would have stayed until at least eight o'clock, doing her boss's bidding, and after Kiki left, Lola would put in another few hours. Then she'd cruise South Beach looking for a man to fawn over her.

If Kiki was leaving, then all of the half dozen employees were gone, and Lola mustn't have returned. It hadn't been difficult learning all that, since Kiki liked to chatter after sex.

Just to be sure, Con called the main number of Omnibus, knowing that there was one woman in accounting who sometimes did a little overtime and always answered the phone when Kiki was out, but he got the recorded message.

Still, he gave it ten more minutes. While he waited, he reviewed the videotape his phone had captured when he was in Lola's office. She hadn't even noticed that he'd left his phone on her desk when she sent him out to the hall. Stupid, stupid Lola. She'd given him plenty of business over the past year or so, when she needed information on a competitor or a potential customer. Nothing terribly complex, but definitely illegal and she'd never dirty her hands with that. But since her brother had come out of prison and she'd launched this fortune campaign, she'd gone crazy, and gotten stupid.

As he crossed the street, he straightened his tie, his suit jacket open. He looked like any Miami businessman going back to the office to grab his briefcase and pick up his messages after a day out with clients. In the building, he took the elevator to the fourth floor.

He pulled out his key ring and slipped it into the dead bolt on the office doors, peering through the glass at the desk where Kiki usually sat. It had been so easy to make a copy of her office key the first night he'd slept with her. He didn't need it, but the key made it all so simple.

Inside the lobby he rebolted the door, stood perfectly still for thirty seconds to determine if there was any sign of life, then went straight back to Lola's office. He'd copied that key, too, of course.

Just to be absolutely sure, he knocked. Then he entered, scanning the neat office to see if anything had changed. The video showed him where the keypad access was, but not what it opened. He'd have to use his auditory skills, which, in his not-so-humble opinion, were unparalleled.

He locked the door behind him and went to the bar, opening the door beneath to an empty cabinet. He flattened his hand on the side, feeling nothing at first. The second pass revealed a crack in the wood, and he bent down and stuck his head in to open it.

The keypad behind it was flat and simple.

He took out his phone and played the video again, this time with his eyes closed. He listened to the tones that would be inaudible to most people, and the notes that even those who could hear the noise wouldn't be able to discern as "music." But Con could.

There were five altogether. Two that could pass for C, one B flat, a D, and . . . he didn't get the last one. He played it again, forcing everything out of his brain but sound. The last note was flat. Too flat for him to identify.

The pad had ten numbers, laid out the opposite of a phone. He started at ten, pressed each one once, and heard the notes. The four was the C, the six a B flat, and nine was a D. Two of the keys, number one and number two, were flat. He'd have to guess what they were. If he guessed wrong, he might have a chance to try again. Or he might trip an alarm.

He'd have to be ready to bolt, and hope the alarm wasn't silent. So before he pressed, he had to be sure his hunch was right about the safe. It couldn't be anywhere on this side of the room, because the camera would have picked it up. That left the desk and the area behind it. The sound from the video was a click, then her footsteps, then a slide. A drawer. His guess, the desk.

He stood to check it out, running his hands under the front. The seam was almost invisible, but not completely. And, sadly, the whole thing was kind of obvious. A better woman would have been more creative.

In the distance, he heard the elevator ding. Soft enough that no one else in this office would ever have heard it, but Con did. There were other offices on this floor. Still, he kicked into action.

Clearing the keypad, he pressed the buttons in order.

He took a chance on the two, held his breath for a millisecond, then heard the soft click at her desk. *Yes.*

The drawer under her desk slid right out, sounding exactly as it had on the video. There were a few more pictures, which didn't interest him. A gold cross on a chain, which was of no value to anyone but its owner who, judging by the size of it, was a child. And there, under the cross, a rectangular paper from a fortune cookie.

"Sorrow is never the child of too much joy."

He slipped the fortune in his pocket, closed the drawer, returned to the bar to shut the cabinet . . . and froze when he heard a footfall in the hallway.

Then the sound of a key—or maybe a pick—on the door to Lola's office. He glanced around. Two choices. The window, which could open wide enough for him to climb out and balance on the ledge, or the bathroom, which left him trapped.

The lock clicked; someone had a key and would enter in less than two seconds. He silently opened the bathroom door and flattened against the wall. If someone came in, he'd take him or her right down.

Whoever it was knew exactly where to go. The sound of footsteps told Con the visitor, definitely a man, was at the bar, and the cabinet door instantly made its minuscule squeak. The pattern of beeps was almost immediate. The soft snap of the secret drawer. Two footsteps to the desk. The rolling sound.

A pause, a curse, and then a loud crash. Wood splintered, glass shattered, then another few seconds of furious breathing.

"That motherfucking bitch lied!"

Another crash of glass and metal, footsteps, the door, then silence.

Con waited until he heard the quiet bell of the elevator, then inched the door open. Everything on the desk had been smashed, the chair was broken, and shards of a crystal lamp sparkled all over the floor. The rest of the drawer's contents were strewn on the floor. Con scooped up the chain, dropped it into his pocket, and surveyed the mess.

Whoever that was, he'd ruined a perfectly neat job.

And he'd made life far more difficult for Con Xenakis because now he'd have to convince Dan Gallagher it *wasn't* him.

Fuck. Maybe he *should* stick to what he did best. Steal.

No, he had a bigger, better plan. And regardless of the mess in this office, he had the ticket in his pocket.

"She drives a mean-ass boat." Dan checked the ammo clip in his Glock, then slammed it into the weapon with the heel of his hand. "Having her get us there and wait while we search the shed is a no-brainer."

From his perch on the armrest of the sofa, Max's look said he was not convinced.

"Trust me, Maggie's a natural, and she knows the Coral Gables waterways better than either of us." Dan said. "Whatever was in that shed took two men to handle, and getting in and out is faster and easier by boat. Especially if someone's home."

Max just picked up a hooded black sweatshirt and stuffed it into a duffel bag they would take on the boat, as silent as always.

After dinner they'd worked out several variable plans, and agreed on the objective for the night: find out what was being shipped and stored in that shed. From there, they'd decide whether they'd bring in the DEA, the FBI, or more Bullet Catchers. Dan wanted enough to seal a case against El Viejo, Ramon, or whoever was involved. If they all went back to jail for another fourteen years, that would be just fine. Especially if they didn't find the fourth fortune.

They hadn't heard a word from Xenakis all day. Big surprise.

"You don't put your principal in harm's way," Max said. "That's a guiding tenet of our job, brother."

"So is 'use the best man on the team for the job.' Maggie happens to be the best person on this team for the boat-driving job. Plus, she's not just under my protection, she's more deeply involved in this than I am, and she's working with me, not under me."

Max chuckled. "If she's not under you, that explains your shitty mood."

Dan ignored him.

Max unholstered his Ruger. "You know, that's your problem."

Dan did *not* like the direction of this conversation. "What is?"

"Sex."

He snorted. "Not much of a problem for me."

"Exactly. Sex has always been your sport of choice, and you're the best player on the field."

"Please take your stupid analogies and shove them up your former linebacker's ass. Like you didn't get laid at every possible chance before Cori."

"Still do. But only with the woman I married."

"Would you please go back to your normal state of grunting only when spoken to?"

"I'm serious."

"You always are." Dan grabbed his own black sweat-shirt and pulled it on.

"He always is what?" Maggie stood in the doorway dressed in jeans, a dark long-sleeved top, and black sneakers. All she was missing was some face grease and she'd be in night camo.

The idea made him smile. As did the sight of her. "He's always a great big pain in the ass. But he's my pain in the ass, so let's take him for the ride."

"Brandy called," she said, coming into the room. "A man named Donovan Rush just showed up to be her personal bodyguard, and two more Bullet Catchers are protecting the bar. She said they flew into the Marathon airport in a corporate jet like the cavalry on steroids."

Dan chuckled at the image.

"Thank you." Maggie put her hand on his arm. "I appreciate you doing this. All of this."

He held her gaze, ready to kiss her just for being that close and that pretty. "No problem. It's what we do."

She tightened her grip slightly. "You do it really well."

He didn't give a shit if Max *was* two feet away. "Damn right." He brushed her lower lip with his finger, wishing it was his tongue.

With a long, sweet look, she backed up. "I'm going to grab a bottle of water, and then I'm ready to rumble."

When she left, Dan was still smiling.

"Like her, do ya?" Max asked.

"What's not to like?"

"The fact that she has a son."

Dan choked softly. "He's *my* son."

"My point precisely."

"What the hell is that supposed to mean?"

"Let's see if I have this quote right. It was 'Do I wish it was me up there, perusing a baby name book? Hell no . . . I like the status quo.'"

"And here I didn't think you ever listened to me."

Max laughed. "I listen, I just don't take you seriously. File this under 'Be careful what you think you don't want, then you get it.'"

"I hate when you get deep."

"Just practical. What are you doing with her?"

Dan gave him a puzzled look. "Nothing, as you just noted with the comment about my shitty mood."

"What do you want from her?" Max asked. "Because the signals are loud, but they're not clear. Can't you tell she's confused?"

Confused? Signals? "Max, I'm trying to find a missing load of cash. I'm trying to nail a drug ring while I'm at it. If, in the meantime, I get a little close with a woman who I already know is a good match in the sack, then so be it."

Max looked disgusted. "Don't screw with that kid's head. Or hers. Understand? She's not like all those women you mess around with. This is a different playing field."

"How's that?"

"She's the mother of your child. And you've messed her up once before. Though obviously she's forgiven you."

Had she?

Before he could answer, Cori came in. "Peyton's asleep. Quinn's watching a movie. You." She pointed at her husband. "Be safe."

Max took one step toward her and wrapped his arms around her, kissing her on the mouth, then on the forehead, then murmured something in her ear that made her laugh.

Since when was Max funny?

Dan turned and left them alone, running smack into Maggie in the hall.

"All set?" she asked.

"Except for this." He pulled her into him and kissed her hard on the lips, just so his signals were *clear*.

She broke the kiss slowly, looking more interested than confused. He should know better than to trust Max's interpretation of what a woman was thinking.

"What was that for?" she asked.

"For luck."

Her eyes widened. "Blink twice. Quick. That's really bad luck to say out loud."

He laughed softly. "You blink for me. While you're at it, keep your eyes closed."

When she did, he kissed her again, tunneling his fingers into her hair, slanting her face to cover every bit of her mouth, and tonguing the roof of her mouth just to feel her body tighten in response.

"Move it." Max nudged him in the back.

Dan released her with a meaningful look, and the glint in her eyes confirmed she understood.

They loaded up the smaller of Max's two boats, an easily maneuverable open-bow Contender, while Maggie familiarized herself with the instruments and checked the chart plotter to map out a course for the short run to the mainland. She asked Max a few questions. Then they took off across the bay toward the maze of canals that ran behind Coral Gables' multimillion dollar homes. And one ratty mess of a former drug house.

Max planted himself on the bow peering ahead into the darkness. Maggie stood confidently behind the wheel, her gaze moving between her charts and the reflective channel markers that rose up from the black water of the bay.

Dan wrapped his arms around her waist, the only thing between them a thigh-high helm bench, not nearly wide enough to separate his front from her back. She looked over her shoulder at him.

"You're such a natural on a boat," he murmured in her ear.

"I got used to them, and I like the water. I hated having to sell Smitty's, and so did Quinn."

"I have one," he said.

"In New York City?"

"In upstate New York. I have a restored Chris Craft Cobra up on Lake George."

She drew back, eyes wide. "Nice."

"It is. Maybe you can come up sometime."

"With Quinn?"

"Of course with Quinn."

She turned to face front, her body stiffening a little as they bounced on a wave trough. He tightened his grip around her narrow waist, her head fitting under his chin perfectly.

"Or maybe Quinn can just go up there alone and see you."

"I'd prefer if you came with him."

"Why?"

He covered her ear with his mouth, her hair whipping in his face. "If you have to ask, I'm doing something wrong."

"Oh, you're not doing anything wrong." She turned her face toward his. As he kissed her, they hit a high wave and bounced out of each other's arms.

Max turned, and pointed toward the channel marker. "Let's take this entrance and work our way over to the Gables."

As soon as they entered the canals, Maggie took them down to a quiet, no-wake five miles per hour. They kept the legal minimum lights on the boat, snaking through the waterways that made Coral Gables more like Venice than a South Florida metropolis. Almost every home had a dock, many covered, most mooring to impressive mini-yachts, sailboats, and cabin cruisers.

When they reached the entrance to the canal that ran behind Viejo's house, she slowed the speed even more.

Dan reached into his pocket and pulled out her comm device. "Here you go, Maggie. Your wireless." He slipped the bud in her ear, turning the tiny microphone toward her mouth. "You can hear me this way." And he'd hear her every breath.

"There," he said, flicking her three silver hoops in his fingers. "Except for these, you look like a Bullet Catcher. One more time, let's review the plan. You and Max wait at the dock while I go up and check out the house and make sure we can get into the shed. If anyone comes up the canal, Maggie, you leave. Circle around until they're gone."

"You'll have no way out."

"That's fine. I'm armed. Once I know we can get back in that shed, I call in Max and we'll go to work. If not, we'll look at options for getting back in."

"If someone's there?"

"We might bail." He glanced at Max. They'd worked all this out in prelim. "Or might reassess."

"If someone's visible from the dock?" she asked.

"We cruise right on by." And he and Max would drive back and enter on foot later.

He moved to the starboard side as they got closer. They passed a poinciana tree that marked the edge of the property, and a long row of queen palms.

"Looks black as night at Casa Viejo," Maggie said, peering up toward the house.

Looks could be deceiving. As they reached the uncovered dock where the Cigarette boat had been tied up during the last pickup, she veered closer. Before he climbed out, Dan pulled her into his chest again to whisper in the ear with no comm device.

"Be careful. Follow directions."

She nodded, but didn't turn. He put a finger on her chin and tried to nudge her around, but she looked straight ahead. "You be careful, too," she said, noncommital.

He ran his hand down her arm until he reached her three bracelets, then transferred one to her other arm, sliding it up with ease.

One bracelet: *Meet me in my room.*

He could swear he felt her shiver. With that to look forward to, he leaped onto the dock and headed into the mangroves.

CHAPTER
FIFTEEN

"LOOKS DESERTED." DAN'S voice, amplified through a state-of-the-art ear speaker not much bigger than her baby fingernail, was as effective as the real thing. Toe-curlingly warm and inviting.

She glanced down at the bangle he'd just used for what might be the smoothest move in the history of seductions. No, he never forgot a thing.

Max stood starboard, one hand on the weathered dock to hold the boat in place, the other at his ear. "Where are you?"

"At the pool. West side. I'm going to circle the house."

Maggie closed her fingers over the helm, the vibration of the twin outboards rumbling through her. She imagined Dan at the gate, rounding the bushes, passing the laundry room, stealthily eating up ground on his mission.

"All quiet," he said softly. "Looks dark. Doesn't mean deserted, just dark. I'm rounding the front and heading back to the shed."

She exhaled and Max turned to look at her, making her remember she was miked, too.

"Part one complete," she said with a quick smile.

"From here," Dan replied, "a cakewalk."

Max cringed.

"Did he just make a face?" Dan asked.

"Uh, yeah," Maggie replied.

"I hate that word," Max said. "Every time, it brings trouble."

Maggie's heart flipped a little.

"Don't tell her that," Dan said. "She believes in that stuff."

More than he could imagine.

A few more minutes passed. The only sounds other than the idling engines were a dog barking in the distance and the steady song of the cicadas. And her heart, which thumped loud enough that they probably heard it in their earpieces.

"All right, kids, I'm at the shed." Dan said. "The lock is on, but . . ." A long pause. "Our secret entrance is intact. Let me get in there and see what we've got."

She imagined him sliding through the opening. The boat rose and fell on a swell, taking her stomach for the ride. Was she really worried about him? Did she really care?

Yes.

When did that happen?

About fourteen years ago. Some dreams die hard. That's what it should have said on her fortune cookie. No. *Some dreams die hard, stupid.*

"Well, what do you know," he whispered. "Santa's been here. Come on, Max. And bring the tools. These crates are nailed shut."

In one easy move, Max grabbed a duffel bag on the bench and stepped up to the dock. The boat rocked with the change in weight; then he turned to her. "You leave at the sight or sound of another boat. We won't lose contact."

She nodded and moved her hand from the wheel to the throttle, and scanned the canal up and down. Nothing.

He disappeared into a break in the mangroves, as soundless as Dan.

"You okay, Maggie?" Dan's voice rolled through her like warm syrup.

"I'm fine."

"No lights? No boats?"

"Don't worry about me, Dan," she said. "Just find what's in those crates."

"I'm coming up the back," Max said.

For the next minute or two they said nothing, and the only sound she heard was scuff and bump as they worked. A few words exchanged. Max swore. Dan blew out an irritated breath.

"Jesus, this is it? Anything inside that one?" Dan asked.

"Nope. Rock solid."

Before she could ask what they were talking about, the low chugging throb of a speedboat came down the canal.

"Someone's coming," she said.

"Go, Maggie. It's a Cigarette boat. Just roll east as fast and quietly as you can."

Her "Okay" was almost drowned out by the backfire of a go-fast engine being held to a speed much slower than it was built to run.

Maggie pushed the throttle forward and steered into the canal.

She turned to squint back into the darkness, already two properties away. Then she looked forward, following the thin beam of the bow light. Four more docks; then she'd turn into the T in the canal, where she could wait or circle all the way around behind the next street. Once the other boat had passed the house, she could head back to the dock.

But if she wanted to turn before that, she was moving far too slowly to reverse directions.

She glanced over her shoulder as the speedboat's engine exploded with one more ear-cracking shot of built up exhaust, then went silent.

"Aw, shit." Dan's whisper was barely loud enough for her to hear it.

One hand on the wheel, she stared behind her, but the moon was only a sliver, giving just enough light for her to make out the bobbing of a low-slung boat without a single light on board.

"They're docking," she whispered.

"Get out of there, Maggie," Dan urged. "We'll hide. There's a ton of cover here. Just *go*."

"We gotta move now, Dan." Max warned.

"We have to check that one. Before he takes it."

Maggie pressed the throttle forward but not enough to get the attention of whoever was docking at Viejo's.

"I think there's just one person," she whispered.

"Get the hell *out* of there, Maggie."

She moved on, but more slowly than she knew he'd want her to. Wasn't she more valuable as their eyes than if she were hiding down the next waterway? "One guy. Definitely. Tying up."

"Drive, Maggie." Dan's voice was tense. "I *mean* it."

"He's off the boat. He's going up there."

"Let's go." That was Max, with urgency. "Just leave it. We got one open, Dan. We saw what's in there."

"You go first," Dan said. "And I'll just . . . get this."

Shuffling. Movement. Scraping metal, exerted breaths.

The driver of the boat disappeared into the mangroves, through the same break in the branches Max had used.

"He's on the property," Maggie said. And a hundred and fifty feet from the shed.

"Max." Dan's voice was low and dead serious. "You better get back in here."

"Not now. He's in sight. Going to the house."

"You better get back in here," Dan repeated. "And Maggie, I need you to get back here as fast as you can."

Now he wanted her back there?

"Fast, Maggie." Something in his voice left no room for question. Something was very, very wrong.

She used her left hand to throw the wheel, then alternated with both hands on each throttle handle, silently thanking Smitty for teaching her the twin engine turning trick.

In her ear, she could hear movement, action, words she couldn't make out. She shoved the left throttle forward and yanked the right one back.

Sweat rolled down her back as she worked furiously to turn the boat around.

In her ear she heard muffled sounds but couldn't imagine what Dan was doing. Maybe he'd found drugs. The evidence they needed to nail Viejo and Ramon again, another way to keep Quinn and her safe from them.

Or maybe he'd found the unlaundered money!

She gave the wheel a shove to the right, nudging the rudder, and the craft started to circle back, close to the sea wall on one side, but clear enough for her to continue. As she did, she glanced up at the house just in time to see a light go on in the one window visible over the trees.

Someone was in the house. How long did they have? Long enough to get whatever they'd found to the boat?

"Maggie, how close are you?"

"I'm one property away from the house," she replied. "Should I meet you at the dock?" She'd have to do some fancy maneuvering to get around the Cigarette boat, but she could get close enough and they could jump.

"Fast!" he ordered. "Kick up the engines and move!"

She did, powering down the canal, her focus on the dock ahead. "I'm going to go around the boat and sidle up to the eastern side. Can you jump?"

She saw the mangroves rustle and shadows move as the men broke through the foliage. "Can't jump," Dan said. "You have to get closer."

He was carrying something. "Can't you just throw it in the back?" she asked.

Just as she reached the stern of the docked boat, she got a good look at the two men on the dock. Max waved her around the Cigarette boat.

Dan held the limp, naked body of a woman in his arms.

Max leaped off the dock onto the bow and reached up, taking the body from Dan.

"Go, Maggie!" Dan vaulted into the boat as Max laid the woman on the bow deck. "Go!"

As she threw the throttle forward, the deafening crack of a gunshot echoed over the water.

Dan threw Maggie to the deck and Max took the wheel.

"Stay under me," Dan ordered as he unholstered his weapon and aimed. But he knew he couldn't hit whoever had a rifle in the upstairs window, and another bullet whizzed by, missing them.

Dan held Maggie immobile on the deck as Max drove away, and in a minute they were out of range.

"Who is that?" Maggie asked, staying low.

"I think you know her as Lourdes."

"Lola? She was—"

"In a crate. And she's alive, but barely. Faster, Max!"

Dan rose up as they got half a mile away from the house and no one made any move on that dock. Instantly, Maggie started to crawl to the body in the front.

"Lourdes?"

Confident they weren't being followed, Dan went with her, yanking off his sweatshirt to cover the woman. At the wheel, Max was already doing the same thing.

"Oh my God, look at her face."

Someone had cut Lola, and cut her bad. Scabbed lines slashed her cheeks, her breasts and torso, and her thighs. Nothing deep enough to bleed out, but enough to badly scar. Her eyes fluttered; then her head lolled to one side. Her whole body quivered with shock, which was the only way Dan knew she was alive.

Maggie covered her with the sweatshirts and scooted closer, cradling her head just as Max hit the open water of the bay and took off with more acceleration.

"Should we take her to a hospital?" Maggie asked.

"No." Lola shook her head slowly, fighting for consciousness. "No hospital."

Maggie held her closer. "Are you awake? Who did this to you?"

Lola opened her eyes and worked to focus on Maggie's face. "Mag . . ." She shivered again with a shock wave. "I don't know," she managed to say.

The boat bounced hard on a wave, knocking Lola's teeth together and making her moan.

"Hang on, Lola." Maggie looked over at Dan. "She was in a crate?"

He nodded, checking the bay behind them.

"Why?" Maggie asked. "Why would someone do that to her?"

"The fortune," Lola said with a soft moan. "He wants the fortune."

"Did you give it to him?" Dan asked.

"I told him where to get it, but it was gone. That's when he did . . . this to me." Her voice cracked and Dan turned to see her looking up at Maggie. "How bad is it?" she asked in a rasp.

"Not bad," Maggie assured her, stroking her hair soothingly. "Let us take you to the hospital. Mercy is really close."

"Please, no. I can't. Just. Home."

"You're not safe at home," Maggie said. "Can you describe this man?"

"Yes. I think so. Not now."

Dan and Maggie shared a look, and he could see the sympathy in her eyes.

"Did you find anything else in the shed?" Maggie asked him.

That was the other thing pissing him off. "Tools."

"Tools?"

"A crate full of wrenches, hammers, and nails, packed for shipment, and heavy as solid steel." Meaning they weren't hollow and stuffed with cocaine. They'd checked one before the boat arrived.

Lola managed to lift her head. "Where are you taking me?"

"My house," Max said, flipping his phone to his ear. "I'll get my wife's doctor to look at you, and if he says you go to the hospital, you go."

She barely nodded, falling back on Maggie's lap until they docked. Dan carried her up to the house, where Cori waited on the patio. She directed them to the wing of rooms off the laundry and kitchen, where the housekeeper lived when Cori and Max weren't in residence.

When the doctor arrived at the gate, Cori left and Maggie helped put Lola in a robe and on the bed. Dan waited in the doorway, assessing how much he could trust Lola. Not much.

"Lola . . . Lourdes," Maggie said, kneeling in front of her. "Do you know exactly what it said on the fortune you have? Can you remember the words and numbers?"

Lola nodded. "Of course I can."

"I have to know them," Maggie said.

Even in her post-traumatic state, Lola's look was sharp. "Give me yours," she said.

Dan took a step into the room. "Listen to me." When he had her attention, he leaned closer. "I don't know what you're trying to prove, or if you think for one minute that you can get your hands on that money and keep it. But you are inches away from a visit to the FBI, Ms. James. In case you don't remember me, my name was Michael Scott and I have some very strong ties to that agency."

She drew back, her mouth open.

"So if you want to keep your company clean and your good name intact, you will tell us everything you know. And not just the words and numbers on that fortune, but the names of everyone else who wants it, and why, and the details of how you ended up in that shed and who took you there. Is that clear?"

Behind him, Cori tapped on the door. Next to her was a short man with salt-and-pepper hair, a thick mustache, and dark, serious eyes.

"This is Dr. Mahesh," Cori said. "And this," she added, holding out an envelope to Dan, "was just delivered by the security guard. It was left at the front gate a few minutes ago."

"For me?" Who knew he was there?

As the doctor stepped in, Dan went into the hall and tore open the envelope. In it were Maggie's and Quinn's passports, a marriage certificate, and a gold cross on a chain. And tucked in the corner of the envelope, a Chinese fortune.

Last was Constantine Xenakis's business card, with bold, black script on the back.

"I want a meeting with Lucy Sharpe."

That was the payment?

" 'Scuze me, doctor," Dan said, stepping back into the room. "I need to ask her a question."

The doctor moved and Dan got right into Lola's face and held up the cross.

"Where did you get that?" She snatched at it but he pulled it back.

"Where did you have it?"

"Hidden. In a safe. The one I sent *this* guy to." She touched a cut.

"Was that where the fortune was hidden, and the rest of the things you had stolen from Maggie's house?"

She nodded.

"Tell me the numbers and words. *Now.* No hesitation."

"Sorrow is never the child of too much joy," she said softly. "Five-eight-nine-two."

A perfect match to what he held in his hand.

He gave her the cross and walked out, not the least bit ready to trust her, or the thief.

CHAPTER
SIXTEEN

"IT'S SMACK DAB in the middle of Lake Marafreakingcaibo," Maggie said, standing in front of the giant flat screen monitor and pointing to a lake a hundred and thirty miles long and seventy-five miles wide. "Zoom in some more on that satellite view, okay?"

As Dan did, his phone vibrated with a text from Max. *Lola's asleep. So are we. Solutions in the a.m.*

"Look at all that cloud cover. We can't even see what's there," Maggie said, frustration and exhaustion darkening her tone.

"Everyone's gone to bed over there, Maggie," he told her, setting the phone down. "Lola's staying at least until tomorrow, and she might be able to shed some light on this."

She turned from the screen, which backlit her curls and bathed her in soft blue light. "You kicking me out?"

"Only if you want to go. We can work on this all night if you like, or . . ."

She smiled at his hesitation. "Or not."

"Not's good." He crooked his finger to get her closer. "I vote for not."

For a second, he thought she was about to give in. Then she shook her head and scooped up her phone and bag. "I'll see you tomorrow."

He was up in a shot, blocking her way. "The alarm's on. You can't go into the main house now."

"You know the code."

"You'll wake Quinn up. And everyone else."

"That's BS."

It sure was. "Sleep here."

Brown eyes tapered with a knowing glint. "We won't sleep."

"Eventually we will. You can't leave now."

"Why not? Give me one good reason, other than raging hormones and a total lack of common—"

He closed the space and kissed her, still holding her hand as he curled it behind her and drew her into his body.

"I want you to stay," he murmured against her lips, growing harder with arousal as she grew softer with acquiescence. He had her. Almost.

He kissed her again, licking her lips to gain entrance to her mouth and using his free hand to run a heated stroke from her jaw down her neck over her breast and around to cup her backside. She responded with a roll of her hips and a soft intake of breath. Always, always so responsive to his touch.

As he trailed kisses down her throat, frustrated by the high neckline of her jersey, he whispered, "I want you, Maggie May."

She stiffened a little, backing up as the light in her eyes went from aroused to . . . wistful? Hopeful? Something that didn't say *throw me on the bed and screw me senseless*.

"What's the matter?" he asked.

"When you said that, you sounded like Michael Scott. Exactly like I remember him. You . . . *he* . . . used to say the same thing. Same tone. Same nickname."

He slid his hands up her body, over her breasts, and under her jaw, where he cupped her face and held it to his. "That man was a cover. He didn't exist on the outside. But the one inside that shell, *this* man . . ." He tapped his chest to make his point. "Always wanted you and still does. Only this time, you know what you're doing, and it's real."

"It wasn't real before?"

"This is even more real."

"And even more dangerous," she whispered.

Maybe. But this time when he made love to her, he wanted her to know exactly what she was doing and whom she was doing it with.

"Maggie, I'm about to explode with how much I need you, but the last thing I ever want to do is make you feel bad about me again."

She searched his face so intently, it was as if she was trying to see right through him. Or into him.

"There was so much about him I loved, until the end. It may have been a cover, but I was in love with . . . that man. And sometimes, when you remind me of him . . . I forget what you did, and remember how you made me feel back then."

"I remember, too," he whispered. "But this isn't about then, Maggie. This is now. I want to make love to you as me—not him."

"But some things are so familiar," she said, regarding him thoughtfully. "It's hard to separate the past from the present." Then her finger was on his lips, outlining them. "Your mouth, for example. You kiss the same. Like . . . you own every kiss."

He burned to own another one, but he waited.

"I can't believe I didn't recognize you just from these lips." She stared at his mouth. "And your teeth. Did they overlap like that?"

He shook his head. "I wore a semipermanent cap. It was part of the cover."

She nodded. "But you can't change your lips." One more time, she circled his mouth. Then she trailed a line down to his chin, back and forth, then wider to cover his whole jaw. "Or this handsome jaw. Though as I recall, you didn't shave every day."

"Beard growth helped cover my face. And longer whiskers were easier to dye. Do you really want to talk about this now?"

Her finger stroked from under one ear to the other, the feather touch making a faint scratching sound that tensed his muscles.

She leaned into the hollow of his throat, and he braced for a kiss there, but she just inhaled softly.

"You have a distinct scent, even after a shower. Kind of . . ." She breathed in again. "I don't know. Like *you*. I smelled it in the shed."

"I was sweating like a pig."

"You were aroused."

"A permanent state, around you."

She stroked his right shoulder, still using a touch so light he almost didn't feel it, following her finger trail with an intent gaze, drinking in every inch of him.

"You're bigger here," she noted. "More muscular than when you were, what, twenty-two?"

"Twenty-five."

She nodded slowly. "I thought you were younger."

"Part of the cover."

Her attention had moved to his other shoulder, her finger traveling down his bicep, over a vein, down a scar.

"Much stronger," she said. "You were lankier then."

She surprised him by pulling his T-shirt up. He slid it over his head and dropped it, one step closer to naked, which was all he wanted to be with her.

She ran her hand over the rise and fall of his muscles, and down the middle, frowning as though something wasn't quite right. "You had dark chest hair. More than this."

"I shave it when I work out a lot," he said. "And then, it was dyed."

She shook her head, circling her finger over a patch of coarse chest hair. "You were so thorough."

"It was part of the job."

Her hand stroked lower, until she reached the snap of his jeans, strained by a hard-on aching for release. She closed her fingers over him. "This is the same."

"Always, with you." He couldn't bear it any longer. "Now, Maggie?"

She closed her eyes for a second, dragged her hands back up his torso, and locked them behind his neck. "Now."

Finally.

Dan moved like a man on a mission, stripping her top off on the way to the bedroom, unclasping her bra and tossing it with one hand while the other set to work on her jeans. She almost laughed at his determination, except hers matched it.

As he eased her back onto the bed, he dragged off her jeans, panties and all, his eyes devouring every inch. The only light was from the living room, but from the look on his face, that was enough to see what he wanted and like what he saw.

He did this, she remembered. He had this magical way of seducing her with his admiring looks and, oh, those hands. He touched her breasts, caressing one, then the other, already licking and suckling and nudging himself between her legs.

Still kissing, he reached down to the other side of the bed to his bag and produced a condom.

There would be no stopping this train, and she didn't want to. Her hips rose to meet his, her center already wet and ready for him, her heart thundering with each well-placed kiss on her throat, her cheeks, her mouth.

His tongue plunged into her mouth as the tip of him slipped between her legs. Every touch was more urgent than the one before, each murmur of her name a little more desperate for entrance.

She opened her legs and he thrust into her. Fast, hard, pulling a shocked cry from her that he soothed with another onslaught of kisses. He stroked once, then again, the thickness and length of him wildly, beautifully familiar, and yet so extraordinary for her body that it hurt as much as it thrilled.

He stopped, fully hilted, working to catch his breath. "Are you all right?" he managed to ask. "Does that hurt?"

"Yes to both," she admitted.

"Slow?" he asked, moving out, then in, to match the word.

"Slow's good."

He kept that pace for two, three thrusts, but tightened and groaned, and quickened again.

"Fast is okay, too," she said with a soft laugh.

He smiled, biting down on his lip with the effort not to

go even faster. "I don't want to hurt you. I never wanted to hurt you, Maggie. Never."

She reached up and stroked his cheek, damp with sweat, rough with whiskers, the words she knew she had to say on her lips—but somehow, they couldn't come out.

He drew out an inch, then back in again, his look expectant, waiting. She brought his face to hers and turned his head, pressing her mouth to his ear.

"I forgive you." She kissed his cheek. "I forgive you, Dan."

As she said his name, he seemed to let go. He kissed her shoulder, then worked his way back to her mouth, kissing her as though it was the only way he could thank her for that.

Then he arched into her, breaking the kiss, plunging in again and again and again, until any pain disappeared and a burn of pleasure crackled through every nerve in her body, and she forgot about everything that had ever happened with this man except right now.

And right now was sheer bliss.

The climax started slow, then intensified with each move, over and over as he stretched her inside with impossible sweetness until she gave in and let go, rocking against him in perfect, perfect rhythm.

Just as lost, he let out a long, low moan of satisfaction and came in five, six, seven thrusts that peaked and slowed until he collapsed on her, and neither one of them could possibly move.

I forgive you.

The echo of her own words filled her ears like his strangled breath. Had she really forgiven Michael Scott for his betrayal, his lies? Had she really opened up her body to this man . . . again?

She kicked the regret away and squeezed him, wanting Dan—this warm, protective, honest, decent, fearless man—to forever replace the memory of anything and everything Michael Scott had done.

Maybe not everything.

But everything that happened that black, miserable night, when he pushed her away, ran from her, shed his jacket, revealed the truth and . . . "What did you say to me?"

"I didn't say anything yet," he said. "But we could start with how much I—"

"No, that night. In the rain. At the warehouse."

He lifted his head, looking at her with a flicker of uncertainty in his eyes.

"You turned to me when you left, right after you took off your jacket. You remember. You turned and said something."

The light in his eyes went from uncertainty to . . . fear? Was that possible?

"I've always wondered," she admitted. "I mean, I guessed it was 'I'm sorry' or 'Run, Maggie' . . . But I want to know. Just for my own curiosity. What did you say?"

"I don't re—"

"*Don't* lie. Not now . . . not like this." With their bodies still connected, the sweat from making love still on them.

For an eternity, he just looked at her.

"I love you," he finally said.

She sucked in a small breath. "What?"

"That night, when I turned back to you . . ." His voice was barely a whisper. "I said I love you."

Her heart squeezed in her chest. "You did?"

"I did say it." His gaze locked on her. "And I meant it."

"Oh." The word was little more than a breath, and she smiled.

He *loved* her. Once, long ago, in those dark days. She closed her eyes and rested her face against his, an entirely different bliss rolling over her. Maybe this was how he felt when she'd bestowed her forgiveness—absolved, somehow, for so many misdeeds she'd spent years regretting.

"You loved me," she whispered in the darkness.

"Very much," he added. "And I've never said it before or since."

"I wish I'd known," she said softly.

"Would it have made a difference, all these years?"

"No. Maybe. I don't know." It would have made her feel less used. But she'd forgiven him for that, and he'd given her this gift, and it wasn't worth telling him at this point. "I'm glad I know now."

"So am I." He eased off her, slowly pulling out and leaving her feeling empty without him. He immediately tucked her deeper into his side. "Don't leave me tonight."

Tonight? She could stay like this forever.

She curled into his hard, hot, wonderful body. "Tell me again."

"Okay." She could feel him smile against her cheek. "I loved you."

Right then, she wished with every wishing trick her Baba had ever taught her, that there was no such thing as a past tense. But there was, so she'd better use it.

"I loved you, too."

CHAPTER
SEVENTEEN

IN THE FAR recesses of Maggie's sleep, she heard laughter. She turned over, longing for quiet and another hour, when the sound rose again. It was Dan's laughter, and someone else's . . . lighter and softer.

She popped up, blinking sleep away, remembering where she was.

Throwing off the covers, she looked down at her still-naked body, then at the door. They hadn't closed that last night. She looked at the clock radio: seven thirteen.

Quinn would be up by eight!

She vaulted from the bed and seized her clothes.

"Shit!" Her top and bra were on the other side of that door, thrown on the floor.

She pulled on her panties and jeans, then headed for Dan's bag, which had had a seemingly endless supply of condoms last night. She grabbed the first T-shirt she found—navy blue, with a gold FBI insignia on the chest—and yanked it over her head.

Then she went into the bathroom, rinsed her mouth

out, ran her fingers through her hair, and wiped some left-over mascara from under her eyes.

When she opened the bedroom door, two faces turned to greet her from the bar at the kitchen. Dan, who looked mildly surprised, and a woman with features so bold and arresting that Maggie couldn't look away.

Dan hopped off a bar stool to approach her as Maggie studied the woman, mesmerized by her fluid, natural grace as she stood to what had to be damn near six feet with a thick mane of shoulder-length black hair.

"Hey," Dan said softly, putting an arm around Maggie and dropping a soft kiss on her hair. "I want you to meet somebody."

From the tone in his voice or maybe the authority in the woman's stance, Maggie knew exactly who she was.

"Lucy Sharpe." The woman held out a hand tipped with deep red nails that matched the velvety gloss on her lips.

Rumor has it they're an item.

I don't want this person on this chaise, in my head.

She quieted the voices and returned the strong hand-shake, doing her best to match it.

"This is Maggie," Dan said.

The note of pride in his voice put confidence into her handshake, and a warm feeling through her body.

"I can't begin to thank you for all your company has done to help my son and me," Maggie said.

Lucy waved an elegant hand, a diamond ring winking on it. *I'm happy she's found someone,* Dan had said.

"It's a pleasure to help someone I know has helped Dan in the past."

Maggie almost laughed at the euphemistic stretch of history. "What brings you here?"

"I came down with my men who flew into the Keys,

and decided to bring the plane up to Miami in case you two needed it. And after looking at that map and the four coordinates you mapped out last night"—she gestured toward the computer screen—"I think you most certainly will need it today."

"You want to fly down there?" Maggie asked Dan. "To Venezuela?"

"I think so. We've been talking about it, and it seems like the right next move."

She ignored the little kick of jealousy over the "we." Shouldn't he have been talking to her about it? Of course, she didn't own the plane. Or a security agency.

"What about Lola?" she asked. "Is she still here? She can probably answer a lot of questions."

He nodded. "She's just waking up. Why don't I walk you over there?" The rest was implied: *so you can dress and get out of here before Quinn wakes up.*

"All right." She turned to Lucy. "I assume you'll be here when I get back, so we can all discuss the next best move together."

She nodded with a hint of a smile. "Of course."

As Dan walked with her to the door, Maggie didn't see her clothes on the living room floor. When he caught her looking, he just winked.

Out on the patio, he snuggled her as he closed the door. "Good morning. Sorry if that was an unexpected awakening."

"I admit, I would have preferred to wake up next to you."

They started walking across the patio. "Me, too, but she knocked at six thirty, which is a few hours into the work day for Lucy."

"She's quite . . ." Gorgeous. Intimidating. Larger than life. "Something."

Dan chuckled. "Everyone has that reaction to her at first. Really, she's just a very smart and capable lady."

Who he might have loved once. Maggie gave him a quick look, and he must have seen the question in her eyes.

"Don't listen to rumors, Maggie May." At the French door that led to the guest wing, he brushed her curls back and tilted her head toward him. "You look good in that shirt. And better out of it."

She gave him a rueful smile. "Where's mine?"

"Hostage. You'll have to come back and rescue it."

"Did you hide it before she came in?"

He shrugged. "I don't waste my time trying to keep things from Lucy. She figures everything out, usually twenty minutes before every one else does." He lowered his head to kiss her just as the sheer curtain on the inside of the French door fluttered.

They backed away from each other instinctively, looking at it.

"If we're not careful, everyone else will figure this out in twenty minutes," Maggie said.

"I don't care."

She did. "I'll be back in a few minutes. I'm going to shower and change." When she opened the door and stepped in the hallway, Quinn's bedroom door slammed shut.

Maybe it wouldn't even take twenty minutes.

It took all he had not to interrogate Lola James, but Dan managed to keep his tone casual as they gathered in the guesthouse a little while later. Lucy stayed, quietly taking it in from a seat at the kitchen bar. Max sat next to her, a laptop open.

Maggie tucked her bare feet under her on a club chair with a view of the wall-size screen, and Lola, sporting scabs from her cuts, slumped miserably in the corner of the sofa, staring at the map of Venezuela on the screen.

She was in pain, though definitely out of her shocked condition. That was the only reason he didn't rattle her cage for answers.

"Exactly when did you learn that the fortune you had was connected to missing money?" he asked her.

"The day my brother got out of prison, and was free for the first time in fourteen years to tell me."

"Or you would have tried to find them all sooner, I suppose."

That earned him a sharp look. "I suppose," she said dryly.

"How did you get those fortunes?" he asked.

"Ramon gave me the cookies, and I shared with my"— she shot a contemptuous glance at Maggie—"babysitter."

"Why didn't he just give them to Maggie and tell her to hang on to them?"

She narrowed bloodshot eyes. "Probably because he knew she'd just hand them over to you the next time you two fucked like bunnies."

Fury whipped through him, but he didn't blink. "How many are there, Lola?"

"Four."

"Did Ramon tell you that?" That's what he told Dan, but he may have been lying.

"He told me everything."

"Why?" Dan asked. "Why wouldn't he just take the fortune you have, and get the money for himself?"

She shook her head, looking as if he was so stupid, it annoyed her to have to respond. "Because he thinks if he finds the money and gives it to our father, he'll be forgiven for his sins—real or imagined."

"Then why don't you help him do that?"

She shrugged. "Personal reasons."

"You hate your father."

"Of course I do. So do you. So does she." She angled her head toward Maggie. "Viejo knew someone was feeding information to the FBI and he made the assumption it was Ramon. That's how it came out at the trial, since you were conveniently dead and she was conveniently gone." She leaned forward. "Wasn't this meeting supposed to be about finding the guy who did this to me?"

"Constantine Xenakis?"

"*He* didn't touch me. But he obviously beat the guy who did cut me up to my office, and stole the fortune."

Con was smart enough to steal the fortune from her; he was also smart enough to work with her to try and derail Dan and Maggie's efforts. Earlier, he and Lucy had pieced together how Con found Dan at Max's house—he knew plenty about the Bullet Catchers, and no doubt knew they were close friends. He must have found out where Max's wife lived and took a chance.

The Con Man was smart, no doubt. But whose side was he on—other than his own?

If he hadn't cut Lola, and she was telling the truth about the guy she'd described when they started this meeting—auburn haired, dark eyed, muscular, with a mole under his jaw—this player wasn't anyone they'd come across yet.

"How many fortunes do you have?" Lola asked suddenly. "You have mine and you have Maggie's and you said you have Ramon's. This other guy must have the fourth, or he wouldn't be so hot on the trail of the other ones. And he must know what it's worth or he wouldn't want it so much."

"Or maybe he works for Viejo," Dan suggested, "and his job is to get them all so no one finds them. Viejo might already know exactly where the money is hidden."

She shrugged. "He might. And if he hasn't laundered it yet, it could still be there."

Dan turned to the screen and pointed to the southwest corner of the lake, not zooming in enough for her to know they had a fourth coordinate from the FBI files, giving them a precise quadrant. "This area of Lake Maracaibo mean anything to you?"

"Yes. My uncle had a house down there in the lake."

"*In* the lake?" Maggie asked.

"A stilt house. They're all over Lake Maracaibo, especially in the south, where there are no oil derricks and plenty of fishing. That's all they are—fishing huts up on stilts, and I was down there with my uncle when I was seven or eight." She squinted at the screen. "I'm pretty sure it was right there. About thirty miles off shore from a town called . . ." She tapped her chin, thinking. "Puerto Concha. A village on a river that leads to the lake." She shifted her gaze to Dan, then Maggie. "Is that it? The location of the money?"

When he didn't answer, her eyes widened with interest. "I should have thought of that. It would be a perfect place for my uncle to hide it. There's nothing around it for miles—at least there wasn't all those years ago. But it's not very secure. The place only has three walls and a thatched roof, a dock, and a toilet. I suppose that he . . ."

At her hesitation, Dan forced himself not to prod her. But Maggie was already leaning forward.

"He what?" she urged.

"He could be dropping it in the water in some kind of protective covering."

Maggie looked at Dan. "Is that possible?"

He doubted it. He doubted a lot of what Lola said, but they had little else to go on at this point. "Anything's possible."

Lola crossed her arms and studied the screen. "It would make sense that Viejo would put it there, far away from the plantation where he lives. But how would that sick old bastard get down there?"

"He's sick?" Dan asked.

She closed her eyes, disgusted. "Black hearted, corrupt, depraved, and mean. That's my dear father." She pushed herself up. "Are we done here? I want to go home."

"You're not going home," Lucy said, standing up. "That wouldn't be safe."

Lola turned and scanned her from head to toe with a mildly interested look. "I'll be okay. This time I won't open my door for anyone."

"We'll arrange round-the-clock protection for you, Ms. James. There will be someone waiting for you as soon as you get back."

Lola eyed her again. "Back from where?"

"The FBI offices. I'm taking you now."

"What?" She jerked forward. "I'm not going to the FBI."

"Of course you are," Lucy said smoothly. "This is an open federal investigation, and you've been face-to-face with someone who might be involved. I understand you often work with the authorities to maintain the integrity of your business."

Lola just stared at her, clearly recognizing she didn't have a chance against the other woman.

Dan smiled at Maggie. "Looks like I might need a skilled boat driver again."

"Let me get my stuff and go say good-bye to Quinn." She started to leave, but Lola reached out and grabbed her hand.

"So it's just one big happy family now?" Lola looked from Maggie to Dan. "How nice that you found each other after all these years."

Maggie pulled free. "I wish I could say the same about you."

Fighter jets and a familiar theme song blared from the media room, telling Maggie exactly where to find her son, and, more importantly, what his mood was.

Top Gun was his comfort movie of choice; he'd watched it about seventy-five times in a row the year that Smitty died.

She pushed the heavy door open and instantly covered her ears at the deafening surround sound.

"Quinn!" she shouted over it.

He sat in the middle of eight theater-style recliners, leaning all the way back, his gaze unwavering on the huge flat screen. He'd never hear her. She walked deeper into the room, but he didn't move.

"Quinn," she said again when the sound dipped for a second.

Still he didn't turn.

She marched to the bottom of the slightly elevated floor and stood right in front of the screen. "Turn it off or you will seriously regret this."

Barely moving a finger, he touched some kind of remote panel and the room went silent.

Asking him what was wrong was a waste of time. He wouldn't tell her anyway. "I'm leaving for a few days."

His gaze was on the screen behind her, as if he were just waiting for her to leave so he could hit Play. Irritation and frustration zipped through her as she kneeled on the seat right in front of him.

"Why are you doing this?"

"Why am *I* doing this?" The fury in his voice surprised her. This wasn't just 'I caught Mom kissing a guy.' "Why are *you* doing this?"

"I told you, I'm trying to keep you alive."

"All night long?" he said. At her look, he nodded. "Yeah, I came to find you last night. I had a stomachache."

A pang of guilt hit. Then she remembered that he hadn't come looking for her with an upset stomach for years. "You're lying."

"Am I? Then I guess I come by it naturally."

She sucked in an audible gasp. Did he know about Dan?

"You're doing an awful lot of sneaking around and changing the truth these days, aren't you, Mom?" He gave her a smart-ass look. "Where are you going?"

"Venezuela."

His eyebrows raised. "What for?"

"To get what we need to make sure you're safe." She leaned forward. "Honey, I don't like this any more than you do."

"I think you like it just fine. And you like that guy, too."

"Yes, I do," she said. "Very much." Way, way too much. He didn't say anything.

"You're not jealous, are you?" she asked, adding a teasing smile to soften the blow.

"Of some hotshot bodyguard with expensive cars?" He puffed out some air. "As if."

Her heart melted, as it always did when he acted tougher than he was. "You stay safe while I'm gone, okay? Do everything Mr. Roper says to do."

A tap at the door got her attention. "You in here, Maggie?" Dan came in, carrying his small duffel bag. "You should put your stuff in here, so we only have one light bag to carry."

Quinn didn't turn to see Dan, or smile at him as he usually did.

"Gimme a kiss, Quinn." She leaned forward and he met her halfway, giving her more cheek than kiss. "I'll call you," she added.

Dan dropped into the recliner at the end of that row. "Here," he said, giving her the bag. "I'll catch a few minutes of my favorite movie while I wait."

Still Quinn didn't look over or react.

"This is the 'hit the brakes and they fly right by' scene, right?"

Quinn nodded, his gaze on the frozen image behind Maggie. She gave a little shrug to Dan, and walked out. The sound came blaring back on, and all she heard was Tom Cruise's voice.

CHAPTER
EIGHTEEN

IN AN OPEN-AIR vehicle that resembled a rickety Jeep, Dan navigated a treacherous combination of dirt, potholes, and huge puddles at the foothills of the mountains. Maggie held on to the roll bar with one hand, the rusted door with the other, and never complained. She hadn't even bitched about riding a bus with chickens from the San Carlos airport to the city to rent a Jeep. He took his hand off the gearshift to give her bare leg a squeeze.

She let go of the roll bar and held his hand for a minute, saying nothing but making him feel something. Close. Connected. Crazy about her again. They shared a look and he knew she was feeling the same thing.

"Not at all what I expected El Viejo's homeland to be like," she said as they slowed down at a group of five or six shacks and a ramshackle store, which constituted a village here.

"There are two Venezuelas," Dan replied. "Over-the-top wealthy, and this."

At one hut, children played in hammocks while a

weary mother pounded laundry on a rock. The kids waved and a flock of herons took off into the hills.

"You think we'll make it tonight?"

He glanced at the sun, which was much closer to the western mountains than when they started. "I don't know. Puerto Concha should be the next town, and that's where we have to find a boat. We need to get down the river, which could take an hour, then out to the lake, to our location, look around, and go all the way back to San Carlos. We're so close to the equator, it'll be light a lot longer, but we'll be tight on time to make it all by nightfall."

The pilots were waiting at the airport with the Bullet Catcher plane, because if they'd left it, it would have been stolen or scrapped by the time they got back. Not too many Lear jets landed in the San Carlos airport.

In less than half an hour, they reached Puerto Concha. The next job was to find the home of a man named Jose Navarro, who was a friend of a friend of Lucy's and who would take them down the river to the lake. The connection was tenuous, and as of Dan's last call to Lucy, she still hadn't spoken to Navarro himself. But Dan had enough cash on him to buy a boat if they had to.

"Calling it a town is generous," Dan said dryly as they rumbled down the dirt road and passed yet another Catholic church and at least the twelfth statue of Simón Bolívar they'd seen since their plane landed.

He parked at a break in the buildings, where fruit and food stands lined the road, checking the address on his makeshift map. "Let's go find Señor Navarro. I think our luck is holding."

She groaned. "What is *with* you? Don't tempt the universe like that."

"I like tempting the universe." He took her hand as she

came around the back, slipped his arm around her, and pulled her close. "It's gonna be a cake—"

She shut him up with a long, slow kiss. "Don't say it."

"Walk," he finished. At her look, he gave her a little nudge. "*Walk* forward. To that chicken spit with roasted plaintains. I'm hungry."

They ate broiled chicken wrapped in newspapers as they walked by the vendors, checking the little buildings to find the address they had for Jose Navarro.

A young Indian boy came scampering up to Maggie. "Do you need a boat, lady?"

They glanced at each other, then the boy.

"Tourists want to see the lightning!" he continued with a wide smile. "I can take you to the lake before the lightning starts."

Dan reached into his pocket for change. "We're looking for Jose Navarro. Do you know him?"

"He lives there." He pointed to a red wooden structure across the street. "But he's been gone for five, six days."

Dan ignored Maggie's "I told you not to jinx us" look and checked his phone. *No Service.* It was spotty here, at best.

"He went to find more tourist business," the boy said, his accented English fairly easy to understand.

"We do need a boat," Dan said, deciding that Navarro might never materialize. "Can I rent yours?"

The boy shook his head. "No, sir. No rental. But I will take you to the lake, because you will never find it without me. I make the trip every day. I know the best waters, the fastest route. There are several ways on the river." He made wiggling motion with his hand. "Several, uh, trib . . . trib . . ."

"Tributaries?" Maggie offered.

He nodded. "Yes. You get lost without a guide. I'll take you for American cash." At Dan's hesitation, he said again, "I take tourists all the time to see the lightning."

"What's the lightning?" Maggie asked.

"Catatumbo lightning." The boy opened and closed his hands as if flashing a light. "Big, bright light in the sky. Red and purple. All the tourists want to see it. My boat is very sturdy. Very fast."

"Are you sure Jose Navarro is gone?" The kid could be trying to muscle in on the little business they got down here.

"Go knock on his door. If he doesn't come out, I'll take you anywhere you want on the lake. I promise lightning tonight. The weather is perfect, and we haven't had any for five nights." He pointed to the opposite end of the town. "My boat is right on the river. Very comfortable. Not expensive." He added a grin. "Less than two hours to the lake."

"We need to go to a specific location," Dan said.

"The lightning is everywhere," the boy replied. "But I take you wherever you want to go."

"Let me try Navarro first. Wait here, Maggie."

He knocked on the red shanty and an older woman selling fruit shook her head and yelled, *"Él ha ido!"* He's gone.

"Let's give the kid a chance," he said to Maggie when he returned. "Otherwise we're going to end up spending the night here."

Two hours and one almost catastrophic motor break-down later that their young driver, Javier, managed to fix, they were still meandering down a winding river that cut through the hills and jungle.

Dan pulled his shirt over his head and stuffed it into

the bag between them in the tiny fishing boat. "According to the GPS, we're almost at the lake. It'll be cooler on open water."

Across from him, Maggie dropped her head back, looking up at the sky and the occasional tree that hung over the river. "What's the lightning he was talking about again?"

"Catatumbo lightning," Dan said. "I've only seen it once. It's a huge cloud-to-cloud display over the lake, something to do with the petroleum in the water causing an accumulation of methane in the ozone. It's pretty, but my memory says it happens after midnight and can be followed by hours of torrential downpour. So God willing, we'll be there and back before the show."

He took out his phone again, but there wasn't even a flicker of service. "I'd like to find out how it went with Lola at the FBI, but I can't get a signal."

"What do you think is going to happen there? She was just going to give them a description of her attacker, right?"

"Oh, we had a little extra surprise planned with the SAC, Thomas Vincenze. That's what we were talking about when you woke up."

"What kind of surprise?"

"Evidently Omnibus isn't quite as clean as we first thought."

"Drugs?"

"No, nothing that serious. Fraudulent insurance claims. She's had quite a few, and they've been lucrative. And Con Xenakis may be meeting Lucy sooner than he thinks, because he's done more than a few deals to help Ms. James 'recover' items that were 'lost' by her cargo company. If they can find him, they'll bring him in, too."

"So Con and Lola may be working together, and lied to us." She gestured in the direction of the lake. "And we're following directions we got from them."

"True, but why would they send us to the wrong place? Just to get us off their case? I don't think either of them is that smart, or has anything to gain by it. Plus, someone did cut Lola up pretty bad. Xenakis may be an unprincipled thief and mercenary, but I don't get the impression he's vicious."

"There's the lake!" the boy announced, rocking the boat as he stood. He looked over his shoulder and grinned at them. "Javi got you here!"

"Step it up, Javi," Dan said, rolling his hands to indicate the boat moving faster. "We want to leave before nightfall."

Javi looked baffled. "You miss the lightning, then. I'll wait with you. It's no problem, señor."

"Not necessary. Just move."

Maracaibo wasn't technically a lake but a fat bay about a hundred miles long and nearly as wide. In this southwestern corner, far from the oil rigs in the north, the water was purer and the villages tiny. A few huts peppered the shore, with some farmers and locals milling about.

Across from Dan, Maggie took it all in, occasionally lifting her camera to take a shot like any other tourist.

"Twenty-five kilometers, northeast," Dan told Javi, glancing at the GPS and then gauging the light. They still had time to get there, explore, and make it back to the Jeep. He could get them to San Carlos in the dark.

"Look!" Maggie pointed to a shell-colored dolphin that leaped next to them.

"A pink dolphin," Javi hollered over the revving motor as they picked up speed. "That's very good luck!"

She loved that, excitedly taking pictures as the dolphin leaped next to the boat. Then she turned to Dan, her eyes bright. "I feel really good about this. This is a really good sign."

Dan leaned over and kissed her. "That's my sign," he said, barely loud enough to be heard over the motor. "For luck."

Camera in hand, she wrapped her arm around his neck and pulled him closer. She kissed him back with much more passion than he'd offered, parting her lips. With her free hand, she pressed against his bare chest, caressing it as she deepened the kiss.

"Oh, you're on your honeymoon!" Javi exclaimed.

They parted reluctantly. "No," they said in unison.

But Javi shook his head in disbelief. "You're going to a *palafito* for the wedding night, *sí?*"

"Not the night, Javi," Dan said. "Just an hour, then we head back."

"What's a *palafito?*" Maggie asked softly.

"A stilt house." Dan replied. "And spending the night in one alone with you wouldn't be the worst thing that ever happened."

Her look said she agreed.

"But we'll find a nice hotel in San Carlos," he promised. "With no live chickens."

They held hands as they bounced over the gentle waves, the late afternoon sun finally far enough behind the mountains and the wind strong enough so that they felt cool for the first time since the plane had landed.

And then, on the horizon, Dan saw a small structure on stilts in the exact location that the GPS was sending them.

"You see!" Javi pointed at the spot. "A *palafito!*"

The closer they got, the more Dan felt certain it was deserted, and absolutely on top of the coordinates, right down to the seconds in either direction. It rose from the water on weathered, wooden stilts with a covered porch that faced west, what looked like one room under a tarred roof, its sides lined with wide windows and a tiny dock. Piping ran down from the house right into the water.

Javi motored up next to the dock, where Dan tied the boat and instructed Javi to wait for them. "You go first," he said to Maggie, giving her a boost.

She hoisted herself up and Dan grabbed the duffel, shouldering it as he climbed onto the dock. As he passed Javi, he saw the kid eye the gun in his holster.

"Don't move from this spot," Dan repeated.

The response was another glance at the gun and a solemn nod.

"It looks empty," Maggie said, already headed to the ladder that led up ten feet to the patio. She started up, and Dan followed. At the top was a six-foot-wide opening to one large room, and an enclosure around a closet that held a toilet and sink.

Dan crossed the room, testing the wooden floor and checking for hollow areas where something might be hidden, heading toward a pile of canvas in the back.

"Anything?" she asked.

"It's a hammock, I think. Yeah." He flipped it around in his hands. "This would be the furniture."

He started his search, carefully tapping boards, opening the single cabinet built into the wall, examining the ceiling, completely concentrating until he heard a distant splash. He pivoted and darted to the front, pulling his gun. Javi was rowing like crazy, and well out of range of a safe shot.

"He thinks we want to be alone," Maggie said, putting her hand on Dan's arm so he didn't shoot.

"Or someone paid more than we did, and told him to leave us wherever he was taking us."

Either way, they were stranded.

Alonso Jimenez heard the distant ring of a phone. Blinking away sleep he reached for the tiny device that he used to communicate with one person only. And he'd been trained not to use names.

"Sí?"

"I've found him. I've found the boy."

The boy who wasn't his grandson. "Bring him to me."

"It won't be easy, Viejo."

More, always more, with this one. "Then take a wrench, *bárbaro!*"

"Easy, old man."

Alonso picked up the condescension in the voice. This one knew who had control now. He closed his eyes and leaned back. Was it time to give up? Did those years in prison really suck the juice from his heart? Was he impotent in all ways, now?

"Just bring me the boy," he said. "And tell me you've got a plan for his mother and father."

"The plan is well under way by now."

"And the shipment? Did it go?"

The silence was too long.

"Did it?" he demanded.

"We're having some problems on this end."

Once he lost control, he lost everything. And it seemed . . . he'd lost everything. "So fix them." The command was . . . impotent.

A man without power was no man at all. And a Venezuelan man without power might as well be dead. He closed the phone and set it on the table next to his cold bowl of *arroz con leche*.

A real man would go to that warehouse now.

Mañana. He would go to the warehouse tomorrow. First, he would sleep some more in preparation for his last act of revenge.

CHAPTER
NINETEEN

THEY WERE OUT there like proverbial sitting ducks, especially since there was no satellite signal. They were so vulnerable, surrounded by thirty miles of lake in one direction and fifty in the other, the mountains of Venezuela the only sight of land they had. And the three flimsy walls—two of which were only three feet high—and bamboo roof with gaping holes would provide little shelter from the coming rain.

Maggie settled against a wide beam, her bare feet peeking out from khaki cargo pants, her white T-shirt sticking to her skin, as Dan tried again in vain to get a call through to the pilots or Miami. Nothing.

He finally stopped pacing, trying various spots for satellite reception. "We're stuck."

"Maybe Javi will come back for us in the morning," she suggested.

"Maybe whoever paid Javi to strand us out here will come back and try to kill us."

She shot him a look. "I realize you're wired to think that way, but who knows we're here?"

"Whoever knows about the fortunes, and gave us bogus information. Ramon could have been lying about reading the clues. Con and Lola could have cooked up the whole thing to get us off their backs. The FBI notes could have been wrong. People know we're here—we just don't know who they are or why they want us here. Hell, Viejo could have orchestrated this for revenge."

He put his gun and phone down, then stretched out next to Maggie. "The view's nice, I'll give you that."

"The colors keep changing," she said. "First it was a muted peach, then it was fiery tangerine, and now it's a soft, ripe plum."

"Someone's hungry." He twisted around to grab the bag and dug for some protein bars and two bottles of water. "Pretend it's peaches, plums, and tangerines." He gave her a warm smile and in response got . . . tears? "Hey, what's the matter?"

"I miss my son."

He nodded, giving her arm a rub. "I bet you do."

"I mean, when I look at you. He has so many of your expressions. Funny, how those are genetic and not just picked up arbitrarily."

He did his best quintessential teenager impression. "Dude, that's, like, so tight."

She laughed and unwrapped a protein bar, leaning back to gaze at the natural beauty around them. "What did you and Quinn talk about when I left the media room?"

Not a thing. The kid was locked up and the key'd been tossed. But there was no reason to upset Maggie by sharing that. "I told him that Max was going to let him drive the Testarossa in an empty parking lot later in the day."

Her mouth dropped open. "Wow. I bet that perked him up."

Not enough. "I believe he said 'cool.' Then we just talked about the movie. How we both fast-forward through the face-sucking scenes. His words, not mine."

"He didn't always skip through those parts," she said as she broke off a piece of the bar. "A few years ago, when we had 'the talk' and I explained what a man and a woman do when they are in love, you know what he said? 'Oh, so that's what Maverick's doing to the instructor.' "

That made him laugh hard. "So it was up to you to tell him the facts of life, huh?"

"As well as I could. A few of the guys at the bar might be augmenting my efforts. I found a *Penthouse* in his room, and I know where he got it because one of my regular customers quotes that magazine like it's the last word on human behavior."

"Must be tough, doing that all alone."

She shrugged. "We're muddling along."

"You're doing more than muddling, Maggie. You know he's a good kid."

"He's moody and, in case you hadn't noticed, he's mad at me right now." She rolled up the protein bar paper with her last bite, tucking the trash in a side pocket of his bag. "He doesn't like change. Even temporary."

"That's not a trait I can take any credit or blame for. I live for change." He pulled her closer to lay her head down on his thighs. "Here, get comfortable and watch the show."

"So you get bored easily." There was the faintest note of accusation in her voice. "Is that why you've never settled down?"

"That's why I do what I do for a living," he told her, stroking her hair. "Every few weeks or months, a new country, a new principal, a new assignment."

"A new woman."

He caressed her cheek softly, the smooth olive skin warm under his finger. "That could change."

As soon as he said it, and her pulse kicked, he waited for regret. The last thing he needed to do was give false promises to the one woman he'd already hurt more than any other.

But oddly, he didn't regret saying anything to Maggie. So he just cradled her head and lifted her face, bending over to kiss her forehead. Then her cheeks. Finally, her mouth. She rose up partially sitting, deepening the kiss to a natural, warm exchange. Not sexual, just intimate.

When she broke the kiss, he cuddled her into his chest and rested his forehead against hers.

"Why do you live for change?" she asked. "Something in your past?"

"Sorry—no torturous memories, no bleak childhood. I had decent parents, a cool sister. Well, she's a pain, but we're close. I grew up in Pittsburgh, had Roper as my best pal, aced my way through Penn State, the FBI, and the Bullet Catchers. It's all good." So why was intimacy difficult, while the sex was so easy?

"I have enough mess for both of us," she said dryly. "But maybe that's why you like change. Everything comes too easily for you."

"I do like a challenge," he said. "Don't get enough of them."

Behind her, the flash was so bright, Maggie whipped around with a quick intake of breath, turning just in time to see a fiery red-orange spark electrify the entire sky, followed by a millisecond of incandescent light that bathed the blackness in a shock of white.

The Catatumbo lightning.

"There's no thunder," Dan said, wrapping his arms around her waist, her back to his chest so they could watch together. "And that's a blessing, because if a boat comes anywhere near us, even rowed, I need to hear it."

In seconds, it happened again, more dramatic because the color was magenta, and the white light bounced between two clouds as if the gods were tossing it back and forth.

"I've never seen anything so majestic," she said.

"You probably think it's a sign."

She chuckled. "You know, I didn't even think of that. What I think is that if we have to be stuck in the middle of a lake, it can't get any better than this."

"Oh, it could get better." His lower half stirred, already well aroused. He slid his fingers under her T-shirt and touched the warm, sweat-dampened flesh of her belly. "Much better."

With a sweet sigh of consent, she tilted her head, offering him her neck. Her curls had long ago been tied up in her little palm-tree ponytail, and he trailed a few kisses along the tender flesh, enjoying how that made her stomach muscles clench and goose bumps flourish on her back.

He glided his hands upward, closer to her breasts. She turned her head to get to his mouth.

Meeting her lips, he flicked the front catch of her bra and captured her breasts in his palms. Her tiny, budded nipples made heat shoot straight down to where his erection pressed into her backside.

"I've always loved your breasts," he said, adoring them with his hands, circling and tweaking her nipples.

"You once told me they were small but mighty. I must have used that description a hundred times."

"Did you think of me when you did?"

"Yes." She arched, pressing more flesh into his hands and more pressure on his hard-on.

More lightning flashed in black cherry strobes, followed by jagged white slashes in the sky. Electricity crackled as she turned to face him, their tongues curling, fusing, fighting with the same spark that lit the sky.

"When you thought of me," he said, her ass in his hands as she straddled him and wrapped her legs around his hips, "was it ever anything good?"

She smiled wickedly. "Yes. It was."

Intrigued, his hands stilled. "Really? What?"

She toyed with the bottom of her T-shirt, whispering, "I'm hot." She pulled her top over her head, taking the bra with it, then leaning back to slay him with a full view her twin peaks, rosy and damp and just heavy enough to make him want to close his mouth over one, then the other.

"I used you right back."

For a moment, he wasn't sure what she meant. "You used me?"

"Later. For fantasies. For pleasure." She grazed her breasts with light fingertips, torturing him with the image.

His mouth went bone dry as he watched her twirl her nipple between her finger and thumb, her eyes shuttering momentarily.

"What did you think about?" His voice was barely a rasp.

"You. Us. What we did."

The clouds flared again, electric purple pulses that lasted for five or six suspended seconds, just long enough for Maggie to reach up and whip the elastic out of her hair and shake her curls over her shoulders. She kneeled, her eyes sparking like the lightning, her body lithe and damp and perfect, her fingers already at work undressing herself.

As fast as the last flash of lightning, she went to the back of the hut, picking up the hammock canvas.

He just watched her move, mesmerized, still half in shock that she had fantasies about him, half in lust over the sexiness of her naked body. She spread the canvas on the floor and kneeled on it. "Come here."

He did, kneeling right in front of her. "What do you fantasize about, Maggie?" He reached to kiss her, but she ducked away from his touch.

"Something I've only ever done with you." She tugged the tie of his camo pants, pushing them down to reveal his erection. She dragged the pants over his thighs, then pushed him to stand up. He did, taking a quick scan of the water and horizon from every direction. A blinding yellow bolt careened across the sky and water as she closed her mouth over him.

His back arched at the first sensation of her tongue.

She gave him a quick look upward, her dark eyes wide as she released him from between her lips. "This is how I come. Every time."

She dropped her head and bent over him. How *she* came?

He braced for the impact of her mouth again, but she didn't take him. Instead, she blew a cool breath over his hot skin, eliciting a drop of creamy liquid on the head. He could only see her thick waves, her profile from above, dark lashes brushing over her flushed cheeks, her tongue flicking out to take a sweet lick of his flesh. Then she cupped his sac with one hand and used her finger to stroke the smooth skin between. He hissed in a breath, groaned it out.

"You love that," she said, knowing.

"Yeah." Enough to die if she stopped.

She quickened her touch, slamming more blood into his cock. *This* was her fantasy? The way she pleasured herself? Then she swiped her tongue over the head, and every remaining drop of blood in his body coursed to the fiery spot where she licked him.

She pressed a kiss on his shaft, then fluttered her tongue and lips down the sensitive vein that she'd long ago discovered.

He gripped her shoulders and held on for the ride of insane, indescribable pleasure as she feathered kisses and licks along the length of him. "Maggie."

She lifted her head and looked up at him. His fingers knotted into her hair. "This can't be your fantasy, baby."

She smiled. "We're just starting. It gets better."

She closed her mouth over him, sliding her palm down his shaft while the head sank deeper into her velvet-soft mouth, her teeth scraping just lightly enough to make him drop his head back, eyes closed, balls tight, willpower gone.

She sucked lightly, then a little harder, faster, bringing him right to the edge of control. Then she stopped.

He let out a groan of disappointment, but she took his hands and pulled him down to the floor with her. "You know what happens next in my fantasy?"

He kissed her, tasting his salt, licking it off her tongue and giving it back. "Yes."

Reaching for her, he kissed her as he laid them down on the scratchy cloth, the colors of the sky changing in a frenzy of red and orange and pure white flashes all around them.

"How often did you think about this and touch yourself?" he asked, stroking her cheek.

"A lot."

He was glad he hadn't completely robbed her of happiness all those years ago. "So you didn't always hate me."

"I didn't hate this memory. Now stop talking, and make it real for me."

He kissed his way down her body at a leisurely rate, despite the ache in his balls that made him want to get there faster. He took his time suckling her breasts, licking the concave of her stomach. Finally, he spread her thighs gently and placed his very first kiss on the wet, warm center of her womanhood.

She melted under him, letting out a soft moan of pure pleasure, spreading her legs and lifting herself into him. He swirled his tongue, sliding up and down the slit, his mouth covering her mound, his hands closed over her tensed thighs.

She urged him on with her fingers on his shoulders, responding to every sensation but definitely wanting more.

He turned head to foot so his body was opposite her, sliding one of her thighs over his cheek, positioning himself so that she could reach his shaft.

She opened her mouth and drew him in, so deeply that he had to stop tonguing her, to let the wave of insane pleasure roll over him.

Under his lips, her clitoris thrummed. Blood raced through his veins as fast as the nonstop lightning, molten and furious, his senses torn between the savage pleasure erupting in his body and the delicious taste and feel of her in his mouth.

This was her fantasy. *He* was her fantasy. All those years, all those nights she was alone.

For a second he stopped, breathing hard against her womanhood, helpless, lost, close to the brink. He thought of her many, many times, too, but no fantasy was as good as this.

She sucked harder, her fists wrapped around the base, squeezing, pulling, stealing his orgasm.

He slammed his mouth back on her, annihilating her with his tongue over and over, until she bucked against him and he shot into her mouth with mind-numbing intensity.

Their bodies shuddered and her heart galloped so hard he could practically feel the blood rush through her whole body. Slowly, she pulled her mouth off of him.

"I have to kiss you." he said, already turning to get face-to-face. He did, the juice of his ejaculation mixed with the remnants of her moisture on his tongue. He glided his hands over her body, dying to touch how he wanted, where he wanted—and he wanted it all.

And finally, as if the gods had been holding back the cooling rain just for them, there was thunder. A low, distant rumble that vibrated the floor.

Except that wasn't thunder.

It was a motorboat.

Chapter
TWENTY

THE TRICK, QUINN decided as he threw back his comforter, would be keeping Goose quiet. He had to get into that office, and as far as he knew, they didn't lock the door. The Ropers slept upstairs, so if he could leave Goose for ten minutes, he ought to be okay.

As Quinn stood, Goose looked up from his corner of the bed with doglike interest.

"No biggie, boy. Just gotta pee. You chillax."

Goose didn't chillax, but he didn't jump off the bed, either. Quinn went into the bathroom, peeing as loudly as he could so that Goose believed him. Then he turned on the water faucet and left it on. Goose had no concept of time. If the water ran for fifteen minutes, he'd just think Quinn was still washing his hands.

He peeked through the doorway at the dog, a dark shadow on the light blankets. Back to sleep. Good boy.

He made it out the door and down the hall without hearing a bark. He knew his way around this place pretty good by now. It was honkin' huge, but he'd chased the kid around so many times, he'd memorized every corner. In fact, it was playing hide-and-seek with Peyton today that let him hear what Mr. Roper had said to that tall lady he worked for.

Not every word, since he was across the hall. But enough that he could figure out they were talking about his mom. And enough to make him curious as hell. Had his mom really been in a drug ring? The girlfriend of a drug dealer? And pregnant when she ran away?

That would mean . . .

But she'd never lie to him like that. *Never*. He had to find out.

When Peyton had found him and screamed happily, the conversation had gone silent. With Peyton in tow, he'd glanced into the office where they'd been talking, and Mr. Roper was holding a file. With the ease of a Tom Clancy spy from that new Splinter Cell game, Quinn had cruised right on in, made small talk, and caught the name on the file. *Varcek*. His middle name.

So that alone gave him the right to spy.

The office was wide open now. He marched right over to the desk, where four or five manila folders stood in a metal-pronged holder. *Varcek* was the third one.

He grabbed it and hustled back to his room, locking the door with shaking hands. Goose started to bark but Quinn hushed him, jumping on the bed to flip open the file and read.

With every word, he couldn't fight the lump of fury and hurt in his throat.

Every single thing she'd ever told him had been a lie. She was a runaway, some guy named Ramon Jimenez's girlfriend. Which meant that guy was his . . .

He threw the file down, the papers scattering. Goose instantly perked up.

"Dude, we've been totally fucked." Quinn looked at the papers and swallowed hard. "Why not just tell me?" he asked the dog, who laid his head on Quinn's leg. "She was never going to tell me. Never. And what about Dad? Did he know? Did she lie to him, too? Even when he was dying?"

That was the kicker. He angrily grabbed a T-shirt, stuck his feet in Adidas flip-flops, and dropped his cell phone into the pocket of his sleep pants. He had forty dollars and his passport, which for some reason his mom had left in his backpack last night.

He was outta here.

Rage made him shake, tears spilling now out of his eyes. Every foul word he knew buzzed through his head as he took a few things from his drawer and threw them in his backpack.

He could get out of here without making a sound. He'd watched Mr. and Mrs. Roper work the alarm system, and he'd memorized the code they'd made no effort to hide.

He'd just run.

On foot? That was crazy. He'd never get past that guard at the island gate. But if he was in a car . . .

Goose followed him into the kitchen, where, right next to the alarm pad, the Ropers kept all of the car keys in a little cubby. Since they were so flipping rich, Quinn had his pick among four.

Well, shit. If you're gonna go, go balls to the wall.

He hit the alarm and opened the door that led to the garage. He opened the Ferrari door with quivering hands, then let Goose climb over the console like he was jumping into his mom's truck, instead of a six-bazillion-dollar Testarossa. He adjusted the driver's seat, to where he'd had it when Mr. Roper let him drive, turned on the ignition, and cracked his neck like he'd seen race car drivers do.

They'd get him, of course. Probably before he hit the causeway. Maybe he'd be pulled over. Then he'd get a record—just like his lying mother.

The garage door went up and he stepped on the gas, eased up on the clutch, and shot forward.

"Shit!" He got the car under control, cruised down the driveway, waited until the huge iron gates opened, then gunned it down the one road that led to the main gate. He checked his rearview mirror. Nothing yet, but something told him Roper would be up and out in ten seconds flat.

He didn't look at the guard or slow down too much, leaving the private island. The gate opened for him and he gave the gas pedal a push, rounding a little circle, crossing another bridge, then turning right on the big Tuttle Causeway that passed the cruise ships.

All was still clear in the rear. Unbeliev—

Panic curled through him at the sight of a blue light flashing behind him. What should he do? Pull over? Drive faster? He swerved as fear shot through him, then hit the brakes. He was *so* grounded for the rest of his life.

He pulled the car over to the side of the bridge. But that wasn't a cop car. Man, he was pulled over by an unmarked. The guy getting out of the driver's seat wasn't even in uniform.

But, oh *fuck,* he had a gun out.

Hands shaking, Quinn managed to get the window down, wishing like hell that Mr. Roper would suddenly come blazing out of Star Island to stop this.

"Yes, officer?" Should he call a plainclothes that?

"Quinn Smith?"

Holy crap! The guy knew his name? Maybe Mr. Roper called the police the minute he heard the garage door. That had to be it. He relaxed a little and nodded.

"Yes, sir."

"Out of the car." He lifted the gun and Quinn almost choked. Goose barked, but Quinn gave him a signal to quiet.

Why the gun?

"What about my dog?"

"We'll take care of your dog. Bring your bag so we can inspect it."

He grabbed the backpack, then opened the door, his legs shaking almost too much to stand. But he managed, holding his hands up like it was a freaking movie.

"Walk back to my vehicle, son."

He did and Goose went crazy, barking as Quinn scanned the bridge for one of Mr. Roper's cars, peering down to the Star Island entrance, praying to see lights. He was so, so sorry he'd done this.

The man opened the back door and Quinn blinked in surprise. There was another man back there. He turned to look at the cop, but he got shoved so hard it took his breath away as he stumbled into the back.

Not again! He wanted to scream, but shut his mouth when the man in the back pointed another black pistol in his face. "Hello, Quinn."

"Who are you?"

The man just smiled as the driver gunned into traffic, throwing Quinn against the seat.

"What do you want with me?" He didn't even care that his voice cracked like a baby's.

"Let me see your bag."

Quinn shoved it at him and the man ripped at the

zippers, digging through his clothes. "All ready for a trip, young man? In your Ferrari?" He laughed, low and ugly. "Oh, look at this." He pulled out the passport and flipped it open. "Excellent. Anything else of value?"

"Forty bucks. You can have it if you let me go."

He just snorted and dug some more, shoving beefy hands in the side pockets and jabbing all around.

"What are you looking for?"

"This." He pulled out a tiny slip of paper. The little piece of paper that his mom said had sentimental value and she wanted it to stay with Quinn. Because he was supposed to be safe at the Roper's house. He cursed himself and his stupid ideas.

"Better put your seat belt on, young man."

He didn't move. "Where are we going?"

"Away."

Out the back window, the blue and white flashes of Miami police cruisers lit up the night, just as a giant black Escalade—one of the Roper's cars—tore out of Star Island and headed in their direction. But all of those cars screeched to a halt around the Testarossa he'd abandoned on the side of the road.

At least they'd get Goose home.

The car he was in blended into traffic and disappeared from their sight.

"They're circling us." Dan stood hidden in a corner where two windows met, his weapon aimed at the boat half a mile away.

Maggie had dressed for escape and crouched on the floor where he stood.

"So it's not our pilots," Maggie said, hope dwindling in her voice.

"No."

"And it's not Javi?"

Dan inched out after a lightning flash, using the momentary whiteness to get a look. "Not our boy come to end the honeymoon."

"What size is it? Could it be someone night fishing?"

"There are two men in a single outboard about twice the size of Javi's." He stole another look, squinting into blackness. "And the only thing they're trying to catch is us."

A small noise caught in her throat and he lowered himself beneath the sill, closer to her. "But they won't."

A burst of reddish light from the sky illuminated the terror in her eyes.

"I swear they won't, Maggie. I'll kill them from up here. I have plenty of ammo, I'm a great shot, and I don't care who the hell they are. They're dead—I'm just waiting to take my shots. And then"—he pulled her closer and kissed her—"we have transportation, because we'll take their boat."

The motor revved and he stood again. They were moving in, but not close enough to risk a shot.

"How can you shoot in the dark? As I recall, you don't have the best night vision."

He just smiled. "So I have a flaw."

"Right now, it's a doozy."

"We've got light. It's just intermittent." And it was slowing down. His memory was that the Catatumbo lightning peaked after about two hours, then waned for a half hour until the rain began. They were nearing the end of that half hour.

These clowns had been circling for almost a whole hour, no doubt waiting for the cover of darkness and a downpour before they attacked. Which worried him.

Another bolt of lightning sparked, much weaker now, and shorter. All he got was silhouettes, and no chance of getting off a shot.

"We must have something they want," she said. "And if it would save our lives to give it to them, why don't we? We don't have to be Rambo and just kill them."

"The only thing anyone wants is the location of the money. That's why I think they trapped us here, even though I'm sure it's not here." His mind whirred with possibilities until he hit on one, hard. "Think about this, Maggie. If we've come to this very place, it means we have all four fortunes. We think we know all of the coordinates. But what if one of them is wrong? If someone knows three of them, and they make it not too hard for us to get them—like Ramon and even Lola did—then when we arrive at our destination—what do they have?"

"A fourth coordinate by process of elimination," she said.

"Exactly. What better way to find out the fourth than to give us a fake one? Now they have all four, and—"

"All they have to do is kill us, put our bodies in the bottom of Lake Maracaibo, using the coordinates to the real location to get the money." Her eyes widened. "You can't let them do that."

"I don't intend to."

All of a sudden, the motor screamed, the sound intensifying each second.

Dan jumped to his feet to get into position. "Just stay flat on the floor and close to the wall, Maggie. And keep that duffel bag on your shoulder in case we have to run." Or jump.

The boat was flying straight at the stilt house, full power, and a flicker of lightning revealed that one man was steering a rudder in the back and another was standing on the bow, ready to throw something.

Son of a bitch, they were going to blow the place up.

Dan reached down and put a hand on her shoulder. "Listen to me. I'm going to fire out this window, but I may not hit him. While I'm shooting, you get down on the dock as fast as possible, and if you have to, jump in the water. Hide in the water. He'll go for the house, not the dock. You're safer there."

"How? Why can't I stay up here with you?"

He swallowed. "I think they have a grenade."

"Oh, shit."

"No kidding. I'm going to shoot until I kill the bastards, hopefully before they let the bomb fly. Do as I say, Maggie." He eyed the boat again. *Come on, get closer.*

"What if you blow up?"

"Take the boat to San Carlos, then fly home."

"Dan!"

"Go!" He pulled her up, a little rough. They had seconds, less. "Go now, Maggie!" He gave her a solid push toward the opening, then catapulted to the window and started shooting.

Nature blessed him with one more bolt of illumination, just long enough for him to see an arm flail and a fist-size pellet fly through the air. Maybe he'd forced an early throw. Maybe he had time.

The grenade sailed through a hole in the bamboo, landing on the floor. Dan dove onto it, then twisted and blindly flung it back outside with all his strength.

An explosion rocked the hut like an earthquake, trembling the shaky stilts and sending a massive spray of water everywhere.

"You got them!" Maggie yelled.

He launched to the window just as a bonfire of flames mushroomed from the boat, and splinters of wood showered a twenty-foot diameter around the explosion. As it died down, he scanned the water, looking for any sign of life.

Maggie climbed back up the ladder and stood in the opening to the hut. "Nothing survived that."

Dan blew out a breath. "Including the boat."

CHAPTER
TWENTY-ONE

MAX'S FISTED HANDS were the only sign of how much anguish he was in. But Lucy knew him so well, she could feel the waves of self-loathing and anger pouring off him as he paced the office, stabbing his cell phone over and over again.

It had been almost seven hours since Quinn had disappeared. Seven critical, interminable hours during which they couldn't reach Dan and Maggie to tell them that Quinn was missing.

"Where the hell is he?" Max paced the office he'd already crossed a hundred times, checking his phone yet again as if he could have missed a call from Dan, or the pilots who had launched the helicopter search ordered by Lucy.

It had taken far too much time for them to get a chopper.

Lucy sat on the sofa, her own misery just as deep and just as contained. BlackBerry in hand, she texted Sage, who ran the Bullet Catchers' Research and Investigation Division—until next month, when she and Johnny Christiano would be getting married and moving to Italy to run her European operations.

And she texted Jack, who made her smile with every word he wrote. Even with their history, Jack was concerned about Dan, and the upsetting news he faced when they found him.

Her text to Jack was interrupted by a call; the FBI, North Miami Beach. Her friend Thomas Vincenze already had launched a region-wide search for Quinn. She signed off with Jack and took the call, giving Max a hopeful look.

"Tell me you have news, Tom."

"Not on the kidnapping, Lucy. Every possible route out of Miami is being searched and we're widening the child-abduction rapid deployment team, working with Miami-Dade police on a minute by minute basis. But that's not why I called. The evidence Dan Gallagher wanted has been returned to the files."

The fortune? "Can you deliver it to me?"

"I can," he said, without hesitation. "But in the meantime let me read it to you, because it does not coincide with the notes he copied."

Meaning they were at the wrong place in Venezuela. And they were out of touch . . . or worse.

"Go ahead." She wrote down the words and numbers and double-checked them, then held the paper out to Max. "Run it through the GPS and see what this does to a location if these are the latitude minutes and seconds," she said softly. Then, to Thomas, "Who returned them?"

"I don't know," he said, unhappiness clear in his voice. "The evidence clerk left me a note that they'd been returned, and now she's under investigation for a lax security system."

"Looks like you have your work cut out for you, Tom," she said.

"Don't I know it. I'll call you within the hour when we get the next update."

"Thank you, and please, send the fortune over. I want to assure Dan we have the correct information."

"As soon as I can get a courier," he promised, signing off.

Max was already on the computer, frowning at the results, tapping keys in frustration. "Damn it," he grunted, looking up when Cori came in with fresh coffee for them. His whole demeanor relaxed at the sight of her.

"No word from him?" she asked, sinking onto the armrest to stroke his back.

"Not yet." he said tersely, focused on the screen again.

"Max." Just the word pulled his attention back to her. "It's not your fault a thirteen-year-old pulled a stupid stunt in the middle of the night and got himself kidnapped, when he knew he was in a safe house for that very reason."

Max glanced at the file they'd found in Quinn's room. "I shouldn't have left that out."

"He was close enough to figuring it out. I figured it out with one good look at the boy."

"He wasn't looking for it. Neither was Maggie when Dan showed up, so it's no wonder Quinn didn't see it." Max shook his head. "Cori, can you imagine how Dan's going to feel? Just put yourself in his shoes. In Maggie's."

"I can't even look at Peyton right now without crying," she said softly.

He gave her hand a squeeze and went back to the computer as Lucy came to see the results of the new coordinates. As she did, her BlackBerry buzzed again, this time with the name she wanted to see most.

"It's Dan," she announced, putting the phone on speaker. "Thank God," she said loudly, the thumping blades of a helo almost drowning out her voice. They had him. "Where are you?"

"We just got picked up at the stilt house. No satellite for hours."

"I know," she said, her heart sinking as she braced to tell him the news. "And I bet it was a false lead."

"A lead and a trap."

She quickly told him about Thomas's call, knowing all this discussion was delaying the most important news of all—the news that would have them on that plane in San Carlos and straight back to Miami, no matter what the new coordinates showed them. Dan delayed it even further by giving them an account of what they encountered at the Lake Maracaibo location.

"I've got a new location, if these are real," Max said into the speaker. "The town of Las Marías, just outside Maracaibo."

"We'll fly up there as soon as we get to the plane in San Carlos. But it could be another goose chase. What makes you think these numbers are right, Lucy? Or that this Thomas guy is even legitimate?"

She knew Dan's voice so well. He was tired, tense, frustrated, and sick of dead ends. And it was only going to get worse.

She and Max shared a look, and there was enough silence that Dan must have picked it up.

"What's going on?" he demanded.

Max waited one second too long, so Lucy jumped in. "It's Quinn, Dan."

"He took off in the Ferrari," Max said.

"He *what?*"

"And he's missing."

Silence. Long, aching, silence that Lucy wanted to fill with explanations and promises and reassurances that the best abduction team in Miami was on the case.

"How long ago?" His voice was emotionless, as if he was trying not to let Maggie know yet.

"About eight hours," Max said.

"Eight *hours?*" Dan lost the flat voice. "What happened?"

Max filled him in, talking fast in case they lost the satellite link.

"We'll find him, Dan," Lucy insisted. "The FBI and the Miami-Dade police have blocked . . ." The sound of the helo blades disappeared and Lucy held Max's dark gaze. "I think we lost the connection."

"I think he hung up," Max said, with the weary knowledge of a lifelong friend.

Cori put her arms around Max's thick neck and rested her head on his shoulder, the comforting gesture making Lucy ache for Jack.

She crossed her arms and looked hard at Max, her mind working in high gear. "Someone sent him to the wrong place. Someone who knows what's going on with these fortunes. We have to figure it out on this end and assure they find the right location, and take down whoever is end-running them."

It was all she could do for her friend right now.

Something was very, very wrong. Maggie knew that before Dan disconnected the call, and there was a sickening swirl in her stomach.

As he put his mouth to her ear and delivered the worst

possible news, all she could do was stare at him, her teeth starting to chatter.

Missing.

Kidnapped.

She put her hand to her mouth to hold back a scream, though her throat was chocked tight.

"Don't worry. We're going straight back to Miami," he said.

She shook her head uncomprehendingly. "Why *wouldn't* we?"

He explained that the last fortune had inexplicably been returned to the FBI evidence file, and didn't match their coordinates. "But we're going home. We're going to find him."

She reeled. "It's been eight *hours.* He could be anywhere. He could be here, if Viejo wanted him badly enough."

"It wouldn't be easy to get him out of the country."

"But someone could," she insisted.

"Yes, someone could," he agreed. "Like a person who ran a cargo company. Or a con artist with connections in prison who can make false docs. Hell, the head of the Miami FBI could get a kid out on a private plane."

Maggie slid her hand into Dan's. "They're going to want a ransom," she said. "They probably want the fortune, so let's give them the *real* fortune. What if this latest coordinate is right? We could fly there right now on this helicopter and find that money."

"We could also go to San Carlos and be back in Miami in a few hours."

"We're so close, Dan," she insisted, gripping both hands now. "Getting this call right now, when we're in this helicopter . . . it means something.

"What if the money's right there? The money we need

to save Quinn." She pulled him closer, desperation making her determined to prove her point. "If we go back there, all we can do is give them our theories, what Ramon said and Lola did. That won't get Quinn back. But if we have that money in hand, they'll give us Quinn."

"We don't know that. Paying ransom is very, very risky."

"We don't have a choice. *Please.*" She squeezed his hands. "Let's go and see what we find. We're almost there. If we don't, we might regret it forever."

He regarded her long and hard. "I'll kill someone if anything happens to that boy."

"You can get in line behind me."

"I feel responsible," he said.

"Because he took a joyride in a sports car when he knew he was being protected? He'll feel my wrath when we find him." If they find him. She clung to the anger; so much better than giving into the fear.

"It wasn't a joyride." He spoke so softly, she barely heard him over the deafening roar of the engines and blades.

"What?"

"He was running away. In anger."

Her heart slipped a little. "Why?"

"He found a Bullet Catcher file on you. It had been amended to note that you were pregnant before you arrived in the Keys."

She just stared at him, then closed her eyes, her head throbbing with pain. And now, he was somewhere unknown, terrified, alone, betrayed. She knew just how he felt.

"Call her back," she said quietly. "Tell her we're flying to Maracaibo."

He did, and requested that a car be waiting when they reached the airstrip. Captain Simon would take the helicopter back to get the plane, and meet them here in a few hours. That's all Dan was allowing. A few hours to get to Las Marías, look at the location, and leave.

They disembarked the moment the chopper touched down, holding hands as they ran across cracked concrete to where a man stood waving to them, indicating a black pickup truck. Dan spoke to the man, gave him some cash, and then they took off.

Despite the predawn darkness, it was hotter than the worst August afternoon in the Keys, the air so thick with humidity she was damp before she closed the door.

"Work the GPS for us, Maggie," Dan instructed as he put his gun on the seat between them. "I'll need a free hand for my weapon."

"Is it dangerous here?"

"Maracaibo is a pit from the depths of hell," he said. "*Maracuchos,* the local marauding thugs, are some of the meanest humans to ever crawl out of it."

"Las Marías, too?"

"I've never been there, but my instinct tells me it isn't going to be Beverly Hills."

He gunned the truck out of the airstrip and they traveled through the winding streets, a maze of shanties, skyscrapers, and open areas where farmers were already setting up markets in the alleys between whitewashed apartment buildings. Maggie's gaze darted between the deserted streets and the GPS, a stress headache feeling like a nine-inch nail from temple to temple as she called out the directions. The neighborhoods grew seedier, the potholes got deeper, the night seemed to get darker instead of breaking into dawn.

Dan reached over and put his hand on her arm. "I don't know if this is the bravest thing I've ever done, or the stupidest."

"Brave and stupid go hand in hand when you have a child."

"So I'm learning."

"Turn left in half a mile. When you love someone, you just do what has to be done." Maybe he didn't know that, yet. Maybe he'd never loved anyone. Maybe not *everything* came so easily to him.

He glanced at her. "I totally underestimated you, Maggie. Then and now."

Her headache slid down to the vicinity of her heart. "You thought I was just a wild child. A runaway from my crazy home, taking up with druggies; then when you find me all those years later, I'm just a single mom working in a bar."

"I don't know what I thought," he admitted. "But you are one of the most beautiful women I've ever known, and one of the sexiest, and also one of the strongest."

"If we don't find our son, Dan, I won't be strong. My life will be over. So let's get that money. And let's get him back."

The way he exhaled said he didn't agree but was doing it for her. "I feel like we've been sent on a scavenger hunt in this country, and I'm not at all sure what we're going to find. But here we are; welcome to Las Marías."

Filthy, narrow streets barely big enough to fit one car, rows of tenements and warehouses. At the corner where they had to turn, four men stood on one side of the street, two of them taking swings at each other, one staggering drunk, another massively barrel-chested, and all openly armed. As the truck approached, they stopped and stared.

Maggie's heart pounded hard, and she didn't look to the side as they passed; Dan closed his fingers over his gun.

He turned left, out of sight, and she watched the side-view mirror for any sign of them.

"All right," she said, returning to the GPS. "We're basically there. It's on this block."

One side was a parking lot with nothing but Dumpsters, a gutted bus, and trash. On the other side were two warehouses divided by a narrow, garbage-strewn alley. The only opening to the buildings appeared to be in the alley.

"Bring your gun," Dan said.

As she reached in the bag for Smitty's gun, he turned around to park with the driver's side right at the entrance to the alley. "We'll leave it unlocked in case we have to run for it. Come out on my side."

She slid across the bench seat and climbed out, looking up and down the empty, silent street. Dan stood right behind her, guiding her toward the alley, one hand on her shoulder, the other holding his weapon. The gun she held added to the sense of surrealness, sneaking through a Venezuelan alley, armed, her son's life in the balance.

Trash rustled.

"Rats," he whispered when she startled.

Lovely. "Is that a way in?" She pointed to an undersize entrance to the building on their right halfway down the alley, partially opened. Dan inched it out with his foot, his gun raised as he looked in. "Nothing that I can see in there. Let's try the other building."

Almost at the very end of the alley, they spied a metal door with a simple padlock.

"If someone's hiding money in there, wouldn't they use a better lock?" Maggie said.

"That would draw attention to it," he replied, testing the lock.

"Can you pick it or shoot it?"

"Both, but picking will be quieter." He pulled out his tool, working on the lock for a few minutes before it opened with a quiet ping. He slipped a flashlight out of the bag and directed her behind him. "Let me check it out first."

More movement in the trash sent a shiver through her, but the rats on the ground were less terrifying than the ones they'd passed on the street. She glanced at the road where the truck was parked, but all seemed perfectly still.

"Whoa. Prepare to breathe through your mouth," Dan said. "Stinks."

She stepped over the threshold. The stench was overwhelming, like something had died in there. She covered her mouth and gagged.

"Look at these crates," Dan said, his undertone of excitement drawing her in. "They're exactly the same as those in the shed at Viejo's house. Exactly."

This time the shiver that ran down her spine wasn't fear, it was a thrill of anticipation. "Are you sure?"

"Yes." He set the flashlight on the floor so it spread an umbrella of light over the area at the far corner of the warehouse. The open area was lined with deep shelves for storage, most of them empty. But in one corner there were half a dozen or more shipping crates, all with reinforced wood corners and steel hinges.

As she got closer the stomach-turning smell got worse. But Dan was already at work on one of the crates, using a crowbar he found on a shelf to force the lid open.

He had to holster the gun to use both hands and he worked furiously. "This is a custom crate. Exactly what was in the shed. This came from Miami, I have no doubt."

He popped the top open and scooped up the flashlight to peer inside, swearing under his breath. "Looks like more damn tools." He reached in and pulled out a thick, industrial-strength wrench. "No drugs."

"We're not looking for drugs," she reminded him. "We're looking for laundered money."

"You're right." He turned the flashlight on the wrench, peering hard at it. He bit it, then examined it more closely. He pounded it on the crate, ran his finger along it, and finally looked at her in wonder. "You are so right, Maggie. We are looking for money—and I think that's exactly what we just found."

Every hair on the back of her neck stood up.

He held the wrench higher, the light casting an eerie shadow on his face. "It's *gold*. If I'd had more time in the shed, I would have figured it out. These aren't tools, they're melted gold refashioned into something that will slip through customs unnoticed. I worked on a similar case years ago, with gold being used to make lighting fixtures and mailboxes. This . . ." He held it up, victory in his eyes. "Is laundered money."

They'd *found* it! They had what they needed to get Quinn back, what his kidnapper wanted. "Now what? How do we get it out of here? Don't even *think* about some scheme to get this back to the government, or lure someone here with the coordinates. This . . ." She marched to another crate, pounding it to make her point. "Is Quinn's ransom."

The opened lid bounced under her hand, sending a wave of the foulest stench rolling out from the crate. "Oh my God," she said, backing away. "That smells . . . like . . . "

Nudging her to the side, Dan lifted the lid, then let out a grunt. "A dead body."

She staggered backward, bile rising up in her mouth so suddenly, she had to throw up. Holding it in, she ran to the door with a strangled, "I need air."

Before Dan could stop her she bolted into the alley, running around the back of the building to vomit. She gagged again afterward, then tried to catch her breath, her blood thumping in her ears.

A dead body.

The sound of footsteps in the alley pulled a shocked gasp from her. She froze, horrified, flat against the building as she listened.

Did Dan hear them coming?

The crack of a gunshot made her jump and slam her hand over her mouth to keep from giving herself away. Did she dare stick her head around the corner to see if Dan had escaped? He wouldn't know where she went; he'd run to the car if he escaped. Should she scream or run or—

Another deafening explosion of gunfire, two shots fired back to back. She stared at the alley, paralyzed. Then a shadow moved, a foot scuffed. Someone was right around the corner, about to find her. About to kill her. She lifted her gun, ready to fire.

Another scuff, inches away. She took a breath, clenched her jaw, and prepared to kill to stay alive.

Someone came around the corner, and she stared in horror at the familiar eyes that were wide in terror, a gun pointed directly at his temple.

"Just do what he says, Mom. Drop the gun, or he's gonna kill me."

CHAPTER
TWENTY-TWO

TWO MEN STOOD over the open crate ten feet away from where Dan lay, swearing in Spanish as they pulled nails, then a wrench from the crate. He knew enough of the language to know that they'd been duped, expecting money for the shot they'd just taken.

They might not like what they'd found, but one of those tools had just saved his life. The metal was warm against the skin of his belly where he'd shoved it when he heard the footsteps, where it had deflected a bullet aimed at his gut.

But he didn't dare move. They thought they'd killed him, and were too pissed or distracted to notice there was no blood coming from the hole in his shirt. At least they didn't know about Maggie.

"No lo siga." Don't follow him. *"El es un asshole."*

Who was an asshole?

Was someone else out there? With Maggie? Moving just his eyes, he managed to locate his weapon about a foot away.

"Mierda!" One lifted the lid of the body crate and

waved the stench away. *"Maracucho cabrón."* He dropped the lid with a soft thud and spoke in rapid, hushed tones to the other one, and Dan was only able to decipher bits of what they said.

They were going to take the tools anyway, even though they wanted money. Let the guy go to the country? Is that what they said? Take . . . her or him to the plantation? The *plantation*.

He wasn't sure, but these two weren't alone—someone could be out there with Maggie.

Dan lunged for the gun. One of them whipped around, reaching for a weapon, but not fast enough. Dan fired right at his face, then again at the stomach, taking him down as the other fumbled to find the gun that he'd put down.

It gave Dan just enough time to roll up and charge forward, shooting him in the leg. He scooped up his duffel and ran into the alley. The truck was still there; no sign of Maggie.

He turned in the opposite direction, to the street that ran behind the back. It was empty, but for more trash and her little .22. He swore, bending to pick it up. Next to it lay three silver bracelets.

Three means . . . *follow me.*

To the plantation?

He bolted for the car, leaving bodies and an injured man and damn near a hundred million in gold behind. Nothing mattered but Maggie, and getting to Viejo's plantation.

If only he knew where the hell it was.

Maggie closed her fingers over the torn vinyl seat in the back of the van. The vehicle careened down city streets at a dangerous speed, and in an even more dangerous direction. West, to the mountains, to Monte Verde. To El Viejo, who knew her every secret now, and would exact his revenge on her.

And on Quinn.

They couldn't see each other, sitting back to back on the floor of a gutted out, windowless van. Their hands bound together, Maggie could feel her son's body trembling in fear, and the occasional sniff told her he was losing the battle not to cry.

During the few moments when she didn't use every brain cell to pray for her life and Quinn's, she stole glimpses of her captor.

How could they have overlooked him? He'd been with El Viejo right from the start. Before Maggie arrived, and before Dan. And after it was all over, he was still there, safe in one of his many disguises. Including the most powerful one: FBI agent.

Had Dan ever questioned Joel Sancere's role from the day he got "sick" and stayed with El Viejo to this week when he scoffed at the rule-bending and offered his unsolicited advice about who she should trust? Not really.

He faced them, leaning against the back doors, his threatening stare and gun trained on them, his heavy shoulders square and unyielding.

She took a breath, working up her nerve. "Why are you—"

He lifted the gun, silencing her.

"Mom. Don't," Quinn insisted, his voice husky from crying. "The guy's a jerk. Just don't."

The sound of Quinn's voice squeezed her heart. It was the first thing he'd said since they were taken at gunpoint into the waiting van.

"Are you okay, honey?" she asked.

Their captor frowned, but didn't move his weapon.

"I'm scared," he admitted softly. "And I'm really sorry."

"Don't be scared," she said, the words sounding hollow as the van took another terrifying turn at sixty miles an hour.

She could only imagine what had happened back in the warehouse. Was Dan lying there dead? Her whole body ached at the thought.

Maybe he'd escaped. Maybe he'd found her bracelets. Maybe he'd understand the clue.

But how would he know where to go?

It was hopeless. Viejo would never let her live. And Lola had faxed that birth certificate to him, so he knew the truth about Quinn. He'd never let him live, either.

Through the screen of thick wiring that separated them from the driver, she could see mountains. They were leaving the city.

"You shouldn't have meddled in my case."

Maggie looked at Joel, surprised. "*This* is how you handle a case? Abducting kids and witnesses? Shooting a former agent?"

"What I meant to say was that Dan shouldn't have meddled in the case."

She bit her lower lip and turned away.

"I had it completely under control."

"Yeah, I see that," she said under her breath.

"I've been working Viejo for years," he said, leaning forward. "Shipment by shipment, box by box, I've been getting the money back to where it belongs. The government."

She gave him an incredulous look. "I was in that warehouse. I saw the tools made of gold. None of that is being shipped to the federal government."

"You're wrong, my dear. I'm merely the conduit, taking Viejo's unlaundered cash and getting it into a safe place where it will be turned over to the U.S. Government. When I have it all, which should be very soon, I'll be a hero."

She dropped her gaze to the gun. "Hardly."

"It's all part of undercover work. Sometimes you have to use some of the bystanders. You understand that, Maggie. You were a bystander once."

And you were used. "So the FBI knows you're here?" Was that possible?

"Nobody knows any of us are here. The decision to finish this job when Viejo got out of prison was all mine. I'd built a relationship of trust with him back in the nineties, and it wasn't hard to do it again. He thinks I'm a rogue agent, but I'm just doing what your buddy Dan would do: bending the rules to get things done."

"Then let us go," she said. "Finish your job. Take the damn gold and hand it over. Why are you taking me to him?"

"He wants you and I told him I could deliver. He has to believe I'm working with him, getting that cash melted into tools, returning it to him. And I have, little by little. Once I figured out where he was stashing it, I could get it all back and give it to the government."

"And be a hero."

He shrugged. "I had to try something different this time. It works for other people. It worked for Dan. It wasn't exactly ethical to screw a teenage girl to get information."

She glared at him, noticing the mole under his jaw, and

remembering Lola's description of her attacker. "And what about cutting Lola? What do you call that?"

"I had to get that fortune."

"And Brandy? Down in the Keys?"

"Blame Ramon."

"Dan trusted you," she said. "He never doubted you."

Another shrug. "Of course not. I'm one of the good guys. I hate to break it to you, but I can't stand your buddy Dan. Anything that made his life suck made mine better."

Made—past tense. "What happened in that warehouse?"

He gave her a nasty grin. "Old Irish eyes ain't smiling anymore. But to be fair, you shouldn't have killed my guys in the boat. They were just local fighters trying to make a little extra cash."

Maggie's throat closed too tight to respond.

"But you did your job, Mrs. Smith," he said. "You got me the final coordinates by playing right into my hand. I thank you, and the government should thank you. But I don't know if Viejo will let you live long enough to be rewarded."

"You wrote the wrong numbers in the FBI case notes, didn't you?"

"Hey, Dan was the one who believed what he saw. Who can stop him and his Bullet Catcher machine when they get on a roll, huh?" His voice with rich with ridicule, and envy.

"How did you know I still had one of the fortunes?"

"Because I study people, Maggie. I knew you were superstitious. And I knew you were pregnant. Remember? Juan cleaned out the trash at the house, and you took at least four pregnancy tests and did a lousy job hiding the evidence. And of course I've had my eye on you and Quinn for years."

Her stomach lurched. "You have?"

"You think I'd let an important contact disappear? A key to solving an open case?" He snorted. "I knew when you got married. I knew when you took fishing vacations, and bought boats, and every time your husband refinanced his bar. I like what you've done with it, by the way. I think you and your new partner could probably dig yourself out of debt one day."

He'd been *in* there?

He read her look. "Who do you think's been supplying Viejo with pictures of his grandson all these years? He has a weakness, and I had to exploit it. Unfortunately, that bitch Lola had to wreck it by sending him the birth certificate."

She just stared at him, wondering how many times she'd come face-to-face with this man, served him drinks, nodded at him in a grocery store line . . . and never knew who he was.

The van turned sharply and started up a steep hill.

"Monte Verde: a beautiful plantation in the mountains of Venezuela, where your son can meet the man who's not his grandfather. He'll be pissed because I promised him all three of you, but I couldn't resist the pleasure of putting a bullet in that son of a bitch's heart."

Sancere's gaze slid to Quinn, who leaned hard against her back. "He's not a kind man, son. Brace yourself. He'll probably start by cutting your balls off and making you eat them."

"Stop it!" Maggie tried to jump up, but the gun in her face stopped the attempt.

"Shut up!" His voice turned harsh. "For all his tough

talk, your little boy is such a baby, crying. Guess he didn't get his Daddy's nerves of steel, huh? Too bad. He's about to need them."

She felt Quinn shudder and ached to hold him. But all she could do was squeeze her hands against his and try to give him strength while he sobbed.

CHAPTER
TWENTY-THREE

DAN KEPT THE accelerator to the floor and tore the shit out of the little truck, bouncing over potholes the size of small craters while he demanded that Lucy's assistant suck the Bullet Catcher database dry until she found the location of Monte Verde. They had a general idea but Avery hadn't yet given him the exact coordinates, and he had to make a choice in westbound roads.

He picked the one with the church on the corner— Santa María de la Magdalena, which he took as a direct message from Maggie's grandmother.

His cell phone rang with a digital beep of hope, and he grabbed it and hit Talk. But it wasn't Avery Cole calling from the Bullet Catcher headquarters; it was Lucy calling from Miami.

"Tell me you have news about Quinn," he said.

"No. But I'm at the FBI offices in North Miami, and we might be able to help you."

"Did Avery tell you where I'm going?"

"Viejo's plantation. Is that where the money is? Not the Las Marías location that you were sent?"

"That's where Maggie is." He hoped. "I lost her. I found the money and lost her." He clenched the steering wheel to keep from pounding it in frustration.

"Special Agent in Charge Tom Vincenze is with me."

Dan's gut tightened even more. Something smelled at that office, and it started stinking right about the time this guy started, friend of Lucy's or not. "I'll confirm the location of the money, or most of it," he said calmly. "If someone there will tell me the precise coordinates of Monte Verde in Venezuela."

"We can do that," the man said.

"And find my son. Now."

"We're working on it, Dan."

"I need satellite images of the plantation. I need to figure out a way in there without being seen. I need to blindside them, and fast, before anything happens to Maggie."

"I might be able to help you." A woman's voice joined the conversation. "I spent summers there when I was young."

Lola? "What are you doing there?"

"Ms. James is working out a deal with the FBI," Lucy said. "Apparently she has a few insurance claims that are under question, but Mr. Vincenze is willing to overlook them if she can help."

When Lucy pulled strings, it could be a damn beautiful thing.

"We have the location," Vincenze said. "Here are the coordinates."

"They better be fucking right," Dan muttered. He punched them into his GPS as Vincenze read them, splitting his gaze between the winding mountain road and the image that popped up on the screen.

Yes. Santa María Magdalena had sent him on the right road.

"How'd the fortune get put back in the ev files, Mr. Vincenze?" he asked pointedly.

"We're investigating," Vincenze said. "Only three people had access to those files. The evidence clerk, the agent of record, and me."

"Who's the agent of record? Joel Sancere?"

"Joel!" Lola exclaimed. "That was the guy who attacked me. I couldn't remember it, but that was the name he used the night I met him in South Beach."

Sancere?

Was it possible? That stickler for truth, justice, and the American way?

"Where is he?" Dan demanded. "Get him in on the line."

He heard Vincenze deliver an order, while Dan's wheels ate up the butchered asphalt below him.

"I can see where you're going with this, Dan," Lucy said.

"Except that the guy never broke a rule, let alone a law. But after what I saw in that warehouse, it makes sense."

"How's that?" Vincenze asked.

"Who better to know exactly how to transport cash to New York, exchange it for gold, then find a few unsavory jewelers who would refashion it into tools that could be legally shipped by the U.S. Post Office? I worked on a case exactly like that . . . with Sancere."

"That's very interesting," Lucy said. "Because we traced the packing slip you found at the house, and it originated in the diamond district of New York."

"He's off duty and not answering his cell," Vincenze reported. "We'll get him, though."

Would *he* have kidnapped Quinn? Why? As a favor . . . to . . . Viejo?

Dan flattened the accelerator and wished like hell he had a real car.

And then something dawned on him. Why else would Maggie leave without a fight? *Quinn.*

He blew around a slow-moving truck, glancing at the GPS. Still miles away. When he looked up, a bus was headed right at him. He threw the car back into the right lane, getting a loud, furious honk in response.

"Be careful, Dan," Lucy said quietly.

"*Screw* careful. Everything that ever mattered to me is about to be delivered into the hands of a brutal murderer bent on revenge. Everything that ever mattered," he repeated softly, the words stunning him with their truth.

"I know exactly how you feel." Lucy whispered. "And my child is going to need an older cousin to look up to."

And he'd have one, Dan swore silently.

"There's only one drive up the hill to the house," Lola said. "You can't get there without being seen coming in."

"There has to be another way."

"There is," Lola replied. "But you'll have to make it on foot, and it's complicated."

"Spill."

"I found her in a warehouse in Las Marías."

At Joel Sancere's words, Alonso Jimenez's dark eyebrows lifted. "You did? Did you find anything else there?"

"Gallagher. He's dead now."

Maggie stayed very still, unbound now, but standing with her hands behind her as they'd been told, Quinn next to her in the same position.

Viejo's eyes narrowed at Joel. "Did you find anything else?" he demanded.

"No sir."

He found gold, but didn't say that, Maggie thought. Which meant Joel might not have been lying to her about why he was doing this.

Viejo's lip curled and he returned his focus to Maggie. "I speak English. Did you know that?"

She shook her head, expecting his wrath but getting barely a glimmer of the fire that used to burn in his eyes. His olive skin had turned sallow, his once haughty cheeks had sunk, his robust chest was now bony.

But he still carried a gun on one hip and a sharp, serrated dagger on the other. He was still capable of murder, especially here in an isolated house on top of a mountain, when no one knew where they were.

And no one ever would. Sancere would cover his tracks from within. Dan's death and hers would be chalked up to *maracuchos* on the dangerous streets. Her son would be just another unsolved abduction story.

Hate burned through her. She couldn't just stand here and let Quinn die. She had to do something. She had to fight.

But Viejo never looked away from her. Not once did he even glance at Quinn. For some reason, that scared her even more.

Sancere was still with them, but the driver had stayed behind, climbing out of the van and hoisting himself on top with a rifle. As if anyone was coming to save her.

She automatically reached for the bracelets she touched during any crisis in her life, but her wrist was empty. The bracelets her grandmother had given her lay on the ground in Las Marías. And so did Dan.

"I know lots of words in English." Viejo continued, his voice thinner and weaker than it used to be. "Words like . . . whore." He curled his lip at Maggie. "Your mother is a whore. Did you know that, young man?" He still didn't look at him; just at Maggie.

She felt Quinn's body tense.

"Don't listen, honey. Don't give him any power. Don't let him make you mad."

"I know the word *fuck*." Viejo spat it out. "Do you know that word, boy?" He still faced Maggie. "Your mother knows that word."

"Stop it!" she hissed. "He's a child."

"Oh, yes." Viejo nodded. "But not a child of my family."

"Should he be punished for that?" she challenged.

"Mom." Quinn gave her a harsh look. "Don't. Just don't."

Viejo slowly drew the dagger from its sheath. He always carried that black-and-pearl-handled knife. How many men had it killed?

She glanced at Quinn, who stared at the knife in horror.

"He should not be punished for that," Viejo said, with an uncharacteristic quiver in his voice. "But *you* should be punished. You little fucking whore, who gave away secrets for sex and ruined my life."

Now he sounded like Viejo again. Her knees felt as if they would buckle, but she forced herself to stand still.

"And you will be punished," Viejo finished. "You will be punished by the sounds of your own son's screams." He nodded, looking over her shoulder. "Take her."

She stiffened as Sancere grabbed her arm and jammed the gun between her shoulder blades. "No. *Please,* no."

Tears swam in her eyes as she tried to drop on her knees to Viejo. "Please, please don't hurt him. Do anything to me. *Anything*. Kill me, I don't care. Please . . ." Her words mixed with sobs as Sancere yanked her backward.

Quinn stood absolutely still, silent tears pouring down his cheeks.

"I'm so sorry, honey." She looked at Viejo. "Please—God, please don't hurt him. Viejo!" She screamed the last word as Sancere threw her into a hallway, his gun still in her back, her arm twisted so far that white dots of pain flashed before her eyes.

Sweat rolled down Dan's temples and back, blinding him as he crawled between the coffee plants to spot the white van at the top of the hill. They'd left a lookout with a rifle, which confirmed his suspicions. Maggie was in there, and possibly Quinn.

He knew a way in now, but to get there without being seen by the guard, he'd have to go the long way, per Lola's directions.

He crouched low between two rows of plants. When the rifleman turned the other way, he ran in the opposite direction, careful not to rustle a leaf in the silence that hung over the hills. He didn't stop until he'd circled a quarter of a mile, and could see the back of the hacienda.

The office was in the back, Lola said, running the entire length of the house. There were bedrooms on the sides, and a main room in the front. The balcony, designed to look out over the entire plantation, was built out of the roof in the front, reached by circular outdoor stairs on the side of the house. And if Lola was telling the truth, there was access from the balcony into the attic, built into the roof tiles.

Getting up there without being seen would be the trick. He'd never make it up the stairs unobserved. But if he crossed the roof from the back, he could drop onto the balcony and then sneak into the house.

He crawled, flat to the ground, toward the covered porch, scanning the windows and listening for any sounds.

Silence.

When he reached the porch he slithered up, staying well below any windows, which were closed tight in the air-conditioned house, as Lola had told him they would be. They were also locked, along with the one door into the house, all with multiple dead bolts. The office looked deserted when he peered in, so he hoisted himself onto the windowsill and grabbed hold of the thick decorative wood trim at the top, pulling himself up without a noise.

Using a wooden window divider as a foothold, he reached up to the gutter and pulled himself higher, getting his other foot on the top of the window. The gutter bent under his weight, but he made it onto the roof and started working his way over the hot terra-cotta barrel tiles. Even this early in the morning, they scorched his hands and warmed through his clothes.

Dan crested the roof peak and looked down at the balcony. He'd be in the guard's view for about a minute, so he'd have to move fast before the guard turned. He scooted across the roof tiles and a loose one slipped, scraping downward until Dan snagged it, just before it could tumble and crash below.

The guard jumped off the van but didn't turn.

Dan held the wayward tile in one hand, and gripped for his life with the other. He couldn't pull out his weapon even if he wanted to take a shot. But the guard stared down the driveway in the opposite direction.

Dan risked moving again, still holding the tile, finishing the crawl one-handed. But he made it, reaching between the curved wooden balustrades to silently place the tile on its side. Then he hoisted himself over the railing and landed right on the spot Lola had promised would get him into the house.

There was the small door, a crawl-through to an attic. He pressed one side but nothing happened. Then the other side, and the door slipped open.

Score one for Lola.

He crawled partway into the dark attic, using the light from the small opening to scan the floor. Where was the hatch above the closet? As he pulled his whole body through, the door closed behind him and eliminated all the light. He turned to reopen it, giving a good shove, but it had jammed shut. Just as he thrust his shoulder into it, a scream of pure, raw despair penetrated the attic and sliced through him.

Maggie.

One wrong step, one noise, and he'd give himself away.

And Maggie, already screaming for her life, would be dead.

CHAPTER
TWENTY-FOUR

MAGGIE WAILED, INCAPABLE of staying calm. What would that monster do to Quinn?

Joel threw her into a bedroom, slamming the door and shoving her so hard she reeled.

"Shut up. You won't hear what's happening out there."

"I don't want to hear!" she screamed, throwing herself at him, ready to face his gun to save her son. He easily knocked her back, the impact throwing her onto the bed.

He stood over her, broad, thick, and far too muscular for her to possibly fight, pointing the gun at her. Did he think she cared that he could kill her? It would just put her out of her misery.

From the living room she heard a thud, and Quinn yelled.

She closed her eyes and stifled a cry of her own; then Joel's knee jammed between her legs. He waved the gun up and down over her body.

"It could have been me, you know."

What was he talking about?

"Who got to fuck the girlfriend. One of us had to."

She clenched the bedspread to keep from punching his face with hatred. It would only cost her. She closed her eyes and tried to hear Quinn.

"We flipped a coin, and of course Gallagher won." He kneed her harder, right in the crotch. "Thought he liked you, didn't you? Thought he was so enamored with your spiky hair and all your earrings that he just couldn't keep his hands off you?"

She turned her head, willing him to stop, waiting for the next sound from Quinn.

He froze the gun right over her heart, just as Quinn yelped. *What was happening to him?*

"We laughed our asses off, too, cause neither of us really wanted to stick it to the skinny teenager with no tits." He rubbed the gun over her breasts.

Vomit rose but she swallowed, refusing to let him know he could make her sick. If he raped her, he'd lose control. Then she'd get the gun, kill him, and save Quinn.

He replaced the gun with his other hand, cupping her breast. "That Gallagher knows just what to say to women. Fucking world-class liar. Bet he told you he likes 'em small."

She refused to react, but that just made him squeeze harder. "They're a little bigger now, but still not in Gallagher's league. Bet he fed you some good lines these past few weeks—told you how he couldn't resist you, how he had to have you, no matter what the risk right under Ramon's nose. Did he Maggie? Did he shovel that bullshit on you again?"

She just stared at him. Her heart ached. Her body ached. Her soul ached. All for her son. Did Sancere think this could make it any worse?

"Or did you believe him, Maggie?" He gripped her so

hard, pain shot straight through to her head. "Did you believe that he risked his life just to fuck you in that shed? Did you?"

She bit her lip and tasted blood.

"Did you fall for it again, Maggie?" He was so close, she could smell his stale, hot breath. "Did you? Tell me!" He dug his fingers deeper.

She refused to react, refused to give him the satisfaction.

"He didn't even like you, you know that? You were *work*, sweetheart. A means to an end. Don't you know that?"

He ripped her shirt up, exposing her, staring at her, his lips quivering.

Quinn hollered, louder this time. And oddly hollow. She'd heard him scream in pain before, but this was different. This was unreal. Oh *God*, this wasn't happening.

"You think he really wanted you?" Sancere spat on her bare breast. "He could have anyone, that son of a bitch. You think he'd want a runaway whore like you?"

Maggie closed her eyes and thought about Quinn as a toddler. A baby. She should have told Dan more about their child before he died. Before they all died.

"He *had* to fuck you so you'd tell him everything we needed to know."

Please, Baba, please make this stop.

"It was his *job*." He slammed her legs open with his knees and pushed his crotch against her. She was no match for his weight and power, crushed as he yanked at her hair so hard she felt it separate from her scalp. "We flipped a coin."

Then she heard another thud, closer. Above them? Did he drop his gun?

"Heads you get her . . ." He ground his body against

her as he growled out the words. "Tails I get her. You know what he said when he won the flip?"

She just closed her eyes.

"He said, 'I lost the toss, Joel.' He lost and *had* to fuck you for the family secrets." He started to laugh, a vicious, low growl. "That's right. He *lost*."

Another thump. Was that in the closet? In the room? She pushed against Sancere with all her strength, but it was useless.

"He lost." He slammed his body against hers.

"He *lost*." Something crashed behind him.

"He lo—"

Suddenly, he was off her, lifted like a rag doll. Maggie blinked at the unexpected reprieve, opening her eyes and seeing . . .

Dan. He hoisted Joel up with one hand and cracked his fist in his face with the other. As he doubled over, Dan ripped out his gun and aimed it right at his heart.

"You sickening little worm." Dan put the gun at his forehead. "Tell her you're lying!"

Maggie rolled off the bed and dove for the door. "Quinn!" The door was locked from the outside. Frantic, she shook the handle.

"Tell her, you son of a bitch!" Dan demanded.

"Dan!" she screamed. "Quinn's out there. Viejo's torturing him!"

Dan shoved Sancere onto the bed, taking his gun. "Here." He held it out to her, pinning Sancere with his knee and pistol. "Shoot off the lock."

She held the weapon in two hands and tried to squeeze, but it was nothing like her .22. Grunting, she used both index fingers, pulling as hard as she could on the trigger.

"I . . . can't . . . do . . . it."

Dan was next to her in one step and grabbed the gun in his left hand, never taking his eye or his own gun off Sancere, and blew the lock off.

She threw the door open and lunged into the living room to see . . . nothing.

"Quinn!" she screamed. "Where are you?"

She heard a shot, and froze in horror, then realized it came from behind her, where she'd left Dan with a gun on Sancere.

All she could do was stare at a pool of blood, rich and red and fresh, spilled over the orange tile floor. She put her hands up to her mouth and screamed. "Quinn!"

His mom's scream sent shivers through Quinn—but nothing like what the crazy old man was doing. Freaking killing himself, and making him watch!

Every time he looked away or closed his eyes, the crazed Viejo picked up a gun and aimed it at Quinn.

"Mira esto, muchacho!" What did that mean? Watch me, boy?

The guy slipped deeper into Spanish with every cut into his own wrists, telling Quinn to scream as he forced him into another room and locked the door.

Now Quinn sat here, trapped by a flesh-cutting lunatic standing over him.

"You make me bleed, *cabrón!*" Viejo growled. "Your bastard blood makes my heart bleed."

"I'm sorry," Quinn managed, tearfully. "I'm really sorry. But, please. My mom—"

Warm blood dripped onto Quinn's torn sleep pants, and above him, the old man brandished the knife.

"Scream for her," he hissed. "Make her writhe in pain, like she gave me."

Quinn just stared, dumbfounded at all the blood.

"Scream! Loud!" The knife grazed his neck.

Oh, *shit*. He gave it his best holler, trying to sound like he was in pain.

"Not good enough!" Viejo pressed the tip harder.

"Okay, okay!" Quinn let out a wail he thought matched his mom's.

That satisfied Viejo for a second. "Now you watch me die."

"No. Please, no." He squeezed his eyes shut.

"You were going to be the heir to all of this." The old man waved the knife around. "Ramon's son. My grandson. *Why aren't you my grandson?*" He screamed the question in Quinn's face.

Wasn't he Ramon's son? Mom was pregnant, and he was her boyfriend . . .

Quinn's hands gripped the armrest. *Just die, you old rotten bastard. Let me go.*

"I'm so sorry. Please. Don't kill yourself." Although that was better than killing Quinn.

"So now your father is dead, too."

Quinn nodded, pressing back into the chair to escape the blood flowing from the wounds. *Oh God, let this be over. Let this be a nightmare.*

"Did you see him die? Did you see the bullet go into his chest?"

His dad—a bullet? Not the Ramon guy, then who? Smitty? He'd say anything to get this guy off him. "My dad wasn't shot. He had a brain tumor."

The old man jerked up, the sudden move making him sway. "Your *real* father. That bastard FBI narc."

"Him?" Quinn pointed to the other room in horror. "The guy who kidnapped me?'

The man choked a dry laugh. "No, the one who lies dead in my warehouse. Gallagher."

Dan Gallagher was his father?

The sound of a gunshot rocked the house, and Quinn jumped up as another shriek echoed. *Mom!*

Without thinking, he tried to push Viejo back. The old man stumbled, but managed to pull out his gun and forced Quinn back into the chair.

His mom screamed again, and the old man lunged forward. He slammed the gun into Quinn's hand, the other holding the dagger right on his neck.

"Shoot me."

"What?"

"Kill me."

He shook his head. "No way. I'm not killing you. I'm not killing anyone."

The door knob rattled frantically. The knife pierced his skin. Pathetic eyes locked on Quinn's.

"Take this gun and put it at my heart and pull the trigger. I will not die by my own hand. And I will not wait around for God to do the job!"

Shaking, Quinn took the gun. "Come on, don't make me do this." His voice cracked and he glanced at the door. "Mom?"

The knife went a little deeper. "Be a man and kill me."

He didn't want to be that kind of man.

"Point it at me!" Viejo ground out, pressing the knife in deep enough that searing, hot pain made Quinn moan.

Quinn jumped at another crack of a gunshot and the sound of splintering wood.

The old man straightened, keeping the knife against Quinn's neck so he couldn't turn.

But Viejo looked stunned. Shocked. His face drained of color, but the knife stayed on Quinn's neck.

"Put the knife down, Viejo."

It was *Dan*. Quinn's head swam with fear and shock and mind-boggling revelations.

"*You* kill me, Gallagher. Your son doesn't have the nerve."

"My son doesn't have the reason. I do."

The knife relaxed, the old man's shaking hand finally letting off the pressure. Quinn put his fingers to the wound, feeling the stickiness of blood.

Viejo stared over his head, the knife quivering in his hand as he slowly pulled away. Then his gaze moved back to Quinn, defeat in his eyes.

"I have nothing left." He flipped the knife and buried it in his own gut.

Quinn launched the chair backward to get out of the way, tipping it and falling, but was caught by Dan as another gunshot exploded through the house and tires screamed out of the driveway.

"Mom!"

"Stay with me, Quinn." Dan dragged him through the main room to the front door, a cloud of dust where the van had been.

"Forget it. You'll never find him." The voice, weak with pain, came from behind. The asshole who'd kidnapped him lay in a pool of blood from a leg wound, his face contorted. "Ramon Jimenez knows every back road in these hills. He has Maggie, and if you think Viejo wanted revenge, you don't even want to imagine what Ramon's going to do to her."

Anger shot through Quinn as he pounced, but Dan grabbed his shirt and held him back.

"Did you bring Ramon here?" Dan demanded. "Is he in on this with you?"

Joel tilted his head, struggling with the pain. "Do I look that stupid? This wasn't about the money. Not . . . for . . . me. I wanted to do . . . the right thing."

"You failed. Miserably."

"Let's go get Mom," Quinn insisted.

"We will."

"Give it up. Ramon's probably killed her by now."

"Then I'm going to do what I should have done to you ten minutes ago. For lying to her. For touching her. For hurting her." Dan lifted his gun.

"No. I am." From the office, a dagger came whizzing through the air straight at Joel, landing square in his neck. Dan spun Quinn away, but he still saw it.

"He's a traitor and he had to die." Viejo crumpled to the ground, barely able to hold his head up. His eyes landed on Quinn. "I wanted you to be mine."

"Where'd they take my mom?" he demanded.

"Ramon likes the Vera tree. His mother's buried there."

"Let's go," Dan said.

They tore ass through the powdery dirt of coffee plants to the bottom of the hill, where a little black truck was hidden between some tall trees. Still holding the old man's revolver, Quinn ran to the passenger side while Dan leaped into the front.

"How do you know where the Vera tree is?" Quinn asked.

"I don't. We're not going there."

"Isn't that where the old man said he'd go?"

Dan floored it out onto the main road, sending up a rooster tail of dirt as Quinn grabbed for a seat belt that wasn't there.

If he was taking her there, she was already dead. But he had no reason to kill Maggie. "He wants money, and she knows where it is."

"How do you know that?"

"Because if Ramon isn't working with Joel, then—hang on." He took a sharp turn without even touching the brakes, and Quinn held his breath until they were back on four wheels. "Ramon came on his own. He was probably watching the house and saw all of this, waiting for his moment to come in and get her."

"You'd better be right."

Dan whipped by a slow-moving car.

Finally, the adrenaline in Quinn's brain simmered down so he could think straight. He stared at Dan, processing all the stuff he'd just learned piece by piece. He should have seen it at first. The guy was a freaking mirror of him. But, still.

"Is it true?" Quinn asked.

Dan gave him a quick look. "Yeah, it's true."

Quinn looked straight ahead, his heart hammering. "Were you going to tell me?"

"When we got back. Hold on again." He took another badass curve, almost tipping the truck. "I had to let your mom get used to the idea first."

"She didn't know?"

"She thought I was dead."

He turned on the seat in disbelief. "Really? That wasn't in what I read."

"You shouldn't have read anything. And you shouldn't have left Max's house."

"I know," he said, sheepishly. "I'm sorry."

"But I'm so glad I found you," Dan said, his voice thick with emotion.

"You gonna cry?" Quinn asked.

"Only if something happens to your mother. I love her."

"Me, too." Quinn kind of laughed. "I mean, duh. She's my mom." He cleared his throat, realizing that he was going to cry himself. "Anyway, it's cool. Just, please get her."

"That's what we're gonna do." He floored the gas and the engine screamed, trees flying at a hundred miles an hour.

If anybody could save Mom, this guy could. He couldn't resist whispering his favorite line from *Top Gun*. "You can be my wingman anytime."

"Bullshit," Dan shot back with perfect Maverick timing. "You can be mine."

CHAPTER
TWENTY-FIVE

MAGGIE STARED AT the purple-blue snake tattooed around Ramon's arm as he held a revolver in his right hand and the wheel in his left. Then her gaze went back to the unfamiliar road.

They hadn't come this way. They were headed east, back to Maracaibo, to the warehouse. But if Dan was following he'd never find her on this road, because it was surely a secret known only to locals.

They didn't see another car or person as they cruised around the other side of a mountain and rumbled toward the money Ramon wanted so much.

Clouds gathered and a gentle rain shower spattered the van's windshield, whipped away by the wipers. The snake tattoo and the rain and the wipers transported Maggie back to another bad ride with Ramon at the wheel.

"You shamed me." The comment came from nowhere, and was said with such loathing that she glanced at the gun to be sure he wasn't going to fire.

"I'm sorry." She wasn't. But she was very sorry she was here. Sorry she had let Dan go after Quinn and went back to lock Joel in that room, only to come face-to-face with Ramon. Sorry she didn't scream for help—but he'd have shot her then, instead of now.

"You will take me to the money, or you will die."

He didn't speak again, driving wildly around the mountain pass, through a tunnel hidden by foliage. Trash on the floor, a roll of tape, an empty can, all tumbled as they made each turn. Before long the traffic picked up, and so did the rain, intensifying to a downpour, the clouds blocking the sun enough that he had to turn the lights on.

At the outskirts of Maracaibo, the ghettos multiplied. Before long they were rumbling through the streets of Las Marías, past the farmer's market, past the warehouses that all looked exactly alike.

"It's near here," she said, looking around. "But it's hard to say exactly where because it was dark."

He lifted the gun. "Does this help your memory?"

No. "We need to find an empty parking lot. With a bus. And an alley." The streets all ran together with no distinct landmarks. Just battered warehouses, dilapidated huts, the occasional *groceria* or fish house.

"If we go up and down every street, I think I'll know it." And maybe that would be enough time for Dan to put two and two together . . . although it would be a stretch to come back here. Still, it was the only hope she had.

Ramon started down one street, turned at the last building, went down another, then another, then another. Each time, his frustration grew and he waved the gun at her.

Finally she saw the bus covered with graffiti and rust.

"There! That's the bus, so that's the alley. The warehouse on the left. The money is in there. It looks like tools, but it's gold."

He pinned her with a hard glare like the one she remembered from the night of the bust. "It better be, Maggie."

He parked the van behind the bus, blocking it from street view, and made her get out first. The rain soaked her almost immediately. She considered running, but where? He'd shoot. He might anyway, now that they were there.

In the alley, the rats were still. The door was open. And the smell of death rolled over everything.

He pushed her inside and she stumbled, then squinted into the darkness. It was quiet. And almost completely empty.

"Where is it?" he demanded with another hard push. "Where the fuck are these crates, you lying whore?"

There was just one now, and she knew it had only a dead body in it.

"Maybe this is the wrong warehouse." It wasn't, but she had to buy time.

"Or maybe you are fucking with me again, Maggie." He raised the gun.

"No, there's another place! Another possibility."

He flipped the lid of the only crate, made a face, and let it thud down. "You're lying."

"I don't—"

"Yes, you do. You lie better than anyone."

She would now. "Ramon, there are a few more roads. Take me back to the car. Let's look." She'd run, and risk being shot. She could escape him in these streets. She had to. "Please. No one could have taken all that money in that amount of time. There were so many crates." His eyes widened. "All filled with gold tools."

He pushed her toward the door, jamming the gun in

her back. "One more chance is all you get. Then you'll be in that crate with him."

They ran through the rain, reaching the parking lot just as the lights of a car washed the area in yellow. Ramon shoved her into the driver's side, pushing her across the seat, then turned the ignition on. Maggie glanced into the side-view mirror. It was the black truck. It was Dan!

She couldn't let Ramon know. As soon as he pulled out, she'd get Dan's attention. She'd lean on the horn or scream or *something*.

But Ramon looked at the mirror and stopped. Did he recognize the truck? Had he seen Dan? She worked to keep her expression impassive, but her heart hammered as he kept his eye on the side-view mirror.

The truck slowed at the alley.

"I think we're close," she said calmly. "If we just—"

His hand cracked over her mouth, a ring hitting her teeth. "Shut up." He reached to the floor and grabbed the duct tape. Yanking off a long piece, he slapped it over her mouth.

"Turn around." She turned toward the window, struggling to breathe as he taped her hands behind her. "Feet," he said. "Give them to me."

She lifted her legs and he bound her ankles, the tape screaming as he unrolled long strips.

"Lie down," he ordered as he climbed out. "All the way down and stay there, or you're dead."

As she flattened herself on the seat, Ramon slammed the door shut, but she rolled over enough to see what he was doing.

He was inching around the bus, his gun out, ready to shoot.

She lifted herself higher, just enough to see the rearview

mirror. The truck had stopped right where they'd parked it the last time they were here. Where he could make a quick getaway.

Ramon moved into position, his weapon out. Was Dan in the warehouse? In the alley? Was Quinn with him? Ramon could shoot them both.

How could she warn them?

The brights! If she could just get to the stick on the steering column, she could flash the brights. Would Dan see? Would he remember the old signal?

She inched forward, her memory slipping back to Ramon's old taunt.

You know how to do that Maggie, or are you so stupid you can't flash the brights?

She got her cheek on the end of the flasher. In the sideview mirror, she saw Ramon straighten.

She pressed her cheek to the stick and moved her head. Everything got brighter. She did it again. And one more time.

Please, Dan. If you're ever going to read a sign from the universe, let it be now.

Dan had one foot in the alley when he saw it. A light, barely noticeable in the rain, from behind the burned-out bus.

The flash of the brights.

Maggie.

He pushed Quinn back into the warehouse.

"Hide, behind the crate," he ordered. "She's out there. So's Ramon."

"How do you know?"

"She sent me a sign." Brilliant, resourceful, wonderful Maggie. "Whatever you do, don't move. Now *go.*"

Quinn made a disgusted face.

"The stink's your cover. No one will go near it. *Stay there.* I have to get her from around the back."

"Okay," Quinn said, sounding braver than Dan knew he felt. "I've still got this gun and I'll use it if I have to."

"Just stay out of sight."

Dan flattened himself against the wall and slithered out to the street perpendicular to the alley, then ran alongside the building and back up the next alley, darting across the street where the parking lot was.

Staying close to the buildings that lined the sidewalk, he moved to a place where he could see behind the bus—and saw Ramon in firing position behind it.

Dan silently sped across the lot behind Ramon.

One more time, light spilled from the front lights and Dan's heart filled with love. She was risking everything to let him know it wasn't safe.

He'd do no less.

He crouched down, steadied his Glock, and aimed for Ramon's head.

The light flashed again and this time, Ramon launched up and spun to the car, his face furious. Just as he did, he saw Dan. For a second, they stared at each other like gunfighters.

Then Ramon opened his arms as if he were going to drop his gun—but the barrel was pointed right in the open passenger window.

Dan fired the instant he did, and the double explosions rocked the air. Ramon's face flickered with shock and outrage; then he fell to the ground.

"Maggie!" Dan ran to the van and threw himself at the open window.

She lay bound and gagged on the front seat, a bullet

hole in the vinyl next to her, her eyes wide with terror, but very much alive.

"Maggie." He yanked the door open, pulling her up to him, working the tape off her mouth, kissing her eyes, her tears, and her mouth.

"You got the signal," she murmured. "You remembered. You understood."

"Of course I did." He kissed her again. "Are you all right? Did he hurt you?"

"I'm fine. Quinn?"

"He's in the warehouse. He's safe. He's perfect. He's *ours.*"

She dropped her head on his shoulder and he hugged her, then turned her to tear the tape off of her hands and feet. Her whole body was trembling.

"Everything's fine. Everything's going to be okay." When she looked at him, her expression was miserable and full of doubt. "Maggie, you know everything Sancere said was lies. You know that, don't you?"

She didn't react and his heart dropped down to the equator. How could he ever undo that damage? How could he make her believe him?

"Of course I know that," she finally whispered. "You loved me then."

He kissed her, then looked her in the eyes. "I love you *now.*"

EPILOGUE

FROM HIS TWO-TOP by the window at Smitty's, Dan watched the front door open at exactly midnight. Constantine Xenakis ate up the floor with every step, his silvery blue eyes lasered straight ahead on Dan.

He reached the table, nodded to Maggie who watched from the bar, then flipped the other chair around and folded himself in it, crossing his arms on the backrest.

"It's been three weeks," Dan said. "Where the hell have you been?"

"Around."

"Robbing banks and mugging little old ladies?"

Silver slits narrowed at him. "I kept my end of the deal, Gallagher."

"Yes, you did." Dan took a swallow of beer, watching Xenakis over the bottle. "And I'm going to keep my end. I was just waiting to make sure you'd show."

"What happened to the money?"

"Property of the U.S. Government, with all but about two million accounted for."

"Glad to hear it."

Was he? Dan pushed the beer to the side. "Let me ask you a question, Con."

He got a shrug in response.

"What do you want with Lucy?"

"Your job."

Dan laughed. "In your dreams."

"Then just one assignment. Consider it . . . a test run."

There was something compelling about the guy, but Dan couldn't pinpoint it. "Lucy already tested you, as I understand it. You didn't pass."

"Things change. People change."

Dan gave him a dubious look.

"You have," Xenakis countered, notching his head toward Maggie. "When you first walked in this place, you'da never given up your golden ticket for a woman."

"I'm not giving up anything," Dan said. "I've only gained."

"All I'm asking for is a chance," Con said. "If I screw up, it's my deal."

Dan nodded. There was *something* about the guy. "I do like to send in a new recruit every once in a while. And there's nothing Lucy loves more than a test."

"So make the call."

Dan's gaze drifted to Maggie, in conversation with Brandy. She laughed at something; then, as if she felt him looking, glanced at him. And didn't look away.

He never wanted to look away.

Xenakis tilted his head toward Maggie. "You chose wisely."

"I haven't chosen anything yet. It's all up to her," Dan admitted, picking up the beer. "Pack for New York. You'll have to interview first. You live through that, you can probably live through anything."

"I've lived through everything," he said, standing up to leave. "That's why I want to do this."

Dan had his phone in his hand before the door closed. Lucy wasn't number one on his speed dial anymore, but he had her on the first ring.

"Please tell me you need a plane to bring you back," she said.

He chuckled. "I could use it, but not for me. I found you a new Bullet Catcher."

"Xenakis?"

Always three steps ahead of the world. "I think you ought to give him another chance."

"I don't know. The job is undercover salvage protection. He might fold when he sees the shiny stuff."

"Or he might surprise you. Sometimes it takes a thief to stop one."

She laughed, the familiar, comfortable laugh that he missed. Just as he missed talking about the business, and brainstorming solutions. He didn't want to stop working for Lucy, but . . .

"When?" she asked.

"I don't want to leave her."

"You know, you can have both," Lucy said. "There's no law that says you have to be in New York. I have planes, there are phones, we can make this work."

Would it be the same? Would he still be the number two man in the company?

Maggie sailed by with a tray in her hand, grazing his shoulder with her fingertips as she passed. "Ten minutes, Irish, and I'm yours for the night."

For the night? He wanted *forever*.

"Just think about it," Lucy said. "In about six months, I'm going to take a leave myself. That'll be close to the end of Quinn's school year. Maybe the three of you can come up here and you can run this operation for me while I tackle motherhood, then go back when I've got things under control."

"As if you ever don't."

"Say that when there's a nursery next to the war room."

That made him smile. Along with her idea. "It's doable, Luce. Assuming Maggie agrees."

"She'd be crazy not to." Her voice was warm. "And believe me, once you try this happily ever after stuff, you'll be hooked. I am."

So was he. "As always, thanks for the ear, Juice."

"Anytime. Send me Xenakis. We'll see what he's made of."

As he signed off, Maggie put her hand on his empty beer bottle and angled her arm to let her bracelets slide over the neck. One, *ding,* two, *ding,* three, *ding ding ding.*

Then she smoked him with a look that said upside down was the special of the house.

"We can go to my house tonight. Uncle Eddie called and wanted to take Quinn fishing early tomorrow. It's been a long time since he's seen Eddie, and I don't want him to lose touch with Smitty's side of the family."

"Home it is," Dan said. "And if I have to help Milk Man wash dishes to hurry things up, I will."

She laughed. "It's Milk Dud, and I'm ready to leave now."

Dan stood and waved to Brandy, who winked.

Outside, the temperature was cooler now. He'd planned something special for Christmas, but after the conversation with Lucy, he didn't feel like waiting.

The house seemed quiet without Quinn and Goose, and quiet was good for tonight. While Maggie showered, Dan set to work, then poured her a glass of her favorite wine and grabbed a bottle of water for himself.

He was waiting in the chair in the bedroom when she came out.

"You know what I was just thinking about?" she asked, fluffing her damp curls, a towel tucked around her body.

"Me?"

She smiled. "How'd you guess?"

"It's mutual. You go first."

She took the wine he offered and curled up on the bed. "Your Chris Craft. That's an amazing boat. Any way I could ever see it?"

The perfect opening. "You'd have to go to New York."

She sighed. "No chance of shipping it down here?"

"Why would I do that?"

"To make Gumbo Jim and Tommy Sloane cry." She smiled. "It's your turn. What were you thinking about?"

"Your grandmother."

She brightened. "How sweet. She'd like you, you know. She had a soft spot for men who made her laugh. What made you think about her?"

"The tarot cards. Can you read them?"

"Not as well as she did, but I think she just made stuff up, anyway."

"All of it?"

She stood and walked toward the dresser.

"You know, I think I'm giving up the whole signs-from-the-universe thing. I don't need guidance from my dearly departed grandmother, who didn't really give me anything except my silver bangles, and"—she opened the top drawer—"her tarot—"

For a long minute, she said nothing. She just looked at what he'd left there, staring at it while his heart kicked up to double time.

Finally she lifted out the jeweler's box as gingerly as if it could explode in her hand. "What is this?"

"A gift. Something I've always wanted to give you."

Holding it, she sat on the bed. "Really." She pulled the white silk ribbon, her hands trembling slightly. "Always?"

He leaned forward, propping his hands on his knees. "Ever since I heard you jingle."

She gave him a quick look, then lifted the lid, blinking at the contents. "Wow. They really sparkle." Plucking the three slender, diamond-encrusted bracelets from the satin lining, she sighed softly. "These are really beautiful."

"Not to replace your grandmother's," he said.

"No, but . . ." She slipped them on and shook her arm to let them ding together. "For special occasions." Twisting her wrist, she admired them, a wistful look on her face. "Thank you. I love them."

"I love *you*. I love everything about you, Maggie."

Her eyes filled a little. "I love you, too, Dan. I love the happiness and wholeness you've brought my life. No matter what you decide to do, or how often you visit—"

He was on his knees before she could finish. "I don't want to visit. I want to stay."

She melted a little. "For however long you like."

"Forever. When I can't be here, you come there. You and Quinn. I won't live without you, Maggie. I love you too much."

She tried to speak, but struggled. Laughing it away, she tapped his shoulders. "Look at you on your knees."

"The perfect place to be, for this." He lifted the satin lining of the jeweler's box to reveal one more circle of diamonds, a perfect match to the bangles. "I believe this is the traditional position to ask this question."

She stared at the ring for a moment, then blinked, sending a tear down her cheek.

Dan reached up to cup her face in his hands. "Marry me, Maggie. Marry me and let me stay with you forever, next to you, under you, beside you. I never want to spend one day without you and your laugh and your love and your jingle."

Her hand trembling, she picked up the ring and held it out for him to slide on.

As he did, he looked up and held her glistening gaze. "I should never have left you the first time," he said. "I loved you then, I love you now, and I will love you for the rest of our lives."

She took his hand and kissed it; then she held out her left hand and admired the ring.

"Now *that*," she whispered, "is a very good sign."

Turn the page
for a top secret look
at the next exciting novel
in Roxanne St. Claire's
sexy Bullet Catchers series,

Make Her Pay

Coming soon from Pocket Books

LIZZIE'S WATCH ALARM vibrated at three a.m., when the hundred-and-twenty-foot vessel was silent but for the hum of the generators. The other divers, the captain, and crew were all asleep. She tiptoed barefoot out of her cabin.

Her feet soundless on the teak floor of the narrow hallway, she barely breathed as she glanced up the stairs to the main deck, where all was dark and silent. Pausing for a second, she pulled a dark hooded jersey around her, took a deep breath, and darted down the steps leading below.

At the bottom, the generators were louder, the engines clunking softly. Grasping the key she'd taken from Charlotte's stateroom during the hoopla when one of the other divers had emerged from the sea holding the beaded silver chain, she headed toward the lab. In the midst of the celebration, it had been easy to slip down to the conservator's stateroom and steal the key. She'd return it tomorrow while Charlotte and Sam Gorman had breakfast, no one the wiser.

The metal door of the cleaning lab squeaked, making her cringe, as she entered.

Inside it was dark, except for one wedge of pale moon light through skinny horizontal slatted portholes. But she didn't need much light. She'd been in the lab enough times to know exactly how the worktables were arranged and where the chain would be hanging on alligator clips in an electrolysis tank.

She took a few steps to the left, reached out to touch the table, and then glided her hands to the row of tanks. From her jacket pocket she pulled out a latex glove, slipped it on, and then dragged her fingertips over the thin metal bar over the stainless steel plate.

But there were no clips draped with a silver beaded chain.

Hadn't Charlotte started the electrolysis yet? She'd naturally done the initial cleaning that afternoon, and then she should have prepped the chain for the electrolysis that would take up to twenty-four hours.

But the tanks weren't even on; there was no soft vibration of a low-volt current. So where had she put the chain?

The nitric baths, no doubt. There were beads on the chain and it wasn't all silver, so Charlotte probably added a wash of nitric acid as an in-between step. Damn. Getting the chain out of a nitric solution would be much tougher.

But not impossible.

She pulled the other glove from her other pocket and headed to the closet-sized room at the opposite end of the lab, where the nitric acid baths were. Lizzie slipped a pinpoint flashlight out of her pocket, because accidentally knocking over even a five-percent solution of nitric acid could cause chemical burns.

Stepping deeper into the closet, she aimed the flashlight at the tiny worktable along one narrow wall and—

Thwack!

The door slammed behind her just as a powerful arm encircled her whole body from behind. A warm hand smashed over her mouth, silencing her scream as the flashlight clunked to the floor.

She jerked one way, then the other, but she was no match for the mighty arms that immobilized her. She tried to see him, but all she could get was an eyeful of shoulder. *Big* shoulder.

"Looking for something in particular?" His voice was a low, menacing rumble, sending shivers over her skin.

She jerked hard, grunting into his hand. "Met me mo!"

"No can do, sweetheart." He punctuated that with a

squeeze, forcing her body against his, her backside right up against his hips.

White-hot terror seized her. In all the dive trips and salvage efforts she'd been on, she'd never been on a ship that had been attacked by pirates. But on this treasure hunt? Entirely possible.

She tried to swallow, tried to breathe, but he just pinned her tighter. She fought again, but he was rock solid and unyielding.

"Mwat do you want?"

"What do *you* want, is the question."

She tried to wrest away one more time, but it was fruitless. She forced herself to be very, very still despite the adrenaline coursing through her, fueling her fight.

Three or four interminable seconds rolled by, her heart whacking at her rib cage in triple time.

"Good girl," he said softly, the tone ominous enough to almost stop that beating completely. "This is a very bad room for a wrestling match."

Yes, it was. Unless you had gloves and long sleeves on, like she did. Only her face was vulnerable. Did she dare?

What was worse, a minor burn or . . . rape and murder?

No contest.

"Now, here's what we're going to do," he said, his mouth still pressed to her ear. "We're going to back out of this closet, very calmly and quietly, before you help yourself to a single item that doesn't belong to you. Then you'll pay for your misdeeds, and the punishment will be severe."

If he let go of either arm, she could grab a cup of acid and back toss it in his face. And scream like hell for help.

"Let's go," he said roughly, lifting her off the floor.

She had one finger free, her arm trapped under his. If she could just . . . close around his pinkie and *yank*.

His knuckle snapped and he loosened his grip just enough to free her arm. She went straight for the row of tiny cups, seizing one in a gloved hand.

He jerked her backward, but not before she tossed the contents of the cup over her shoulder. Instantly, he whipped them both to the right, hard enough that remaining acid splashed over the rim of the cup.

With a shriek, she flipped the whole cup just as he threw her to the floor, covering her body from the rain of acid.

"What the hell!" he grunted, writhing over her.

"Get off me!" She shoved at him, not knowing if any of the acid had touched her clothes, or his. "Get the hell off me, you bastard!"

She tried to scramble away, but he snagged her sweatshirt. "Take it off!" he insisted. "Now! Take it off!" He grabbed the zipper and started to yank.

"No!" She slammed her hands into his chest, just as she felt the air on her arm, where a hole in her hoodie suddenly appeared and grew, the acid on it centimeters from her skin.

"You'll burn! You have to take it off!" He pushed the jacket down, stripping the sleeves as he pulled her to her feet and ripped off her cotton tank top, leaving her entirely bare.

"Your pants! Hurry, before you burn!" He seized the waistband of her sweats just as she saw two gaping holes widening over her thigh.

"Off!" he demanded, dragging them down her hips and taking her underpants with them. In one more lightning move, he flung them away. "Water! Wet your skin!"

He pushed her to the sink and flipped the faucet on, the water shockingly cold on her arm. Then he tore his dark shirt over his head and ripped his jeans off, whipping his clothes into the same corner he'd thrown hers.

"More water," he said, pushing her closer to the sink and cupping his hands. "Give me your leg."

Who *was* this guy?

She lifted her leg and he started splashing handfuls of water over her thigh with one hand, and onto his shoulder with the other.

"Why the hell did you do that?" he demanded. "You could have blinded me."

"That was the idea. You *attacked* me."

He snorted softly, looking at her face. "I caught you stealing. Big difference." He lifted his own leg to the sink and started splashing.

"I was not—" She grasped the side of the sink, adrenaline pumping through her like a straight shot of whiskey, her body rubbery and wobbly as she stared at the huge, dark, naked, furious stranger next to her.

"Who *are* you?"

"The new diver."

Oh, no. Oh, *no*.

"The new . . ." Her voice gave out under the force of his laser-beam glare. Embarrassed, she looked down . . . right at the dark nest between his legs, his manhood fully exposed against the wet thigh he held up to the sink.

The new diver.

Please—this *wasn't* happening to her.

She finally managed to meet his cold blue eyes again, her stomach flipping around like a hooked fish. "I thought you were going to rape me," she said quietly. "Or . . . worse."

He stopped splashing water long enough to drop his gaze over her body, as if he were . . . considering it.

"This isn't enough," he said gruffly, still studying her.

"What?" What the hell did that mean?

"We have to shower. There could be droplets on your skin, and they'll burn. They might already be burning. Come on."

She hesitated for only a millisecond; he was right.

"In my cabin." He shoved her toward the door.

He really *was* the new diver. The one who was coming . . . *tomorrow.* The one who was going to sleep in the small cabin next to the lab because it was the only unoccupied bunk on the boat.

The new goddamn freaking diver. "I thought you were . . ."

"I know. Rapist. Killer. Pirate. I got the picture."

"It's only five percent nitric acid," she said as she led him through the shadowed lab.

"It'll still burn you. And scar." She turned to look over her shoulder. His gaze was sharp as steel and trained directly on her bare bottom.

Flynn had told them they were getting a new diver. But he failed to tell them the new guy was tall, dark, and so far past handsome that he was in another time zone. And she'd tried to burn *that* face?

He nudged her into the hallway and the first cabin, then whipped open the door to the head, a typical combination toilet and shower in one fiberglass closet.

With one hand, he shoved her into the tiny area, lifting the shower hose off its hook as he flicked the water knob.

"You know what they say, don't you, Lizzie Dare?" He stepped inside, stealing every remaining inch of space with his big, bare body. He pulled the door firmly behind him and looked down at her with a dangerous gleam in his eye as he pointed the ice-cold spray right at her breasts. "Payback's a bitch."

Sexy suspense that sizzles

FROM POCKET BOOKS!

Laura Griffin
THREAD OF FEAR
She says this will be her last case.
A killer plans to make sure it is.

Don't miss the electrifying trilogy from
New York Times **bestselling author Cindy Gerard!**

SHOW NO MERCY
The sultry heat hides the deadliest threats—
and exposes the deepest desires.

TAKE NO PRISONERS
A dangerous attraction—spurred by revenge—
reveals a savage threat that can't be ignored.

WHISPER NO LIES
An indecent proposal reveals a simmering desire—
with deadly consequences.

Available wherever books are sold or at www.simonandschuster.com

POCKET BOOKS
A Division of Simon & Schuster
A CBS COMPANY

19582

Get intimate
WITH A BESTSELLING ROMANCE
from Pocket Books!

❀

Janet Chapman
THE MAN MUST MARRY
She has the money. He has the desire.
Only love can bring them together.

Starr Ambrose
LIE TO ME
One flirtatious fib leads to the sexiest
adventure of her life....

Karen Hawkins
TALK OF THE TOWN
Do blondes have more fun? He'd love to know—
but it takes two to tango.

Hester Browne
THE LITTLE LADY AGENCY
IN THE BIG APPLE
She's a manners coach for men, and
she's working her magic on Manhattan!

Available wherever books are sold or at www.simonandschuster.com

POCKET BOOKS
A Division of Simon & Schuster
A CBS COMPANY

19584

Experience the
excitement
of bestselling romances
from Pocket Books!

Eileen Carr
HOLD BACK THE DARK
When a clinical psychologist and a detective
investigate an unspeakable crime, they learn that
every passion has its dark side.....

Laura Griffin
WHISPER OF WARNING
Blamed for a murder she witnessed, Courtney
chooses to trust the sexy detective pursuing her.
Will he help prove her innocence...or
lead a killer to her door?

Susan Mallery
Sunset Bay

What if you got another chance at the life that got
away? Amid the turmoil of broken dreams lies the
promise of a future Megan never expected....

Available wherever books are sold or at
www.simonandschuster.com